Rae Rivers

I am an avid reader and writer with a passion for writing juicy romance novels. I live in Cape Town, South Africa, with my gorgeous husband, two beautiful children and a zoo of house pets. Besides writing, I love family time, the outdoors, travelling, watching TV series, reading and chocolate. For more information about my books, or me, please visit www.raerivers.com. You can also follow me on Twitter @RaeRivers1 and Facebook www.facebook.com/RaeRiversBooks

PRAISE FOR RAE RIVERS

The Keepers: Ethan

Book 3 in The Keepers Trilogy

RAE RIVERS

A division of HarperCollins*Publishers*
www.harpercollins.co.uk

Harper*Impulse* an imprint of
HarperCollins*Publishers*
1 London Bridge Street
London SE1 9GF

www.harpercollins.co.uk

A Paperback Original 2016

First published in Great Britain in ebook format by Harper*Impulse* 2016

A catalogue record for this book
is available from the British Library

ISBN: 9780008181253

Set in Minion by Palimpsest Book Production Ltd, Falkirk, Stirlingshire

Printed and bound in Great Britain

MIX
Paper from
responsible sources
FSC
www.fsc.org
FSC™ C007454

As always, to my incredible husband and children who are my biggest fans and most beautiful cheerleaders. I love you all so much.

Also, to my Dad who was always so proud and enthusiastic about my writing. Fly high and free. Love and miss you always.

The Keepers Trilogy

The Keepers: (Free prequel)

The Keepers: Archer

The Keepers: Declan

The Keepers: Ethan

CHAPTER ONE

Thursday afternoon
Bennett Estate, Rapid Falls, Canada

He felt her heartbeat beneath his fingers.

A slow, steady rhythm that quickened the moment he touched her. Tightening his grip on her hip, Ethan circled her, his senses tuned in to his surroundings – the crunch of forest debris beneath his boots, the trickle of water from the river behind him, her quiet breathing.

The setting sun had masked Jenna's skin in a golden glow, the single braid of blond hair darker than usual. She stood poised with quiet confidence, her legs parted. She held the bow and arrow with practiced skill, the ease at which she handled the weapon never failing to impress him. Dressed in a tank top, army pants and boots, she looked prepared for combat.

He kept his gaze on the warrior woman, not surprised when her expression remained even, her back straight, as though the closeness between them had made no impact.

But her heartbeat gave her away.

"Ready?" he murmured, stifling a smirk.

"Of course."

He tapped her elbow. "Straighten your arm."

"You're giving me archery tips?" Her brows raised, a mild grin playing on her lips. "*Me?*"

He nudged her arm for good measure and smiled. "If you need more time –"

"I'm ready, Ethan. Stop trying to distract me."

He held out a hand toward the river, coloured with a touch of pink. "Don't blink, it'll be fast."

"I'm faster."

"Cocky, are we?"

"Confident." On a gentle hiss of air, she drew back the arrow, ready for flight. "Stop stalling."

Grinning, he mentally ditched the larger rock he'd had in mind and opted for a smaller one. Nothing like upping the challenge at the last minute.

He rotated his hand, the movement sparking a small whirlwind on the riverbed. A rush of energy swirled through him, bringing the familiar comfort he always felt when connecting to nature.

Air. His elemental power.

"On the count of three," he murmured and began the count-down. In lightning speed, he directed the wind away from them. It hoisted the rock into the air with a force that launched it across the sky.

She released the arrow, followed by a triumphant cry when it connected with the target.

Smiling, she lowered the weapon and wiggled her butt and shoulders in a victory dance that extracted a laugh from him.

"You haven't won yet, Pocahontas," he reminded her.

Light blue eyes sparkled with mischief. Her bright smile empha-sised high cheekbones and perfect teeth. She handed him an arrow. "Your turn. I showed you mine. Now you show me yours."

He flashed his wildest grin. "That sounds kinky. Even for me."

She laughed again. "In your dreams, stud muffin."

"*Stud muffin?*" He shot her a look of disgust and snatched the bow from her, reaching for a confidence he didn't quite feel. He wasn't a bad aim when it came to archery, but Jenna's talent for the sport outranked his.

"You remember what this final challenge means, right?" she called over her shoulder as she combed the riverbed for a rock.

"How could I forget?"

Their afternoon of combat practice in the forest surrounding their estate had once again turned into a contest. One he wasn't guaranteed of winning. Not with her. Where she lacked his bulk, she made up for it with determination and skilled martial arts manoeuvres that frequently left him breathless. Lately, she'd been pushing harder, channelling her frustrations into their training sessions the same way he did.

She reached for a rock and straightened. "You miss this shot and you'll be buying me beers on our next night out."

"*If* I miss. Not gonna happen."

"Right. Let's get on with it then. I'm eager for the bragging rights that I was the woman to kick your ass."

Yeah, he'd hate that.

Even if she was a Keeper, like him. A skilled warrior with heightened physical abilities who'd befriended his sister several years ago whilst training at the academy. They'd been inseparable until Jenna had been selected by The Circle, a group of ancestral witches who governed the rules of magic, to leave the academy and infiltrate their enemies, posing as one of them.

They'd assigned her to Kate Carrigan, a hybrid witch she'd protect above everything else.

Because that's what Keepers did.

And protecting Kate meant rubbing shoulders with the very people wanting to harm her.

Bad ass.

Carrying four rocks, Jenna walked back to him and dropped them onto the ground at his feet. Her delicate brows lifted at his scrutiny. "You're staring. It's kinda creepy."

3

"Just thinking how awesome you are."

Although she'd meant for the punch to his arm to be playful, it still packed a powerful blow. "Flattery won't score you a win. Time to settle this once and for all. Pay attention, stud muffin."

"You really should stop calling me that."

Her grin was all mischief. "No harm in trying to throw you off your game."

"Scared you'll lose?"

"No. Now stop stalling and man up."

She reached for a rock on the ground, the movement shifting her t-shirt to expose smooth, tanned skin above her belt. The glimpse of ink surprised him.

A tattoo?

The urge to reach out, to explore, went ignored and he averted his gaze when she straightened. "How about we up the reward?" he asked.

"Feeling confident, are we?"

"Always. That make you nervous?"

"No."

"Fine," he said. "I'm upping the stakes. You win and I'll not only be your personal beer slave, I'll –"

"Do it shirtless too."

He frowned.

"Come on," she prompted with a laugh. "You're that certain you're going to lose?"

"Fine, it's a deal. But if you're choosing your prize, then I'm choosing mine."

She laughed. "I think me running around shirtless would ruffle a few feathers."

His included. And it wouldn't be pleasant. The thought of her shirtless in public arrowed all kinds of objections through him.

"No," he said firmly, refusing to dwell on why. "There's something else I want."

"Ooh, you sound serious." She walked around him, straightening his arm that held the bow. "So what's your prize?"

"You'll tell me where you went last night."

Her eyes widened. She met his gaze, a prickly silence overshadowing their previous playfulness. Her expression shifted from surprised to hesitant – both reactions he'd expected.

"You'll be wasting your win on that answer, Ethan. It wasn't important."

"The fact that you snuck out at midnight without telling anyone tells me it was."

"I needed air." Frowning, she nudged the arrow at him. "Take the shot. It'll be dark soon. You're meeting your brothers at the restaurant in an hour and I'm on witch duty."

"So you agree to the new terms of the challenge?"

"No."

"Come on," he mimicked. "You're that certain you're going to lose?"

"Fine. You'll never win anyway and if you're upping the game, I am too."

He raised a brow.

"Don't look so shocked. You're the one who took us beyond the beers and shirtless fun." She flashed him a smirk that softened the irritation in her eyes. "Next time you go on a *business trip*, I want to go with you."

"You loathe boardrooms."

"I do, but we both know your recent trip to New York had nothing to do with a meeting."

Their gazes locked, the air sizzling with tension as she waited for him to contradict her. For a wild moment, he considered denying it.

"Searching for Hazel alone is dangerous and you know it." Her expression tightened at the mention of the dark witch caster. Born to a lineage of witches who thrived on black magic, Hazel Brogan was a despised enemy and their greatest threat. After spending more than two years with her, Jenna had firsthand experience of everything the witch was capable of.

"Do my brothers know?" Hell, he'd never hear the end of it if his older brother discovered he'd been hunting their enemies. As it was, things were tense between them.

"You really think Archer would've kept silent if he knew?"

"I can't sit around anymore waiting for our enemies to attack. And they will, Jenna. You of all people know that. Why wait? We find them, we end this."

"We're not murderers, Ethan."

"You're starting to sound like my brother. You really believe the best thing to do is to wait for them to strike?"

"No."

"So why the lecture?"

"There's a fine line between crazy and courageous."

"Yeah, it's called common sense. I'm not stupid. I've been careful."

"Doesn't make poking around a witch's lair less dangerous. So we have a deal?"

"Provided you don't tell my brothers."

"I won't." She held up the rock. "Ready to miss your shot?"

Grateful for the diversion, he adjusted his grip on the bow and arrow in his hands. "Careful, Jenna. Over-confidence is a warrior's downfall."

Her grin derailed the moment of tension. Placing her hands on his hips, she twisted around him. "I'm all confidence and all warrior."

He readied the weapon. "Never underestimate me when I want something."

He became vaguely aware of her scent. Soft and fragrant, a subtle hint of pine cones. Counting back, she moved behind him, closer than required.

A ploy to distract him, no doubt.

But Ethan kept his focus, aligned his eyes with the arrow, and drew back his arm.

She leaned forward, her mouth against his ear, her hands on his hips. He zoned in, locking in his target, and slowly released the arrow.

"It's you who shouldn't underestimate *me*," she whispered as her hand swept lower, her fingertips brushing his crotch.

He inhaled sharply at the unwelcome arousal and the arrow took off on a burst of air, missing its target completely.

Her soft laugh broke the silence.

He tossed the bow and caught her arm. "Using feminine charms to disarm me?"

"Not my fault you weren't concentrating."

"I was, until you put your hand on my gear." And his body had acted wildly in response to her. Hot damn.

Her smile smacked of mischief. "I still won."

"Foul play."

She gasped when he tugged her closer. For a moment, they stared at each other in quiet amusement, their faces inches apart. When her heartbeat quickened, a testament that he wasn't the only one affected by her little game, he couldn't resist a grin.

"Take it like a man, Bennett." Her husky voice stroked his arousal. "You lost."

"I'm all man – which is exactly why you did that."

"All's fair. . ."

He moved swiftly, a speed he never tired of. Air escaped from her lungs in surprise as he backed her against a boulder. Securing her body with his, he reached for her hands, pinning them beside her.

"What are you doing?" Her breathing had turned choppy, her breasts rising and falling in tiny movements against his chest.

Damn sexy. Annoying.

"Is this fair enough?" he asked, his raspy voice surprising him. Hell, he was more aroused than he was letting on. His gaze fell to her mouth and for an insane moment, he wondered what she'd taste like.

7

A small smile curled her lips. "Easy, Casanova. There's a big red line we're stomping all over."

"You're the one who nudged the line first, Jenna."

"We've been nudging it since the day we met."

He blinked, surprised by her admission. Ah, so she'd felt it too.

He dipped his head, his mouth hovering against the corner of hers. He had the sudden urge to kiss her. To surprise her the way she'd done to him.

But held back, that big red line flickering like a runway.

They were Keepers, housemates, colleagues. Friends. A romantic fling didn't fit into that combination. At all.

But still, he couldn't resist teasing her.

He trailed a finger across her golden skin, pausing at the opening of her shirt that dipped between her breasts. "Next time, play fair and keep those curious hands off the merchandise."

"Curious —? It was simply a distraction!"

He grinned wildly at her breathy protest and pressed his hips against hers, taking pleasure in the way her eyes widened when she felt his arousal. "Whatever you want to call it," he whispered against her ear, "clearly, it worked."

CHAPTER TWO

Heat flooded Jenna's cheeks.

He towered over her, the intensity of him unsettling her. Dark hair, eyebrows, and long lashes. She lowered her gaze from his blue eyes, which smacked of mischief to his lips. A thin upper lip, indented with a perfect V in the middle, and a fuller bottom lip. Lips curled into a challenging grin.

Jenna shoved him away. He relented with a low chuckle and retrieved the bow off the ground.

She was blushing. Blushing! Not something she ever did, but her ploy to distract him had backfired in a way that had left her hot and bothered.

What the hell was she thinking?

Despite the attraction that always sizzled beneath their friendship, she'd so far managed to keep their relationship on a professional basis.

Until now.

"It's late," she said, her stomach twitching with butterflies – a rarity for her. "We should get back to Sienna and Kate."

Two witches they were duty-bound to defend. Sienna Beckham, a potent elemental witch and Kate Carrigan, the hybrid witch with the strength of a Keeper and the ability to nullify magic – both fiercely hunted for their powers.

Two women Ethan's older brothers adored.

"No rush. They're with my brothers. Besides, I think you and Declan could use some time apart."

She wrinkled her nose at the mention of his brother's name. Declan, the fire warrior with the personality as explosive as his powers. "It's that obvious?"

"I heard you arguing this morning." He tapped his ear. "Super-hearing and all that."

"I'm sorry."

"Don't be. Declan's an ass on the best of days." He placed a hand on her shoulder, turning her to face him. "He's worried about Kate, Jen. It's not personal. You protect the woman he loves."

Worships. Adores.

According to Ethan, they'd never seen Declan so enamoured with another woman before. After almost losing Kate to their enemies recently, Declan had become impossible when it came to her safety.

A given considering their enemies still lurked. With the ability to negate magic and break spells, Kate could swing the eternal war of good versus evil in their enemies' favour.

The fact that Kate had become part of Ethan's family, a woman they'd all grown to love, was irrelevant to those bastards.

"He doesn't trust me with her. Questions my every move." She reached for the bow, knowing she was doing a lousy job at hiding her frustration. "I'm her Keeper. Declan knows what that means."

"We all do."

Of course. It was the foundation of her friendship with Ethan. He understood their world and what it took to protect their witches. Like her, he lived for being a Keeper, but knew it came with a mammoth responsibility and continuous worry that often shrouded everything else.

Jenna inhaled noisily and straightened, shelving the conversation. "Enough doom and gloom. I'll handle Declan."

His eyes followed her movements, studying her, like he always did. "Of course you can."

She watched him walk away, his swagger different from the men she'd watched in New Orleans. He radiated confidence, but in a quiet way. The kind that made you underestimate him. He was an air warrior, connected to an element of nature that many people underrated.

But she'd seen him in action. With the ability to manipulate air, he was able to wield the wind and weather to his will. The man could whip up a storm that would put the New Orleans' floods to shame.

Not that he would. But he could.

As for her stunt a moment ago . . . touching him had been inappropriate but it had snagged her a win – one she'd been desperate for. She couldn't tell him where she'd been the night before. Or why.

Seeing him flustered – if only for a split second – had been a bonus.

There was a rustle of trees behind her. She turned around to see a single black crow squawk twice on a nearby branch before taking flight.

Ethan leapt across the river, landing with ease on the opposite side of the riverbank, the jump effortless and agile. He was tall and muscular without being bulky. His toned muscles bulged beneath the black t-shirt he wore. Whistling softly, he straightened and waded through bushes in search of the arrows they'd lost.

Realising she was gawking like an idiot, Jenna shook her head to get her brain moving again.

The sudden squawk of a second crow startled her. The bird circled above before nose-diving to the ground. It landed silently and tucked away its wings.

The setting sun had tinted the sky and mountains in pink,

the river a glow of beauty. The town nestled amongst vineyards and greenery in the distance. A peaceful, close-knit town where everyone was up in everyone's business and things like home-baked pie, honesty, and solid friendships still existed.

She hadn't grown up in Rapid Falls like Ethan and his family. She'd met his sister, Sarah, at the academy and frequently travelled home with her during the holidays.

Two women from different backgrounds. Sarah had three older brothers and came from a prestigious family who owned a wine estate. They'd lost their parents in a fire when they were younger. Jenna had once had a family until the night their city had been raided, their homes attacked. Her parents had sent her away, urged her to seek shelter at the academy until they could come for her.

She was still waiting.

But through her darkest moments, she'd never given up hope that her parents were still alive. That they'd still come for her.

She'd never told anyone, not even Sarah. Her death had left a void inside Jenna that could never be filled. She'd never found friendship like that again – had never bothered searching for it.

Not that she'd met many friends in the last two years. Hazel and her people had used bullying and violence as a means of gaining – and maintaining – friendships. She'd soon mastered the art of feigning whatever was needed in order to stay under their radar.

A means of survival few people would understand.

Several excited squawks from the tree above brought her attention back to the present. Five more crows had arrived.

The arrival of a dozen more sent a ripple of unease down Jenna's spine.

The sky in the distance had darkened, the pretty pink dissolved by a black cloud of doom that moved toward them at a rapid rate. It looked like a thunderstorm rolling in, destroying all traces of the beauty she'd previously admired.

"Ethan?" He'd seen it too and stood with his back to her, staring off into the distance. "Please tell me that storm's yours?"

12

"It's not. And I don't think it's a storm."

The crows above her took flight, circling, their high-pitched shrieks soon joined by numerous others. Uneasy, she gaped at the blackness creeping in.

A plague of crows. Thousands and thousands of squawking birds, sucking everything joyful out of their surroundings.

Shit.

Wings flapping, nose-diving, shrieking with excitement, the birds engulfed them.

Jenna crouched low, swatting them away as they circled from all directions. Pecking, scratching, screeching. Her desperate attempts to swat them away were wasted on the sheer number of birds.

"ETHAN!"

He'd already jumped to her side of the river, waving his arms to fend off the invasive attack. "Jenna!"

She couldn't see, couldn't breathe, engulfed within the stench of wild madness. Her foot caught on a tree root and she cried out as she collided with the rocks. Pain arrowed through her, along with the vile taste of panic.

A hand closed over hers, a lifeline through the chaos.

"Jenna!" Ethan squeezed her hand. "Close your eyes!"

She felt the flutter of wind, gasping in relief when several crows relinquished their grip.

Ethan crawled closer. He covered her body with his, tucking her head against his chest. "Close your eyes. NOW!"

She did and pushed her face into his shirt.

Heat fired beneath her cheek as energy swirled through him, erupting in a vigorous whirlwind around them. The crows flapped furiously for control, squawking in protest.

Ethan held her, shielding her body with his.

The whirlwind turned into a small tornado, sweeping the birds across the river, gathering water and other forest debris.

Everything fell quiet.

Blissful stillness tinged with choppy breathing as they struggled

13

to catch their breaths. In the distance, the tornado faded, the sky still marked with a few lurking crows lucky enough to have avoided the turmoil.

Blowing out air, she shifted her gaze to Ethan's. He was scratched and bloodied. A quiet fury burned in his eyes.

He ran his fingers through her tangled hair. "Are you hurt?"

"I'm fine." She leaned back on her knees and exhaled. "They came out of nowhere!"

"That was the biggest damn infestation of crows I've ever seen."

She shook her head. "That wasn't an infestation, Ethan. It was an attack."

A heavy silence filling the space between them.

"It's Hazel," he said, the words coming out in a low growl. He leaned back on his haunches, a harsh frown narrowing his eyes, and met her gaze. "Dammit, she's back, isn't she?"

"She never left. She's simply been quiet."

Until now.

CHAPTER THREE

A matter of time.

Jenna had known that. But the few months unmarred by Hazel's darkness had been blissful, despite the constant anxiety that churned inside.

But it was over.

Ignoring the surge of panic at the thought, Jenna walked into the Bennett cellar, not bothering with the light, and retrieved another bottle of wine from the shelf.

The temperature was cool, maintained for optimal storage of wine. Dark shelves lined the walls, stacked with bottles of wine; some home-brewed using their own grapes, some from other wine estates. It smelt of grapes and cork, a delicious aroma that brought comfort.

The sound of her friends' laughter drifted through from the living room, high-pitched and excited. A given, considering the amount of wine they'd consumed. She desperately needed another glass to ease the tension knocking at her insides. Ever since the incident with the crows earlier, a permanent sense of doom had hijacked her mood, her body wired with an adrenaline high she'd found impossible to shake.

She headed back to the doorway, gasping as a familiar tingle of pain spread across her hip.

Oh, no.

She fumbled for the light switch and lifted her t-shirt. Even though she knew what awaited her, her heart still plummeted at the fresh mark etched on her flesh.

Beside two others that had appeared a few days ago. Faint images, similar to a birthmark but darker. Like a tattoo. She'd always had a mark on her hip – the mark of her lineage, one she kept hidden from everyone. But lately, the damn thing kept sprouting. They held no meaning, but a few magical tattoos appearing on her body out of nowhere spelled trouble.

"Jenna, where's the wine?" Sienna called from the living room, startling her.

She lowered her t-shirt, drew in a deep breath, and went into the kitchen. The house was mostly in darkness, dimly lit by a few lamps that offered warmth to the old house. It had been renovated over the years, carefully furnished with a style that smacked of wealth. Thanks to generations of family money and a thriving wine estate, the brothers lived a life of luxury Jenna had never known.

The opposite of the poverty she'd endured whilst growing up.

She hadn't yet told them where she came from. *Ameera.* The secret realm that harboured supernatural beings, most of which had a hunger for violence and chaos. A place where danger lurked at every corner. A city of neglect and violence. Destruction and despair.

The brothers knew of Ameera's existence, but for them their knowledge of it was derived from stories and folklore.

For Jenna, Ameera was home.

Or at least, it used to be. A long, long time ago.

Shaking her head to ward off the sadness that always came when she thought of her family, Jenna walked into the kitchen.

The room still smelt of their dinner, a chicken dish Sienna had prepared to perfection.

Flames burning in the fireplace against the living room wall masked the spacious room in a flicker of orange. It was almost too warm for it as the harsh winter cold had finally relented, but needed for the black cauldron boiling steadily in the centre of the hearth.

Sienna and Kate sat on the floor in front of the pot, surrounded by cushions from the leather couches, empty wine glasses in hand. Bottles of herbs littered the coffee table, their ingredients for tonight's potion.

With her long red hair, pale skin and green eyes, Sienna appeared gentle and feminine, but beneath her beauty was a power that could be lethal if not controlled. Where most elemental witches could channel one element of magic, Sienna could channel four. Earth, Air, Fire, and Water.

Next to her, Kate sat relaxed and happy despite the fact that, like Sienna, she was one of the most hunted witches on earth. Her long dark hair had been stuffed into a messy knot above her head; her bare feet revealing toes painted in bright blue nail polish.

This was the hybrid witch Jenna had sworn to defend. It was her calling, her destiny, something ingrained within her that couldn't be explained. Only the Bennett brothers got it and for that their bond had been instant – despite the challenges she faced with Declan.

The two women broke out in a cheer when Jenna sauntered toward them, opening the wine.

"Have I ever told you how much I love living with wine farmers?" Sienna asked, her voice tinged with laughter as Jenna refilled her glass.

Kate grinned, holding up hers, and hiccupped. "Yip, it certainly has its advantages."

"Farmers?" Jenna echoed, pleased her voice held no trace of her previous unease. She laughed and tipped the bottle in their direction. "Suddenly I'm having flashes of red-checked shirts and pitchforks. I think *wine makers* are the words best suited to your guys."

Sienna laughed. "I can so *not* see Declan in a red-checked shirt waving a pitchfork."

"Don't forget the gum boots and tractor!" Kate added, erupting into a fit of giggles that gave way to another hiccup.

Jenna laughed at the image they'd created. The brothers owned the estate that supplied the grapes for their infamous Ice Wine, a delectable dessert wine their town was renowned for. But in truth, it was their estate manager, Tara, and loyal staff who ran the winery.

They were at the restaurant for the evening, a newly renovated project of Ethan's that would be opening its doors the following day. The three women had opted for a girls' night in. Needing to eat, they'd made dinner. Needing to forget they were facing an inevitable war, they'd brought out the wine. The rest had gone downhill from there.

But it'd been a fun night.

The lights flickered on a buzz of electricity as a loud hiccup escaped Kate. Eyes widening, she slammed her hand across her mouth.

Sienna discarded her glass and settled in front of the cauldron. Smiling, she raised a brow, her hand poised over the bubbling liquid. "Ready?"

"Are you sure about this, Sienna?" Jenna frowned as Sienna scooped the liquid into a bottle the size of Tinker Bell. "Tell me again why we're doing this?"

"Because we're teaching Kate how to make potions. Being a witch without potion knowledge is like a Keeper without speed. Not cool."

Kate hiccupped. "And because it'll cure my hiccups."

Jenna couldn't resist the grimace. "You seriously trust this stuff?"

"Drink up. It's my grandmother's recipe." Sienna handed the

potion to Kate, slapping away Jenna's interfering hand. "Stop it, you're going to spill!"

"If this harms one hair on Kate's head, Declan –"

"I'm not afraid of Declan." Sienna laughed, giving a dismissive wave of the hand. "He's my Keeper. He'd never harm me."

"Kate's his woman."

"Ooh, trump card. Clever."

Another hiccup.

Jenna sent her a narrowed glance. "Didn't you and Sarah once explode your grandmother's kitchen or something?"

"A minor miscalculation."

"*Miscalculation*? You blew up Rose's kitchen! Give me that!" Jenna reached for the bottle, but Kate shifted out of her reach and tossed the liquid down her throat.

Jenna's jaw dropped and they stared at each other in silence.

"You're both looking at me as though I'm about to combust into a bearded lizard or something," Kate whispered and then she laughed. A loud and hysterical laughter that escalated as though the potion had unleashed a giggling teenager.

Sienna grinned.

"They're gone!" Kate said, sobering, and held out a hand for silence. No hiccups. Beaming, she gave Sienna a high five and they both burst out laughing.

They sounded so free, joyous: everything Jenna and the Bennett brothers fought so hard to preserve. It was contagious and by then, Jenna couldn't hold back her smile.

CHAPTER FOUR

Another sleepless night. Another nightmare.

Jenna sighed and opened the freezer, brightening when she saw the new tub of ice cream. Since Sienna had discovered Jenna's weakness for mint ice cream she kept the freezer stocked with a steady supply.

Jenna grabbed a spoon, opened the tub, and hopped onto the counter. At the rate she was devouring her midnight stash, she was sure to gain a few extra pounds.

Hopefully, her morning training session with the guys would help to offset the damage.

She was on her fourth spoonful when she heard movement on the stairs. She tilted her head, spoon dangling above the ice cream, and waited, refusing to acknowledge the way her heartbeat had upped its rhythm.

Because it had *nothing* to do with the fact that those stairs led to Ethan's room. Right?

He paused on the last step when he saw her. She hadn't bothered with the lights, relying on the yellow glow from the patio light outside. Besides, she'd know her way around the kitchen blindfolded. Hell, she'd done this pyjama drill enough times.

His hair was ruffled, like he'd run his hands through it a dozen times. He wore a t-shirt that hugged the muscles in his chest and arms and cotton pants, the ones with a flimsy drawstring that hung low on the waist. Firm, athletic, tanned.

She swallowed, tasting mint.

He didn't seem surprised to find her there but raised an eye at her midnight snack.

"Want some?" she asked, putting the spoon into her mouth.

A mild grin curled his lips and he crossed the room, stopping to grab a spoon out of the drawer. He scooted onto the counter beside her and reached for the ice cream. "Another dream?"

"Yeah. You?"

His brows creased but he didn't ask her to elaborate. He probably knew she wouldn't tell him anyway. He shook his head. "Work."

"Figured so. Your hair's a mess."

"What's my hair got to do with work?"

"You wear it neater than I do." Grinning, she motioned to his hair with the spoon. "*That* spells all kinds of tossing and turning."

His lips twitched in one of those half smiles she loved.

She refilled her spoon, trying to ignore the flutter inside triggered whenever she was alone with him – a sensation that had magnified since their tussle in the forest earlier. "You worried about the opening?"

"We're as ready as can be," he replied, in the quiet voice that always seemed to stir her senses. His frown grew deeper. "The town is still infested with crows. Nothing like what we experienced, but bad enough. They're everywhere."

"Shitty timing with the opening of the restaurant and the festival this weekend. The entire town will be there."

And Hazel's timing was no coincidence. Their enemies loved public events as it meant tons of witnesses, most of them unaware of the supernatural happenings right under their noses, so magic was on a tight rein.

Whilst Keepers and witches protected the secret of their magic,

21

their enemies flaunted it in their determination to achieve their goals of power, exposure and control.

But Ethan couldn't delay the opening of the restaurant any longer.

Jenna lowered her spoon and sighed. "There will be so many people there. The idea of taking Sienna and Kate out after what happened today –"

"We can't keep them locked up."

"It's dangerous."

"I know."

Of course he did. He'd been protecting Sienna far longer than she'd been protecting Kate. But there was so much more at stake now.

She scrunched her nose. "As much as I love being a Keeper, it sometimes sucks big monkey balls, you know?"

His rumble of laughter reverberated across the room. "That about sums it up." He laughed again and she smiled. Sobering, his gaze met hers. "We won't let anything happen to them," he said softly, his tone taking on a more serious edge. "To be honest, I wish Hazel would hurry the hell up and appear."

His words didn't surprise her. She knew how much he hated waiting for an attack. They all did, but for Ethan it was different. He'd grown tired of constantly being in defence mode, always primed in case their enemies showed up. Despite knowing that Archer would never agree to an attack, Ethan had tried everything to find Hazel. He'd grown impatient, frustrated, a side of him she hadn't seen very often.

"A part of me is relieved she's showing presence again," Jenna said. "Her silence has been unnerving."

"Damn right."

The dark witch caster had been far too quiet ever since Jenna had rescued Kate from her in a New Orleans cemetery a few months ago. She'd almost lost Kate that night – an offering in one of Hazel's sacrificial rituals. Hazel had intended using Kate's blood to free her nephew, Mason Brogan, imprisoned and desiccating in an abandoned storage room on the Bennett estate. Once they'd harvested Kate's blood, they would've killed her and scavenged her magic – a victory that would turn the war in Hazel's favour.

But Jenna and Kate had escaped.

Ethan dumped his spoon into the tub, not surprising her. Talking about Hazel was always an appetite-killer. "Despite my search, my questions, no one will reveal where Hazel's hiding. Even witches that side with us."

"They're afraid, Ethan. Hazel is all power and fear. Few people would dare cross her."

"You did."

"That's different. I had Kate to protect." She didn't elaborate, didn't have to. He'd put himself in danger countless times defending Sienna. Their witches, their lives, came first above all else. Even their own.

"Are you afraid?"

"When it comes to Hazel, it'd be stupid not to be. All the more reason you shouldn't be gallivanting the streets looking for her."

"*Gallivanting* is not quite the term I'd use."

"It's still reckless."

"The waiting is killing me."

"Your brothers find out you've been searching for her behind their backs, they'll be furious."

"They'll get over it."

"Not if you die."

His expression hardened and he tossed his spoon into the sink, his blue eyes flashing with a sadness that needed no words. *Sarah*. Losing their sister had nearly destroyed them. "I've been discreet, Jenna."

"Underestimating Hazel and her reach is foolish. I figured it out. It won't be long before your brothers do too."

"Stay out of it. I'll tell them when the time's right."

Something about his expression told her it wouldn't be any time soon.

"I won't say anything." She placed the tub on the counter, along with her spoon. "Provided you take me with you next time you go looking for them."

His smirk triggered the dimple in his cheek. "You're resorting to bribery?"

"I won today's challenge, so you have no choice. Besides, it'll be safer if there are two of us."

"Safer? If anything, you coming with me makes you a liability. Anyone wanting to get into Hazel's good books will rat you out in a heartbeat."

His words stung, mostly because they held a truth to them that left Jenna with a permanent sense of dread in the pit of her stomach. For Hazel, no betrayal ever went unpunished. Jenna had witnessed that too many times. Freeing Kate and destroying the blood that would set Hazel's nephew free had sealed Jenna's fate. She knew there'd be consequences.

"Guess I'll have to watch my back, then." She gave him a small smile and hopped off the counter to rinse the spoons. They could've waited until morning, but she needed something to do.

She was grateful when he didn't press, but a quick glance in his direction told her what she already knew. He had his quiet, thoughtful, smouldering gaze pinned on her. Almost as though he saw right through her.

Damn, she adored all three brothers, found them all attractive, but something about Ethan's all-knowing, quiet stares seemed to touch her in places the other two brothers couldn't.

He moved so quickly, a soft rush of air filling the silence, and when she turned around, he was there. A rock-solid wall of muscles and simmering heat. A sizzle of awareness raced down her spine, his closeness snatching her breath away.

"Don't do that," he murmured. When she tried to avert her gaze, his fingers tipped her chin upward. "Don't pretend like it doesn't matter."

Her throat tightened, the reply trapped between the worry and emotion. Clearing her throat, she shrugged. "I did what I had to do, Ethan."

"And you're marked because of that."

"I had to protect Kate."

"Doesn't make it an easy burden to carry."

His features were illuminated in a soft shade of yellow from the light outside. His dark blue gaze held her captive. An all-knowing look that threatened her facade. Air evaded her, along with a reply, and she stepped back but flinched when her arm brushed her hip. Damn, her flesh still ached from the new mark.

"Rough day?" he asked, his tone softening with the familiar playfulness she loved. A small smile played on his lips. No doubt a ploy to return them to neutral territory.

She smiled, grateful for the reprieve. "Nothing I can't handle."

"It wasn't *all* bad."

Her stomach flipped at the reminder of their intimacy in the forest. Her cheeks heated and the image of a sorority girl with a crush came to mind. She bit back a groan. Could she be more pathetic?

"It's late." She cleaned up and wiped her hands on a cloth. "I should go to bed. I'll need my beauty sleep for combat practice with you and your brothers in the morning."

Their sunrise training sessions in the forest had become a daily ritual. It kept them in shape and improved their skills.

And helped to work off the ice cream.

"Jenna." His fingers toyed with hers. "About what happened earlier at the river, with us . . . I'm sorry. I was out of line."

"Me too." Relieved to clear the air, she withdrew her hand, flicked his shirt, and smiled. "But I still won our bet, so that makes me your travel buddy. And you're still buying me beers. Shirtless."

"You won't let that go, will you?"

"Not on your life."

25

CHAPTER FIVE

The tranquillity of the forest did little to ease Jenna's worry. Her body tingled in anticipation, her senses primed as she made her way through the trees.

A thin fog blanketed the ground and the air felt crisp and cool. The sun would be up soon, along with the trio of Bennett brothers, ready for their daily training session.

She could hardly wait. Her entire body felt coiled, ready to unravel at any moment. A kick-ass fight was just the kind of outlet that would help.

Until then, Jenna would revel in the quiet, walking, searching. Like she'd done countless times when she'd thought no one else was watching.

But Ethan was onto her.

She clamped the worry that flared at that thought and shone her flashlight at the path ahead. It highlighted the remains of an old well, unused and dilapidated, but served as a beacon that would help her find the entrance to the underground storage rooms, where Hazel's nephew was kept. Sienna and her grandmother had

26

spelled Mason years ago, the night Sarah had died. A horrible fate for a horrible man but a fitting punishment for someone so evil.

Jenna wasn't here for the warlock, but at some point Hazel would come for him. Not that she'd easily reach him as Sienna had sealed the tunnels with a spell, but still. Hazel was close. She could feel it and if that were true, they would've used their favourite mode of transport into Rapid Falls – a portal.

Portals were instant doorways to anywhere in the world. They allowed Hazel and her followers to move between cities with ease. Quick entrances, quick escapes. And a whole lot of damage caused in between.

That was the mild part.

The most dangerous portal was the one that led to Ameera. A door that remained firmly sealed because opening it meant anything could emerge and enter the mortal world. *Their* world. The portal was the only thing that separated the two realms.

Because of the risks involved, The Circle had bound the spell to open portals a long time ago, but it had been stolen by a dark witch caster, an evil lineage of witches with a love of black magic.

Hazel's lineage.

Over time, on the rare occasions they'd opened the portal to Ameera, it had been brief and they'd ensured no one escaped.

But Jenna had.

The last time the portal had been opened had been the last night Jenna had seen her parents. The night her mother had sent her through the portal, along with a young orphaned witch her parents had taken under their wing, hurtling them into another world that was far prettier and more peaceful.

But just as frightening.

Jenna had been here ever since and after that night the door to Ameera had remained shut. Jenna had long since given up hope of ever returning until she'd been sent for Kate – and met Hazel. Even though she'd known the risks, she'd hoped that Hazel would attempt opening the portal to Ameera.

If only briefly, enough time for Jenna to return to find her parents.

Jenna's chest tightened, like it always did when she thought of them. She hated the weight of despair that had reared its head. She'd mastered the art of keeping it all buried. But lately, memories of her parents had begun to consume her.

A rustle of leaves in the distance startled her. Turning off the flashlight, she quietly scanned the forest.

Her senses flickered and she held her breath, searching, listening. And then she heard it again. A shuffle of movement. Quiet breathing. A heartbeat.

She wasn't alone.

She stepped behind a tree. A large shadow appeared in front of her, the movement so sudden and fast that leaves scattered. She dropped the flashlight and ducked. Moving with lightning speed, she lunged.

It was like slamming into a brick wall but he grunted and went down. Jenna scrambled on top of him, using her body weight to pin him down. She threw the first punch, but her fist connected with a palm.

"Dammit, Jen, what the hell was that for?" Ethan growled, his words stunning her into stillness.

Jenna gaped at him, her heart lurching with relief. She punched him on the shoulder, but it lacked the force the previous one had. "Why did you sneak up on me like that? I could've killed you!"

He snorted. "Like I'd ever let that happen."

"What are you doing here?"

"What are *you* doing here?" He lifted his head, glanced at the door behind her. It was overgrown and bushy, but he'd know what was behind it.

Damn.

Her mind scrambled for a reply but none came. What the hell could she say anyway? If he ever discovered she'd been searching for a portal – preferably one to Ameera, of all places . . . yeah, he wouldn't like that. At all.

Besides, she wasn't ready to tell him she was the daughter of Keeper parents exiled to a prison world on another realm. Ha, she almost laughed at how absurd that sounded. Not the kind of thing one could easily divulge.

But still, she was busted and she needed an answer.

"You followed me!" she accused, hating the slight hitch to her tone. But dammit, he'd frightened her! Messed with her plans. And he was onto her. She wasn't sure which of the three she loathed more.

"You wouldn't tell me where you've been going at night."

"Ethan!"

"Why are you here, Jenna?"

She sat back, not caring that her waist ground against his. She tilted her head and looked at the door, grasping for an explanation. Anything that would ease his suspicion. "I came to check on Mason."

Silence.

His brows lifted. "Right. And?"

"I haven't gone inside yet." She swatted his chest. "You have no right to follow me, you ass!"

"I have every right. Especially when I think you're bullshitting me."

She climbed off him, hating how transparent she'd become with him. "I had a dream that made me want to check on Mason."

It was the truth. Kind of.

"What about the other night?" He rose, watching her. "Also a dream?"

"It's none of your business, Ethan." She tried to push past him, but he caught her arm and drew her back to him. Her body collided with his, a barrier of broad shoulders and hard muscles.

"This is my witch, my home," he murmured. "*My* business. And you shouldn't be in the forest alone, Jenna. It's too dangerous."

The cry of frustration erupted before she could reel it in and she shoved him away. "Everything's dangerous, Ethan. Everything! I'm so damn sick of it!"

She snapped her mouth shut, shocked at her outburst.

Silence stretched between them and when he stepped forward instinct had her taking a step back, but he kept coming until she was backed against a tree.

Awareness surged through her. The air caught in her lungs. She could feel him, smell him. His strength and masculine power immobilised her as he pressed forward, using his body to anchor hers.

She lifted her chin in quiet defiance, meeting his gaze, refusing to reveal how she felt. Cornered. Breathless. All too aware of the heat and man that had her pinned to a damn tree.

"We live in a permanent sense of fear, Jenna," he said quietly, his words a rumble of sexiness that made her heart skip a beat. "I despise it as much as you do. But the only thing that keeps me from going mad is knowing I'm not alone."

The dim light from the discarded flashlight highlighted his features in a shimmer of orange.

Something calm and enticing washed over her. Her ability to breathe had totally escaped her.

His fingers brushed away a lock of hair from her face, his touch gentle, despite the soft scrape of his calloused palm. "At some point you need to realise you're not alone either, Jen. Knowing that makes all the crap more bearable."

"Ethan —"

His eyes narrowed. "I get that you're secretive about your past and your time with Hazel." She looked away, but his fingers caught her chin, bringing her back to him. "That's okay. But you're not alone. As long as you know that."

She couldn't speak, the words trapped in her throat, emotion rolling through her in ways she usually avoided. All she could do was nod.

He stayed that way for a moment longer, simply looking at her, stroking her hair, his eyes flashing with something she couldn't quite define.

With a small smile, he withdrew. "My brothers are near," he said, his voice gruff. He cleared his throat and looked away, searching the forest. "Let's check on Mason and get the hell out of here. I hate this place."

CHAPTER SIX

The sound of clashing sticks and steady breathing permeated the quiet morning air. The Bennett brothers' daily training was in full swing. It was warm, the forest streaked with gentle rays of sunlight that filtered through the trees.

Ethan and Jenna circled each other, both using long sticks to either attack or defend in a whirl of swift, steady movements.

The dance was smooth, rapid, focused. Tainted with an underlying frustration that seemed to have upped a notch this morning. A result of circumstances or the fact that he'd followed her?

I came to check on Mason. Right.

He had no reason to doubt her, but instinct told him she hadn't been entirely honest. There was more. To her excuse. *To her.* He knew that, but the woman kept a Great Wall of China between herself and everyone else and he wasn't sure if he had the energy or the inclination to break through.

Because breaking through walls meant caring. And that stirred up heaps of crap he usually avoided.

She mirrored his movements perfectly, making it impossible for him to gain an inch of ground. She shielded his every blow, constantly engaging with an overbearing force that had him more on the defensive than offensive.

Adrenaline soared, their bodies sleeked in thin layers of sweat, and they fought on, breathless, determined, the practice session as thrilling as it was necessary.

Jenna used her stick to field his next hit, retaliating with one of her own. He moved, but not fast enough, the weapon connecting him on the shoulder with a powerful force, missing the side of his head by an inch.

"Whoa, Jenna!" He broke away, frowning at her as he rubbed his shoulder. "Rule of combat practice – attack the aggression, not the aggressor."

"You should be defending your red zone, Ethan. You left yourself wide open." She poked his chest with the stick.

His hand shot up, clutching her weapon. Grinning, he gave a hard tug, taking pleasure in the way she launched forward.

In a swift movement, he had her pinned beneath him, the stick at her throat.

He raised a brow. "Wide open?"

With a loud grunt, her knee jerked upward, dislodging his hold on her. She was on her feet in a flash, smiling. Panting, she backed off, lowering her weapon, but sprang into action the moment Ethan's brother, Declan, pounced.

Stick raised, she swung around and ducked as Declan charged. He wielded his own stick, bulldozing full steam ahead with his surprise attack.

Their fight was swift, their bodies moving between the trees with breathless pace.

"Wow, Declan, frustrated much?" Jenna moved around him in a steady flow of fancy footwork, easily defending his blows with her own.

"Scared of some friendly banter, Blondie?"

She lowered her body, ducking his next attack, smiling with satisfaction when her stick connected with his legs. She pulled back, circling him, a mild grin breaking free. "Is that what this is? *Friendly*?"

"Of course."

"Right."

They stood staring at each other, breathlessly assessing the distance and range of the weapons between them.

Simultaneously, they charged.

Sticks clashed, louder and with added hostility as they performed a perfect mirroring drill, anticipating each other's moves with ease.

Ethan glanced at Archer, watching the tussle quietly, arms folded across his chest. His oldest brother exerted a permanent control and calm that Declan lacked. They were so different in so many ways.

Declan lunged for Jenna, releasing a growl of frustration. Ethan frowned at the scent of aggression that lined their fight – a fight born out of need for building strength and endurance.

But this was different.

Archer's expression tightened and the slight narrowing of his eyes hinted that he sensed it too.

Declan stepped back, twisted his stick, and charged. In a blur of speed, Jenna took a running leap. Anticipating her move, he joined her, sailing through the air with ease.

Their collision was loud, powerful, their sticks clattering on impact. They were still fighting as they fell, their landing less skilled. They parted, straightened their sticks, and stared at each other, frustration sizzling between them.

Jenna glared at him, her jaw clenched, her shoulders rising and falling in breathy gasps of air. With a soft curse, she lowered her weapon, shaking her head.

"Had enough?" Declan goaded as she turned around.

Ignoring him, she walked away, but drew to an abrupt stop as a single line of fire reared to life in front of her. She spun around to face Declan, her mouth opening in surprise.

Another line of fire roared to life in front of her, cutting her off. She slammed her stick on the ground. "Dammit, Declan! Cut that out!"

The line of fire chased around her, closing in. Realising she was about to be imprisoned, she bolted for the remaining gap between the blaze, cursing when Declan added more heat, more energy. The circle closed before she reached it, flames rearing up with a force that had her backing to the centre of the circle.

The sound of fire crackled around her, the flames almost at shoulder height.

"Something wrong?" Declan called out, his voice laced with mild amusement. "Come on, Blondie. Can't fight your way out of this?"

"You're being a dick, Declan."

"We're at war. You need to be prepared."

"You're questioning my combat skills?"

"It's not your combat skills in question. Hell, even *I'll* admit that your moves are impressive."

Surprise etched her expression at the admission.

"But you refuse to use your elemental powers," he added. "That makes you weak."

Her nostrils flared and she tilted her chin upward. "Tossing around a few fireballs won't necessarily win our war."

Declan's lips curled at the dig, but he let it slide. "Afraid of your powers, Jenna?"

"No."

The flames flared higher. "So show me."

"Screw you, Declan. I don't have to prove anything to you."

"I beg to differ. You protect the hybrid witch our enemies are after. They reach her and the balance of nature is screwed."

"Yes, but the balance has nothing to do with this. With us." She waved a finger between them. "I protect the woman you love, so for you it's personal."

"What are we? Fifteen?"

"I get that being an overprotective ass is your default setting, but Kate is *my* witch and I will die before letting anything happen to her, just as you would for Sienna."

Declan scowled at her, the muscles on either side of his jaw twitching.

"You think I don't know what I'm up against protecting Kate?" Jenna said, her tone clipped with irritation. "I live with a permanent sense of dread, knowing what's at stake if I fail, and I don't need you constantly pushing me, taunting me, and giving me crap every day trying to prove that I'm worthy. We're supposed to be on the same team, dammit!"

"Because you're all about teamwork, aren't you, Blondie?"

"When it comes to protecting Kate and Sienna, I am."

"I can't be on team you until I can trust you can handle this."

"Rather unfortunate considering Hazel's showing presence again. And don't for one moment think she won't sniff out a divide between us."

"As easily as she'll sniff out a weakness."

"I'm not weak!"

He raised a brow and pegged her with a challenging glare. The fire reared higher, the crackling muffling her soft curse.

"Declan," Archer said, stepping forward. "That's enough."

"No." Ethan took his arm. "Leave them."

Archer frowned. "She's right, Declan's being an ass."

"I think she's had her fair share of dealing with asses. She can handle this one too."

Archer paused and glanced at Jenna. A moment later, his pensive expression relaxed and he gave a single nod.

Silence engulfed them, the air sizzling with tension.

It was Declan who broke their standoff. Flames still burning, he swore loudly and shook his head. Turning around, he walked away.

A warlike cry shattered the silence as Jenna launched through the air, breaking through the blaze. She collided with Declan and exploded into a series of martial arts manoeuvres that triggered another fight.

This time, there was more rage, more determination, and they moved so swiftly that it was near impossible to follow them.

Declan fought back with a viciousness that matched hers, but something in his eyes gave him away.

She'd surprised him.

Ethan grinned.

In the end, Jenna creamed his brother in a swift pace that had them gaping at her. Declan was a skilled a fighter as any, but Jenna possessed a natural fighting skill that topped his. In battle mode, the woman was damn near faultless.

Ethan caught Archer's gaze, not missing the flash of satisfaction in his brother's narrowed one.

Delivering a final, vicious kick that connected with Declan's nose, Jenna backed off. Declan cursed as blood splattered and he glowered at his opponent. They were both breathless, bloody, bruised. A fierce silence followed and Jenna circled the warrior, fists up, ready for his retaliation.

Which never came.

Instead, Declan lowered his fists and spat out blood. Breathing heavily, his gazed locked with Jenna's. "It's not quite the display of magic I'd hoped for, but . . ."

"You'd be a fool to underestimate me again, Declan." A smirk softened her anger. "Kicking your butt just proved that."

Declan swiped at his mouth with the back of his hand, his lips twitching.

Ethan's grin widened. She'd impressed Declan and he wasn't easily impressed – or surprised. In a matter of moments, she'd accomplished both.

Damn right.

Jenna lowered her stick. "You have a right to be worried, Declan. We're all worried. But you're forgetting one thing. You've met Hazel twice. *Twice.* I lived with her and her merry band of evil for two years. I know what we're facing more than you will ever know, so choosing not to be on team me is . . . stupid."

With a final glare, she turned around and left.

CHAPTER SEVEN

The opening of the restaurant coincided with the school's annual parade, one of the town's many traditions. Each summer, the high school seniors hosted the parade, an event that had grown so popular over the years that it attracted tourists from all over.

The main road hummed with activity, the restaurants crammed with visitors. The aroma of fried donuts filtered through the air, sweet and enticing. Children ran between the crowds of people that walked the streets, lined with vendors selling homemade crafts or fresh produce. Others lay sprawled on picnic blankets in the central garden. Their laughter and voices mingled with the music played by the band.

The celebrations for Ethan's restaurant opening were in full swing. A joyous occasion that did little to shred Jenna's uneasiness.

Darkness was near. She could feel it.

They all could, but in a world where their kind lived in secret and social obligations like restaurant openings and festivals couldn't be avoided, events that surrounded them with friends determined to celebrate, they had no choice but to mask the worry and pretend that Rapid Falls was the perky, safe little town everyone thought it was.

What a load of crock.

Jenna scanned the street again before going into the restaurant. She slid into an empty seat at the end of the bar and eyed the bottles of alcohol against the wall, longing for the oblivion the clear liquid promised. But no. She hadn't eaten much and needed a clear head.

They'd packed the restaurant to capacity, a steady flow of people coming and going. The aromas of garlic and herbs spiced the air, a contrast to the sweet scent on the street.

The restaurant had been refurbished with a contemporary feel, but the wooden floors, brick walls, and lighting gave it a warm edge.

Sarah's.

An apt name for the restaurant and a brilliant way to honour an amazing woman.

A loud rumble of thunder reverberated above them, followed by Ethan's laugh, which drifted across the room. Two women were draped around him at the far end of the bar. One distributed shots of Tequila.

Mr. Popular himself. Always the first of the brothers the women flocked to – even more so now that Archer and Declan were no longer single. Beneath his easy-going personality were layers of a mysterious, quiet confidence the women adored.

Jenna wondered how many of them actually made it back to his bed. She knew he avoided a relationship the same way he avoided asparagus. Didn't like it, wouldn't try it. His encounters were brief and fun.

Hell, the thought of Ethan doing a naked monkey dance with any of these women added a spark of annoyance straight to her gut.

And she refused to decode why. Nope.

He'd shaved, the subtle scent of his aftershave knocking at her senses every time he came close. He wore a white shirt and blue jeans, the sleeves rolled up to the elbows. Black leather bracelets covered each wrist, along with his Keeper ring on his finger. Despite everything, he looked relaxed. Happy.

She envied the way he was able to flip the switch that instantly turned off the worry in front of others. A perfect mask. If she hadn't known better, known him . . .

Almost as though he sensed her quiet scrutiny, he turned, his gaze connecting with hers across the room.

Jenna's stomach flipped in response and she began toying with the box of matches on the counter. It had the name *Sarah's* scrawled on one side.

Ethan downed another shot, disentangled himself from the women – despite their protests – and joined her at the opposite end of the bar.

Pocketing the matches, she lifted a brow. "Needing a break from their flattery?"

"Trust me, flattery was too mild a word for what that was." He slid into the vacant seat beside her, giving an exaggerated shudder that made her laugh.

"Too much for you to handle?"

"No. I can handle them. But I don't want to. Besides, they're both married."

"They are?"

"I have no idea where their husbands are tonight, but I got a taste of what it feels like to be a burger and beer at a health clinic."

She laughed and nodded in the direction of the kitchen. "How's it going in there?"

"There were a few hiccups and I'm in need of a new pastry chef, but overall the opening's been a hit." He scanned the full restaurant. "Sarah would be proud."

"We should drink to her."

He leaned forward, a teasing grin easing his expression. "And I believe I owe you a beer."

She smiled. "Shirtless?"

"I've never backed down from a bet," he said, fiddling with the top button of his shirt.

Something niggled inside, a mild objection at the thought of his beautiful body on display to everyone here. "Really?"

"It's my restaurant. My party."

"And it's my win, right?"

"Which is why I'm about to lose my shirt in a full restaurant."

Niggle, niggle.

"No," she said softly, covering his hand with hers, surprising herself.

Electric-blue eyes found hers. A small grin hitched the corner of his lips, triggering a familiar stirring in her belly. "You're backing out?"

"It's my win, so I say keep the shirt. The women here don't need the distraction."

Leaning closer, he brushed his lips against her ear. "They don't or *you* don't?" When she inhaled sharply and pushed him away, he chuckled and walked around the bar. "I still owe you that beer."

"If I'm letting you off the hook, stud muffin, you owe me several."

"You're relinquishing your win?"

"Only the shirt. The rest of our deal still stands." But something about his expression told her he already knew that.

He leaned forward, his elbows on the counter. "You insist that searching for Hazel alone is dangerous. How's that different from your midnight cruises?"

"Because I wasn't searching for Hazel."

"So why the sneaking out at night?"

"Why are you keeping tabs on me?"

"Answer my question."

Sighing, Jenna looked away. "I've been struggling to sleep."

"Bad dreams?"

An understatement. *Bad dreams* had plagued her for years – fragments of the night she'd lost her family and the time she'd spent with Hazel. Lately, her dreams had escalated to horrific nightmares, so vivid and real that she dreaded going to sleep. Broken images of screaming women tied to each other, locked in a burning building as a group of people stood by and watched.

Jenna knew the nightmares were about the witch massacre that had occurred many years ago, when a group of witches had exposed their magic to a few ordinary folk in hope of living in harmony. The backlash had been tragic. Whilst their Keepers had stood by and watched, dozens of witches were rounded up and burned, proving how essential it was to keep the existence of their kind a secret.

Something they still fought for, everything their enemies despised. As for the Keepers who'd betrayed their witches . . .

"What are the dreams about?" he asked, the soft words spearing her thoughts.

She looked back at him, caught by the urge to tell him. She'd never shared them with anyone, never dared. Because admitting to the massacre nightmares would spark several unwanted questions, all of which led straight to her family.

He deserved to know the truth – and she'd tell him. Soon.

The thought made her heart skip a beat. Not surprising. The Bennett brothers lived and breathed to protect witches. She'd been born into a lineage of Keepers exiled to live in Ameera as punishment for harming them. It wasn't a conversation she looked forward to.

Especially if it altered the way they saw her.

Shaking her head, she tucked her hair behind her ears, needing to give her hands something to do. "It's not important."

"That's where you're wrong, Jenna." Despite his even expression, his tone held a serious edge. "Considering what we're facing, who we protect, everything that goes on in my home is important."

"Your home, Ethan. Yours. Your brothers, your witch, your town. Arriving here hasn't been a picnic for me. Sometimes I need air and you don't get to monitor me, so back off. Please," she added quickly, not sure why she'd felt the need to.

He studied her for a long while before nodding. "Fair enough. But next time you go for a midnight cruise on your own, you should let someone know."

"Same goes for you and your business trips."

The lights flickered several times, extracting a ripple of surprised murmurs across the room. The crack of thunder echoed in the distance and Ethan glanced outside, a deep frown hardening his expression. "The storm's getting closer."

"The crows, the storm . . . Hazel's near and I hate that we can't stop her."

"We'd need to find her first."

She caught the frustration in his tone. "Even if Archer agreed, it's no use. You've been tracking her for weeks and still have no idea where –"

A trickle of awareness raced down her spine, and a moment later Archer slid into the seat beside her. He had the ability to manipulate water and was the quietest of the three brothers, always brooding. But now, his green eyes blazed with fury and a muscle worked in his jaw.

He shot Ethan a raised brow. "You went searching for Hazel?"

"Eavesdropping again, brother?"

"Your recent trip to New York. Is that what you were doing?" Archer's tone held a dangerous edge, but failed to evoke a response from Ethan. Archer turned to Jenna. "Did you know?"

"Leave her out of it, Archer," Ethan said quietly, his voice unwavering. "We agreed we'd try locating Hazel."

"We agreed we'd put out feelers, ask around. Not go hunting for her." He slapped Ethan's shoulder with the back of his hand. "*Alone*, Ethan? What the hell were you thinking?"

"I'm sick of waiting for her to show."

"She will, and when she does we'll be ready for her."

"But how many lives will be lost until she does?"

"Did you find her?"

"A few of her hideouts, a few followers."

"But no Hazel?" When Ethan didn't reply, Archer scowled. "Did they see you?"

"I'm frustrated, not stupid."

43

Archer gave Ethan another smack on the shoulder. "Hunting down an evil witch caster alone *is* stupid."

"It would've been nice to have company, brother, but you refuse –"

"We're Keepers, Ethan. We vowed to protect, defend. We fight for peace. Going on a killing rampage is not what we vowed to do."

"And sitting back letting innocent people die is?"

They glared at each other, tension simmering between them. Jenna caught a few curious glances sent their way and she quietly leaned forward, placing a hand on each of them.

"Guys, there are people watching," Sienna muttered, coming up behind them. Her tone reminded Jenna of one a mother would use to reel in her squabbling children. "We can discuss this at home. Tonight's supposed to be fun. For our friends, at least."

Scowling, Ethan leaned forward, his face close to Archer's. "Our duty is to our witches, to the people –" he nodded in the direction of the crowd behind him, "– and the balance. We'll always honour that, but things have changed, brother. Our enemies are stronger, people are dying. The same rules don't apply anymore."

Archer's eyes flared. "You think I don't know that, brother? But if we start hunting our enemies, what separates us from them?"

Ethan didn't reply. He stared back, his eyes a grey storm of emotion, the truth of Archer's words striking a chord for them both. What Ethan was suggesting went against everything they believed in, everything they were. But sitting back and waiting for an attack seemed just as wrong.

The muscles in Ethan's jaw slackened and he swallowed. Glaring at his brother, he turned around and headed for the door.

CHAPTER EIGHT

Anger churning in his gut, Ethan dodged a grey cat on the sidewalk and bolted up the steps to the roof. The brisk breeze that trailed behind him went ignored.

He went to the railing and drew in a few deep breaths.

The band had tempered their music, opting for more mellow songs to suit the mood. Dozens of fairy lights were cast across the street, creating a blanket of white below him. The air smelt of rain. At the end of the street, the senior kids were preparing for their march, a flurry of wild decor, extravagant floats, and costumes that ticked every colour of the rainbow. Visitors had cleared the street in anticipation, the sidewalks crawling with a stream of people.

Sienna and Kate had settled at a table in the park. Declan and Archer hovered nearby, their heads bowed together in a heated discussion.

Arguing about him, no doubt. He knew they'd be furious he'd gone to search for Hazel alone, but what was the alternative? To wait for another attack?

His chest tightened.

Being a Keeper was all he knew, a destiny he treasured, honoured, but sometimes, like now, he resented the hell out of it because of the stifling confines that came with it. Keepers were good, noble, respected – dedicated to protecting witches and the balance of nature. Protecting the innocent. That was the easy part, something he'd sworn to do, but over time, as their enemies had grown stronger and claimed more loved ones and innocent lives, something had altered inside him. A rebellion against everything he was.

Their war was a constant, monotonous battle, where they only attacked when absolutely necessary. Self defence.

They defended.

And it was bullshit.

Their enemies had killed his parents, Sienna's parents, Rose, his sister, and many other innocent people. They'd attacked Sienna. Kate.

And yet, despite all that, their nobility and duty prevented any retaliation.

A rush of air swept across the floor, unsettling a pot plant at the top of the stairs. The railing groaned beneath his grip, caving from the pressure. He relaxed his hand, the motion triggering the flow of colour to his whitened knuckles. He frowned at the indentation he'd left in the metal.

Turning back to the street, he breathed in again, but it did nothing for his agitation, only calmed the breeze. The overturned plant he'd deal with later.

"Ethan?" Jenna murmured from the top of the stairs. She'd moved so quietly and he wondered how he'd missed her approach.

A few strands of blond hair had escaped the messy knot at the nape of her neck, softening her features. She wore a sleeveless black shirt tucked into jeans, the cut neat and simple. Not a frill or bow in sight.

She held up two beers, the sight of her easing his frustration. But instead of going to him, she held back and glanced at the steps. "I can leave if you'd prefer to be alone."

The flash of uncertainty in her eyes surprised him. She was a powerful warrior. A kick-ass *ninja*. Always sure. Always certain. Seeing that flicker of doubt intrigued him. Why, he wasn't sure. But it did. More than he'd care to admit.

He motioned her closer with a wave of the hand. "Plying me with alcohol?"

"Always good for easing tension." She edged into the dim light, handing him a beer. Her lips were pressed in a thin line and for a moment he wasn't sure if the worry was directed at the reality they faced . . . or him. She sipped her beer and scanned the street. "Wow. It's beautiful from up here."

"It's one of my favourite places. It all seems so serene from up here, doesn't it?"

"Which is why I come here." He nodded at the crowd below. "It's nice to see everyone so happy. It validates everything we do. They have no idea how fragile their serenity is."

"If serenity even exists. We've had quiet times between trouble, but they're more like beats, pauses, in a whirlwind of threats."

He didn't reply and sipped his beer, absorbing the truth of her words. Cynical but so true.

And it sucked.

She glanced at his brothers in the park below. "They look serious."

"Archer's the poster boy for serious." His brother had a forehead permanently creased into a frown. So different to Declan, the wilder, more reckless brother, who operated without a filter.

"Ten bucks you're in for a mammoth lecture when we get home."

"Like I care." Arguing with his brothers seldom bothered him. Tolerating them was easy. He'd had years of practice. He took what he needed, ignored the rest. Suited him fine.

The grey cat appeared on the top step, leapt onto the metal railing and walked toward them. Silent, casual, purring quietly. A burst of music filled the air, the sound echoing in the darkness that stretched beyond the town. Moments later, the steady rhythm of beating drums joined the melody, followed by an eruption of cheering. Startled, the cat meowed and sauntered off.

Ethan pointed at the parade in the distance. "Your timing is impeccable. This is the best spot to watch the parade and the fireworks."

"Just as well I brought beer."

"You'd make an awesome date."

She snorted. "I haven't had many of those."

"I find that hard to believe."

"Being known as the orphan girl at school had little appeal to the guys." She shrugged her shoulders. "And once I discovered my strength and abilities, I kept screwing up. Still do. No matter how hard I try to be more feminine, to hide my strength, it always emerges in some way. Besides, it's not much fun walking on eggshells around a man 'cause you're terrified to hurt him."

He smiled, all too familiar with that feeling. The strength they possessed was exhilarating, but in the company of ordinary humans, restraint was always a challenge.

She grinned. "Thank God for Kate. She keeps me busy, gives my life a purpose. Keeps me from knitting socks and making soup."

He laughed, not quite able to see her as a knitting, soup-making type of woman. Far from it.

The parade began their march through the street, the band pounding away at their instruments. Floats of all different sizes and colours moved along the street, creative and cleverly designed. Colour and excitement lit the air as the fireworks erupted. They were perfectly timed to the music, extracting murmurs of awe throughout the street.

His brothers had taken up a spot on the table in the park, Kate and Sienna between their legs on the bench in front of them. The women were smiling up at the fireworks, chattering wildly. Despite how calm they appeared, Ethan knew they were all wary.

Two grey cats sat nearby, unperturbed when the sky suddenly erupted into red and white sparks. A mild grin curled Jenna's lips and she sipped her beer. A gentle breeze toyed with the strands of hair framing her face and he had the urge to reach out and tuck them behind her ear.

His gaze shifted to her lips, full and soft and promising. Tempting. His abdomen tightened at the thought.

A steady pulse beat in her throat. Another round of fireworks lit up the sky, illuminating her face in a colourful glow. *Beautiful.*

He saw the moment it changed for her. The shatter of stillness.

Her expression tightened and she straightened, staring at the street below. "*Ethan,*" she said, grabbing his arm. "The cats!"

****

A hot spurt of alarm hit Jenna as she pointed to the cats below. One by one, they transformed effortlessly into humans. The shift was so subtle, so graceful and quick, that it went unnoticed.

"Oh no," Jenna breathed, an icy sensation raking down her spine. "They're shifters, Ethan!"

"What the hell?" he grumbled, reaching for his phone.

"Hazel must've opened the portal to Ameera."

What that meant sparked a torrent of emotions that Jenna was quick to sidestep. She couldn't think about that. Not now.

Ethan had Archer on speed dial, his barked orders swallowed by an explosion of fireworks that lit up the sky in a rainbow of colours. The fires in all the metal bins that lined the street flared brighter.

The bins exploded, in sync with the noise of the fireworks, white sparks flying everywhere. A few people noticed, moved out of the way, but the noise and sparks were so perfectly timed with the parade that it caused little alarm.

One by one, like a snake slithering toward its prey, the bins exploded, moving toward the parade.

Archer and Declan were already on their feet, Sienna and Kate sandwiched between them.

Smoke filtered from the sidewalks. It triggered a few surprised looks from the marching crowd, but they moved on, caught in the excitement of the night.

Energy, noise, and colour filled the street. Music played, people laughed, unperturbed by the explosions. It was all part of the show.

The smoke thickened. A few people coughed and backed away from the parade, arms flailing.

Fireworks exploded. Bins exploded. Perfect synchronisation. Light bulbs erupted. A tree caught alight.

By the time the cries of alarm added to the chaos, Jenna and Ethan were already running.

CHAPTER NINE

They raced down the stairs and onto the street, merging with the crowd. Confusion had broken up the parade. The music stopped, the explosions continued. Everyone began running. Screaming.

Ethan bolted into the panicked crowd, dodging people and fire, his focus zeroed in on one woman across the road. Sienna.

Jenna felt it too. That burning need to protect her witch above everything else. Despite the anguish. Despite the screams. Their witches came first. Always. She raced through the crowd, searching for Kate through the thickening smoke. *Kate!*

Declan came up behind her, taking her arm. "You have to get Kate home!" he shouted, tugging her with him as he walked.

"Where is she?"

He turned into the alleyway beside the restaurant. A wave of unease crashed through her as her instincts lit up like a runway. In a brisk movement, she yanked her arm out of his grasp and spun around, delivering a powerful kick that sent him reeling against the wall.

She launched at him before he could recover, slid around him and grabbed his neck between her arms. A death grip that could snap his neck in a heartbeat.

"What the hell was that for?" He gripped her arms, trying to break free. "Kate's in trouble, you crazy woman!"

"You think I'm stupid?" She tightened her grip, taking satisfaction from his grunt. "Declan would never, ever leave Kate alone during an attack, so next time you try your Mimic crap with me, try a better story."

He grumbled something beneath his breath, his words barely audible, and grew still. Then he laughed. The image of Declan disappeared to reveal the man beneath the facade. She recognised his mop of black curls and his jagged teeth. One of Hazel's sidekicks, although Jenna had hardly spoken to him in her time with them. A Mimic. Known for his ability to imitate others.

And now there were shifters too – able to shift into cats at will. Both dangerous and deceptive.

"There are innocent people here!" Jenna said. "Are you all insane?"

Safety aside, a magical display like this risked exposure and severe consequences.

"Mildly, but watching you and the Bennett brothers fight to keep our secret is so entertaining."

Jenna didn't respond, distracted by a movement in the distance. Two cats sauntered toward her, unperturbed by the chaos in the background. In a sleek, agile movement, they effortlessly shifted into their human form, two women Jenna had never seen before. They were small in build and had dark hair, porcelain skin and narrow, bright green eyes that smacked of malice.

Jenna heard the rush of air a moment before she felt the impact from above. A third cat collided with her, a light force that instantly grew stronger as it shifted. But Jenna was faster. She dropped the Mimic, simultaneously delivering a vicious elbow to her attacker's face the moment she became human. The shifter crashed into a dustbin but was on her feet in an instant. She had a similar appearance to the other two, almost identical.

They circled Jenna, snarling softly, the sound emanating from the back of their throats. Three against one. And the damn Mimic. Just her luck. Jenna braced herself as they closed in.

"STOP!" A voice demanded from above. "Get away from her! Hazel was clear this one was hers."

A young woman leapt from the roof and landed on the ground in front of them. She had short jet-black hair, eyes outlined in dark makeup. Small in build, but a fierce and powerful witch Jenna instantly recognised.

Megan. The young witch her parents had taken in. Despite their mercy, love, and guidance, she'd joined Hazel's cause anyway. The last time Jenna had seen her had been the night they'd tried to sacrifice Kate.

Jenna's hands closed into fists, her body flooded by conflicting emotions always sparked by an interaction with Megan. Good versus evil. Right versus wrong. Two women on opposite sides of the war. Bound by a twisted childhood friendship.

Their gazes locked, silent animosity bristling between them. A shared past, a secret they both fiercely protected.

"We were only having some fun," the Mimic replied, watching Megan with wary eyes.

"Get out of here," Megan ordered, turning to the shifters. "And tell your people to tone it the hell down. We're here to deliver a message, not spark a damn war!"

They hurried away, leaving behind two estranged woman and a heavy silence.

Anger soared through Jenna as instincts demanded she avoid Megan. The witch who wouldn't hesitate to harm them.

The witch who had just helped her.

An age-old voice reared to life within her, a whisper of a twisted loyalty Jenna had always felt but never understood. So compelling. So wrong. Manifested during the years her parents had fostered Megan. They'd both been seven years old when they'd met and had become firm friends. Sisters.

Enemies.

"It would've been nice to have a warning before you invaded our town," Jenna said.

"I warn you and I'm dead, Jenna. Besides, why would I bother? You destroyed any ounce of relationship we had when you betrayed me in New Orleans."

"You were about to kill my witch!"

"A witch we needed."

It was an ancient war between them, an inner battle they both fought. In truth, their friendship had altered the night Jenna's mother had sent them through the portal. They'd parted ways. Jenna had joined the academy and Megan had aligned herself with the very people Jenna's parents had despised. In time, they'd grown to be enemies, allied in opposite armies.

But somewhere beneath all that was a slither of respect and loyalty neither of them could shed. A legacy of the parents who'd raised them in a glimpse of time when they'd mattered to each other.

And if their alliances ever found out, they'd both be shunned. Or dead.

"I told you never to set foot in Rapid Falls again," Jenna hissed through gritted teeth, temper flaring.

Megan grinned. "But this is where all the good witches are."

"If you harm my witch, no amount of –"

"I'm not here for that. Not today." Megan's expression grew serious, her brows creasing with worry. "Hazel's opened the portal to Ameera, Jenna." Hearing the name aloud sent an icy spurt of alarm through Jenna. Their gazes locked, the mention of their old home jarring the rivalry between them. "I have a message from her."

"Forever her sidekick."

Megan let the comment slide. "She'll keep the portal open until Sienna hands over the Brogan Grimoire."

Ah, the damn Brogan Grimoire. Sienna's mother had once sealed the book with a powerful spell. According to her grandmother, a

54

Beckham spell and four enchanted stones would unseal the book, but so far Sienna hadn't been able to crack it.

Hazel was convinced the book contained the location of the witch massacre – a minefield of potent energy left behind by the slaughtered witches. If she ever found where that magic was buried, she'd have access to a power that went beyond anything they'd ever seen. She'd be unstoppable. So the book remained in hiding, safely tucked away at the Bennett Estate.

"Sienna will never relinquish the Grimoire," Jenna said.

"You know what will happen if that portal stays open!"

"And you know what will happen if Hazel finds that magic!"

"Ameera is so much worse now –"

"*You've been back?*" Jenna cut in. When Megan looked away, her lips thinning into a grimace, Jenna gasped. "Hazel's in Ameera, isn't she?"

"Jenna –"

"Did you find my parents?" A surge of desperation had Jenna in front of Megan in a sudden movement. "Did you see them?"

Megan's unfaltering gaze met hers and held, an ocean of memories bristling between them. "No."

The ache in Jenna's chest was almost unbearable. "Why's Hazel in Ameera?"

The question served as a stark reminder of everything that stood between them and Megan jerked back, her expression hardening. "Like I'd tell you."

A scream in the distance jarred Jenna into action. Anxious to find Kate and instinctively knowing that Megan wouldn't offer any more information, she backed away, scowling at her. "Stay away from my witch, Megan."

Turning around, she bolted for the street.

The fire had spread, claiming trees and plants along the way. The awning above a boutique window went up in flames.

A child stood in the centre of the chaos, clutching the arm of a teddy bear, crying hysterically. Jenna raced forward, scooped him up and pushed him into the arms of a young woman with saucer-wide eyes.

It began to rain. Soft droplets that soon grew heavy and persistent, dousing the flames. *Archer?*

A ripple of energy washed over Jenna, one she instantly recognised. Kate's magic. Her body soared with relief when she spotted her witch beside Sienna in the distance, surrounded by the three brothers. They were all drenched from the rain. Kate wore a blank expression, almost oblivious to the chaos, but Jenna knew better. Her witch had gone into that quiet, private place that would stop the madness.

Jenna was beside her in a heartbeat.

Instantly, as though Kate had flicked a whip, everything began to settle. The explosions stopped, the panic lessened, and the shifters retreated. Clearly, they'd been warned that the hybrid Null was no match for them. More so now that Kate had been practicing with her grandmother every day for the last few months. Honing her powers, developing her skill. Lethal.

When Kate snapped out of her trance, blinking rapidly, Jenna reached for her arm, frowning at the slight tremble beneath her touch. "It's okay, I'm here," Jenna said. "Are you hurt?"

Kate shook her head but leaned in, holding Jenna's arm.

"Where the hell have you been?" Declan snapped, scowling at Jenna.

"Bumping heads with your lookalike."

"A Mimic?"

"Yeah, and he was much friendlier than the genuine version." She pointed to the retreating shifters. No sign of Megan or the Mimic. "They're leaving already."

Cursing, Ethan spun around, but Archer was in front of him in the blink of an eye. A barricade of rigid resistance.

"Ethan!" Archer grabbed his shoulder, adding more resistance when Ethan ignored him. "Stop, dammit!"

"Let me go, brother." Ethan kept moving forward, taking his

brother with him. An inescapable force. "They attacked a town full of innocent people, Archer! This is bullshit and you know it!"

"You can't go alone! We don't know how many there are." Archer's shoulders heaved and his eyes flashed with something wild. He jabbed a finger at Declan. "Go with him. We'll take care of Kate and Sienna. Go."

Declan jerked forward, his protective instincts itching for a fight. But he hesitated, his gaze moving between Archer, Kate, and Sienna.

His brother. His woman. His witch.

Jenna stepped forward and touched his arm. "Go with Ethan, Declan. We'll be fine. I promise."

Declan's frown deepened, words unnecessary. They both knew what was at stake. Exhaling harshly, he scanned the crowd. With a quick nod, he pulled out the keys to his Harley Davidson and tossed them to Jenna. "Stay in town. It's safer. We'll come back for you."

As the two men took off, Jenna wondered if their witches were safe anywhere.

CHAPTER TEN

Usually, Jenna loved the feel of a Harley between her legs. The freedom, the speed, the power. Pure bliss.

Not tonight.

If anything, she felt ill. Fear and worry had taken up residence within her, her mind reeling with all kinds of thoughts that only escalated the closer they got to home.

The portal to Ameera was open.

The shifters had already filtered through and it wouldn't be long before other supernatural beings and creatures followed. Greed, destruction, and violence had depleted their resources ages ago, feeding a growing restlessness and hunger throughout the city. They knew there was another world outside their realm and had been searching for a way in for so long.

Something Hazel seemed quite happy to provide.

If the portal stayed open, it was only a matter of time before both worlds would be altered forever.

The thought frightened Jenna, but she couldn't deny the nugget of truth gnawing at her. After so many years of searching for a way back to Ameera, she finally – *finally* – had a way in.

She could find her parents.

Jenna's chest burned at the thought and she realised she'd

stopped breathing. The pressure eased when she drew in a deep breath, but it did nothing to ease the ache in her heart. She released the throttle, slowing the bike, and turned toward the Bennett estate. Home.

It was late, dark, and so damn cold. The rain had stopped, but thunder and lightning still worked its fury across the sky.

Sienna and Archer trailed in his SUV behind, the glint of their headlights a small comfort in a lot of tension. They'd opted to drive separately. Easier to split up if needed.

The aftermath of the attack had been a crazy whirlwind of fire engines, police, and ambulances that had their local sheriff, Pam, in a frenzy. Debris and glass littered the blackened sidewalks. Injuries were minor, so the sheriff had sent people home.

Kate sat behind Jenna, arms around her waist. They huddled together on the bike, gliding along the mountain pass on the gentle hum of the Harley.

They arrived home without trouble and Jenna exhaled as the huge gate closed behind them. Soft lighting illuminated the driveway all the way to the house. A safety they longed for. Levi, their Golden Retriever, stood on the front steps, always eager to greet them.

Only this time, there was no wagging tail. Or friendly face. The dog stared into the darkness, growling. Jenna's stomach lurched when she saw why. Two black shadows had emerged from the forest and were racing across the lawn on all-fours.

Hellhounds.

A force crashed into them from behind, the impact so powerful it threw Kate off the bike. Jenna skidded across the road, weighed down by the machine on top of her.

Jenna cried out as the gravel tore her flesh, but before the bike came to a stop, she was already scrambling beneath it, frantically searching for her witch.

Three enormous hounds surrounded Kate. They had large heads, pointed ears, and eyes that glowed like embers. They circled:

dark bodies crouched in attack mode, growling through upturned lips and sharp canines.

She'd seen them before. Back home in Ameera, now *here*.

One of the hounds glared at Jenna. With a howl, it turned and sped across the lawn toward her. The other two hounds were quick to follow, abandoning Kate. They circled Jenna in perfect synchronisation. Saliva dripped from their mouths, their snarls as frightening as their sharp teeth. Large claws protruded from their paws as they moved.

Jenna reached for the bike as Levi tore across the lawn, barking viciously. "Levi, NO!"

But Levi charged the hound closest to her.

Jenna climbed onto the bike. It revved to life and she sped across the lawn, drawing to an abrupt stop – just long enough for Kate to jump on behind her. With another loud roar of the engine, Jenna took off on a burst of speed and aimed for the house.

Abandoning Levi, the hounds set chase, quick to reach them.

Plan B.

"Hold on tight!" Jenna shouted, turning toward the forest. A dodgy decision, but their options were limited. And dammit, where the hell was Archer?

"Trust me, I'm not going anywhere!" Kate tightened her grip. "They're so fast! What the hell are they?"

The moment they reached the umbrella of leaves, blackness engulfed them. Jenna steered the bike between the trees, grateful for the single beam of light at the front. She zoned in on their surroundings, her Keeper instincts slipping to the forefront like she'd flipped an internal switch. Jenna gave into them, gliding through the forest as though she knew it by heart.

In a way, she did. She'd jogged these woods every day since her arrival in town.

The hounds made no sound, but she knew they were close. She could feel them. Smell them.

"Jenna!" Kate screamed when one came catapulting between

two trees. Jenna changed direction and the hound soared above them, connecting with a tree, yelping on impact. The other two had raced ahead, readying themselves for the ambush.

A barricade of canine force.

Jenna looked around, mentally scrambling for other options. The volume of adrenaline pouring through her veins sharpened her senses, numbing the fear. It was exhilarating.

The sound of the river in the distance set a new plan into place. "Kate, hold on!" she called over her shoulder, slowing the bike so suddenly that they both slid forward. In a swift movement, she changed direction and accelerated. "Time to lose these beasts!"

Kate tightened her arms around Jenna. "If the beasts don't kill us, your driving will!"

"My driving skills might be the only thing going for you right now. Show some respect."

The sound of water gushing nearby gave her hope and she sped through the trees, searching for the bridge Ethan had shown her the previous day. An old wooden bridge at the foot of the mountain. It joined two valleys, each side consisting of high rocks covered in moss, trees and ferns. A waterfall ran down the rocks behind it, flowing into the river below.

At the time, she'd even stopped to admire the beauty. Now, it might be their lifeline.

Finding it was easier than she'd expected. She slowed the bike, cringing at the sound of the heavy breathing and snapped growls behind them. The bike rattled along the wooden slats, the wheels skidding in the sand as they came to an abrupt stop on the oppo-site side.

Jenna's head reeled from her sudden movements. *Insane.* She scrambled off the bike, pulling Kate with her. "Where are they? Can you see them?"

"No, but I can hear them. They're close," Kate replied breath-lessly, scanning the valley.

Jenna tilted the bike toward her and twisted open the fuel cap.

She reached into her pocket for the matches she'd taken from the bar and shook the box at Kate.

Kate's eyes widened. "What are you doing?"

"Serving hot dogs."

"You're cracking jokes? *Now*?"

"You'd rather I was quivering in fear?"

"Seriously, Jenna, no comedic timing at all."

Even though it was dark, Jenna could hear the smile in her tone. Jenna grinned, tossed her the box, and aimed the bike toward the bridge. "On the count of three, you light the match and throw it into the fuel can. I'll do the rest."

"You're going to blow up Declan's bike?" Surprise laced Kate's words but she didn't argue and readied the match. "On the count of three –"

The rustle of trees signalled the hounds' arrival. All three of them.

"Now!" Jenna snapped, scrapping the countdown.

Kate dropped the match as Jenna gave the bike a mammoth push, along with a spurt of the throttle before releasing it. The bike charged along the bridge and smashed into the railing. Metal scraped and glass shattered, followed by a burst of air as the fuel ignited. Flames engulfed the bike and a deafening explosion echoed through the darkness.

Whining, the hounds paced the edge of the rocks, eyeing the fire, their bodies illuminated in a yellow blaze.

A second explosion claimed the bridge, devouring it within seconds. Wood splintered, ropes snapped, and the flaming bike plummeted into the river below, taking the middle of the bridge with it.

The hounds howled. They eyed the waterfall, the flames, and their prey standing out of their reach. One mock-charged, causing Kate to reel back, but it backed off as it reached the edge of the rocks.

"It's okay," Jenna said breathlessly, eyeing their predators.

"They're terrified of fire." She focused on steadying her breathing. Her body felt charged with fear and energy. The fear she despised. The energy she welcomed. The immediate threat had passed, but they had no idea what else awaited them in the forest.

"You've seen them before?" Kate asked. "What are they?"

"Hellhounds."

"What on earth is that?"

"Not something you want to mess with." As a child in Ameera, hellhounds had been the equivalent of the monsters under the bed that haunted children's dreams. Although they usually kept to the outskirts of the city, Jenna had always been terrified of them. "They came through the portal."

"How do we know there aren't more on this side of the river?"

"We don't, but now we know to look out for them."

With a final howl, the hellhounds fled.

Kate blew out air, her gaze shifting to the remains of the bike below. "So, Miss 007. We're stuck in the forest and you've destroyed our ride home. What now?"

"We'll stay close to the river. There's an old well further down. It'll be tricky to find in the dark, but if we can access it we can access the tunnel that leads to the house." An old underground tunnel the brothers had cleared in case they needed a quick escape. She pulled out her phone to call Ethan. "With luck, Sienna and her muscles can meet us along the way."

"Sienna would've spelled the entrance shut."

"You're the witch who eats magic. Piece of cake."

"*Eats magic*?" Kate laughed, but her voice sounded tense. "That description totally kills my image."

"Who cares if it'll open the tunnel?"

"Are you sure it's safe?"

Jenna's grin widened as she put her arm around Kate. "Don't worry. I won't let anything happen to you."

"I should hope so. I'd hate to be hound food."

"Declan would kill me."

63

"Nice to know he motivates you."

"Speaking of Declan . . ." Jenna grimaced at the bike. "I just blew up his bike."

They both knew how much Declan loved his bike.

"Think he'll be mad?" Jenna asked, even though she knew she'd just plummeted to the bottom of his Christmas list.

Her question went unanswered as they stared at the fading flames in silence.

And then Kate giggled.

CHAPTER ELEVEN

The air in the tunnel was hot and musty. Dozens of cobwebs hung from the low ceiling, difficult to spot in the narrow flashlight of Jenna's phone. It was a long, uncomfortable walk but the tunnel served its purpose.

Ethan and Declan were waiting for them, Sienna and Archer behind them. They all sported scratches and bruises, worried frowns and pissed-off expressions. But the tension in the air eased the moment they were reunited.

After exchanging relieved hugs and quick updates, Archer and Sienna led Kate out of the tunnel and into the basement. But Jenna didn't follow. Instead, she turned to Declan, hovering beside her like a riled-up bear. She swiped at the moisture on her forehead and sighed. "You really want to do this now, Declan?"

"Damn right." His words were quiet and fury clouded his expression. He pointed after Sienna and Kate. "Archer wrapped his car around a damn tree thanks to air bags exploding for no reason and Kate –"

"Is unhurt and home safely," she interrupted, reaching for patience. "I said I'd take care of her and I did, Declan. That tunnel was torture and I'm not in the mood –"

"Were you hurt?" When her brows lifted, he moved around her.

His hair was messier than usual, his shirt torn, a hint he'd had a struggle of his own. "Dammit, Jenna, were you hurt?"

"Like you care?"

"Kate cares so I care and if you're watching over her, then I need to know you're in top form."

A small smile broke free. "Careful, or I might think you're worried about me."

"Keep dreaming, Blondie." Frowning, he took her arm. "I told you to stay at the restaurant."

"Things settled quickly after you left. It was safer to leave." She yanked her arm free. "I brought her *home*, Declan. That was the best of a lot of crappy options."

"What happened?" Ethan asked, dropping a hand on his brother's shoulder, easing Declan away from her. His knuckles were red, swollen and scratched.

"We were ambushed in the driveway," Jenna replied, her lowered tone losing the defensive edge, "by hellhounds."

"Hellhounds?" Ethan gaped at her. "They're legends. We've never –"

"They came through the open portal to Ameera," Jenna interrupted. She explained what had happened and the more she spoke, the more their agitation grew. "We had no choice but to head for the forest."

Ethan ran a hand across his face. "Shifters, hellhounds, what the hell's next?"

"I saw Megan tonight. She had a message. Hazel wants to exchange closing the portal for her Grimoire."

Declan snorted. "Right. Like we'd agree to that."

"Of course not but . . ." Jenna inhaled quietly, her gaze moving between theirs. "If the portal stays open, what we saw tonight won't scratch the surface of what's to come."

They nodded, a heavy silence wedging between them.

Ethan moved to the side of the tunnel and held out a hand, motioning her forward.

She glanced back at Declan. "Oh, and I should mention you'll need a new bike." Her heart thudded at the intensity of his glare. Slowly, silently, he raised a brow. "It was either saving Kate or your bike. I went with Kate."

"That was the explosion we heard?" His nostrils flared. "How's it possible that in one night, *one fucking night,* creatures from hell set fire to our town and targeted Kate?"

"Oh, and that's the other thing," Jenna said quietly. "I don't think they were after Kate. They were after me."

****

They were after me.

Jenna's words echoed in Ethan's mind as he climbed the stairs to his room.

Hot damn, but hearing her say that had given him a good dose of the shivers. She'd said it so casually, as though being marked by vicious wolves on a magical high was the most normal thing in the world.

But he saw right through her. Beneath the bad-ass front she maintained around his brothers existed layers of worry that seldom showed.

Everyone had gone to bed, even though the morning sunlight would soon filter through the windows. They'd kept most of the blinds shut to keep the rest of the world out for a few hours.

He revelled in the silence of his room. Quiet and in the furthest part of the mansion. His space. Designed as a spacious apartment attached to the house, complete with an open-plan living area, kitchenette, and bedroom. Decorated the way he liked it. Simple and sparse.

The exact opposite of his lifestyle.

He never brought women up here. Excluding Jenna, but that was different on so many levels. Other than Sienna, she had the only woman pass he'd ever issued.

He'd soon figured out she shared his need for space – time out from the touchy-feely shit and all-knowing looks happening downstairs. Their single status amongst a house full of lovebirds had bound their friendship immediately.

His dates used to be fun. But now, with all the crap he and his brothers faced on a daily basis? Not so much. Although great women, making smalltalk over dinner with them had grown increasingly harder, soon frustrating the hell out of him – to the point that he'd begun to swap nights out for nights in.

With Jenna.

And they weren't even having sex.

He blinked.

Where the hell had *that* come from?

He tossed his jacket over the leather couch, ignoring the way his body had reacted to that thought.

Right. Water.

Clearing his throat again, he walked to the kitchen. It was small but stocked with the basics.

In the months following Sarah's death, other than venturing out to work, he'd holed up here. The main house had been too empty, sad. His sister's death had sent Sienna and Declan hightailing it out of Rapid Falls. He'd missed Sienna, worried about her, but Declan's departure had been a blessing. Had he stayed, his brothers would've killed each other, the rift more than a simple spat.

Guilt. Anger. Resentment.

And a shitload of grief that paled everything else.

Managing the restaurant renovations and the winery had fallen on Ethan's shoulders. He'd had no choice. With Archer's focus on finding Sienna, and Declan drowning his sorrows in whiskey and women, someone had to man the hell up.

Declan and Sienna had finally returned two years later to fend off Mason Brogan's younger brother, Warrick. They'd killed

68

Warrick and ensured Mason remained entombed in an underground storage room on their estate. A victory, but one that had come with a price. They'd almost lost Sienna. Instead, they'd lost Rose, her grandmother.

Kate and Jenna's arrival a while later had tallied their head count to six people living under one roof. Despite the size of their house, Ethan had soon felt crowded. After having only Archer as company for so long and with two budding relationships between his brothers and the women, the communal areas were quick to resemble an international airport on a romance high.

So Ethan often retreated upstairs.

Not that he minded. Kate, Sienna, and Jenna were welcome. They belonged here. But still.

He grabbed a bottle of water from the fridge and headed to the bathroom, knowing the shower would do little to cleanse the frustration gnawing at his gut.

At least it would cleanse the grime of the night.

His mind reeled with everything that had happened. The crows, the shifters, the hellhounds.

Jenna.

The shower was brief and hot, the air permeated with soap and steam when he finished. He walked to the door, towel-drying his hair with a vigour that resembled his mood.

Jenna's sudden appearance in the bedroom doorway drew him to an abrupt stop.

"Oh!" Her jaw fell and her hand came up to cover her eyes. Her cheeks coloured, not surprising considering he was as naked as the day he was born.

"Looking for something?" he drawled, lowering the towel just enough to cover his crotch. His ass was on its own.

She shuffled in the doorway. Hair in a ponytail, black robe and barefoot, no armour in sight. Vulnerable. *Beautiful.*

The hint of her feminine side always intrigued him. He'd connected to her as a Keeper, one to another. He'd fought beside her, witnessed her strength, but thanks to sheer willpower and many cold showers, he'd never dared to dwell on what he'd find if he delved further.

A whole lot of woman beneath the warrior.

Her fingers covering her eyes opened just an inch. "Ethan!" she cried, her voice laced with exasperation.

And Jenna never did exasperated. Ever.

He bit back a grin. "You should've knocked."

"Your door was open."

"I wasn't expecting company."

"Clearly." She peeped through her fingers again. "You're enjoying this, aren't you?"

"Tremendously."

"Well then, in that case, let me join in too." Surprising him, she lowered her hand and zeroed her gaze on him. *Down there.* Still blushing, but taking her fill.

This time, if he had the ability to blush easily, he would. Hot damn. Chuckling at her candour, he flashed a wide grin and slowly fastened the towel around his waist. "Happy?"

Her gaze did a lingering sweep across his body. "I've always wondered if your female fans were after your money or your body."

"Now you know."

"*Definitely* the money."

He laughed and went to her, wondering why she was here, surprised at how much it pleased him – and how easily she made him forget everything else. It was always like that with her. "Attacking my manhood again? I thought you learnt your lesson in the forest."

"I wasn't attacking anything."

"Yet we're back to my manhood."

"No we're not."

"I'd be more than happy to –"

"Not in your wildest dreams, stud muffin."

"– make some coffee, if you'd like."

70

A sheepish grin spread across her face. "That's not what you were going to say!"

"You'll never know, will you?" He took her wrist and drew her inside, frowning when she flinched. He froze. "You're hurting."

She didn't reply. Didn't deny it either.

A ripple of unease crashed his amusement and he quietly scanned her body for signs of injuries. She'd fobbed him off earlier in the tunnel when he'd asked if she'd been hurt. He'd suspected it then. He knew it now.

"What's wrong? And tell me you're fine and I'll feed you to Declan," he added.

She rolled her eyes. "Declan doesn't scare me."

"I know. That's why you're perfect for Kate. Now answer my question."

Her shoulders fell and she blew out air. "I have some serious road rash on my back from the fall on the bike. Usually it would heal, but I caught a few shards of glass." She held up a small first-aid box with her other hand. Damn, he hadn't even seen the white box that always followed trouble. "I tried removing them but . . ."

With a single nod, Ethan put a hand on her waist, led her inside, and shut the door.

CHAPTER TWELVE

Asking for help hurt almost as much as the pain.

Jenna swallowed the pills Ethan had given her, watching him as he rummaged through the first-aid box on the kitchen counter. A mild frown drew his brows together and a muscle worked in his jaw.

He was worried. About her.

His wet hair had been finger-raked into place. Glorious tanned flesh contrasted the white towel. He had broad shoulders and a smooth, muscular back. He wore the mark of a Keeper, a large pentagram tattoo, on his upper right arm. A perfect resemblance of their connection to earth, his connection to his siblings and their witch. Five elements of nature. Earth. Fire. Air. Water. And Sienna, the spirit, that connected them all.

He turned around, the front of him even more muscular than the back, ripples of abs that continued into the towel around his waist. A towel that covered a very smooth, *naked* waist she had no business ogling.

But darn, she couldn't help it. Fully dressed, she found it hard to tear her eyes away from him. Seeing him half-naked? Impossible.

She averted her gaze, suddenly all too aware of how under-dressed they were. Something stirred inside, a swirl of desire that mingled with the curiosity, and she couldn't deny the trickle of satisfaction that followed. She'd been alone for so long, trapped with people she despised. Survival – for herself and Kate – had been first and foremost on her mind. Not sex. It had been years since she'd felt any attraction to a man.

Until Ethan.

Oblivious to her scrutiny, Ethan tossed the box onto the couch beside her and headed to the bathroom. He stopped in front of a wooden drawer against the wall to pull out some clothes.

The glimpse of scarred flesh beneath his left arm surprised her. It ran along the entire length of his side from his hip to shoulder. A scar?

An old one. One his magic had never healed.

He shut the drawer and disappeared into the bathroom.

Puzzled, she sipped her water and looked around the room. A king-size bed nestled between two large windows overlooking the vineyards. The blinds were closed, the room lit by a single lamp. The wall opposite the bed had been tiled in natural stone tiles, a fireplace in the centre. Immaculate – which didn't surprise her. Everything about him was neat. His kitchen, the restaurant, the way he dressed, even his hair. He was an overworked, cranky housewife's dream.

With a charming smile, heaps of mystery and a body that could easily change the cranky status quo in a flash.

The thought sparked a grin and she leaned into the couch, wincing at the sting of pain in her back. She adjusted her robe.

Fluffy and soft. A little comfort in a lot of pain.

Ethan returned to the couch, dressed in a white t-shirt and a pair of black draw-string cotton pants.

Darn. She'd liked him naked.

The smell of soap and man permeated the air and she released a dreamy sigh.

If he noticed, he didn't say anything and sat beside her. He held up a shiny gadget he'd taken from the first-aid box, snapping the points together. "Ready?"

She groaned. "Why do I get the feeling this'll be painful?"

"Once the glass is out, it should heal soon."

Quicker than he'd expect. All Keepers had the ability to heal rapidly, but she was different. She healed instantly.

"It's still gonna hurt like hell. Why weren't Keepers blessed with a higher pain threshold?"

"Because we're mortals. Not gods."

"So why couldn't we be mortals with higher thresholds?"

"Don't be a sissy. Pain keeps us real."

"I can think of other things that keep me real."

He smiled. "The painkillers will help."

"Maybe." She waved a hand at his clothes. "But I preferred the towel. It made for a great distraction."

A smile curled his lips and she stared at them, wondering what he'd taste like.

His grin widened at her scrutiny. "Clearly you're in more pain than I thought."

Not for long. Once he removed the glass, her magic would heal the flesh immediately – if she allowed it to. But he couldn't know that. Not yet. Exposing her magic would expose her lineage – and she hadn't had enough painkillers for *that* conversation.

He made a circular motion with his finger. "Turn around and lower your robe."

"I hope you use better word choices for the women you bed."

His smile was pure mischief. "Trust me, babe, when it comes to bedding a woman, I have a separate vocabulary."

"That would explain your popularity." She laughed and turned around, lowering the robe off one shoulder, just enough to reveal the wound whilst still keeping her tattoos hidden. Until she figured out what they meant, they were for her eyes only.

He didn't answer and she glanced over her shoulder. A fierce frown had tightened his expression.

"Sexy, huh?" she said, opting for a cheerful tone. "A casualty of being caught between the road and the bike. Not my most graceful moment, but it all happened so damn fast."

With a quiet grunt, he picked at the shards of glass embedded in her flesh. "You're right. This will hurt."

Like a bitch. "Nothing I can't handle." She bit her bottom lip to keep herself from wincing. "You should have stayed in the towel, though. Given me something to think about while you do that."

"Something wrong with your imagination?"

"No need for my imagination. I've seen you naked."

"You haven't seen the best part."

"Just as well. That might make things weird between us."

He picked at the glass, dropping the splinters into the empty bowl beside him. "Weird can be fun."

Amusement coloured his tone, words meant to tease, but stroked her imagination. "I haven't had fun for a very long time."

His hand stilled and he leaned forward, touching his lips to her ear. "Well, maybe you should do something about that."

She stifled a shiver and elbowed him. "Stop messing with me."

He laughed and touched her shoulder. "I'm distracting you. We're done, they're all out."

"Already?" She'd expected worse.

"Nothing like a little friendly banter to dampen the pain."

"Whiskey works just as well."

"Maybe, but that was way more entertaining. It should heal soon."

"I know." She'd already felt the stir of energy, the magical touch that would wipe her slate clean. It was always exhilarating, but for now, she held back, reeling in the swirl of power. A pro at keeping her magic hidden. Adjusting the robe, she twisted to face him, relieved the pain had lessened. "Thank you for helping me."

"Of course. You were hurting." He discarded the bowl, wiped his hands on a towel, and leaned back against the couch. "We should get some sleep. We have a lot to discuss and my brothers won't rest for long."

For a while, they stayed silent, their mood shifting as reality crept in.

She tilted her head to look over her shoulder. His eyes were closed, his previous playfulness replaced by weariness. He'd lowered his guard, a warrior at rest. Beside her.

A beautiful man in the wake of a very ugly night.

"Will there ever be a time when we're not fighting the world?" she asked softly.

"We're not fighting the world, Jen. We're protecting it."

"Would be nice to have an off day now and then." A small smile broke free and he tugged her closer. With a large sigh, she nestled into the cushions beside him. "How are we going to stop Hazel?"

"We found a way to stop her nephews. We'll find a way to stop her too."

Sighing softly, she relaxed against the couch, against him. It felt good to have him near. It eased the anxiety gnawing at her, if only for a moment, and when she tilted her head so that it rested on his shoulder, he didn't pull away.

Instead, he rested his head against hers. The gesture triggered a small smile, giving her a case of the warm and fuzzies she'd seldom experienced.

They stayed like that for a long while, words unnecessary, revelling in the stillness they always found with each other.

She opened her eyes, fighting the fatigue. "I should go to bed."

"Hm." He sounded just as sleepy, but neither of them moved.

"Don't mention this to Declan, okay?" she whispered, closing her eyes.

"Don't worry about Declan. He's the least of our problems."

CHAPTER THIRTEEN

Jenna stirred two hours later, curled up on the couch, her head in Ethan's lap.

In his lap.

Lovely.

Her cheeks flared with heat and she sat up, hoping like hell she hadn't drooled on him. She wiped her mouth, relieved to find it dry.

He'd slept upright, his head resting against the back cushion. Sleep had eased his frown, masking the quiet thoughtfulness that often simmered in his eyes. He had tousled hair and a jaw covered in stubble. Rugged and asleep – a glimpse of him she'd never seen before.

Unable to tear her eyes away, she took her fill, fascinated by the vision of morning male beauty. Even in sleep, he looked powerful. Wide shoulders and a body of muscles that strained against his white t-shirt. He still wore his leather necklace, the pendant hidden beneath his t-shirt – one she recognised. His one hand rested on her waist, the other on his thigh. Beautiful hands. Working hands. His sleeve had crept up, revealing a glimpse of tattoo. She swallowed, caught by the urge to run her fingers across the ink. Or cuddle up to him again.

And she never cuddled. Ever. If anything, physical affection was something she usually avoided — a result of being raised for so many years in the mortal world without any. After leaving her parents in Ameera, she'd soon learnt that acts of kindness and attention usually came with a price.

But something about Ethan's presence, the calm that radiated off him as he slept, drew her in.

"Stop staring at me," he said quietly, eyes still closed, "it's creeping me out."

Despite the flush that crept into her cheeks, she smiled and hugged a cushion against her chest. Like that would conceal everything. "I'm looking at your pendant."

Long, dark eyelashes lifted to reveal beautiful, sleepy blue eyes. "Liar."

She tossed the cushion at him.

Ignoring it, he grinned and rolled his shoulders, breaking out into a yawn. "Are you okay?"

Besides the sudden rush of butterflies to her stomach? Yeah, great. "I'm fine."

He glanced at his watch and groaned. "Damn, only two hours?"

"We've got by with less sleep."

"I know but it still sucks. In my next life, I want to be an accountant. They get eight hours' sleep a night, don't they?"

"The honest ones maybe."

"Cool, done deal then."

She couldn't quite picture him as a number-pusher. "But think of the adrenaline rushes you'll miss. I don't think accountants get to ward off an attack of crows, chase a bunch of shifters and flee from hellhounds."

"Exactly." He stood and headed for the bathroom. He returned a few minutes later and within moments, the aroma of fresh coffee filled the air, enticing and comforting, the machine quietly bubbling away as it brewed the liquid.

She ran her fingers through her hair and hoped there were no mascara remains beneath her eyes. She slipped into the bathroom to check anyway. Nope, all clean. But the bathroom smelt like him. His soap, his scent. An aroma that quickened her breath. Stifling an inward groan, she splashed her face and rinsed her mouth.

He was waiting for her at the couch, two mugs in his hand. He'd finger-smoothed his hair, his cheeks covered by a thin fuzz she found far too sexy. "No doubt, my brothers are downstairs in full planning mode. I find them more manageable with a dose of caffeine."

She smiled and took the mug, the gesture as sweet as it was appreciated. She needed the caffeine kick after last night. The thought triggered a wave of dread as reality came crashing down on her.

"I almost lost my witch last night, Ethan." The frightening reality they always feared and fought to prevent.

"Maybe, but you didn't, Jen. You brought her home."

"I was watching for everything but the hellhounds. By the time I saw them, it was too late. They moved so damn fast."

"Hazel's crazy and unpredictable. We do the best we can. Now that we know the portal's open, we'll be more careful."

"And what happens when our best isn't good enough?"

It was a fear they faced every day.

He sipped his coffee. He wore a ring on each hand, almost identical. The mark of a Keeper. Antique silver rings, each etched with a pentagram. A symbol of everything they were, everything they fought for.

Most Keepers only wore one. Ethan wore two – his own and the ring that had once belonged to his sister.

Jenna looked at hers, similar but more delicate. It felt good to be able to wear it again. "In all the time I spent with our enemies, you know what I missed the most?" She flexed her fingers, showing him her ring. "This. After a while, once the loneliness kicked in and I became immersed in the violence and darkness, it was easy to forget why I was there, what I was fighting for. I could've used the reminder."

Ethan discarded their mugs and took her hand. But he stilled. His eyes narrowed as he twisted her wrist, palm facing upward.

Her stomach plummeted when she glimpsed the tattoo partly visible beneath her sleeve – a tattoo worn exclusively by their enemies. "Ethan . . ."

His thumb grazed it, his gentle touch a contrast to the irritation in his eyes. "They branded you?"

She tried not to flinch at the quiet anger in his tone. "If I resisted, they would've known."

Now she was marked permanently as one of theirs. She despised the symbol, ached to have it removed from her skin. It resembled everything she'd survived, fought, loathed. She straightened her fingers, her gaze shifting between her ring and the tattoo. "Ironic seeing these two symbols beside each other, isn't it?"

"I think it's apt."

"Hardly. The one symbolises evil. The other good. They contradict each other."

"A perfect reminder of everything we stand for. You should wear these symbols with pride, Jen. You singlehandedly snatched Kate from right under their noses. You saved a very special woman and strengthened our side. That's pretty damn bad-ass."

His words chipped at something inside, a wave of relief nudging at the humiliation she'd felt since they'd branded her. Exhaling slowly, she closed her fingers around his and squeezed softly.

"Thank you," she whispered, lifting her head. Pensive blue eyes stared back at her. His expression had eased but he radiated a quiet intensity that sent a shiver down her spine.

He stroked a lock of hair against her cheek, his touch triggering all kinds of electric sensations through her. His eyes had darkened, never leaving hers. And this time, it wasn't anger she saw but something else. Compassion. Desire.

For her.

The sizzle of electricity didn't surprise her. It had always been there. But their responsibilities and everything else had always stood between them. They'd never challenged it, never dared to.

Until now.

His fingers dipped into the curve of her neck, cupping her jaw in the palm of his hands. His touch was light, tender, and goosebumps erupted across her skin.

She offered him a small smile, needing to ease the heat between them. "We should keep our focus on finding Hazel."

"My focus hasn't deviated."

"Then stop looking at me like that." *Or mine will.*

"I'm a distraction?"

Yes. "No."

A smile hovered on his lips. He was so close, the heat of him making her breathless and unsteady. When he dipped his head forward, she stopped breathing entirely.

"You're lying," he whispered, his breath fanning her lips. He smelt like coffee and man and soap, the enticing scent igniting a shiver of excitement.

"That's twice in one morning you've called me a liar, Bennett."

His grin was way sexy and all-powerful. "Guess I see right through you."

She swallowed, caught by his boldness, and leaned into him.

With a satisfied smirk that sent her pulse racing, his mouth covered hers. His lips were soft, demanding, his stubble gravelly on her skin, but the kiss was so heated, the rush of desire and excitement so overwhelming.

And just as intense as she'd known it would be.

One hand curled around her waist, drawing her closer. Her fingers plunged into his hair and she relaxed, leaning into him, revelling in his rock-solid strength. The evidence of his arousal pressed against her hips and her libido soared with anticipation.

He kissed her until she was breathless.

But just as swiftly as he'd moved in, he withdrew. Inhaling

deeply, he took a step back but kept his eyes pinned on her. They'd turned a shade of blue she'd never seen before. Dark and hungry.

A loud knock on the bedroom door broke the silence as Declan pushed it open and walked inside. He froze in the doorway, frowning when he saw them. Together, drinking an early morning coffee, dressed in sleepwear. *Flushed.*

Fantastic.

Declan glanced at the bed – still made, thank God – and raised a brow at Jenna. "Since when did you take up residence in Ethan's bed?"

Jenna bit back a groan. "Declan, this isn't –"

"Any of your damn business," Ethan interrupted. He took in Declan's harsh frown and grim expression. "What's wrong?"

Declan crossed the room and opened the blinds. The light outside was dull and eerie, a contrast to the perky morning Jenna had expected.

Thick clouds had moved in, the air speckled in a blackness that marred the beauty of the mountains and vineyards.

"Bees?" Ethan turned to look at his brother. "What the hell, Declan?"

"Get dressed and meet us upstairs. Both of you. Pronto," Declan added, walking back to the door. "Reports are streaming in from all over. Hazel's unleashed a shitstorm."

CHAPTER FOURTEEN

Jenna met him outside the attic door.

She'd showered and opted for black clothing. The colour of his mood. She looked poised and controlled, not the breathless, flushed woman she'd been in his arms less than half an hour ago.

Without saying anything, they went inside. The aroma of herbs filled the air, along with the spice of tension. The spacious room had been transformed into a magical haven for Sienna. A shelf lined one wall, crammed with books, Grimoires, and dozens of jars and bottles. Two creased leather couches faced a window that stretched from the floor to the ceiling, the view marred by the bees outside.

Sienna sat at the table holding an iPad, Archer and Declan towering over her. With folded arms and feet planted firmly apart, they looked like scary bodyguards standing to attention. Grim expressions, pissed-off glares.

Ethan's mood had met its match. "What happened?"

Declan grunted. "Hazel and her minions of darkness had a busy night."

"It wasn't only Rapid Falls on their radar yesterday." Archer took the iPad and held it up. "It's all over the news."

Ethan reached for the iPad, Jenna peering over his shoulder, and scrolled through the images and news reports. Bleak images of people and places in the wake of Hazel's destruction. He looked up. "Insects?"

"Bees, roaches, grasshoppers, snakes . . ." Sienna shuddered. "She opted for cities and towns far apart, creating enough devastation to catch our attention, but not enough to alert the authorities that it's magical."

"It gets worse." Declan added. "Four Keepers went missing yesterday. Another one this morning. All their witches recounted the same story. They were attacked by shifters, were-cats."

"Were any of the witches harmed?"

"No. They weren't even touched. The Keepers were attacked and moments later they vanished."

Ethan heard Jenna's sharp intake of air and turned back to the iPad. Images of three smiling faces stared back at him. They'd been hiking in the mountains. Below was a single photograph of their body bags on the ground beside each other. According to the headline, they'd been attacked by a pack of wolves.

Hellhounds.

With a low growl, he held up the iPad and pinned Archer with a fierce glare. "This is all Hazel. The insect infestations, the missing Keepers. And now this. Still want to sit back and wait?"

"*Ethan.*" Archer's tone held a warning that went ignored.

Fuck that. "We have to stop her!"

"We don't know where she is."

"Even if we found her, we'd never pin her," Declan said. "The portals give them a mobility that makes them unreachable. You saw last night how fast those shifters vanished."

"We let them get away!" Ethan exhaled noisily and tossed the iPad onto the table. "We defend and protect because we're so damn responsible. Noble. And in the meantime, we're losing this war!"

"Ethan," Archer said, "we've been through this. We're not murderers. That's not what we signed on for."

"Neither was losing our parents and sister in this damn war!"

Ethan jabbed a finger at the iPad. "Four Keepers are missing. People were hurt yesterday thanks to *natural crap* we know weren't natural. Three kids were mauled by fucking hellhounds! It won't stop here and you know it!"

Archer slammed his hands on the table. "You want to Van Helsing them down before they hurt more people. I get it. You think I don't want that too? *But we can't.* We're Keepers. We don't kill just because we can."

His words struck Ethan where they mattered most and he glared at his brother, torn between the urge to protect – and destroy.

"Even if we agreed to kill Hazel," Jenna said, breaking the silence, "we can't. Not until we're able to close the portals. Especially now that she's opened the one to Ameera." Her expression darkened, her eyes clouded with something Ethan couldn't decipher, but she turned away when she caught his scrutiny. "She's not our biggest problem right now. The portals are."

"Jen's right," Sienna added, "and considering what's happened lately, those trapped on the other side have already started crossing over. Soon, we'll be facing enemies far more dangerous than witches and warlocks."

"What are we dealing with?" Ethan asked. They'd heard stories, legends, but the door to the other side hadn't been opened in so long.

"Shifters, vamps, werewolves," Jenna said quietly, "and that's just to name a few."

"How many?"

"Enough to make The Circle bind the spell that could unleash them," Sienna replied. "Before the portal spell was stolen, they used to banish evil warlocks and witches to Ameera as punishment."

Ethan raised a brow. "A prison?"

"Rose suspected a few Keepers were banished there as punishment for what happened to their witches the night of the massacre."

"I thought they'd all been killed?"

"That's what we were told. Tragic really, as amongst them was the last Salubrious ever seen."

A Keeper with abilities different to theirs. Ethan rubbed his temples and shrugged. "Not so tragic considering what they did to their witches."

"Either way, they wouldn't have stood a chance. They were as good as dead the moment they betrayed their witches. Here, they'd be loathed by others like us. In a place like Ameera, they'd be hunted by our enemies."

"Outcasts and in danger in both worlds. A fitting punishment," Declan added, his tone taking on a disgruntled edge.

"You weren't there that night, Declan," Jenna argued softly. "You don't know what happened."

"Dozens of witches were murdered, Jenna. Their Keepers stood by while it happened. If Rose was right and they were banished to Ameera that would never be enough to avenge what they did."

Jenna clenched her jaw and turned away. But something about her demeanour had changed, enough to catch Ethan's attention. It was so quiet, subtle, that no one else noticed but he'd spent enough time with her in the last few months to know she was upset.

"How do we close the portals?" he asked, trying to read her expression.

"Hazel's the only one with the spell," Sienna replied, turning to Jenna. "Only she can close them. Did you ever see her open one?"

Jenna shook her head. "If you had the spell, could you close them?"

"Any witch could. It's a glorified entry spell, but in order to close them, I'd need the exact spell."

"When I realised that Hazel's a dark caster, I tried searching for it. I wasn't sure what to look for and then . . ." Frowning, Jenna lowered her gaze and shrugged. "Things got heated so quickly and I had to get Kate out of there."

Her admission sparked a beat of silence. They knew what would've happened had she not saved Kate. They also knew the danger Jenna faced because of it.

Ethan glanced at Declan, not surprised to see his frown had

grown more pronounced. Like it always did when the details of that night surfaced. But this time, there was something more. A flicker of admiration in his eyes. For Jenna. Ha, imagine that. Stifling a comment, he turned to Sienna. "What would the spell look like?"

"According to my grandmother, it's a small spell book – like a Grimoire, but mostly about the portals and how to access them."

"A book?" Jenna's eyes fired and she stepped forward. "If we can find Hazel, we could steal it."

"*Right*," Declan drawled, flashing Jenna a fake smile. "Piece of cake."

"Bite me, Declan."

"Hazel's crafty. It's not like she'll keep the book on her kitchen table."

"I didn't say it would be easy."

Unease rippled down Ethan's spine. "You want to go back?"

Jenna nodded. "I lived with her for two years. She has habits. At least now I know what to look for."

"She'll kill you in a heartbeat!" Declan reminded her, pacing the wooden floors.

Although determination lined her features, Ethan saw a flicker of fear that she quickly covered by turning away. She planted her hands on her hips and glowered at Declan. "I'm not going to waltz into her den. I had two damn years of being crafty. I can handle this. Unless you have a better suggestion?"

"It's a stupid plan."

"Right now, it's our only plan."

"She can do it." Ethan's voice cut through their argument, steady and stern.

Declan scowled at him. "Great, now you're on her side?"

"I'm on the side that scores us a portal spell and Brogan-free margaritas."

"Assuming there'll be no more Brogans crawling out of the woodworks. And dammit, those bastards keep spawning!" Declan blew out air and ran his fingers through his hair. "Besides, this conversation is a mute point considering we have no damn clue where that witch bitch is hiding."

"She's in Ameera," Jenna said, ignoring Declan's double take. "I figured it out from something Megan said last night."

"That means nothing if we can't find the portal."

Jenna's expression brightened. "Could you show me where you last saw the shifters last night? Megan was here to deliver a message so it's possible they all returned to Ameera. If we can find the portal, we can follow them. Find Hazel."

"*No.*" Archer held up a hand. "No one's using the portals. It's too dangerous."

"Archer, this is the first time we have a vague location for one!" Jenna argued.

"We're not using the portals!" Archer's voice boomed through the room. "For all we know, it's a one way ticket to Ameera. It's too damn risky."

"Hazel's after chaos and disorder. Leaving the portal open will ensure that."

"We're not going. It's a realm we know nothing about!"

"A realm *you* know nothing about!"

Archer spun around to glare at her. "What the hell does that mean?"

Jenna's mouth clamped shut but she matched his glare.

"*Archer.*" Ethan's tone fired with warning. Watching his brothers interrogate her had ignited a flare of irritation, along with a surge of protectiveness. He scowled at them. "Back the hell off. Both of you."

"If Hazel's in Ameera, she'd probably have the spell book with her," Sienna said, taking Archer's arm and drawing him away.

"This is the first time we know where she is," Jenna said. "We find her, find that spell, we can close the portals. She'll be trapped there. No killing, no war."

A heavy silence enveloped them as they weighed up the implications of Jenna's words.

"Jen," Sienna said softly, "Archer's right that finding the portal is dangerous. I'm worried –"

"It might be our only chance at finding Hazel."

"It's not the portal I'm worried about. Or Ameera. It's Hazel. Before you betrayed her, you were on the same team. Now you're not. That makes her lethal to you."

Jenna looked up, meeting Sienna's worried gaze. But she didn't flinch. Or blink. "I can handle her, Sienna."

"She uses dark magic that's unfamiliar to us. Her powers and spells . . . they're unpredictable. And she's fuelled by evil and hatred. That combination is a level of danger we've never faced before."

Jenna held her gaze but didn't reply. Probably because she knew Sienna was right.

But what was the alternative?

"Declan and I found no trace of the portal," Ethan said, not giving a damn when Archer's glare slid to him.

"But you have a vague location of where one might be. That might be enough." Jenna touched her left wrist, stroking the tattoo. Her gaze met Ethan's and something in her eyes sparked his own excitement. "You couldn't find it but *I* can. Until now, I had no idea where to look. Show me the area where you last saw the shifters and I'll find you the portal."

CHAPTER FIFTEEN

The sun had begun to set and the smell of dinner wafted through the air when Jenna escaped to her bedroom, the need for space overruling the need for food.

The sheriff had left and the brothers were on a conference call with a few other Keepers. Jenna's suggestion to find the portal and steal the spell had met one heated discussion after the next. Tensions were at an all-time high, spiked by Hazel's threat of keeping the portal open.

Drawing in a deep breath, Jenna slowly exhaled. Her chest felt tight, almost as though there wasn't enough air in the hallway. She blamed it on the house. The arguments. Their inability to reach a decision. Hazel. Megan's message. And the truth that gnawed at them all.

The war around them had only begun.

It terrified Jenna. She knew what Hazel was capable of. She'd witnessed countless times how brutal Hazel could be to the witches and warlocks who opposed her. There'd been too many times she'd felt helpless, torn between protecting them and Kate. She'd helped where she could, even risked blowing her cover once, but she'd only been able to save a few.

As for the ones she couldn't help . . . those were the ones that frequented her dreams.

But despite the hell she'd lived every day, she'd stuck it out.

Because The Circle had chosen her. Despite her background, her parents. *Her*. And who turned down The Circle?

Her Mentors at the academy had conveyed their message. She'd been told to infiltrate their enemies – a group of warlocks and witches. At the time, the group had been led by Harper Avery, a Brogan sidekick. She had to discover what they knew of Kate and intercept any attacks against her. That had been her mission.

Kate. Above everything else, everything she'd endured, *Kate* had been her priority. Find her, protect her, and bring her home.

But everything had changed when Jenna had realised that Hazel was a dark witch caster. Her Mentors had wanted confirmation and the portal spell – a task Jenna had already taken upon herself before they'd given the order.

A search she'd abandoned when they'd closed in on Kate. Leaving the spell behind had been torture but she'd had a witch to protect, a duty to uphold.

Jenna's stomach turned, agitation pounding inside her chest with a force that left her breathless. The moment she shut her bedroom door, she sensed she wasn't alone. Instincts bristled and she spun around, air trapped in her lungs.

Ethan sat on the couch in the corner, a mild grin playing on his lips. He'd changed into a suede jacket and dark jeans, a hint he was on his way out. His elbows rested on the armrest, his fingers steepled beneath his chin.

Damn, he looked good in her bedroom.

She closed the door, her body flushed with a pleasure she refused to acknowledge. She tried to breathe, tried to hide her surprise, and opted for a casual tone. "Need something?"

"Yes. Air."

"You realise that's odd coming from you, right?" A half-smile

91

appeared, but he didn't reply. His presence filled the space in the room. A room that was private. All hers. "Shouldn't you be on a conference call?"

"My brothers can handle it."

Sitting on the couch, he seemed so placid, but she could see by the fire in his eyes that something was brewing. She'd seen that look before. The warrior was up to something.

She should be worried, but in truth the thought enthralled her. That side of him always had. Despite his easy, calm nature there lurked a quiet strength and darkness that could be dangerous if unleashed.

Ethan rose and crossed the room, his strides slow and even, and stopped directly in front of her. "You're staring. Again."

"You're up to something. I'm trying to figure out what."

"What makes you say that?"

"You're supposed to be in a meeting but you're here."

"You have a problem with me being here?"

"No."

"Your heart's beating very fast."

"Using your Keeper powers against me is unfair," she said, but didn't deny it. Her heart raced like crazy and she hated that he could hear it.

"Are we going to talk about that kiss?"

"Not on your life."

"It was a great kiss."

"Maybe, but we both know it shouldn't happen again."

"Maybe, but we both know it will."

His boldness made her grin and she raised a brow. "What are you up to, Ethan?"

"What makes you think I'm up to something?"

"Because you're here, in my room, waiting for me, and I know you're not here to talk about our kiss." And he radiated an energy that sent prickles all over her. Good energy. The contagious kind.

He edged forward, his body brushing against hers. She backed into the door.

"I came to ask you something." He placed both hands on the door, his arms a barricade of muscles on either side of her head. He glanced at her lips before slowly, slowly, lifting his gaze. "The portal. Going to Ameera to find Hazel. Stealing the spell. . ." His words were a low rumble of sexiness in the quiet room that took her breath away. He paused, allowing his words to take a beat. "Did you really mean all that?"

She nodded, not trusting herself to speak. The man had parts of her fluttering that shouldn't be fluttering. Not here. Not for him.

"You think you can pull it off?" he asked.

Another nod.

"You can find the portal?"

"I'll certainly try."

For a long while, he simply looked at her, like he was pondering his next move. She left him to it, curious, and tried to ignore the heat and energy simmering between them. Anticipation joined the ranks of other sensations already there, the intensity of the moment rooting her to the spot. She considered pushing him away, but even breathing was impossible. Not with him all over her. Her heart pounded, her entire body alive with a zing that seemed reserved for him.

His gaze lowered to her lips, lingered. Pushing forward, he dipped his head closer.

Just as she thought he'd kiss her again, he reached for her jacket on the hook beside her head.

"Then let's go," he said softly, his grin softening the heat between them.

She blinked but kept her expression a blank canvas, refusing to expose the flare of disappointment. Instead, she took quiet satisfaction from the flash of heat she'd seen in his eyes moments before he'd smiled.

Raw desire. For her. Again.

Wow.

"We're going out?" she asked, the smell of leather filling her nostrils as she pulled on her jacket.

He produced car keys and dangled them mid-air. "Up for a road trip?"

Her eyes widened and her jaw fell. And then she grinned, hope soaring for the first time in so long. "You want to find the portal. I thought Archer shot me down on that."

"My brother has his opinions. I have mine."

"This is different."

"I know." Ethan gave a sigh of resignation. "Archer's overprotective and worried. He's also driven by honour and our code of conduct. It's clouding his judgement."

"He's not wrong."

"He's not right either. Neither am I, but this waiting will only end in more deaths. We all know that."

"If we hunt them down and kill them . . ."

"We're *nothing* like them, Jenna." His words were spoken louder, with conviction, irritation tightening his expression. Then he relaxed. "Besides, I think your plan of sealing Hazel in Ameera might work. If we're crafty."

"I can do crafty."

The corner of his lip twitched. "Archer's doing what he thinks is right. I'm doing what I think is right."

Jenna tugged her hair out from beneath her collar, her body zinging with excitement – and fear. Lots of it. Thoughts of Ameera always did that to her. "But you need an accomplice?"

A small smile broke free. "It'll be fun."

The idea of returning to Ameera was as terrifying as it was tempting. But finding the portal meant finding Hazel – and with luck, the spell.

My parents.

Her heart soared, despite the tug of conscience warning her to tell Ethan about her history with Ameera. But she couldn't. What if he changed his mind?

"It'll be dangerous," she said instead, unable to look at him, afraid of what he'd see if she did. He'd always been able to read her.

"You're afraid?"

"I'm not stupid. I've seen what they're capable of." *And I've been where we're going.*

"But this time you'll have company."

Bingo.

During the last few years, the violence and darkness had been a constant struggle, but the loneliness had been the worst.

"Fine," she said, snatching the keys out his hand. As if she needed convincing. "But your brothers will be furious."

"Think I care?" He walked to the window, reaching for the rucksack on the floor.

"You've already packed?" Was she *that* transparent?

"For us both. Just the essentials."

"You raided my stuff?"

"A toothbrush and a change of clothing is hardly raiding." His smile was all mischief and too damn sexy. "But I couldn't resist adding a few of the lacy panties. Red ones."

"A shame you won't be seeing them on me."

"Is that a challenge?"

"*Dreams*, stud muffin."

His low chuckle made her blush. He pushed open the window and lifted a brow. "Coming?"

"Does anyone know we're leaving?"

Ethan put one leg through the window. "Nope. We're going rogue."

"You realise we can use the back door and still be rogue?"

"But this is way more exciting." He flashed a grin that rendered her breathless.

And jumped.

95

CHAPTER SIXTEEN

The fact that Hazel had opened a portal at the local school irked Ethan.

It reinforced how little regard she had for others. The late hour meant it was quiet and deserted, but soon the grounds would be crawling with people oblivious to the chaos around them.

· *That* part he liked. Blissful oblivion was what he and his brothers fought for. To defend the innocent and their homes.

Cobblestones paved the walkway, dimly lit by a few streetlights. A large fire hydrant loomed in the centre, its shadow twice as large on the uneven ground.

Under different circumstances, the school held a certain charm, fond memories, but tonight it smacked of something else.

Danger. Fear. And the thrill that came with both.

Ethan circled the fire hydrant, a flashlight in one hand. "This is as far as we got before they vanished." He rubbed his palm over the point of the fire hydrant. The shape reminded him of a pawn on a chessboard.

Jenna zipped her jacket, stopping just below the curve of her breasts, and unfastened her watch. Shoving it into her pocket, she reached for the flashlight. She kept close to the walls, alternating glances between her wrist and the bricks, pausing briefly to explore.

"We couldn't find the portal," he said. "What makes you think you can?"

"Because you've given me the first hint of where one might be and I have something you don't." She held up her wrist, palm facing upward. She flinched when he took her hand.

This time, he knew what was there and understood why she'd always worn a sleeve or jewellery.

His thumb traced the tattoo. "You never talk about what happened during your time with them. Or anything that came before that."

The thought struck as it had many times before – how little he actually knew about her. She seldom shared and had mastered the subtlety of fielding questions with ease. Her secrecy annoyed Declan, but for Ethan, everyone had secrets. So he seldom probed, despite his growing curiosity.

Besides, The Circle had sent her and he trusted them. Hell, they'd have his balls if he didn't.

"I've told you what you need to know. The rest is irrelevant. Kate's safe and that's all that matters." She withdrew, covering the mark with her free hand. "I hate bearing this mark, but right now it's our only hope of tracing the portal."

He let the deflection slide. "It is?"

"The portals are well hidden. A bit tricky if you're looking for a ride home in a hurry. Their tattoos guide them. Line up the two, add some light and bam, you're portalling."

"You've done this before?"

"How else do you think we travelled between cities? The portal to Ameera should be the same."

Damn, he'd never thought of her as an experienced portal rider before. It reinforced how little he knew about her.

She placed a hand on a jagged brick in the wall. "Right now, this thing is zinging like a beehive so I figure we're close." She began to climb, small movements, feeling her way upward, her feet tracing the places her hands left. Halfway up, she flashed him a grin over her shoulder. "You coming?"

"Of course." But he didn't move.

"You're not afraid to ride the portal, are you?"

He considered dodging the question, lying even, but opted for honesty. "It's never been at the top of my bucket list. And shit, what if Archer's right and it's a one-way ticket?"

Her smile faded as she clambered over the ledge and looked down at him. "Then we're screwed."

"Yeah, but then I'd feel crap 'cause I dragged you into this."

"You don't have to come with me."

"I thought *you* were coming with *me*." He joined her on the roof, glancing down at the school below. He and his brothers had spent many nights up here when they were younger. Beer-drinking, jesting, and messing around. Sarah had often joined them too. But it all looked different now, those memories tainted ever since the night of the carnival. That night had started off fun; he'd even hooked up with an old flame. A few hours later, Sarah was dead.

And only because he'd switched places with her. *It should've been me.*

The thought triggered a flare of guilt, like it always did when he thought of her. The fury and regret that followed was so intense that he gripped the railing beside him.

"Ethan?" Jenna's soft murmur did little to jar the memories and he stared straight ahead, caught by the overwhelming pain that riddled him. It was always like that, hot and blinding – the reason he seldom embraced thoughts of Sarah's death. Jenna's hand covered his, her touch soft, warm. "Hey, are you okay?"

He blew out air and nodded but didn't offer an explanation. He'd never told anyone. A guilt he'd carried alone.

Her soft gasp drew his attention to her hand. The mark on her wrist glowed. She took the flashlight, flicked the switch and shone it around. A gentle swirl of lights sprang to life in front of them, shades of blue that served as an instant doorway.

Jenna tilted her head to look at him, her eyes flashing with fear. Hell, he felt it too.

"Are you sure you want to do this?" he asked.

"It might be our only chance. If we find the spell, Sienna can close the portals. That'll deal with Hazel and any more creepy crawlies itching to get into our world. As for the next part . . ." She shrugged. "I haven't figured that out yet."

"But going to Ameera, confronting Hazel . . . are you sure, Jen?"

"No. But you'll watch my back so we're good. Unless *you're* worried."

He turned, facing the portal. "Let's get this over with."

"Our witches –"

"My brothers will protect them." Leaving Sienna felt wrong on so many levels, and had clashed with several objections since they'd left home, but this was something he had to do.

His phone hummed, the silly ring tone breaking the moment of tension. A theme song from the latest superhero movie. Declan had programmed it himself.

Jenna laughed, the sound delightful in the midst of where they were. His grin was short- lived, erased by the flicker of guilt when he saw Declan's face on the screen. Even though he wasn't in the mood for the backlash from his brothers right now, his need to talk to them before entering the portal was stronger.

"I've been calling you for over an hour!" Declan growled when Ethan answered.

"I've been busy."

"Where the hell are you?"

The familiar sound of ice being tossed into a glass pierced the silence. Knowing Declan, whiskey would follow.

"Ethan?" Declan prompted. Then he cursed. "You've gone in search of the damn portal, haven't you?"

"We found it, Declan."

A chair scraped the floor and toppled over. "Are you insane?"

"We're running out of time and options."

"You can't go alone."

"I'm not. Jenna's with me. And it's safer for Kate and Sienna at home." Surrounded by protection spells, Grimoires and two burly bodyguards. He hoped it was enough.

"You and Blondie are on a suicide mission."

"Someone's gotta man the fuck up."

"It's got nothing to do with that and you know it, Ethan."

Ethan heard the underlying anger to his tone. "I've got to go. I won't be contactable for a while."

"Ethan . . ."

The rasp of his name held all the emotion that Ethan felt. "I'll call you as soon as I can."

"Don't do anything stupid."

"Glad to know you care, brother."

"I don't want to be lumped with a restaurant to run. My glass is full as it is."

Despite the bleakness of the moment, Ethan grinned. "With whiskey, no doubt. And I think the term you were reaching for was *plate*."

"Who cares? Besides, whiskey's a given. It brightens up all this crap."

Ethan scoffed. "There's not enough whiskey in the world that can brighten up the crap we're facing."

"You can't blame a brother for trying. Archer's gonna be pissed, you know that, right?"

"He'll get over it."

"And while you're portal-chasing, I have to deal with him. Fair deal, brother."

"Yeah, payback's a bitch, Declan. You left me with him for two years. I'll be back in a few days."

"This is different. I wasn't in danger. You are. That changes everything."

"Is he there?"

"No. He went to check on Mason."

"Mason? Why, something happen?"

"Yeah, that's why I've been calling, dummy. But your news kinda trumped mine."

"*Declan.*"

"Pam called. A couple of teenagers were hurt at the river earlier. An animal attack."

Ethan straightened. "Hellhounds?"

"No. Large cats. Mountain lions. Or, at least, that's how they were described."

A spurt of alarm crept down Ethan's spine. "The last time we had animal attacks in Rapid Falls, they were a spawn of Mason's magic." He'd spelled domestic cats to be larger and stronger. Vicious and grotesque, an abomination Mason had used for his evil gain.

"Archer's gone to check that no one's tried freeing him."

Without Sienna and her Grimoire – or Kate's blood – that would be impossible. But they all knew it wouldn't stop Hazel from trying.

"Be careful, brother," Ethan said, unable to keep the grit from his tone.

"Likewise." Declan took another sip of his drink and cleared his throat. "Is Blondie ready for this? They get one sniff of her and they'll eat her alive."

He thought about her wrist tattoo and the guarded look that entered her eyes whenever the subject came up. "I think they've been nibbling on her for years, brother. She can handle this."

"Watch your back, Ethan. Both of you."

"We'll be fine. I'll call you as soon as I can. And keep Sienna close."

"Don't worry about Sienna. And tell Jenna that Kate's . . . tell her not to worry either."

"You could tell her yourself, you know."

"Like hell."

He smiled and ended the call, pocketing the phone.

Jenna took his hand, lacing their fingers. "You get this is risky, with a good chance of death, right?"

"Of course."

"And if running head first into Hazel's den and a city of supernatural freaks doesn't kill us, Archer will."

"I'll handle my brother but. . ." his eyes narrowed, "how big's *your* brave?"

"Bigger than theirs. Let's go."

He grinned. "You're so bad ass."

She laughed and tightened her grip on his hand.

CHAPTER SEVENTEEN

AMEERA

A damn roller coaster.

Of all the places Hazel could stick a portal, she'd opted for the top of a roller coaster.

Judging by the rust and overgrowth of bushes that surrounded them, it had been out of order for a long time. Hills loomed behind them and the city shimmered in the distance, signs of life that brought little comfort. The sun was fading fast, its rays peering through the thin fog that hovered over the city.

They were on the outskirts of town, surrounded by bushes and trees, in an abandoned amusement park. The carousal's horses were stripped. A lone swing swayed in the wind to the right of it, the chains rattling softly. A tree lay on its side across the empty parking area, the rest of it overgrown with greenery.

And the damn roller coaster.

"This part of Hazel's sense of humour?" Ethan grumbled, zipping his jacket to ward off the icy wind. He felt dizzy – a side effect of the portal.

It hadn't been that bad, but he still preferred his Aston Martin as a mode of transport.

Teeth chattering, Jenna adjusted her weight on the metal surface. "She likes to keep the doorways out of sight."

"Can't get more out of sight than this."

"If her minions can get down in one piece, we can too."

"They probably keep a stock of brooms up here for that."

Glancing over his shoulder, she looked down and grimaced. "Any chance you know your way around roller coasters?"

"Yeah, don't fall."

She smiled, one that failed to reach her eyes. Shoving her hands into her pocket, she gazed at the city. The smell of smoke lingered in the air, a result of several fires burning in the distance. No doubt an attempt to combat the cold.

"It's so quiet, peaceful," she murmured, motioning to the city with her chin. "So deceiving."

"It doesn't look very welcoming."

"That's because it isn't."

"What's with the amusement park? Bit of an odd fit."

"For the children. Despite the harsh life and dangers here, there are families trying to make a life for themselves. They're not all evil."

"Doesn't look very liveable."

"It's not an easy life here, but it wasn't always so bad. It's always been a violent, selfish city, but there was a time when the entire city was fully functional. Similar to back home. Once you block out the constant threats around you, it's easy to forget you're not on the mortal realm."

Looking at the dilapidated city below, he found that hard to believe. There were dozens of tall skyscrapers interspersed with smaller buildings, most of which were either half-built or damaged. Many of the roads and bridges were destroyed. A jungle of concrete and steel, coloured in grey and grime.

But not a soul in sight.

"What changed?" he asked.

"Greed. Violence. Power struggles between all the species."

"Species?"

She pointed in the distance. "There are four divisions in the city, separated by invisible boundaries. Vampires, werewolves, and shifters. The final division is a mixture of others." Her jaw tightened and her eyes narrowed. "Over the years, they depleted most of their resources. Neglect and destruction set in. More so when everyone realised they were running low on reserves. They've been fighting for a way into the mortal world for years. This is what's left."

To one side of the city, several buildings were flattened, the ground covered in concrete rubble. They faced a gaping black hole in the middle of the ground. It was enormous, surrounded by rocks and sand. The bottom wasn't visible.

"That's the pit," she explained, following his gaze. "There's water at the bottom and no way out."

"Their water supply?"

"No. They use it for punishment and torture. When there's a dispute between rival species, they usually resolve it by holding a fight at the edge of the pit. Whoever falls in first loses the argument."

"They sound charming."

Patches of light flickered in the distance, easing the darkness that had begun to set in. There was a mystery to the city that intrigued him – but it brought a shitload of unease too.

A city that Jenna seemed to know all about.

His head bolted sideways to look at her, her expression catching him off guard. Her troubled eyes stared straight ahead, her features clouded in a sadness he hadn't expected. And whoa, were those *tears*?

Fragments of their conversation reeled into place. "Jen?"

She started and shook her head. "We should get down. It's cold."

His skin prickled as anger rolled through him. He caught her wrist, stepping up to her. "You've been here before." It hadn't been a question. Her face and body language gave her

105

away. But his mind grasped for an explanation, an excuse. Any damn thing.

What the hell?

She lowered her gaze.

"Jenna?" A simple nod was all she offered. He raised a brow, spreading his hands. "Care to elaborate?"

"No."

"You really think you can drop something as big as this and I won't have questions?"

"I didn't drop it on you. You asked and I answered you honestly."

"So, please continue. *Honestly.*"

"No need for snarky, Ethan."

"Confused is more apt. Even a little pissed." He frowned. "I thought the portal hadn't been opened for ages."

"I thought it hadn't." She waved a hand at the destruction of the city. "But that's proof that it has. Opening and closing the portal makes both our worlds unstable. It causes earth tremors, a sign to the locals that one has been opened."

"Why don't we know about this?"

"Hazel's lineage has kept it quiet. If we knew, we'd stop them. Any effects of the portal back home are blamed on a natural disaster. No one ever suspects the portal." She gazed out at the city, her expression grim and pensive. "But clearly, the portal's been accessed more than we thought."

"The shifters, the hellhounds . . . this is the first time anything's escaped."

"Only because Hazel wanted them to. There'll be more, as soon as it suits her diabolical plan. She's always been wary of coming here, so the fact that she has means she's desperate."

"Why didn't you tell me you've been here before?"

"It was a long time ago. There's a lot I don't tell you, Ethan, but it doesn't change whose side I'm on."

"And you're sure it's mine?" She flinched but held her ground and he loathed the hurt that crept into her eyes. Hurt he'd caused. He cursed softly. "You should've said something."

"It's not something I ever talk about." Irritation laced her tone and she yanked her hand back. "And yeah, maybe I should've mentioned it, but talking about it dredges up crappy memories I'd rather avoid!"

"Jenna –"

She turned away, testing the metal bars. When they didn't budge, she stepped forward, repeating the motions.

"You know I'm not going to let this go, right?"

"Of course. I'd be worried if you did. We're at war and we're alone." She motioned to the city with a brief nod. "Two people facing a ton of danger. You'd be a fool not to want to know more about the only person watching your back."

Her words stirred something inside him. A connection to her, unlike anything he'd ever had with another woman before. She got it. Their world. Their battle. Their code.

Their gazes met, a silent understanding easing its way between them.

"I will explain," she said softly, "but I need time. It's difficult being back. But I'm on your side, Ethan. All the way. Just know that."

That was enough. For now. Despite her secrets, he trusted her. And usually, he had a damn good sense of judgement. He just hoped like hell he wasn't way off this time. "So for now you expect me to continue as though this conversation never happened?"

"Not expecting. I'm asking. Please."

Something in her tone, her eyes, tugged at him and he found himself nodding. "Fine, but I won't be sidelined for long, Jenna. No matter how difficult it is for you to face your fears or secrets or whatever goddamn crap you're hiding. I want to know what the hell's going on."

Her eyes flared but she didn't protest. "Fair enough. And just for the record, I had no idea that Hazel planned to open –" The snap of metal pierced Jenna's words as the track gave way beneath her feet. The sudden movement threw her weight and she fell through the gaping hole.

He plunged forward and caught her wrist, the abrupt stop jerking them both. He dug in his heels, reaching for a hold with his free hand. Her body slammed into the track and dangled mid-air like a rag doll.

The metal creaked around them. Her head tipped back and wide eyes peered up at him.

The image of her hanging beneath him, clutching his hand, eyes flashing with fear, struck him somewhere deep inside. Icy fingers gripped his heart and instead of pulling her to safety, he froze.

CHAPTER EIGHTEEN

Sucking in shallow gasps of air, too afraid for more in case the metal gave way, Jenna clung to Ethan's hand for the lifeline it was.

The wind whipped around her, the icy chill cutting into her flesh. Her heart pounded, adrenaline soared, and she waited for Ethan to pull her up, surprised when he hesitated. She blinked, gaping at him. "Ethan, pull me up!"

He didn't respond and stared down at her. Frozen. A harsh frown etched his expression and even though he was looking at her, it was as if he wasn't *seeing* her.

"Ethan?" He'd disappeared, even though he hadn't moved. What on earth? She jerked, terrified she'd dislodge them both. "Ethan!"

He inhaled sharply, his nostrils flaring. With a grunt, he hauled her upward. They collapsed onto the small platform behind him, breathless and panicked.

"What happened?" Jenna gasped.

He growled low in his throat, swiped at his forehead and turned away. But she saw what he'd tried to hide. That flash of terror that had held him prisoner.

"Ethan?" she panted.

"I'm sorry." Cursing softly, he drew her into his arms and

buried his face into her hair. His heavy breathing and racing heart reverberated against her. "I'm so sorry."

"Where'd you go?" Something had rattled him. Something triggered by the fall. She'd never seen him like this before. "You don't like heights?"

"No, it's not that. At all. Lately, I keep having the same dream." He lifted his head, the fierce frown unfaltering. "It's of Sarah. The surroundings and circumstances keep changing but the outcome's always the same." He nodded in the direction of the broken bars. "That was such a clear simulation of my dream that it caught me off guard. I'm sorry if I frightened you."

"Will you tell me about it?"

"She's dangling from a ledge and I'm holding her hand. Every time I'm about to pull her to safety, her hand slips. Every damn time." He rested his head against the metal bars behind him. "And every time I wake up, I'm reminded that she couldn't be saved, that I couldn't help her."

"Ethan, you're not to blame for her death."

His jaw tightened and for a while he didn't reply. He cleared his throat. "After Sienna stripped Mason of his magic, we sealed him in the tomb. His brother, Warrick, was unconscious on the floor." He gritted his teeth and closed his eyes. "I shouldn't have left her with him."

"Warrick was unconscious, Ethan. You couldn't have known."

"She was there protecting Sienna, but when Warrick attacked Declan she died protecting him."

He seldom spoke about Sarah's death. Losing her had affected them all in so many ways, the cuts brutal, irreparable, different, but equally traumatic.

"She was my baby sister and we should've been the ones protecting her."

"She was a warrior. Like us."

He nodded and opened his eyes. "That night changed everything. We'd always been together, inseparable, and then suddenly

110

she was gone. A big fucking gaping hole that couldn't be filled. Sienna left, Declan went on a whiskey spree, and Archer became even more of a recluse."

"What about you?"

He shrugged. "I got on with it. Someone had to hold all the shit together. I threw myself into the restaurant renovations. Figured she would've liked that. After all, the restaurant was her dream. When Declan and Sienna returned, I got caught up in defeating Warrick and Harper and keeping my brothers from killing each other."

"And now? Warrick and Harper are gone. Your brothers have patched their relationship." They'd even reached a level of peace with Sienna and Kate that still evaded Ethan. "Maybe that's why you're suddenly having these dreams."

"It's been more than two years since she died. Why the hell now?"

"You were preoccupied. Now you're not."

He looked at her for a long while but didn't reply.

Instinctively knowing he wouldn't say anything more, Jenna sighed and leaned her head against his shoulder. His arm snaked around her waist, drawing her closer. The movement felt good, warm, and she smiled. "Sarah would be furious to see how we've mourned her."

"Yeah, guess she'd kick our asses for all the moping."

Jenna had been a loner at the academy for so long and Sarah's arrival had saved her. For the first time in years, Jenna had found something to hold onto. *Her purpose.* Sarah had helped her see that. They were Keepers, destined to protect and defend. If she withered away, her parents' honour, their sacrifice, and everything they'd fought for would've been for nothing.

So she'd fought harder, thrown herself into the training, determination overruling the emotion. In the process, her friendship with Sarah had evolved into one she'd treasured.

She could easily picture Sarah's face – short black hair,

mischievous smile, and a zest for life. With three older brothers to live up to, the tiny woman had been dynamite. Feisty, outspoken, and confident.

Jenna nudged Ethan with her elbow. "Remember that drama at the academy when one of the Mentors was trapped in his car?"

"The one almost eaten by the creeper?"

"The way he carried on, you'd swear it was about to devour him." She smiled. "It was all Sarah's doing."

Surprise crossed his face and he grinned, the motion triggering the dimple in his cheek. "That was Sarah?"

"Uh, huh. She was furious because he refused to let us participate in an activity the guys were doing. Told her he'd put something 'less challenging' together for us."

Ethan's smile widened. "So she wrapped his car in a creeper?"

"With him in it." She laughed, recalling the man's outrage. "He never underestimated her again."

His low chuckle eased the tension.

A gentle hum of an engine drew her attention and she stood, searching, instantly tracking the approaching headlights in the distance. She pointed at the train and stood. "Ever boarded a moving train before?"

"We're hitching a ride?"

She flashed him a grin and held out a hand. He took it, allowing her to pull him up. "Riding portals and train-hopping. Who said life was boring?"

"Beats sitting at home arguing with my brothers."

"Still want to be an accountant in your next life?"

He laughed and shook his head.

CHAPTER NINETEEN

Ethan couldn't breathe, the stench of cigarette smoke and sweat and fifty shades of agitation making him feel as edgy as hell.

He stepped up to the door of the train and shoved it open. The fresh air helped, despite the cold, and he inhaled the cool night air.

The locals were familiar with train-hoppers but instantly curious about Ethan and Jenna. He could see it in their open stares and whispers. They kept their distance and Ethan kept his guard up.

But no one seemed interested – or brave – enough to bother them.

Only two lights worked, illuminating the train in a dim glow. The lack of seats had people crouched against the sides of the carriage, their bodies swaying to the rhythm of the train.

A group of teenagers huddled against each other. Their pupils were dilated, their bodies an artwork of tattoos and piercings. The oldest boy, tall and skinny, skimmed a gaze across Jenna's body.

Ethan bit back the urge to reach for her, shield her. *Stake his claim.* But she stood her ground, head held high, and returned the scrutiny with a glare of her own. When the boy finally looked away, Ethan almost smiled.

Almost. Because he knew that others wouldn't be as easily diverted. Not in a place like this.

A movement in his peripheral vision drew his attention. An older woman stood in the corner of the train, watching them. She wore a beanie over curly brown hair and a blue coat buttoned to her throat.

He turned back to the door, just in time to see a stray dog limping beside the track, its head low, unperturbed by the roar of the train. It stopped to sniff a pile of garbage against the fence, scavenging for dinner, but scattered when a vagrant chased it away.

They passed a bridge with a big gaping hole on one side, exposing steel reinforcements that dangled mid-air. The streets were mostly in darkness, lit by the odd streetlight along the sidewalks. Litter and chunks of concrete were scattered everywhere. The buildings resembled construction sites, half-built or dilapidated. Most of the windows were shattered, the discoloured walls covered in graffiti.

Jenna appeared behind him, tugging at the collar of her jacket. She folded her arms, tucking in her hands. Her hair fluttered in the wind and her teeth chattered, but she leaned into the doorway, drawing in a deep breath.

The urge to hold her, warm her, clashed with the agitation creating a shitstorm inside him. Instead, he remained still and studied her, sensing the energy that rolled off her in waves.

Despite the danger, their environment, being back had triggered something in her. *She'd been here before.* Hot damn. What that meant triggered all sorts of questions he was forced to shelve.

For now.

Clamping the frustration, he turned his attention to the rowdy cheers in the distance. A crowd had gathered beside the tracks, surrounding two men in a fist fight, their cheers whipped away in the rush of wind as the train sped by.

A shout rang out from the carriage next door. The door at the back of the train opened with a force that almost dislodged the hinges. A large man stood in the doorway, feet planted firmly apart. He had a bald head and a sleek row of black studs that lined each eyebrow. A thick beard covered most of his face.

The woman in the blue coat gasped and recoiled into her corner.

His presence caused a ripple of movement from the teenagers on the floor, inconspicuous, but Ethan heard the rapid increase in their heartbeats. The kind usually triggered by fear.

One of the youths elbowed his friend. "It's Axel," he whispered, moving toward the wall, eyeing Axel's three buddies hovering directly behind him. They all wore identical studs on each eyebrow.

Axel searched the train, pegging the woman in the corner with a fierce glare. "Where the hell have you been?"

She stood rigid, unflinching when Alex stomped toward her. The thud of his steps echoed through the train, so heavy that Ethan felt the vibrations beneath his feet. With a little more effort, he even felt the vibrations of the woman's racing heartbeat.

Ethan welcomed the trickle of energy that swept through him and dismissed the voice that cautioned to reel it in. Deliberately employing a bored expression, he drew on his magic and targeted the flow of power. The wind picked up speed outside the train, howling against the windows.

He added more power, channelling the air, moulding it to his will.

All at once, the side doors burst open and an icy wind gushed through the train, sparking a ripple of surprised murmurs.

Axel swayed and collided with the teenagers. One laughed, receiving an instant punch in the face for it. The boy reeled, clutching a bloody nose. His friends eased back, surrounding him. All but one. The skinny kid who'd ogled Jenna stepped forward, glaring at Axel, hatred oozing from his posture.

Axel zeroed in on the younger boys. A small smile eased his expression, the kind that lacked humour. "You think this is funny?"

"Axel –" the boy replied, but snapped his mouth shut when Axel grabbed him by the throat.

Grunting, Axel squeezed. The smile had vanished. His bulk and strength gave him the advantage and he added more pressure, smiling when the motion triggered a round of choked gasps.

The woman in the coat stepped forward. "Axel, stop it!"

Axel glanced at the open door opposite him. With a low growl, he swung around and shoved the kid toward it.

In a flash of movement, Jenna was there, using her body as a barrier between the kid and the door. He slammed into her, grunting on impact, and scrambled toward his friends when she pushed him away. Everyone gaped at her.

She turned, finding Axel's gaze. "Pick on someone your own size, asshole."

Axel burst out laughing and hitched a brow. "Who the fuck are you?"

"Someone who despises bullies."

"But it's so . . . fun."

"For you maybe. Not much fun for the kid."

"His problem."

"You're twice his size."

"I'm twice *your* size."

Jenna lifted her chin in quiet determination. "Underestimating me 'cause I'm a woman would make you a fool as well as an asshole."

The group of boys snickered, but were quick to shut up when Axel shot them a glare.

Ethan took a step forward, his reaction hovering between admiration and wariness. Even though Jenna could kick Axel's ass and most likely win, the man's expression sent a ripple of unease through him.

And he had no idea what the hell Axel was or what powers he possessed.

When Axel took three heavy strides toward Jenna, Ethan slid between them. A rock-solid barrier.

Axel halted in his tracks and looked at Ethan, challenge rolling off him in waves. "Let me guess. You don't like bullies either?"

Ethan's brows hitched. "Attacking kids and women? Doesn't say much for you."

"You speak for her?"

"No one speaks for her."

"So back the fuck off and mind your own business."

"She *is* my business."

"Ah, that why you're guarding her like a watch dog?"

"Of course. I protect my own. Always."

Axel's gaze flickered between theirs, settling on Ethan. A pregnant silence filled the air whilst Axel appeared to be mentally sizing him up. Ethan maintained his poker face and clenched fists, his body on full alert. They were evenly matched in height and size but Axel had three beefy backups at his heels.

The train's momentum changed, causing a rustle of movement as people gathered at the open doorway. The woman in the blue coat shifted, her attention still on Jenna. She mumbled to herself, the words a mere whisper that Ethan missed.

A muscle worked in Axel's neck. He took a step back and sniffed the air, breathing it in like he'd smelt something delectable. "I could smell your stench from two coaches down. Fresh blood. Guessing Hazel sent you. You're new here."

What the hell did that mean? "That a problem?"

"For you?" Axel grinned. "Absolutely. But for now, I'll leave you to the others. If I smelt you, they will too. Maybe even the vamps and werewolves too."

"Good to know."

"Let's see how long you last," Axel said, his smile doing little to ease the malice in his eyes. The look on his face reminded Ethan of a predator toying with its prey. Still smiling, Axel backed away when the train slowed. Without waiting for it to stop, he leapt, followed immediately by his friends, their excited calls echoing through the night.

"I could've handled him," Jenna said.

Ethan ignored the irritation in her voice and took her arm. "Of course"

"So why the interference?"

He led her to the door, scowling at the group of teenagers ogling them. Axel's warning made him uneasy. Witches and warlocks were familiar to him. Vampires and werewolves weren't.

The platform consisted of a concrete slab. The steps had crumbled. Music played in the distance, a magnet for the teenage boys.

Ethan followed, moving at the same pace as the others, despite the full run his instincts urged. Jenna sensed it too, the need to blend, matching his strides in silence. The music grew louder as they rounded the corner and walked through a wide arch. It had a faded name scrawled on the wall.

The Square.

A massive courtyard of abandoned bars. Dark grey cobblestones paved the ground, littered with concrete rubble and broken tables and benches. Most of the bars were boarded up – all but one. Soozie's. A waitress swept the floor outside. Two prostitutes stood nearby, both dressed in cocktail dresses that were far too skimpy for the cold. The smell of their cheap perfume wafted through the air.

When the teenagers settled at a table, the women called out a greeting and sidled closer.

Jenna took Ethan's arm and exhaled loudly. "I need a drink."

A beer bottle hurtled through the air and shattered on the ground.

"Something tells me that one drink won't suffice," he grunted.

A dustbin clattered and Ethan swung around, surprised to see the woman from the train standing outside Soozie's. She straightened the bin and climbed the three stairs to the front door, pausing in the doorway to glance at Jenna.

Their gazes locked and held for a long while before she disappeared into the bar.

Jenna nodded in the direction of the woman. "I think we found our drink."

"She didn't look very welcoming."

"That's probably because she isn't."

CHAPTER TWENTY

The first thing Jenna noticed when she walked into the bar was the old plumbing pipes that had been revamped into lights, the bulbs covered by whiskey bottles.

Which made her think of Declan.

The bar had an industrial feel, decorated with recycled material. A high ceiling, low lighting, wide arch windows and raw brick walls. Mismatched tables and chairs were placed throughout the room. A long counter made up of railway sleepers ran along the length of the back wall, the shelves stocked with glasses and empty bottles. A massive clock hung on the wall to the right, a red jukebox beneath it. The song they'd heard had ended, leaving the bar in silence.

The woman from the train stood behind the counter, repacking glasses. She'd shed the beanie and coat and wore a black apron.

"Following me?" she asked, without looking up.

Her quiet, guarded tone had Jenna reaching for an easy smile. "It appears we have the same taste in bars. You open for beers yet?"

"It's early."

"The money's still good."

She glanced at Ethan. He'd disappeared toward the back, no doubt making sure they were alone. With a brief nod, she motioned to the chairs in front of her. "What can I get you?

"Two beers please." Jenna took a seat and glanced around. A blackboard stood against the wall, listing the daily special – soup. No doubt the only food on offer. The ingredients were smudged. "You expecting a lot of people later?"

"Always. Give this place half an hour and it'll be swarming with my regulars. My bar is one of the few still operating."

"I'm Jenna." She jabbed a thumb in Ethan's direction. "And that's Ethan."

"You saved that kid on the train. Not sure if you're either brave or stupid. Not many people stand up to Axel."

"What – who is he?"

"He runs this district and everyone in it. You shouldn't be going around asking that. All it does is mark you as a newbie in town. That's gonna get you killed. You're lucky Axel's had his fill for the night otherwise he'd never have walked away."

"Fill?"

Ignoring her question, the woman offered a hand. "I'm Susan."

Jenna reached out, surprised when Susan recoiled as though she'd been scalded, staring at the tattoo peeking out from beneath Jenna's sleeve. *Oh, crap.*

"Two beers coming up," Susan said softly, backing away. Her strained smile faded as she reached beneath the counter.

The baseball bat came out of nowhere.

****

The shatter of glass, accompanied by Susan's squeal, had Ethan bolting for the bar.

Jenna had the woman pinned to the counter, using her body weight to restrain her. Her brows were puckered, her expression more one of irritation than anger. "What the hell was that for?"

"Let me go!"

Jenna glanced at the bat beside them, surrounded by glass. "A baseball bat? Really?"

121

"Jen," he said, injecting a casual tone to his words. "Get off her."

"She attacked me. With a damn baseball bat."

Apparently, that insulted her more than the attack itself. Which explained the irritation. He smothered a grin and moved closer. "She's half your size."

"Doesn't make her swing less brutal."

He thought of the photograph he'd seen on the back wall. Four generations of women, each wearing pentagram necklaces. "She wasn't attacking you. She was defending herself."

Jenna leaned forward. "I meant you no harm. Why'd you do that?"

"I was wrong about you. You're one of them," Susan hissed. Jenna stilled but Ethan caught the slight flinch. "I've seen that mark around here enough times recently to know who to avoid."

"You're a witch?"

Ethan picked up the bat and placed a hand on Jenna's shoulder. "Jenna, back off."

But she didn't budge.

"She attacked you because of your mark," he pointed out. "I think that makes it clear whose side she's on." He eased her off Susan, not missing the bristle of energy that radiated off her. Susan straightened, her eyes widening when he handed the bat to her.

She placed it on the counter, her gaze on his ring. Recognition dawned in her eyes but she didn't comment. With a soft sigh, she pulled out two beers from the fridge behind her and slid them closer. "You shouldn't be here. We've already had enough trouble from the likes of your kind."

Ignoring her disgruntled expression, Ethan slid into the chair and took the beer. "Thanks. Likes of our kind? And that would be . . .?"

"Warlocks and witches. Keepers."

"Keepers?" Jenna said quickly, straightening.

"Haven't seen any around here in years and this week there've been a few. Only difference is, this lot's furious. Violent."

"Keepers aren't violent," Ethan said. "Not without a reason."

"They are in Ameera. It's different here." Susan's shoulders sagged, a sign she'd lowered her defences. "For so long, I've managed to stay off everyone's radar, but suddenly my bar's a magnet for people like you. Others too."

Others? Ethan sipped his beer, wishing she'd stopped referring to them like sidewalk vermin. "You've had trouble?"

"Bar fights. Arguing." She grabbed two glasses from a tray behind her, motioning to the far wall, which contained a shattered mirror. "That's what you get for turning a blind eye on your kind."

Sidewalk vermin.

"What happened?"

"An argument broke out between Axel, a Keeper, and a warlock. Next thing I know, there's a Herculean brawl that trashed my bar." Ethan skimmed a gaze across the room. It didn't look trashed. "I had a friend who owed me a favour. What brought you here? To my bar? I can't afford more trouble."

"The men who were fighting . . . do you know them?"

"Only Axel. As for the other two, the one wore a ring like yours, the other a mark like hers." She shot Jenna a disgruntled look. "Lots of strangers in and out of here lately and it doesn't take a genius to figure out where you're all coming from."

"You know about the portal."

"The earth tremors have started again so it's obvious it's open. First time in ages. Got people stir-crazy looking for it, but they won't find it unless that dark witch caster wants them to."

"You've met Hazel?" Jenna asked, taking a sip of her beer. Susan scowled at her wrist as though it would sprout something. "Any idea why she's in Ameera?"

Susan shrugged and reached for another glass, but not before Ethan caught the way the lines tightened around her mouth. He'd mastered the art of reading people and right now his instincts were firing all over the place.

He studied her in silence, contemplating his next move, his

finger working around the rim of his glass. She must've sensed the intense scrutiny because her heartbeat sped up.

She was nervous. Good. She had answers for them. He was damn sure of it.

Without taking his eyes off her, he nodded at the door. "Of all the places in Ameera, we ended up here, in your bar. That wasn't a coincidence, was it?" Surprise coloured her expression but she continued to clean the glass. "How did we get here, Susan?"

"We happened to be on the same train."

His hand shot out to catch her wrist. "Bullshit. You wanted us here. What did you do? An enticement spell?" Her eyes rounded and they stared at each other, a heated silence beating between them. He pushed back his chair and stood, bringing her arm closer. "We're in enemy territory, Susan, so right now I'm assuming that everyone's a threat. I don't take lightly to threats or games, or whatever the hell you've got going on here."

She broke free and lowered her gaze. "How did you know?"

"I've lived with witches a very long time. I know when I'm being played by one. Why'd you cast the spell?"

"I knew when you stood up to Axel that you were different. I had to talk to you."

Well . . . *shit*. He hadn't expected that. "I'm assuming that means you don't side with them?"

"The only way I've stayed alive all these years is by not picking a side. I do what I have to. A lot of us do. This place might be a dump, but there are still some good people here. Hazel's meddling with the portal will ruin us."

"So help us stop her. You know that we can or you wouldn't have spelled us here."

"I know," she replied softly, nodding. She glanced at the clock on the wall. "You should go."

"We're not done here."

"No, but you've already been here too long. If I'm going to help you, it's best we're not seen talking to each other."

Ethan clamped the flare of frustration, but knew she was right. "You got a suggestion for a place to crash tonight?" Ethan ignored Jenna's surprised look and hauled out his wallet. "Clean linen and no rats will get you money for a brand new mirror."

"There's only one other mirror like it in Ameera. It's an antique. Costs a fortune."

He smiled. He'd spotted it the moment he'd entered the bar. His mother had loved antiques and their home still contained many items from her collection.

A group of women burst through the doorway in a whirl of high-pitched chatter. They all wore heavy makeup and cocktail dresses that barely covered their asses.

Susan's gaze flickered between Ethan and the girls. With a low grumble of words that sounded like she was arguing with herself, she reached into the drawer beneath the counter. She scribbled something onto a napkin before sliding it across the counter, along with a set of keys. "Directions to my apartment. I'm not staying there as I sleep here most nights. It looks like a dump from the outside but its clean and off everyone's radar. You'll be safe there."

Ethan covered her hand with his. "Thank you."

"Be careful." She gave him the keys. "You're in Ameera. There are enemies everywhere."

Yeah, he'd figured that out already.

Jenna's eyes narrowed. "Why are you helping us, Susan?"

"It's no secret that Hazel's after the magic those dead witches left behind. She accesses that energy, there'll be no stopping her. Not in your world or mine. We'll all be at her mercy, ruined. Not even your Beckham witches will stand a chance."

Witch. Ethan held back the urge to correct her about Rose. Then he raised a brow. "How do you know I protect a Beckham witch?"

She avoided his gaze and backed away. Wiping her hands on a towel, she turned to serve the women. A few minutes later, the jukebox boomed to life again. Two couples appeared in the doorway, followed by a waitress.

"You trust her?" Jenna asked after they finished their beers and made their way to the door.

"We'd be a fool to trust anyone here, but I think she's the least of our problems right now." And she hadn't answered his question about Sienna.

He glanced through the window. A crowd of men had gathered outside. Apprehension trickled through him when he recognised one. Rick, Hazel's right-hand man – the warlock with the ability to create smoke at will. He was older than the others, his arms covered in tattoos.

"*Ethan.*" Jenna's eyes rounded, his name escaping on a rush of air when she saw Rick.

The warlock broke away from the crowd and headed toward the door. She swung around, pressing herself into Ethan, and backed them up against the wall in the corner. He raised a brow and she raised her chin.

And then she kissed him.

CHAPTER TWENTY ONE

A diversion.

That's all the kiss was meant to be.

Ethan knew that, but the moment her mouth touched his, heat fired between them. Her lips were soft, hesitant, and she tasted like beer, smelt like soap. His hands found her hips, his body reacting to hers, despite her guarded kiss. And the danger.

Ethan wrapped his arms around her shoulders, shielding them from the warlock's glance en route to the counter.

When Ethan took full possession of her mouth, her eyes widened. But she didn't object.

Rick gave Susan his order and walked outside, oblivious to them.

And yet Ethan continued to kiss her, the pull of the woman in his arms more enticing than he'd ever imagined. Her body was firm and strong, soft where it mattered. It ignited all sorts of wicked desire through him and he ached to explore more of her.

With a soft groan, she broke away. Her lips were swollen, her eyes wild. She looked over her shoulder. When she turned back, he kissed her again. Slow and tantalising, a delicious torment he couldn't resist.

"Ethan." Her words were a breathy rumble of sexiness against his lips. "Rick's gone outside."

"I know."

"So why are you still kissing me?"

"Trying to be inconspicuous."

She lowered her gaze to his arousal pressed between them, her lips twitching. "Any more kissing and *inconspicuous* won't be an option for you."

He smiled and rested his forehead on hers, shoving aside the urge for more. His heart raced, a rhythm that matched hers, and his heavy breathing fanned her face, mingling with the sound of her own. The need for words had evaporated with the kiss, leaving them both breathless and wanting. But reality loomed, like a great big shark circling them, crashing the heat ignited by the kiss.

"You know him?" He reluctantly withdrew, the absence of her body against his immediately noticeable.

"Yes, I despise the man. I don't recognise the others." Although disapproval laced her tone, excitement, not fear, radiated off her. "If Rick's here, Hazel can't be too far. We're onto them, Ethan. I figured the portal would lead us close, but I never expected to find them so soon."

He straightened her shirt.

She swatted his hand away. "You weren't supposed to kiss me back."

"You were so persistent. I didn't want to blow you off."

"Camouflage, Ethan. That's all it was."

"I was obliged to play along."

"Right." Her mouth curled and she glanced at the door. "Keen to get out of here?"

"Will it involve any more kissing?"

"That wasn't a kiss."

"Ah. Camouflage?"

"Exactly. And it won't happen again."

Unable to stop himself, he slid an arm around her waist. He took great satisfaction when her eyes widened and her breath caught.

His gaze lowered to her mouth. Full lips, rounded in surprise. He ached to kiss her again.

Her pulse sped up, a flutter of movement beneath his fingertips. He tilted his head forward, his mouth close to hers.

"Want to say that again?" he murmured and grinned when it earned him a punch to the gut. He glanced outside. "The coast is clear. Let's sneak out the back and watch from the roof."

"Fine, but no more kissing."

"Spoil sport."

****

Jenna hovered at the edge of the rooftop, watching the street. The late hour had brought more people, the entrance humming with activity. A beefy bouncer had arrived to guard the door, his stern expression evoking cautious glances from the steady stream of people in and out.

They all looked so ordinary. Like normal people out for an evening of fun.

"Any idea what they are?" Ethan asked from beside her.

"It's hard to tell them apart. Shifters. Maybe even witches and warlocks." She shrugged and shook her head. "Definitely no vampires or werewolves, though. They keep to their districts." Most of the time, anyway. Her fingers tingled and her mouth felt dry. Frustration had long since overruled her excitement. "We've been waiting for two hours and nothing's happened."

"We could consider that a plus."

His voice was level, his tone light, but everything about the way he stood, his body rigid, his jaw clenched, told her that he felt it too. The need to charge into the bar, to hunt them down.

To do something.

For Jenna, that was the tame version. Being back in Ameera made her feel restless and agitated, two destructive states she loathed. Seeing Rick again only aggravated her more. She hadn't anticipated seeing him so soon. Tonight. Here. Drinking beer and acting like he wasn't the spawn of pure evil.

She'd seen right through Rick's Italian charm the moment she'd met him – the underlying cruelty he covered to perfection. Cold, evil, calculating.

Two women came out of the bar clinging to each other as they wobbled on high heels and the fumes of alcohol. They were from the group they'd seen earlier – only a messier version. Wild hair and squeals of laughter.

Jenna almost envied them.

Ethan shifted beside her, folding his arms. Her skin tingled, the way it always did when he stared at her. "So we're pretending like those kisses never happened?"

Jenna stilled, surprised he'd brought it up, but she appreciated the distraction. "Absolutely."

"Figured you'd say that."

Even though she kept staring straight ahead, she knew he'd smiled. His head dipped toward hers and he grinned when she froze. Despite her iron will, her heartbeat upped its rhythm.

And he knew it.

His low chuckle broke the silence. "Oh, they happened, Jen," he murmured against her ear, his gentle breath evoking a shiver down her spine. "We kissed. Twice. And it'll happen again. We both know it."

She turned her face toward his, her cheek brushing his, aware of how dangerously close his mouth was to hers. "Maybe, but it shouldn't. We both know *that*."

"Could be fun."

"Could be dangerous."

"Since when do we shy away from danger?"

Despite herself, she smiled. "You realise we're playing with fire, right?"

"We'll make sure to bring enough water."

She laughed, but her reply vanished when beefcakes below

burst out laughing. The sound was immediately followed by Rick's boisterous laughter, flirtatious and easy. It grated Jenna's nerves, just as it had every time she'd heard it during the time she'd lived with them.

She'd underestimated him once. Never again. Hot resentment and anger speared through the memories. *Asshole.*

"I'm gonna assume that comment was aimed at Rick and not me." Ethan's tone was mild, but a slight frown creased his brows.

Jenna blinked. Darn, had she said that aloud? She stared straight ahead, flooded with memories and emotions of a time when she'd been limited, helpless. Alone.

"What happened?" Ethan asked softly.

"He broke my arm." Her words were barely audible and she cleared her throat. "He was bullying an innocent witch and I stepped in. It hurt like hell." She turned, meeting his gaze, connecting to the quiet anger that simmered off him. But he remained quiet. "My arm healed, but I had to pretend it was still broken. I walked around with a sling, acting all pissed off and injured and all I wanted to do was put his face through a wall."

The memory made her sick to the stomach. She'd tolerated his quiet smirks, even though she'd itched to retaliate. But retaliation would reveal her Keeper strengths and blow her cover. To them, she'd been a scavenger with the same vision as theirs, not the Keeper with a hidden agenda.

"I was watched like a hawk after that," she continued. "It highlighted how careful I needed to be. After that, he became more sadistic. Constantly taunting me for a reaction."

Ethan cast a gaze across the city. "Did that happen here?"

"No. New Orleans."

"Tell me about Ameera."

His quiet question didn't surprise her. She'd known it was coming. And when he stepped around her, reaching for her shoulders, she had the urge to shrink back. Run. To guard her secrets. Instead, she raised her chin, trying to ignore the fear that rolled through her. She'd always known the time would come to tell him about her background and she'd always been terrified he'd see her differently when she did.

The conversation they'd had in the attic came to mind and she fought the urge to cringe.

"I've never told anyone about Ameera," she whispered. Her chest ached from the pressure that always came with thoughts of her family. The night everything changed. The images of her father fighting their enemies and the worry on her mother's face were forever burned in her brain.

"You're familiar with the city. You've spent a lot of time here?" he prompted.

She nodded and opened her mouth to reply, but no sound came out. The words remained trapped, forever sealed within her mother's warning. *Tell no one what you really are. Protecting our identity protects our secret. Especially in the mortal world. It's our legacy and despite everything we were accused of, it's our duty to guard it.*

"Jen?"

Tears welled in her eyes and she hurriedly blinked them away, appalled to feel the wetness. A shuffle of movement below drew their attention. Taking a deep breath, Jenna stepped back, grateful for the distraction.

Laughter erupted from the street, a sound Jenna instantly recognised. Megan. She sported the same short, pitch-black hair and heavy eye makeup. Her hands were jammed into her coat pockets.

Slapping a hand on the bouncer's back, Rick slid an arm around Megan and pressed a kiss into her hair. Waving at their accomplices, they took to the sidewalk and began walking.

Jenna shifted uncomfortably, her instincts demanding she stop them.

Ethan's hand covered her shoulder, the motion reeling her in – just as he'd intended, no doubt. She met his gaze. Their conversation wasn't over. He'd want answers and she'd have no choice but to provide them. But the movement below had brought out the warrior in him and he'd shelved the questions.

For now.

CHAPTER TWENTY TWO

Megan and Rick wasted no time. A couple on a mission. They caught the train, rode the line for a few blocks, and jumped off between platforms, disappearing into the darkness.

Ethan and Jenna followed, gliding across the rooftops above, trailing them. Their jumps were made in perfect unison, silent and effortlessly. Despite the icy wind and the tension, Ethan couldn't shake the euphoria that came with the freedom of each jump.

Hiding his abilities around his women had always been a bitch. He'd always felt the need to curb his superhuman strength and haul out the gloves and tenderness. The fear of hurting them had always lingered. Always. It was only now, sailing across the roofs, that he realised how damn stifling that had been – and how exhilarating it felt having Jenna navigate the rooftops beside him.

The roads were quiet, litter scattered everywhere. The buildings were mostly in darkness. A tall fire escape loomed across the entire side of the block, minus its bottom ladder. There was movement further down the street, the walls a shimmer of yellow. Four men huddled around a fire, a pot boiling above the flames. The air smelt like beans. Their makeshift cardboard houses lined the sidewalk behind them.

Laughter erupted from a nearby warehouse, accompanied by

several whistles that attracted Megan and Rick like damn flies to leftovers.

The windows had been painted white. When they stalked around the back, a heavy wooden door opened to allow them in, amplifying the whistles and laughter from inside. There was a grunt, a curse, and the unmistakable sound of fist impacting on flesh that evoked another round of applause and jeering.

"Ethan." Jenna's snapped whisper drew him away from the edge of the roof. She was crouched beside an air vent, her fingers cupped around the dome as she searched for a way in. On the next round of applause, she gave a hard tug. The cover came off easily and he helped her lift it, placing it quietly beside them. Together, they crouched around the opening.

A group of men of various ages, many brandishing tattoos or body piercings, had gathered in a circle, surrounding two men in a vicious fight.

Ethan zeroed in on the man directly beneath him, instantly recognising him. Axel. The man from the train. His friends stood a few feet behind him, watching the fight with enthusiasm. Axel stroked his beard with one hand, twirling the hair between his fingers. He acknowledged Rick with a brief nod.

The two fighters were splattered with blood. Their eyes were glazed, their bruised faces devoid of emotion.

One man charged the other, crashing into a crate of wooden boxes, which splintered on impact. In a whirl of punches and curses, followed by more cheering and laughter from their spectators, the two men attacked.

"What are they?" Ethan murmured.

"No idea." Jenna grimaced when the two men parted, glared at each other and simultaneously broke out into a running leap. They collided with a powerful force and delved into another round of punches.

"How long have they been at it?" Megan called out to Axel.

"They arrived in the city late last night," he shouted back.

135

"Where are the other two?"

"Vamps had a go at them. We staked our claim on these two before they could. Had to keep them locked in the cage for their safety. And ours. Been fighting for over an hour."

"They're still in good shape."

"They're strong, but they're tiring. Think the spell will work?"

"It's already working, dumb ass. The fact that they're fighting each other proves that." Megan turned to Rick. Their exchange was brief, quiet, and Rick withdrew a knife from his jacket pocket.

Taking three large strides to the centre of the fight, he grabbed the man closest to him, swung him around, and drove the knife into his chest. In a swift movement, he repeated the move with the second man.

The eruption of cheers drowned out Jenna's gasp. Rick stepped over the groaning men, tugging on their hands. He circled them, a half-smile twisting his lips. He looked at Axel. "This proof enough that Hazel's plan on the mortal realm is working?" Axel continued to stroke his beard. "So we have a deal?"

Axel's lips parted into a wide smile. "Damn right." In a swift movement, he mounted the injured man closest to him and leaned forward. His mouth hovered above the man's and even though Ethan couldn't see what the hell he was doing, he knew it couldn't be good.

Rick reached for the second man, hauling him up by the shirt. It tore, revealing a mark on the injured man's right shoulder. A mark Ethan instantly recognized.

Holy fuck.

"His tattoo," Jenna hissed, leaning forward, "a pentagram. Shit, he's a Keeper?"

The realisation sent a burst of energy swirling through Ethan, fast and furious, triggering a rush of wind around them. A gentle whistle of wind that grew stronger as it crept down the walls of the warehouse. Windows rattled, extracting a few surprised looks from the people inside.

Rick took no notice, smiling as his accomplices began to close in on the injured men. He turned back to the crowd, his face a mixture of aggression and sick pleasure. Holding up his hand, he uncurled his fist to reveal the two rings he'd taken from the Keepers. "The only good Keepers are dead ones!"

The crowd went wild.

Axel tilted his head back, panting heavily, his eyes wide. As though he'd sampled something delectable. Turning around, he looked at Rick and grinned. "We're done here. The scavengers can finish them off. Let's get moving on Hazel's plan. Tonight."

Scavengers. Witches and warlocks with the ability to absorb the powers of their victims. Dead victims. Ethan bolted forward as he realised what was about to happen, but Jenna grabbed his arm.

"Ethan, stop!" she snapped in a hushed tone. "It's too late. It's over."

He tried to tug loose, but she yanked at his arm, pointing toward the men. Rick stood above them with a knife in his hand. The two men were dead; others were closing in. Blood pooled around them.

"They killed them," Ethan hissed through gritted teeth. "Those fuckers killed them and now they're scavenging their powers."

"Ethan –"

He reared backward as fury slammed through him, so heated and powerful that it scorched everything inside. Energy burst through his body, amplified by the rage in a way he seldom embraced. But this time, he didn't give a damn.

The front door burst open on a gust of wind that blew through the room, gathering sand and dust in its wake.

A few murmurs broke out, followed by a shout as the wind gathered force. It whipped around the crowd, rattling everything in its path, scattering boxes and abandoned tables and chairs. The lights flickered. More energy. More wind. Light bulbs exploded, along with two windows, and glass rained down upon the crowd.

"What's happening?" Rick shouted, crouching beside Megan, his arm raised above his head.

"There's someone here. Let's go!" She bolted for the door, but screamed as a gust of wind hoisted them off their feet. It tossed them through the air and slammed them against the wall.

And just like that, Ethan turned it off.

Everything collapsed to the ground, the room a dusty mess as the sand settled. A few groans filled the room, along with Rick's bellow of rage.

Growling softly, clenching his fists, Ethan inhaled a ragged breath and withdrew the wind. It whipped through the room one more time, escaping through the shattered windows.

But he didn't stop there.

As easily as he could create air, he could deplete it. And he did. With a viciousness he'd never indulged before. A voice niggled inside, a warning, tugging at a consciousness he'd sidestepped, but he couldn't stop.

Instead, he thought of the two slain Keepers and gave in to the overwhelming need that gripped him. *Vengeance.*

Everyone in the warehouse began gasping as they realised the air was thinning. They staggered, arms flailing, gaping at each other in confusion.

"What's happening?" Axel grunted, grabbing Rick by the shirt. "Is this Hazel's doing?" His eyes bulged, panic overriding his trademark fierceness.

Ethan channelled more energy, absorbing more air.

"Ethan."

Jenna's low voice did little to stop him and he focused his rage on their enemies below. Rick clawed at his throat and Megan cried out, her mouth wide as she sucked air.

"Ethan, stop it! You'll expose us!" Jenna snapped, rising. "Ethan, you're going to kill them!"

About sweet fucking time.

He ignored her, sucking every last breath from the room.

"STOP!" Jenna yelled, slamming her hand against his shoulder. The impact of her blow jolted him. He stumbled, straightened,

138

blinking rapidly as the crash of senses returned. "Dammit, Ethan," she breathed, and disappeared.

Staggering forward, he slowly reeled in the flow of rage.

It grew still. Deathly still.

Breathless and disorientated from the roar of fury he'd often felt but refused to welcome, he crouched over the vent. He scanned the bodies scattered across the floor. Horror curled inside as he realised what he'd done. A growl tore through him, almost beast-like, and he stumbled backward, dropping to his knees.

And in that brief moment of weakness, confusion, he saw a blond woman emerging from the doorway on the street below, Megan slung over one shoulder.

But then Jenna was beside him, tugging on his hand, her expression etched with worry. "Ethan, we should go."

Frowning, he glanced at Megan panting on the sidewalk and tried to recapture the image of how she'd got there. But everything was a blur, clouded in rage and magic and power.

He shook his head to clear the murkiness, gripped Jenna's hand, and stood.

CHAPTER TWENTY THREE

Low groans and shuffles of movement from inside the warehouse had Jenna and Ethan scaling across rooftops at a breakneck speed. Three blocks later, they took to the streets in the direction of the train tracks.

Jenna's head reeled from the vivid images of the horrific attack on the two Keepers – men who'd fought each other with a violence usually reserved for enemies, killed for their powers.

What the hell was Hazel up to?

Ethan's retaliation, the eruption of fury, had surprised her – a side of him she'd never seen before. He still bristled with anger and walked with heavy, determined strides, his fists clenched beside each thigh.

"Ethan . . ." she said.

"Not now, Jenna." His words were clipped with a sharp undertone. He kept walking, staring straight ahead, his features hardened by a harsh frown. He kept his head lowered, his hands jammed into his jacket pockets.

"What the hell happened up there?" They turned the corner and she grabbed his arm. "Ethan!"

"Back off, Jenna."

"You almost killed them."

"I didn't."

"If I hadn't stopped you —"

He spun around, glanced over his shoulders to ensure they were alone, and pinned her with a deathly glare. "They injured two Keepers for the damn fun of it and then handed them over to Scavengers. They laughed and cheered and acted like it was a fucking circus! Whatever I did would *never* have been enough to avenge that!"

"You lost control and almost killed them! Besides the fact that you just exposed us, exposed that we're here, Archer's right. If you start murdering them, then what the hell makes you different to them?"

"They're monsters!"

"And killing them just because you can doesn't make you one?"

"We are losing this war, Jenna!" he yelled, putting his hands on her shoulders. "Look around you. Where we are. What just happened! I'm sick of standing by, *defending*, whilst people die and our enemies grow stronger. And now they've roped in Axel so I think it's safe to assume our enemies have multiplied. It's bullshit and you know it!"

They glowered at each other in heated silence, tension simmering between them. He was right. It *was* bullshit, but. . .. dammit.

"If I hadn't intervened, you'd have suffocated them." She lowered her voice. "I'm on your side, Ethan, and I agree that we need to stop them. If anyone here knows what they're capable of, it's me." She stepped closer, placing her hands on his chest, her eyes locked with his. She saw the struggle there, she felt it too. "But we're Keepers and have a code to honour. That's who we are. We lose control and go on a killing spree and we're nothing."

He released a low growl of protest from the back of his throat, the sound reverberating beneath her fingers. "I didn't lose control. I was pissed and lashed out, but I stopped. Those assholes get to live another day. Yay for us."

"We'll find another way to stop them."

He tightened his grip on her shoulders. "Well, bring on the suggestions, Jenna, 'cause next time they touch an innocent person or harm one of our own, control and honour and all that crap won't mean a damn thing to me."

Voices behind them had Jenna glancing over her shoulder. Turning back to him, she nodded and pulled away, surprised when he wouldn't let go. When her gaze lifted to meet his, dark blue eyes scowled at her.

The intensity she saw there stilled her.

"Megan was the first one out," he said quietly, the chill to his words sending a shiver down her spine. "The *only* one out."

"She's smart."

"She was suffocating and then suddenly, she was on the sidewalk." He raised a brow. "Any idea how that happened?"

Her heart skipped a beat and her chest tightened, but she held her ground, held his gaze. Searching, questioning, accusing. He knew. *Shit.*

Despite knowing it was wrong, Jenna had taken brief satisfaction in watching their enemies suffer. Seeing Megan at the mercy of Ethan's wrath had given her sick pleasure and she'd been tempted to leave her. But something had fired deep inside, a flicker of conscience, doubt. More than just the warped slither of loyalty that occasionally reared its head. She needed Megan alive. Especially now. Here. They were rivals, but the one thing they both longed for was discovering what had happened to Jenna's parents.

Megan had an in with their enemies so she'd have access to information that Jenna wouldn't. Even though it had clashed with every instinct she had, Jenna had pulled her out of the building.

"I told you," Jenna said quietly, pleased her tone was steady. "Megan's smart."

His narrowed gaze remained on her. His nostrils flared. "You and Sarah were arguing outside the restaurant the day before she died."

Jenna drew in a deep breath, surprised by the mention of Sarah's

142

name. She elbowed him off her and took a step back, hating the reminder of her last encounter with Sarah. Their disagreement had developed into an argument they'd never resolved.

Because they couldn't. Sarah's death had sealed their fight and Jenna had regretted it since.

"Why was my sister so angry with you?"

"Why are you bringing this up now?"

"Because Sarah was so furious she used her magic and uprooted a tree!"

The damn thing had crushed several park benches and triggered a ton of chaos and unwanted questions. They'd managed to cover it with a viable explanation – old tree and all that – but there'd been a few raised brows.

"It was an accident," Jenna said, wishing her voice hadn't sounded so feeble.

"What was the fight about, Jenna? She was yelling at you about Megan. Why would she do that?"

Because Sarah had seen them together. Overheard a conversation she shouldn't have. She'd misunderstood, partly, and Jenna had never had the chance to set things straight between them.

It took every ounce of willpower she had not to flinch. Not now. Because flinching would give her away. "That argument was between Sarah and me. It's none of your concern."

Anger flared and he stepped up to her. "Everything with Sarah is my concern. She was my sister."

"She was my friend!" she snapped, venom edging her tone. "I will always regret that the last conversation I had with Sarah was that damn fight. Every memory I have is tinged with the guilt of knowing that's the last thing we said to each other."

"We never heard from you after her death. Not even for her funeral."

His words stung and she gasped. Slamming both hands on his chest, she shoved him away, the burst of anger that backed her blow catching him off guard. "Don't you dare do that!" she cried, her voice cracking. "Don't you dare undermine my feelings for Sarah simply because I couldn't be there after her death!"

She shoved him again, the pain and regret and guilt chewing at her in a way that threatened to cripple her. Emotions she'd kept buried, just out of reach, triggered by his damn accusation. "You all had the luxury of mourning her, grieving, whilst I had to suck it up and put on a cheerful front for our enemies and act like I wasn't dying inside. Don't you dare undermine what that felt like!"

"Jenna –"

"You have no idea what it was like for me –"

"You're right, I *don't* know! You're always so damn secretive about everything that happened."

"Because they're my secrets to keep! I've told you what you need to know, one Keeper to another, and only because it affects the safety of our witches. Everything else that falls outside that Keeper realm is irrelevant."

"One Keeper to another?" He gave a brief laugh that rang of more mockery than amusement. "I think we're past that, Jenna."

"We protect two of the most powerful witches in the world. We will *never* be past that."

"Sienna and Kate will always come first, but there's more happening here and you know it."

"Because we kissed?" She gave a defiant lift of her chin. "That's all it was, all it'll ever be."

He was in front of her in a flash of movement. Her eyes widened and she took a deep breath. When she stepped backward, he moved forward, until she was trapped between him and the wall. He placed his hands against the wall, cocooning her head. His gaze found hers, intense and demanding. He was all heat and man and the sheer force of him took her breath away.

"Say that again," he murmured, his voice deep and throaty, wrought with tension. "I dare you to say that again."

"Stop it, Ethan." She turned her head.

He captured her face between his fingers, forcing her to look at him. Tension sizzled between them, fuelled with the desire that always flared whenever he touched her. "Say it."

"Screw you."

"Say it, Jenna."

"No."

He dipped his head closer, so close that his lips were almost on hers. "Because you *can't*."

Her breath caught and she froze, staring at him. He slid his hands down her neck, her shoulders, and gripped her waist, tugging her against his arousal. Her sharp intake of breath pleased him, as did the heat that sizzled between them. She could see it in his eyes, the smirk on the corner of his lips.

"You feel the attraction as much as I do," he murmured.

The challenge sparked a thrill of excitement through her. She didn't reply or bother denying it, knowing he'd see through her anyway.

Suddenly there wasn't enough air. Breathless, heart pounding, she placed both hands on his chest, easing him off her.

The ground vibrated beneath their feet and the soft rumble of a train could be heard in the distance.

Grateful for the distraction, Jenna slid out from beneath him and walked away.

CHAPTER TWENTY FOUR

The train smelt like urine, an aroma that aggravated the hollow, sick feeling in Jenna's stomach.

But at least they were alone.

Susan's neighbourhood was on the outskirts of town and consisted mostly of apartment buildings and a few industrial warehouses. The streets were covered in concrete rubble and litter, empty but far from quiet. Voices drifted from the windows above. Music blared.

"Where is everyone?" Ethan asked, glancing up at the endless rows of clothing pegged to the fire escapes.

"They won't be out on the streets this late. Too dangerous."

"That doesn't bode well for us, then." He scanned the buildings and tilted the piece of paper in his hand toward the single streetlight.

"How do we know this isn't a trap?"

"We don't." He pocketed Susan's directions and climbed over a pile of building rubble. "But Susan's the closest thing we have to a bed tonight. We'll keep our guards up."

They walked in silence, wading through the mess on the streets. Several buildings had collapsed, leaving a trail of debris. The state of the neighbourhood only worsened the further they walked.

There were signs of neglect and poverty everywhere. Derelict buildings, windows covered with makeshift curtains, paint peeling from the walls.

And yet the music and voices continued. Despite everything, people had made their homes here.

Jenna wondered what had happened to hers. Was it still standing? Occupied by others? Her chest tightened at the memories and she tried to push them away, but they kept coming, stronger and more powerful than ever.

The image of her mother's face, her father's voice, their home. Megan.

If she allowed herself to, she could remember everything. In detail. But it always hurt like hell afterward when reality bit and she was reminded how alone in the world she was. The loneliness she could deal with, but it was the not knowing that was slowly killing her. Eating away at her determination to move on.

"Jenna?" Ethan's voice cut through the anguish and she looked up, surprised to see they'd stopped walking. They stood outside an industrial building. Large windows overlooked the street. A wooden sliding door covered the front entrance. Most of the blue paint had peeled, the remaining streaks covered by dirt. "We're here."

"This is where Susan lives?"

"As of now, this is where we live." He unlocked the door and they went inside.

The reflection of streetlights offered some relief from the darkness. The room was spacious, empty. High ceilings and glass windows. A steel staircase to the right led to another level.

The sound of locks clicking into place echoed through the darkness.

"Why do I get the feeling we're lambs heading into a slaughter?" she whispered, her heart upping its beat.

Ethan's grunt mingled with the jingle of keys as he walked to the stairs. "I dare them to try."

She didn't comment and followed him up the stairs to the single door on the platform.

Susan had converted the industrial room into a loft apartment. It was spacious with wide windows overlooking the city. The lights flickered in the distance, almost pretty. The height of the building gave the loft a privacy that most other apartments lacked.

The white plaster from the walls had faded, exposing glimpses of red brick beneath it. The small kitchen consisted of a counter made of the same railway sleepers as the ones from the bar. Two leather couches, one torn on the side, surrounded a makeshift coffee table made from a glass slat that rested on recycled wood.

And the bed.

Low, covered in a black sheet, at the far end of the room. Simple and sparse, but promising a hint of comfort after a shitty day.

Jenna's insides did a little jiggle.

Ethan closed the curtains and walked to the kitchen, stopping to turn on the lamp beside the couch. It offered little light, the dim glow suiting their mood.

"Susan's mirror just got a size bigger," he said, peering into the cupboards. A mild grin on his lips, he pulled out his wallet and stuck a wad of cash on the shelf. Turning, he held up two cans of food and a bottle of whiskey.

Her insides did another jiggle, far more potent than the one evoked by thoughts of sleep.

Jenna smiled, taking a seat at the counter in front of him. "After a really, really crappy night, this is like heaven, so she's officially made my hero list." And that was a very small list.

He scooped up two glasses from the shelf behind him and poured them each a shot. "Drink first. Then food. It's not much, but . . ."

"As long as there's alcohol," she interrupted, taking the glass. She needed the numbing effect the whiskey offered more than the food anyway. Even though her stomach growled, a reminder that they'd missed dinner.

To chase a damn portal.

And now, here they were, in Ameera. The city of the damned. Separated from their witches.

"This is exactly where we need to be, Jenna," he said softly. "What we just witnessed proves that."

She blinked, wondering if she'd said the last part aloud. But she figured he felt it too. Being apart from Sienna and Kate felt wrong. A necessary evil.

She pulled out her phone and glanced at the blank screen. "I wish this stupid thing would work here so we could call home."

"What would we tell them?" he asked, his words clipped with irritation. "That we just witnessed the demise of two Keepers and did nothing?"

"Ethan, stop it. We couldn't do anything. We had no idea –"

"They were stripped, injured, and not once did they bother fighting back. What's with that? We start turning on each other, allowing these assholes to treat us like shit and we're over."

"Maybe they had no choice. Maybe they were spelled. That's the only way we'd turn on each other. There's only one spell strong enough . . ." *Oh, crap.* Her eyes lifted upward, her glass hovering mid-air. "Could they have used a Behesting Spell?"

The weight of what that meant reflected in his narrowed eyes and harsh frown. The powerful spell, designed to make the victim adhere to the caster's bidding, was vanquished decades ago. No witch had been bold enough to touch it and risk the wrath of The Circle.

Except Hazel.

Ethan cleared his throat, a thunderous expression on his face. "So they're taking Keepers, sending them here, and spelling them to harm each other. When they've weakened, they're left for the scavengers to cipher their magic." Frowning, he poured another drink. "But what about the witches that were left unharmed back home? That's a lot of magic they chose not to scavenge."

"From what Axel said at the warehouse, Hazel's using Keepers

149

as some sort of payment for their agreement." She took the drink he handed her and swallowed it in one go. Her throat had gone dry, her stomach queasy. Hoping the alcohol would help, she held out the glass for a refill.

"Still doesn't explain why they left all the witches untouched. And what's in it for Axel?"

"Our magic. Our abilities. Maybe he values that more." Her eyes widened as another thought struck. "The Brogan family have always been after power. Mason and Warrick thought they could achieve that by targeting the witches, but every time the Keepers stopped them. Hazel's smarter. Her goal is ultimately accessing the energy at the site of the massacre."

"She'd have to get through an army of witches to find it."

"But she'd have to get through an army of Keepers first," she breathed. She set her glass on the counter, her body bristling with a rush of adrenaline as everything reeled into place. "That's it, Ethan. The hellhounds were after me, not Kate. The missing Keepers, the fight we just witnessed, the spell . . . it's all part of a pecking order. A master plan." Her eyes found his, the magnitude of those words hanging between them, fuelling the tension as the puzzles of truth slid into place. "And right now, the witches aren't the targets. The Keepers are."

Ethan cursed. "She's not only using them to fuel her agreement with Axel, but eliminating the Keepers would leave the witches exposed."

"Which makes them vulnerable. Destroy the witches and she destroys the opposition."

"So if she discovers where the magic is buried, she'd have a golden fucking pathway right up to all that energy."

CHAPTER TWENTY FIVE

Ethan stood at the window, staring at the city in the distance. His gut churned, the alcohol doing little to ease the worry.

He'd turned off the lights, revelling in the darkness and silence, marred only by the soft sound of the shower running. Exhaustion had set in, along with more unease that had only intensified since they'd uncovered Hazel's plan – or what they suspected it to be.

There were still a lot of holes to be filled in, but they were right. He knew it. And it sucked that he couldn't call his brothers. Check on Sienna. God, how he missed her.

Guilt flared and he drained the last of the whiskey. He turned to the kitchen, debating another drink. Or a shower. Anything to wash away the grime of the day.

He was *here*, searching for Hazel and the portal spell, and even though leaving Sienna still stung, he knew he was exactly where he needed to be.

Jenna too.

He froze, staring into his glass. Is that why she'd agreed so easily to find the portal? To return to Ameera?

The glass shattered beneath his grip. Cursing, he discarded it and went to the sink to rinse his hand. The cut was deep and bleeding and stung like crap. But the damn thing would heal soon.

He froze when he heard Jenna's soft cry. His senses and instincts instantly sharpened, zoning in to his surroundings as though he'd flipped a switch.

Silence.

He shut off the water and was pushing open the bathroom door in a blink of the eye. The sound of Jenna's pounding heart and snappy breathing sent a ripple of unease through him. A candle burned on the basin, the room clouded in steam. The air smelt of soap.

"Jenna?" She turned, unsurprised, and met his gaze, the worry in her eyes sending a punch to his gut. Her hair hung in wet strands around her shoulders. A towel covered her curves. All flesh. All woman. *Beautiful.* His body tightened at the sight of her, but he pushed the thought aside, his concern for her overruling everything else. "Jen, what's wrong?"

It was the slight tremble to her hands that unleashed something inside of him. A surge of protectiveness. Worry. A beast that had him in front of her in a flash of movement.

"Jenna?"

"They keep coming," she whispered. "Out of nowhere. They just keep coming."

****

Ethan's brows furrowed as he scanned the room. "You look as though you're about to toss your cookies."

She felt like she was about to toss her cookies.

Inhaling deeply, she tried to calm the rush of panic that choked her. Her shower had been brief, hot, blissful. Only to be crashed by the pain that always came with the appearance of a new tattoo. Out of the blue.

Symbols and marks, tattooed, on *her*.

Holding the towel across her breasts, she shifted the material to expose her lower back, revealing the inked marks. She turned around, watching him in the mirror. His frown deepened as he zeroed in on her flesh.

"They came out of nowhere a few days ago," she said, her voice shaky. She cleared her throat. A shiver ran down her spine when his fingers grazed her skin, still clammy from the shower.

"Could it be Hazel messing with you?"

"Maybe." It had crossed her mind too. She shrugged her shoulders. "If she's trying to creep me out, it's working."

His thumb brushed the markings. "Do you recognise the pattern or any of these symbols?"

"No." He tugged on the towel, searching for more, but she covered her hand with his and shook her head. "That's all there is."

The muscles in his jaw tightened as he adjusted the towel. Awareness arrowed through her. He was so close, towering over her, all masculine and strength and man.

She was naked. Vulnerable. Not a sensation she embraced. Ever.

The ends of his hair had curled against his collar and fresh stubble covered his jaw. He'd shed his jacket and shoes. The V-neck of his t-shirt revealed tanned flesh and a leather necklace, the silver pendant tucked beneath the material.

Something stirred inside, a familiar sensation he triggered whenever he came too close. She lifted her head, not surprised to find him watching her in the mirror. She'd felt his gaze on her. Felt him everywhere.

She waited for him to say something. His eyes had darkened, the worry that lined his features giving way to something more.

The room shrank around them, blocking out everything else, and all she saw was him. Only him.

"Why didn't you tell me when the first mark appeared?" he murmured, trailing a finger across her skin.

The faint smell of blood filled her nostrils and she glanced at his other hand. "You're hurt."

"Just a mild cut. Answer my question."

"I was hoping to figure out what they mean first."

"So many secrets, Jen."

"Secrets are all I know. They've kept me alive all these years." The truth of that went far deeper than he understood.

"When are you going to realise you're not alone anymore?" His hand moved up her back, toying with her hair. "Because you're not, Jenna. Not anymore."

He radiated heat and a masculine power she'd always tried to ignore. His gaze seared into her and he edged closer, his chest against her back. Gently, slowly, he brushed away her hair with one finger and stroked her shoulder, his touch light.

Electricity sparked between them, ignited by that simple movement.

She swallowed, her heartbeat racing, unable to breathe. Too scared to move, terrified he'd do more. Terrified he wouldn't.

He tilted his head, pressing his nose into her hair. He inhaled, breathing her in, and slowly blinked. His heart beat a rapid rhythm against her back and she almost smiled, relieved to know she wasn't the only one affected by the moment.

Heated. Real. Inappropriate.

His fingers trailed across her shoulder, down her arm, leaving a shiver of wanting. He caught her hand in his and laced their fingers. The movement was so quiet, so still, but charged with an energy and heat that kept her rooted to the spot.

When his mouth pressed against her ear, his breath a whisper against her skin, she shivered and leaned back.

"Remind me about that big red line again," he murmured, his low words reverberating through her.

Hot tendrils of excitement trickled down her spine and she turned her face toward his. "It's a very thin, blurred line right now."

"Damn right it is."

CHAPTER TWENTY SIX

He turned her around, capturing her mouth with his.

The kiss that followed was so gentle, a slow rhythm that fuelled the flame inside her. He stilled, his lips lingering on hers, allowing the moment to take its beat.

When he withdrew to look at her, his eyes questioning, she touched his cheek, keeping him close, not wanting it to end.

"What if this makes things awkward between us?" she asked. She'd hate that. She valued his friendship too much.

He smiled and slid his fingers along her neck, cradling her face. "Then we'll do more of this until it's less awkward."

"Ethan," she whispered, not sure if she'd issued an objection or an invitation. But when her gaze lowered to his lips, his mouth came down on hers in a heated, hungry kiss that took her breath away.

Instincts fired a warning, urging her to stop, but the essence of him weakened her resolve. Desire spread through her like wildfire, along with the overwhelming urge for more. Of him. Of everything he offered.

His evening fuzz brushed her chin and his tongue swept across hers, searching, teasing. He edged forward, until her back met the counter, and tangled both hands in her hair. When he tore his lips away from hers, tipping her head back to nuzzle her neck, she sighed.

The sound drew his mouth back to hers and he devoured her all over again.

He invaded her senses, his touch possessive and demanding until anticipation and hot desire were all she knew.

He tugged her hips against him. The hardness of him made her instantly wet. She felt him everywhere, her body alive with a sexual awakening that had been dormant for so long.

Her towel loosened and she clutched at it with one hand, but not enough to cover all of her. Breathing heavily, he lowered his gaze to her exposed breast, taking his fill. He cupped her breast, rolling her nipple between his fingers until it was hard and aching beneath his touch.

"You are so damn beautiful," he murmured, his voice husky. Raw desire lined his expression, his eyes darker than she'd ever seen before.

With a soft growl, he dipped his head, sucking a nipple into his mouth. The air rushed from her lungs and she arched her back. The sound must've pleased him, spurred him on, as he exhaled noisily and slid his hand between them to find the sensitive nub between her legs. She was so wet for him and she cried out, surprised at how easily she leaned back, her body going slack against his.

His mouth caught hers in a savage kiss, whilst he teased her with a few leisurely strokes that hurtled her into a sea of sensations so powerful she was sure they'd consume her.

When that familiar pinch of pleasure rose up inside, she threw her head back, clinging to him. Her climax was fierce and sudden, her cry one of pure ecstasy. Energy surged inside her, warm and comforting.

A vague voice of warning jarred her senses. But it was too late. And he felt it too.

That magical trickle of warmth that touched everything inside her. Now inside him.

156

A low growl emanated from the back of his throat as his arms came up around her waist, holding her close. They stood in silence, breathless, panting, a quivering mess of desire and heat and wanting. But there was something more. Confusion. Questions. Surprise.

He looked at the cut on his hand. A cut that wasn't there. His questioning gaze met hers. "What the hell just happened?"

The lack of anger in his voice surprised her. Clutching her towel, she took a step back, connecting with the bath. "I don't know."

It was the truth. Sort of.

Confusion furrowed his brows. "Was that you?"

"It was us, I guess. That's never happened before." She cleared her throat and fastened the towel around her. "A reminder that . . . *this* should never have happened."

"You weren't complaining a moment ago."

No, she most certainly hadn't. Because it had felt so damn incredible and it had been too damn long.

"Ethan." Licking her lips, she lifted her gaze to meet the intensity of his. "We shouldn't do this. As amazing as that was . . . we can't." Her heartbeat pounded in her throat as she said the words. Desperate to put some space between them, she hurried to the door.

"Jenna." The quiet murmur of her name had her glancing over her shoulder. "Your magic, you've never shown me. You never talk about it."

"It's habit, Ethan. I spent the last few years hiding it from our enemies."

"But you're not with them anymore. You're with me."

Their gazes locked, the moment rife with emotion, tension. Unable to breathe, she took a step back, but he was there in a heartbeat, taking her arm.

His unwavering gaze sent her pulse soaring. "Why do you do that?"

She raised a brow.

"Withdraw," he explained. "Every time we get too close, you run."

Words evaded her and all she could do was stare. She'd expected a barrage of questions, accusations. Anger. And his ability to see right through her was unnerving.

"Don't hide from me, Jen," he murmured. "Your magic. Your past. Stop hiding."

She thought about denying it, offering an excuse. But couldn't. Instead, she exhaled quietly and opted for honesty. "It's instinctive, Ethan. The only way I've survived for so long is by keeping it all hidden. And it goes back further than my time with Hazel. I don't know anything else."

The emotion in his eyes and the heat that emanated from him set flight to the butterflies in her belly. When he captured her face in his palms, she stopped breathing.

"I want more," he murmured, tilting her head so their gazes were level. "I want to know everything there is to know about you. Your desires, your fears. Even your damn secrets."

"Ethan —"

"I want it all, Jenna, but I get they're your secrets to keep and you're scared to let me in. I also get that any more of what just happened probably isn't a great idea. But it's not the *worst* idea." The corner of his mouth lifted into a teasing smile, increasing the dimple in his cheek. He leaned closer, his lips hovering against hers. "As complicated as this is, it'll be fun. And safe."

Safe. Something she hadn't felt in a long, long time and, somehow, he knew that.

He kissed her, smiling when she quivered. Slow and teasing, the gentle touch of his lips a contrast to the heat that blazed off him.

But he pulled away all too soon, leaving her breathless and wanting. She was all too aware of his arousal pressed against her and couldn't deny the punch of satisfaction knowing she wasn't the only one affected by their kisses.

He wanted her as much as she wanted him.

"And just so you know," he murmured, a mild grin playing on his lips. "After what just happened, that red line between us is damn near invisible."

Without waiting for her reply, he planted a firm kiss on her lips and withdrew. Grinning, he turned around and left.

CHAPTER TWENTY SEVEN

Jenna held her breath as she sailed across another rooftop, her body fuelled with adrenaline that numbed the guilt. It did nothing for the ache in her heart.

An ache that was all Ethan.

I want more.

Their last conversation, the way he'd ravished her in the bathroom, had replayed in her mind as she'd tossed and turned on Susan's bed. She'd insisted they share, but Ethan had taken the couch. He'd fallen asleep quickly, even though the couch was a size too small.

Desperation and anguish and a dozen other emotions had fought her conscience and she'd waited another hour before giving in to the urge that robbed her of rest.

She was in Ameera. At last. She finally, *finally*, had a chance of returning home. Discovering what had happened to her family.

So she'd dressed silently and left, ignoring the rush of guilt that curled her insides. Leaving him behind was wrong. She knew that, but if she hurried, she'd be back before he awoke.

Fat chance.

She'd taken to the rooftops. When she'd reached the higher

buildings, she'd hit the ground running and only slowed when she reached her old neighbourhood.

Jenna kept her senses alert and her gaze lowered. Her legs felt heavy – or was that her heart? Either way, dread had taken over, the thought of returning home suddenly more terrifying than facing Ethan's wrath if he woke up and found her missing.

When she finally turned the corner into the street where she'd grown up, desperation wiped away all thoughts of why she shouldn't be here. So many years had passed, so much longing, speculating. There had to be answers here. She had to know what had happened to her parents, why they'd never come for her.

Then maybe – *just maybe* – she could move on. Live her life. Closure.

Was that even possible?

A row of triple-storey duplex homes lined both sides of the street. They were all joined, tall and narrow. There were no gardens, only weeds and concrete rubble, the ground strewn with litter. The earth tremors had damaged the entire city, even here. Several houses had been abandoned. A few people hovered in their doorways, their attention on a crowd gathered in the distance. Despite the cold, they wore minimal clothing, most likely all they had.

The air smelt like fuel, a luxury in the city. The crowd up ahead erupted into angry shouts, hurling insults at two men bound to a lamppost, secured with ropes. Wood taken from old furniture and doors surrounded the pole, drenched in fuel.

Unease crawled through Jenna, instantly recognising the ritual. A punishment. She'd only seen it once before, the night the people in her neighbourhood had captured a young vampire with a blood lust for teenage girls.

A city of violence, where an eye for an eye was a given.

A woman emerged from the crowd, a vague profile in the darkness, and struck a match. The wood went up in flames. Cheers erupted.

Nausea washed over Jenna. She hurried away, climbed through two concrete slabs, dodging cement debris.

And then there it was. Her old house. Sad, ruined, a shell of what it had once been. It looked nothing like she remembered. *Finally.*

She stared in silence, unable to move. Her eyes welled with tears and she blinked rapidly to clear them. The flames behind her illuminated the house in a soft glow. The walls, once yellow, were now black – the charred remains from the fire that had ravished her home so many years ago.

The cast-iron bars were still intact, most of the windows broken. There was no front door, only a black, gaping hole and a gate. A rusted swing chair stood on the porch, stripped of anything useful. They'd never used it, as sitting outside had been too risky. But her mother had liked knowing it was there.

Willing away the memory and the ache in her chest that came with it, Jenna pushed open the gate, the scrape of metal against sand rattling her nerves.

"What do you want?" a voice called, the sound amplified in the silence.

Jenna spun around. A woman peered out from a window in the neighbouring house. It was too dark to see her features, but by the way she crouched and the sound of her voice, Jenna figured she was older.

"If you're here to loot the house, you're wasting your time," the woman said. "Everything was destroyed during an Annex a couple of years ago. The house is empty. Has been ever since."

The Annex.

One of the most dangerous times in Ameera. Every month, when the full moon peaked, the invisible boundary walls between the species fell away and everyone had the freedom to roam wherever they wanted. A night of chaos, power struggles, looting, and violence that lasted until sunrise when the boundary walls returned. Anyone still out of their district when that happened rarely survived.

Jenna forced herself to take a breath. "And the couple that lived here? Do you know what happened to them? They had two little girls."

"What's it to you?"

Impatience clashed with irritation and Jenna walked closer, removing her wristwatch. She held it up. "Where are they?"

The woman's gaze fell to the watch. "There was a fire. We never saw them again. They weren't the only ones hurt that night."

Jenna's heart quickened at the memories. Her neighbours' screams of panic and confusion. The crackle of flames as the fire had ravished their homes.

But she'd never seen the faces of their attackers. Her mother had shielded her. Run. She'd argued, refused to enter the portal, but her mother's insistence had won out.

You're made for greater things, Jen. Things that can't be accomplished here. They won't think to look for you in the mortal world. You and our secret will be safe there. Trust me. When the time is right, I will find you and I will come for you. I promise.

A promise her mother hadn't kept.

Jenna tasted blood, realising she'd bitten her lip.

The woman wiggled her fingers to summon the watch. When Jenna tossed it to her, she cradled it like a new treasure. Which it probably was. The watch was valuable and bartering was a way of life for many people in the city, her family included.

"Our neighbourhood never recovered and with every Annex, it's grown worse." The woman nodded behind her, motioning to the dilapidated street. "The earth tremors from the portals don't help either. Soon, there'll be nothing left."

Guilt gripped Jenna, making it impossible to breathe. A wave of dizziness washed over her. Turning away, she hurried up the concrete steps.

"You best be careful," the woman called, glancing up at the sky. "The next Annex will be here in a few days and with the open portal and that dark witch from the mortal world in the city stirring up nonsense, the streets are no place for a young girl like you."

"You know Hazel?"

"I knew her sister and husband."

Mason and Warrick's parents. They'd been accused of killing Sienna and Ethan's parents and when they'd fled Rapid Falls, there'd been a car accident. They'd died instantly, leaving their boys behind. "How would you know them here, in Ameera?"

"They were regulars here."

That surprised her. "Why?"

"They often brought supplies, but . . ." she lifted her shoulders in a small shrug. "Whatever they wanted in return, I doubt they found it as they kept returning." She motioned to Jenna's house with a nod of the head. "They were here that night of the fire."

Dread curled Jenna's insides and she swallowed, afraid to ask the next question. "You saw them?"

"No, but others did. After that, they disappeared and the portal stayed closed until recently."

"They died in a car accident."

"Figured something had happened. Pity about the supplies. The little they brought helped a lot. I guess now that the portal's open again, Hazel's planning to continue what they started."

"Be careful. She's dangerous."

"It's not me she's after." She pointed at the house behind Jenna. "Did you know the family that lived here?"

Jenna nodded and hurried inside. She backed up against the wall. Breathless. Panicky. Her mind reeled with everything the woman had said. She'd always hoped the attack on her family was random, victims of the Annex. Her parents had been so careful, brilliant at developing a foolproof cover.

But in a place like Ameera, with a dark witch caster on the hunt, was anything foolproof? Hazel's sister had been there that night. A coincidence?

We never saw them again.

164

An inner voice began to scream and Jenna covered her face in her hands, gasping air, trying to calm the flood of emotions that bombarded her. Forcing several deep breaths into her lungs, she lowered her hands and looked around, drawing on her senses to scope her surroundings. Her heart might be breaking but she hadn't forgotten the dangers she faced.

Silence greeted her. She dug into her pocket for her phone. It was useless here but the gadgets still worked. Activating the flashlight, she shone it around. She sniffed and blinked, fighting the tears.

She never cried. Hadn't dared since the night of the attack.

A thick layer of ash covered the living room floor, along with chunks of wood that looked like charred remains of furniture. A double couch rested against the back wall, blackened, springs exposed. Part of the ceiling had sagged in the kitchen, the floor covered in wooden beams and fragments of cement.

She waded through the debris, drifting to the bottom stairs. Her foot connected with something on the floor. It rolled, startling her, and she hurriedly shifted the beam of light in search of it.

A doll's head lay on the ground. The hair had shrivelled, the face a charred, melted mess.

But she recognised it immediately.

Her mother had given it to her as a birthday gift one year. A treasured toy in a world where toys and birthdays were seldom available or acknowledged.

Breathless, she picked it up, clutching it against her chest. She caught sight of a single shoe on the bottom step. Her mother's shoe. She went for it and swiped at the grime.

It was a simple slip-on, one her mother had always worn – even the night they'd been attacked. It used to be white.

A soft sob escaped, echoing through the empty house, followed by another and when the tears came, she couldn't stop them. The pain was too great, the loss too powerful.

She sank to her knees and covered her face, crying for the

parents she so desperately missed. She'd never even said goodbye in their rush for safety.

But as fast as the tears had come, she turned them off. Instincts bristling, she swiped at the tears and killed the flashlight. Her heart skipped a beat, the prickle of warning followed by footsteps outside.

She wasn't alone.

CHAPTER TWENTY EIGHT

Jenna's senses jerked to the forefront.

In lightning speed, she moved into the shadows and glanced out the window. A woman scurried up the front stairs, hesitating in the doorway. She wore a beanie and a scarf, her hands shoved into her pockets.

Megan.

"What are you doing here?" Jenna asked, her voice gritty from the tears, and suddenly, she regretted them. A moment of weakness.

"*You!*" Megan gushed, stepping inside. She cast a quick glance around the room. "I was right. Back at the warehouse. You pulled me out."

"A momentary lapse of judgement. I should've left you to die."

"You'd never do that, Jenna, and we both know it."

"You killed two Keepers!"

"Oh please, you really want to keep track of who's killing who? We're at war. Casualties are a given." As if to prove her point, Megan raised her hands and whispered a chant. Fragments of cement debris rattled on the ground before rising, hovering mid-air. With a sly smile and another whisper, it soared through the air toward Jenna.

Jenna held up her arms to shield her head, wincing as dozens of cement pieces hit her. Coughing, she straightened as the dust settled, and glared at Megan. Anger flared as she tried to reconcile the girl she'd grown up with to the woman in front of her.

"What the hell was that for?" Jenna cried.

"Payback for New Orleans. I should've known when you came to us that it was a farce. I trusted you! I thought you were on our side."

When Jenna had first joined them, convincing Megan she sided with them had been a challenge. After all, the woman knew her better than most, but Jenna had pulled it off. It had helped that Megan was as determined to hide their connection and history. *Ameera.*

"Hell would freeze over before I support your cause, Megan. I will never –" Jenna stopped, distracted by a movement in the street.

"I came alone," Megan offered.

Jenna eyed her suspiciously. "If you knew I'd be here, why not tell Hazel?"

"How the hell would I explain this?" She waved a hand at the room. "Hazel's not stupid. She'll sniff out the truth in the blink of an eye and will know –"

"That you're from Ameera? That you were raised by good people that took you in when you had nothing? They loved you when no one else would! They believed in you, dammit!"

"Don't you dare preach to me about your parents!" Megan yelled. "Your mother sent us away! That's not love, Jenna."

How could Megan so easily discount everything her parents had done for her? Jenna bared her teeth, clenching her fists. "You know nothing of my mother and what she stood for, what she fought against."

"No, I don't because your parents were always so damn secretive."

It was true. Despite taking Megan off the streets, her parents had insisted they keep their magic a secret from her. From everyone.

They'd owned a store, sold herbs and medicine for healing. Placebo crap that covered their magic. A good front, one that everyone had believed.

Megan's eyes narrowed. "But now, in hindsight, knowing you're a Keeper, I can't help but wonder why. Who were they, Jenna? What were they hiding?"

It was only a matter of time before Megan figured it out. Shit. "They were good people, Megan. A trait you know nothing of," Jenna shot back, her tone clipped with anger and resentment. "And somehow, they must've known that."

The words struck a chord for Megan as Jenna had known they would. Her breathing hitched and her nostrils flared. The energy shifted in the room. A blast of magic smacked into Jenna, hurtling her across the room. She slammed into the wall and slid to the ground.

"Why did you come back here?" Megan asked, circling. "Your parents are gone. There's nothing here for you. All you've done is upset Hazel again."

"Why's Hazel in Ameera?"

"You really expect me to answer that?"

Jenna dashed across the room so fast that Megan barely had time to register the movement. They collided in an exchange of punches and curses, fuelled by divided beliefs and years of accumulated frustration and disagreements. But Jenna was stronger and faster and Megan was quick to break away. Breathless, they circled each other, gazes locked.

"Does Ethan know why you're really here?" Megan panted, her voice dripping with challenge.

"To search for Hazel."

"We both know that was only half the agenda."

"Maybe, but I'll still fight to my death to protect my witch and the people back home. My entire life is about that, Megan, and if you threaten that, I won't hesitate to annihilate you."

"Just like that? Despite what we meant to each other?"

"That was a long time ago, a relationship soured by our different beliefs. We're on opposite sides of the war now."

Megan tensed. The ground trembled with a speed and violence that took Jenna by surprise. A beam dislodged from the roof. It crashed to the ground, splintering on impact. Windows and walls quivered.

"Stop it!" Jenna breathed, reeling back.

"Why? We're enemies, remember?" Megan scowled at her, breathing heavily, exuding a scary energy she'd never used on Jenna before. A frightening force wedged itself between them and Jenna took a step back.

Another beam collapsed above them, bringing down the floor above. Jenna dove for cover but building debris engulfed her. She threw her arms up to shield her head and squeezed her eyes shut as soot and dust blurred the air. The noise muffled her cry as something sharp pierced her flesh. The pain was sheer agony and in an instant, her body clamoured to heal itself.

Megan towered over her, hands outstretched, her face twisted with fury.

But she screeched as she was flung across the room, crashing into the wall. Jenna gritted her teeth and felt for the object lodged in her side. The smell of blood filled her nostrils.

And froze when she saw him. *Ethan!*

He had his arm around Megan, trapped in a death grip. His expression was beyond anything Jenna had ever seen before. A blind rage that overruled everything else.

Megan swatted him, gasping air. Her eyes bulged when he added more pressure. A simple tug would snap her neck like a chicken bone.

"NO!" Jenna screamed and lunged for him. The force broke his hold on Megan and she scrambled out of his reach.

Ethan's gaze found Jenna's, confusion clouding the fury in his eyes. Megan rose, straightening her jacket. She'd lost her scarf in the scuffle. Watching Ethan warily, she fled.

Ethan let her go. He was in front of Jenna in a heartbeat, his face inches from hers. The air had turned icy, but he was all heat and fury. His eyes blazed something lethal. A vein throbbed in his neck.

A shiver of apprehension trickled down her spine, but she fought the urge to step back. Instead, she lifted her chin.

"Megan is one of Hazel's sidekicks," he said slowly, the words dripping with venom. "She supports everything we fight against. She tried to hurt Kate and Sienna. Repeatedly."

"Ethan, it's not what you think."

"We protect those we care about. Those we side with." He jabbed a finger in the direction of the door. "That bitch hurt you and you just *defended* her."

"It's not like that," she whispered, loathing the desperation in her tone.

"Then explain it to me," he said, towering over her. "Because right now it looks like you're in her corner and if that's the case, we have a big fucking problem."

CHAPTER TWENTY NINE

He caught the flash of fear in her eyes, knew he was the reason for it, but didn't give a damn. Screw that. She'd left him behind to meet with Megan. A damn witch who sided with their greatest enemy.

Anger churned, along with a sense of betrayal that scorched like a bitch. He'd tasted betrayal before, but this was different.

This was Jenna.

He swiped at the blood on his cheek – a result of Megan's frantic attempt to claw his eyes out. His mind reeled as he tried to reconcile the woman he knew to the woman in front of him. He'd heard the end of their conversation and it had taken every ounce of strength he had not to tear into them both.

"Last night at the warehouse," he said through clenched teeth. "It was you who dragged Megan to safety, wasn't it?" She gave a brief nod, her hands squeezed into fists against her chest. "I thought you were on our side."

"I am, Ethan. I swear."

"Then explain why the hell you keep protecting the very person who'd kill our witches in a heartbeat!"

"We have history. It's complicated."

"So *uncomplicate* it for me. 'Cause right now, all I see is a Keeper who's playing both sides." He took a step closer, tightening his fists. "And you of all people know how much I hate being played."

"I'm not playing you, dammit!"

"You saved Megan! Twice."

Her eyes flared and she shoved him. Hard. He was about to bolt forward but hesitated when he smelt blood. Her blood. He scanned her for injuries, his stomach twisting when he saw the telltale red stain on her jacket, hitched above a small steel rod that protruded from her flesh. "You're hurt," he said, reaching for her.

"Don't touch me!" she snapped, reeling back.

"You're bleeding, Jenna."

Frowning, she waved him away. She gripped the rod and pulled, stifling a cry. It clattered to the floor, the sound ringing in the silence of the room. She drew in a deep breath, and energy exuded off her in waves.

He moved around her, surprised when she let him. Her grim expression eased and her breathing grew more level. She squared her shoulders and lifted her head, the fire back in her eyes.

"The pain's gone," he said. He could see it in the way she stood, the way she looked at him. He moved aside her jacket. There was so much blood, but the wound had healed. Her expression remained unreadable. "How did you heal so fast?"

She looked at the floor and blew out air. "The reason I never showed you and your brothers my elemental powers is because I don't have any. My magic heals – myself and others too."

His eyes narrowed. "Keepers can't heal others."

Her head lifted and she raised her hand, her fingers cold against his cheek. But warmth soon filtered through his skin, gentle and soothing, erasing Megan's scratch.

He frowned, his mind scrambling to make sense of her revelation. "There's only one lineage of Keepers who can do that and they're as extinct as the damn dinosaurs."

A special lineage of Keepers with the power to heal, the last of them destroyed after betraying their witches the night of the massacre. There'd been two types of Keepers that night. Keepers like him, and others like. . .

"Most of them, yes."

Her expression clouded with something he couldn't decipher. Fear? Hesitation? When she shrank back, he caught her chin between his fingers, bringing her back to him. "You're not like me, are you, Jenna?"

"My magic isn't elemental. It's healing." Her eyes burned with emotion and untold truths between them.

"If that's true then . . ."

Her brief nod confirmed his suspicions. "I'm a Salubrious."

****

Saying it aloud sparked a ripple of unease through Jenna. A word she never used to describe herself.

A Salubrious. A Keeper with the instinct to protect and the power to heal. Fix the broken. Something an ordinary Keeper was unable to do.

She'd never told anyone. She'd been taught from a young age to keep that part of her hidden. Her family had embraced their magical powers but never in front of others. Being such an isolated lineage, their magic would give them away and the threat of their enemies discovering their existence always lingered.

Ethan gaped at her, a harsh frown creasing his brows. Silence stretched between them.

"How's this possible?" he demanded. "How are you here?"

"My ancestors were there the night of the massacre. The last of our lineage in the mortal world. There were other Keepers too. Afterward, The Circle wiped the memories of the humans involved and exiled the Keepers to Ameera as punishment."

"Rose's suspicions were right." He jutted out his chin, exposing the veins that throbbed in his neck. "Why would they keep that from us? Hell, why would *you* keep that from us?"

"To protect us."

"Your family killed their witches and *you're* the ones needing protection?"

"Allegedly killed," she hissed, unable to keep the anger and bitterness from her tone.

"I doubt The Circle would've banished them to Ameera based on *allegedly*, Jenna. They betrayed their witches, watched them burn and did nothing."

She couldn't deny it. Because it was true and her parents had never been able to fathom why. The details of that night were sketchy. After exposing their magic, the witches were rounded up by irate town folk. They were imprisoned in an old building and set alight. Their Keepers had done nothing to help them. An act of betrayal Jenna had never understood. It went against everything Keepers were sworn to uphold and protect. Against that inner desire to defend their witches.

"That's why you're familiar with the city," he said, eyes widening. "This was your home."

"I was born here, but it hasn't been my home for a very long time."

"You come from Ameera? How the hell did you end up in our world?"

"Once a month, when the full moon peaks, Ameera has an Annex." She explained the most dreaded night of the month, but knew her words did little to convey the fear and terror that came with it. Her chest tightened and she lowered her gaze as the memories came. "The night I left, the Annex was different. Earth tremors ravaged our city and the boundary walls were nullified before the moon peaked, catching us off guard. Our neighbourhood was attacked."

She looked away, swallowing, willing away the lump in her throat. Images kept coming, no matter how much she tried to field them.

"Jenna?"

The sound of her name jarred her torment and she looked up, biting her lip. "Somehow, my mother tracked the portal and insisted we leave."

"She came with you?"

"No. Megan and I."

"That's why you're protecting her? You have some sort of screwed-up loyalty?" She turned away, unable to explain or deny it. Hell, she'd bust herself up enough times because of her twisted loyalty to the witch. "What happened to your mother?"

"I haven't seen them since that night," she replied, her voice cracking.

He rubbed his temples and shook his head. "Everything we know about you is a goddamn lie."

"I never lied!"

"Omission, lie, same damn thing. You should've told me!"

"Telling anyone that I'm a Salubrious puts me at risk." She jabbed a finger in the direction of the window. "Sienna was right. We never stood a chance – here or back home. We're loathed by your kind, hunted by enemies and because of that, most of the Keepers there that night are dead."

"And that surprises you after what they did?" He caught her wrist, drawing her closer. Fury dripped from him in a way that unnerved her. "You're from a lineage of Keepers we despise. Your family is everything we aren't."

A small part of her crumbled when she heard the disgust in his voice. She'd always dreaded telling him, knowing he'd view her differently.

"This trip to Ameera . . . this had nothing to do with finding the spell, did it? Hell, did Kate even feature in your plans at all?"

She wrenched her hand free. "Of course she does. Kate – and Sienna – will always come first. Always. But not knowing what happened to my family is killing me, Ethan. I've searched for a way back here for years and when we discovered the portal was open, I had to return. I may be magical, but I'm also human, dammit." Her voice trembled and she drew in a shaky breath. "I had to know. I had to return."

They stared at each other in silence, hurt and anger wedged between them, a barrier of ugliness they'd never shared before.

"I know all about pain and loss and longing, Jenna. I know what it's like to have parents ripped away from you. I get it." His voice softened, but did little for his disgruntled expression. "But I trusted you."

"You can still trust me, dammit! I haven't lost sight of our goal or why we're here."

"You should've told me!"

"I was afraid! I had to protect myself."

"From me?" Her words reignited the fury and he bulldozed forward, only stopping when he had her backed into the wall. "That's why you never told me? You'd thought I'd hurt you?"

When she didn't reply, he slammed a palm against the wall beside her head. She gasped and flinched, gaping at him. The air prickled with tension, rife and frightening.

For a moment, he simply scowled at her, his breathing shallow and rapid. "What infuriates me the most is that through all the years we've known each other, the dozens of conversations we've shared, the battles we've fought . . ." Placing his other hand on the wall beside her, trapping her between his arms, he edged closer, his face inches from hers. "*You* didn't trust *me*."

CHAPTER THIRTY

The Square looked different in the morning light. Deserted, less ominous. A contrast to the way Jenna felt.

Ethan had walked away and she hadn't stopped him. Even though the pain in her chest had magnified with every step he took. She'd wanted to call out to him, ached to make things right, but she knew he needed space.

From her.

That thought made her feel like a leper.

She sauntered into the courtyard, head lowered. The grey cobblestones matched the grey of the sky, the sun hidden behind the clouds. The courtyard was deserted, scattered with tables and chairs and empty beer bottles.

Susan's bar was locked, the blinds drawn, but the sound of voices in the kitchen drew Jenna to the back entrance – faint, inaudible to most people, but she heard them. A Keeper perk.

She approached the kitchen window quietly, crouching low, and peered inside. Susan stood against the counter, a row of pots and pans dangling from the ceiling above her head. A bandanna subdued her hair and she wore an apron over her dress.

Axel leaned over her, his arms around her neck. His lips were close to hers but they weren't kissing.

When Susan whimpered softly, he broke away, panting, dazed, and high on something that wasn't sexual. He flexed his jaw as though he'd just feasted on something tasty. His bearded face cracked a lazy smile.

Susan glanced at the clock on the wall. "Shouldn't you be going? You wouldn't want to keep Hazel waiting."

"Hazel's on my turf. She shouldn't keep *me* waiting." A frown creased his studded brows and he backtracked to the door. "I'll stop by later."

The moment the door closed behind him, Susan paled and slumped against the counter.

Jenna gaped at her in surprise, her anger lessening. Whatever had happened had been consensual, but Susan hadn't liked it. *She faked it.* And Jenna knew all about faking it. There were only two reasons a woman would tolerate the advances of a man she loathed.

Desperation or survival and, sadly, it was often both.

Susan spun around when Jenna pushed open the kitchen door. She saw the anguish in Susan's eyes moments before the steely facade returned.

"You shouldn't have come back to Ameera," Susan said, her voice edged with annoyance, "it's too dangerous for you here."

Jenna's brows lifted. "You're helping us but you're kissing the enemy? Which side are you on, Susan?"

They shared a long, silent look before Susan sighed and shook her head. "That wasn't a kiss," she said quietly, her shoulders sagging. "He wasn't kissing me. He was feeding."

****

Ethan stood on the rooftop of the tallest building he could find. Peering down at the city, he forced air into his lungs, reached for calm, perspective – any damn thing that would cool the rage.

He'd sensed that Jenna was up to something. Her tossing and turning had kept him awake. When she'd snuck out a while later, he'd dressed in record speed and followed her. But had never expected this. A goddamn Salubrious. Ties to Ameera.

And he'd suspected neither.

I'm on your side, Ethan. All the way. Just know that.

He did. Despite all the lies, omissions, or whatever the hell she called it, but dammit, how had he not known? And why the hell had The Circle kept the banishment of the Keepers a secret?

But Rose had figured it out.

He scanned the city, slowly coming to life with the daylight. A thin layer of smog hovered and the air smelt of smoke. The sun's rays filtered through, touching broken buildings and abandoned streets. Two women argued from a nearby apartment, their voices amplified in the quiet.

A couple emerged from a makeshift cardboard house on the sidewalk, rumpled and sleepy. Without saying a word, they sat on the curb, heads lowered.

Jenna grew up here. In this shitty city of the doomed. She'd had a family, a life he knew nothing about. And would she have told him had he not forced her to?

His fists clenched as another wave of anger rolled through him. He wasn't sure what irked him more – that Jenna was a Salubrious, from a family exiled to a prison world, or that she'd kept it from him.

The couple on the sidewalk sprang to their feet so fast that they unsettled an overturned bin they'd used for a table. A pot clashed to the floor but went ignored as they scrambled into their house.

Ethan searched the street, curious as to what had sparked their abrupt retreat. He stiffened when he saw why. Axel. Walking briskly in the middle of the street, like he owned it.

He was on a mission.

And Ethan needed a distraction.

Fuck yeah.

****

A feeder?

Jenna recalled the image of Axel leaning over the dying Keeper the night before. It made sense now. He'd been *feeding*.

"They feed on the energy of people like us," Susan explained.

Similar to Scavengers, but they didn't kill for their fix. Feeding on others strengthened them, but they weren't able to absorb any powers.

Her gut clenched at the thought of their magic being used to fuel their enemies. Magic that was pure and treasured and meant for the greater good. "They know you're a witch?"

Susan picked up a ball of dough, placed it on the counter, and began kneading it with her fists. "There's more to me than that, but they don't know it yet."

"It's a violation, Susan."

"In Ameera, we have no choice. You of all people should know that."

A wave of apprehension rolled through Jenna and she squared her shoulders, taking a step forward. "You said I shouldn't have *come back*. To Ameera. Why would you say that? I never said I'd been here before."

Susan dumped the bread onto a tray and shoved it into the oven. The oven rattled when she slammed the door. Wiping her hands on her apron, Susan turned around and met her gaze. "I was expecting you, Jenna."

Jenna's jaw went slack. "You know me?"

"I know who you are."

"How?"

"I'm a Sage."

No wonder the woman was so sketchy with the details of her magic. A Sage dabbled with simple spells but had the ability to see parts of the future, possessing knowledge of it that no one else had. A power Hazel would snatch up in a second.

"I see things differently to others," Susan explained. "I have visions and lately you keep appearing in them. Last night, after meeting you, I had the most vivid one yet."

Jenna's breathe quickened. "Why would I be in your visions? That's just creepy." Footsteps echoed in the alley behind the bar and she shot Susan a worried look. "Expecting someone?"

Susan leaned over the stove to peer through the blind. Gasping, she quickly withdrew and took Jenna's hand. "Hurry, we have to hide. They can't see us together!"

Susan dropped to her knees, tugging Jenna with her, and crawled under the kitchen table. The handle turned as Susan whispered a chant. Jenna had no idea what the spell was for, but she'd heard enough of them to know when one was being cast.

Unease crawled through her and she was about to object, but the back door burst open and Rick stepped inside, Megan directly behind him.

Jenna jerked, but Susan grabbed her arm with both hands, shaking her head. When Rick's gaze scoped the room, missing them beneath the table, Jenna understood what Susan had done.

A veiling spell.

CHAPTER THIRTY ONE

She'd found Hazel's hideout in Ameera.

What that meant evoked an avalanche of conflicting emotions for Jenna.

She drew in a few even breaths, trying to get a grip on the tension that riddled her. She welcomed the adrenaline rush; it sharpened her mind and instincts, needed considering she was about to enter a house full of warlocks and witches that would kill her in an instant.

But for now, they couldn't see her.

Thanks to Susan's veiling spell, tailing Megan and Rick through the streets of the city had been easy. A ghost that walked amongst the streets, weaving in and out of people who had no idea she was there. The spell had an eeriness to it that Jenna couldn't shake – no matter how much she relied on the invisibility to save her ass.

Several hours later, they'd finally headed to the edge of the city. The terrain was overgrown and neglected, but greener and more spacious. A row of mansions overlooked the city, the backdrop of rolling hills behind them.

They were once homes for the wealthy. Now, most likely, homes for the powerful. But neither wealth nor power had saved them from Ameera. Many walls had toppled over, others covered in creepers. Windows were broken, staircases collapsed. Several roofs had blown off, leaving wide, gaping holes.

The dense overgrowth of bushes and trees had moulded the gardens together in one long, wide landscape.

Megan and Rick took the single row of stairs that led into a courtyard and went into the house. The water feature outside held no water, only an angel statue that missed both arms. Voices drifted from inside.

Jenna's mind raced and her body pulsed with adrenaline and fear. Even with the veiling spell. Being here alone was dangerous. She knew that. But Ethan had walked away. After searching for so long, she'd finally traced Hazel. This might be her only chance at finding the portal spell. They could go home, close the portal, and seal Hazel inside Ameera for eternity.

Could you?

Jenna stilled, allowing the words to seep in. She bit her lower lip, more harshly than intended, tasting blood, loathing the voice that whispered inside her. It echoed her deepest longings, her deepest fears.

If she had the power to close the portal forever, to lock the door on her old home and the truth of what had happened to her parents, would she? Could she?

Her skin tingled as the truth gnawed for attention. A truth she refused to acknowledge. Because acknowledging it would clash with everything she believed in. Everything she'd sworn to defend. The fact that she'd even allowed that question to surface terrified her.

She shook her head, refusing to go there. Not now. Screw the voice. Screw her conscience.

Laughter burst out from within the house, spurring her forward, and she went inside. She debated a swift sweep of the house but the warrior in her urged caution. So she moved silently, her instincts and senses primed, her body on edge, coiled and ready to strike.

The open-plan living room and kitchen had been sparsely furnished. Old, but neat. A grand piano stood in the corner of the room covered with a white sheet that had long since discoloured. Two spears decorated the wall above it.

A man stood at the doorway to the patio. Jenna's heart skipped a beat when she recognised him. John, the Chinese warrior, as skilled at martial arts as Jenna. Maybe even better. They'd spent many hours mastering their techniques on each other. Their sessions had been harsh, often resulting in injuries.

When Megan and Rick walked up behind him, he gave a low whistle. "The mother ship has company and she's in a mood, so approach at your own risk."

But they didn't. Instead, they hovered in the doorway and stared outside.

When Jenna saw why, her breath caught.

Hazel.

The dark witch caster stood beside a muddy pool, the backdrop of hills behind her, deep in conversation with Axel. She'd tied her black hair into a ponytail. It highlighted the bony tattoos across her neck and shoulders. Dark ink circled her eyes.

She looked like a living skeleton, her natural beauty eradicated by the artwork. Her nephew, Mason, wore similar markings, a masculine version of Hazel and just as creepy. Three grotesque cats paced around Hazel. They were massive, far larger than any other wild cat Jenna had ever seen. Big heads, square-shaped jaws, murky brown fur.

Domestic cats, spelled to be larger and fiercer. Mason's trademark and a product of their dark magic. Most likely a ploy to intimidate the locals.

Axel eyed the cats circling them. His studded brows were drawn together in a tight frown. "We had a deal, Hazel. I want out of this hellhole." The way he glared at her and everything about the way he stood, shoulders erect, feet planted firmly apart, made him seem fearless.

Stupid? Or a farce? Either way, Hazel would eat him alive if she wanted to.

"In time," Hazel replied. "You're not strong enough yet."

"Don't insult me."

"You haven't seen my opposition in the mortal world. You may be strong and forceful here, but back home the Bennett brothers and their witches would destroy you."

Pride flared at the meaning of Hazel's words. She saw them as opposition, powerful enough to make her wary. Ha, fancy that.

"I'd like to see them try." Axel stepped up, his face close to hers. Hazel didn't even flinch. "My people can only be satisfied for so long."

"Oh please. If you haven't learnt how to make them *think* they're satisfied, perhaps you shouldn't be leading them."

He jabbed a finger at his watch. "You have until the Annex. Two days, Hazel. You better not back out of our deal."

Her jaw of tattooed teeth curled into a half smile, devoid of humour. "I don't take likely to threats, Axel."

"Neither do I."

"Considering I have the portal spell and I'm the one supplying you with Keepers –"

"We both know the only reason you're bringing those Keepers to Ameera is to eliminate your competition in the mortal world. If anything, we're doing you a favour by feeding on them daily."

"I can always offer them elsewhere if you'd prefer. I'm sure the vamps –"

"Like hell. I've given you safe passage," he waved his hand at the house, "a place to stay and I've agreed to help you fight your battle against the witches and their Keepers. You owe me."

She laughed. "You really think I needed you for a safe passage?"

"You need alliances, otherwise you wouldn't be here." Backing up to the door, he held up two fingers. "Two days, Hazel. And up the supply of Keepers. There are many of us to feed and I hate scraps."

"We're working on it."

Jenna's heartbeat lurched when Axel passed her, missing her by inches. The heavy thud of his boots echoed in the room. Without a word, Rick followed him through the house.

No doubt, the portal would be Axel's reward for helping Hazel. As for her? *An alliance.*

Shit. That's why she was in Ameera. She was building herself a goddamn army.

Hazel's attention turned to Megan. "Did you find Susan?"

"She wasn't there."

"Axel suspects she knows more than she's letting on. If that's the case, I want her found." Striding to a nearby table, Hazel picked up a book and held it up. The light caught the scorpion bracelet on her wrist. "After all the waiting and you summon me *this*?"

Megan blinked. "It's the Brogan Grimoire –"

"It's empty!" Hazel snapped, her voice lined with a hysteria Jenna had seldom witnessed. "The stupid book is blank!"

Jenna jerked forward. *Wait, what?* The Brogan Grimoire?

"You were able to open it? I thought only Sienna could open it." Megan shifted in the doorway, her movements slow and hesitant. Jenna couldn't blame her. In fury mode, Hazel was terrifying.

"It's my family Grimoire. Of course I can open it." Hazel slammed a fist on the cover. "But apparently, being able to read the darn thing is more complicated."

She tossed the book across the patio, sparking a low growl from the closest cat. The book slammed into Megan's chest, but she caught it before it slid to the floor. Wide-eyed, lips parted in surprise, she smoothed a hand over the leather cover, and sent a wary glance at the cats. They circled Hazel, their lips parted to reveal sharp teeth. "It's the right book, Hazel. Mason gave it to me himself. He said the Beckham witches veiled the pages."

Whoa. Mason? What the hell?

A fresh spurt of alarm speared through Jenna. There were only two things able to set Mason free. Either Sienna retracting her spell or Kate's blood.

No!

Breathless, Jenna fought the rush of panic that tightened her stomach. It couldn't be. There was no way Sienna would free Mason and if something had happened to Kate, she'd have sensed it.

Even here, in Ameera?

Damn, what if her connection with Kate had been severed the moment she'd walked through the portal?

Sighing loudly, Hazel stomped forward, snatched the book from Megan and placed it on the table. She held up her hands and whispered a chant. She repeated the words, her muttered ramblings laced with irritation. When nothing happened, she tried again, this time louder and with more fervour.

Jenna felt the prickle of energy wash over her. Instinctively, she moved back, moulding her body against the wall.

"Hazel," Megan said, hesitating, "only a Beckham witch can unspell it. Even Mason couldn't –"

"Oh, please. Don't insult me. I'm not just *any* witch. And my unveiling spell works like a charm."

Several failed attempts later had turned Hazel's cheeks red. With a cry of rage, she picked up the Grimoire and hurled it at Rick.

Apparently, even the all-powerful witch caster was no match for a Beckham spell.

Hazel jabbed a finger at him. "We need the Null. Her blood may be our only chance of breaking that damn spell!"

"She's protected, Hazel," Rick said, tucking the book under his arm, "and she's stronger."

"Find a way!" she screamed, turning around. But her breath caught and she stilled, surprise clouding her expression. She slowly tilted her head, her narrowed eyes flashing with amusement.

And looked straight at Jenna.

"Well, well, what have we here?" Hazel asked in a cool tone that sent a jolt of alarm through Jenna. Her jaw line of tattooed teeth cracked a wide smile.

Megan gasped.

Icy terror spread through Jenna. *Oh, crap.*

Hazel's unveiling spell. She hadn't been able to break the Beckham spell on the Grimoire but had broken Susan's.

It had unveiled *her.*

CHAPTER THIRTY TWO

Jenna straightened her shoulders and lifted her chin, reaching for a steely facade that would cover her fear.

She refused to give Hazel that satisfaction.

The silence was unnerving, marred by the faint rumbling of thunder that echoed in the distance. They glared at each other, thick tension spicing the air. A culmination of years of hatred and violence, an unresolved rivalry.

Dark clouds had swept across the sky, casting a shadow over the city. It looked like a dome of fury about to engulf them.

"Nice of you to pay us a visit," Hazel said, her voice far too cheerful for the occasion. She walked closer, her movements slow, meticulous, her gaze never wavering from Jenna's. "A courage like yours is to be admired, Jenna." Her skeletal teeth curled into a smirk. "But right now, right here, it's just plain . . . stupid."

A crack of thunder startled the cats. Growling, they paced. Restless, agitated, sizing up their prey.

Her.

"Where the hell did she come from?" Rick asked, his wide grin matching John's. Their expressions reminded Jenna of kids on a Christmas morning.

A spurt of adrenaline flooded her veins as energy rolled through her. Energy that wasn't hers. A darkness and strength so powerful that it took her breath away.

Hazel.

With a soft laugh, Hazel flung out her arm and Jenna soared through the air, smacking into the wall. Instead of sliding to the ground, she remained pinned. Trapped by an invisible grip.

An old trick of Hazel's. One she'd often used when trying to prove a point.

Jenna tried to break free but an unbearable weight pressed against her chest, threatening to crush her.

The two men approached, grinning like idiots. Their excitement filled the air, their hunger for violence apparent in their wild eyes and restless movements. Megan hesitated in the doorway, her expression a mixture of fear and worry. The men stopped in front of Jenna, the woman who'd betrayed them and cost them a victory in a war they kept losing. Jenna knew what they were after.

Vengeance. And it wouldn't be painless.

"Don't harm her!" Hazel shouted above the noise of the thunder. "She's mine!"

The crack of thunder was so loud and close that the cats jumped. They paced the patio, growling quietly. It began to rain, soft droplets that quickly gathered momentum. The hills were almost invisible from the grey clouds that covered the valley.

Frowning, Hazel glanced at the sky. "Ah, I see you brought company."

Company? Jenna stared at her. The storm wasn't Hazel's?

Hope flickered and she glanced in the distance, searching for Ethan, torn between relief and worry. Relief that she had someone fighting with her. Worry he'd be harmed because of it.

Hazel jabbed a finger at Rick. "Find her friends. Now!"

"It's only the younger Bennett brother," Megan called after him as he disappeared. "The others are still in Rapid Falls."

"No doubt," Hazel's smile contradicted the malice in her eyes, "to protect their witches from . . . *me*. Which makes me curious why Jenna left Kate unprotected to come here."

All kinds of prickly sensations ran through Jenna at the mention of Kate's name. "Kate has all the protection she needs."

Rick reappeared in the doorway, shaking his head. He clutched a hunting knife in one hand.

Hazel clenched her fists and Jenna's throat tightened in response – even though Hazel wasn't touching her. Air evaded her and she gritted her teeth against the powerful hold that threatened to suffocate her. Or worse, snap her neck.

Just as Jenna's view became murky, a bolt of lightning flashed across the patio, connecting with a nearby tree. A branch broke off with a deafening crack and fell into the pool.

Hazel unclenched her fists, releasing her magical hold on Jenna's throat.

Coughing, Jenna sucked in air. Her throat ached, her lungs burned. "My death won't change anything, Hazel," she called out above the noise of the rain. "Between the Bennett brothers and Kate and Sienna's magic combined, you'll never win."

"But I had a chance before you destroyed everything and stole Kate from under my nose."

"You have no right to her."

"Like that would stop me." Frowning, she took the knife from Rick. "That night you took Kate pissed me off more than you'll ever know, Jenna."

"I'm a Keeper. I was protecting my witch."

"You betrayed me!"

"And honour and loyalty are so . . . you."

Hazel sauntered closer, ignoring her sarcasm, and waved the knife in the air. The frown on her inked brows eased when her lips curled into a smirk. "I warned you I'd make you pay for betraying me."

Jenna struggled against the invisible hold still pinning her to the wall. When the knife pressed against her stomach, she couldn't deny the rush of fear. Hazel's eyes had darkened, the way they always did when she was about to do something horrible.

She ran the tip of the blade over Jenna's skin. "You came into my home, mingled with my people. For months you lied, cheated, and then trashed our plans."

The blade cut into Jenna's stomach and it took every ounce of willpower she possessed not to cry out. Hazel yanked out the knife, grinning at Jenna's grimace, and was quick to stab her again. Jenna grunted and caught her lower lip between her teeth. Blood gushed from the wounds and she felt the familiar swirl of energy that would heal it. *No!* Every instinct she possessed clamoured to heal, but she fought the urge, reeling it in.

"You made a fool of me." Hazel ran the knife across Jenna's neck, piercing flesh. Slow, meticulous cuts of pleasure. "If only Kate could see you now. Beaten. Defenceless. Bleeding out."

"Screw you, Hazel."

Anger uncoiled Jenna's restraint and something snapped inside her. *No fucking way.* With a loud cry, she slammed her head forward, connecting with Hazel's. The impact was quick and hard. Hazel gasped, her eyes rounded and she lowered the knife.

The magical hold on Jenna lessened, just enough to free her limbs. Hope soared and she gave in to the overwhelming urge to heal herself. Renewed energy and strength flooded her body, a fix only her magic offered. The pain subsided as her flesh healed. With her magic came fresh determination and she reared forward, snapped her hand around Hazel's wrist, and yanked.

The knife clattered to the floor. A second yank dislodged Hazel's scorpion bracelet. It bounced across the patio, accompanied by Hazel's bellow of rage.

But there was something more. A sliver of panic behind the anger. Jenna saw it in her eyes as clear as she saw the fury.

"My bracelet!" Hazel screamed, whirling around. She jabbed a finger at Rick. "Find it! NOW!"

Embracing the distraction, Jenna delivered a powerful kick that sent Hazel sliding across the patio, crashing into the cats. The hold on Jenna relented completely and she slumped to the ground.

Glass exploded as a spear soared through a window, slamming into John's leg. Rick barked orders, his voice muffled by another rumble of thunder. This time it was so loud that the windows rattled.

"I want my bracelet!" Hazel screeched, shoving away a cat as she struggled to her feet. Rain pelted down on her. She swiped at the strands of hair that hung limply around her face, coloured with blood from a cut on her brow. Her rain-soaked dress clung to her skinny frame.

Hazel stepped forward, but a bolt of lightning cut her off, more powerful than before, one flash after another, until the entire patio was a sizzle of electricity. Taking on the lightning would be lethal, even for Hazel. She recoiled, screaming at Rick, searching the ground.

Jenna's narrowed gaze followed hers, suspicion trickling through her when she saw what Hazel had fixated on. Not the storm, the attack, or retaliation. *The bracelet.*

"JENNA!"

The snap of her name had her whirling around and her spirits soared when she saw Ethan running toward her. Drenched, bloody, torn shirt. Bolts of lightning surrounded him, striking everything in his path. Hazel screamed and dove for cover.

And then Ethan was there, in front of Jenna, practically giving off sparks as he sizzled with energy and fury. He tugged her up as bolts of lightning fired across the ground. "Let's go!"

"Wait!" Jenna pulled free and sped across the patio. Dodging a cat, Jenna swooped down to snatch the bracelet.

And ran.

CHAPTER THIRTY THREE

Ethan heard the cats tailing them. Smelt them. The stench of hunger, determination, and the rush of excitement that came with the chase. The magic had amplified their abilities and appearance – as well as their instincts.

They were predators at heart and he'd be damned if that made him and Jenna their prey.

He pushed on, Jenna matching his pace, speeding through bushes and trees along the bottom of the hill, the cats gaining steady ground.

"We should head into the city!" Ethan shouted, pointing to the nearby buildings. "It's safer there than the outskirts."

"No. That's werewolf territory. We enter and we're as good as dead."

"We stick around here and we're as good as dead. We've just pissed off the most powerful witch in Ameera."

"I have a plan. Keep going."

There were no signs of their enemies, the storm he'd left behind hampering their chase. He'd given it all, fuelled the storm with as much energy as he could muster. Wind, rain, lightning, thunder. All at once, with as much fury as he could channel.

Damn, it had been ages since he'd embraced his magic to that extent. It had been exhilarating watching the confusion it had created. Even Hazel had been dumbfounded. But they'd trapped Jenna. Taunted her. *Cut her.* And it wouldn't have stopped there.

"Ethan!" Jenna shouted as the cats closed in. They moved rapidly, running across the ground with feline grace, their unwavering gazes tracking their prey. One trailed behind whilst the other two raced ahead, tracing a triangle. A perfect trap.

Like hell.

"We're almost there!" she shouted, stumbling when the ground began to tremble, a steady rumble that was quick to gain momentum. No doubt a sign of Hazel's wrath. Jenna pointed to a clock tower in the distance. It stood between two tall buildings at the foot of the hill. "We need to get there. Can you get rid of the cats?"

He took her hand and changed direction. Jenna followed, matching his stride with ease. A rush of energy joined the adrenaline already pumping through his body, flowing from him as effortlessly as breathing. He knew a torrent of mini tornadoes would be on their trail because of it. Looking over his shoulder, he tracked all three cats, cursing when he heard the telltale voices of Hazel's men approaching in the distance.

The tornadoes gathered momentum, quickly catching up to them. The wind grew stronger. It clouded their vision, stole their breaths. Ethan drew to an abrupt stop and wrenched Jenna toward him. She bumped into his chest as he wrapped his arms around her, tucking her head beneath his.

The tornadoes engulfed them. A force that was as exhilarating as it was terrifying. They split directions, aiming for each cat. The animals never stood a chance. Despite the magic, their strength and power, they faced three powerful whirlwinds and two warriors hell bent on survival. Their yelps and fierce growls were whipped away by the wind as they were sucked into the centre of the storm. A vacuum that offered no mercy.

Still clutching Jenna, Ethan twisted around and channelled the tornadoes toward the house they'd just run from. A loud roar echoed around him and he realised it was him. Furious, spent, breathless.

He felt Jenna's hand slip into his. She laced their fingers, jerking him forward. "We have to keep moving. I have an idea." She nodded at a grey building in the distance. Tall and narrow, the clock tower loomed over several smaller buildings below. With its pointed roof and arched windows and doors, it looked like a castle straight from Rapunzel.

Without the pink and prettiness.

"Werewolves?"

"No. We've passed that district."

Glancing around to ensure they weren't being tailed, they aimed for the tower, soon merging into the streets. The ground was uneven, covered in chunks of concrete. The gravel crunched beneath their shoes, the sound heightened in the quiet street.

The dark and gloomy sky cast the buildings in a grey shadow. They ran the rest of the way, passing a crowd of people gathered on the sidewalk. They were mostly men, deathly pale, and all wore coats and boots.

"Oh crap," Jenna gasped, gripping his arm.

Before he could question her, someone whistled. The sound sparked a flurry of movement as the men gathered behind them, keeping to the shadows of the buildings. They began running, growling. Shouts of excitement rang out, along with more whistles. They'd found a new form of entertainment and Jenna and Ethan were it.

Screw that.

When two men leapt to the ground in front of them, cutting them off, Ethan took Jenna's arm and changed direction. The men charged, snarling at them, sharp incisors flashing behind upturned lips.

Vampires.

Shit.

"Keep going!" Jenna shouted.

They raced forward in the direction of the tower. The vampires were everywhere, keeping to the shadows, running behind them, scaling walls. They moved quickly, their movements spider-like and eerie.

Jenna cried out when a vampire jumped on her from above, teeth bared. She rammed her elbow into his face, the crunch of bone accompanied by his loud yell. Whirling around, she aimed a kick, planting it in the centre of his chest. The force hurtled him across the street.

"Guess you've figured out this area of the city is vamp territory," Jenna panted as they bolted.

"A heads-up would've been nice."

"I didn't think they'd be out yet. They usually only come out after sunset."

That would explain the lurking in the shadows.

A loud screech joined the frenzy as a female vampire soared through the air, pouncing on Jenna. Ethan dove after them, thrusting the woman away. A male vamp took her place, clutched Ethan's arm and yanked.

Ethan grunted as a blinding pain arrowed through his shoulder. He slammed his head back into the vamp's face with a force that dislodged his grip.

Ethan reached for Jenna as more vampires surrounded them. He felt her fear, rage, the heightened adrenaline rush. Knew she would fight as hard as he would, driven by a mutual survival instinct that seared everything else.

But despite their strength and determination, there were too many damn vamps.

"Ethan," Jenna muttered, her voice so quiet that he almost missed it. She glanced at the clouds. "*The light.*"

CHAPTER THIRTY FOUR

He followed her gaze, taking in the grey sky that hovered above like a dark cloud of doom threatening to devour them.

And then it hit him. *Fucking vamps.*

Still circling, eyeing the vampires, he seized the magic buried inside. It flowed through him, an exhilarating rush of power he thrived on. A gust of wind blew through the street, parting the crowd. It wrapped around them, sparking nervous glances when more wind followed. He added more force and sent the wind upward.

The clouds receded, allowing beams of sunlight to filter through. The rays were weak from the setting sun, but strong enough to provoke an outcry as the vampires rushed for cover.

"The roof!" Jenna yelled, taking Ethan's hand.

They hoisted themselves onto a nearby balcony and leapt to the roof, still basked in sunlight. The vampires tracked their movements restlessly from the ground below, keeping to the shadows, shouting at each other. The sun hovered on the horizon, all that stood between them and the vamps.

"I have a new appreciation for the sun," Jenna breathed, looking around.

"It's fading fast. We don't have much time. The sunlight will keep them street-bound for a little longer. After that, we're vamp food."

"Like we'd let that happen." She pointed to the buildings ahead of them, their roofs covered in a faint orange. "That's our way home."

He mentally calculated the distance of the jumps between each building. "It's a lot of ground to cover with very little sunlight left."

"I know, but if we hurry we can make it. Like Declan says, we're superheroes."

It was an old joke, an attempt to ease the tension, but the reminder of his brother jarred something inside him. He scowled at her for a long moment, a big ball of pissed off wedged in his chest.

But now wasn't the time.

She must've sensed it as her brows tightened. "Ethan . . ."

"Not now, Jenna." The words cut her off, his tone harsh. Without saying anything, or waiting for her to follow, he walked to the edge of the roof.

****

The vampires went mad.

Realising they were about to lose their prey, they set chase with an unnerving determination that had Jenna upping her speed.

Even though the vamps couldn't reach them yet.

Breathing heavily, high on an exhilarating adrenaline rush that rivalled all others, Jenna matched Ethan's pace. The higher buildings were trickier to navigate. Many of the roofs were unsteady, covered with cement debris, but were few and manageable. They sailed across rooftops with breathless speed, not stopping to take a beat.

Alone and free – not the two Keepers who'd just stirred a hornet's nest with a group of blood-sucking predators and an irate witch.

Several lights had turned on in anticipation for the darkness, adding a mirage of colours to the city. The storm had subsided and by the time the sun finally relented, disappearing in the distance, they'd reached the borders, leaving their attackers behind.

But they kept going, all too aware that the vampires weren't the only enemies on their trail. The city would hide them, but only temporarily as Hazel would stop at nothing to find them.

Jenna thought of the scorpion bracelet in her pocket. A powerful witch whose retaliation had been hampered by her desperation to retrieve the bracelet. Losing the bracelet had distracted her enough to give them a chance to escape. That alone hinted at its importance. So Jenna had taken it.

Something niggled inside, a nugget of truth demanding to be voiced, but went ignored when she spotted the railway in the distance.

Breathless, they took to the streets. The air smelt of smoke. A group of people stood around a drum on the sidewalk, a fire burning between them. They were surrounded by three toddlers playing with a dog. They all wore blank expressions and mismatched clothing, mended and patched.

Ethan and Jenna kept going, led by the rumble of a train nearby. Catching up with the train was easy, boarding it a little less skilled.

She stumbled as she landed on the floor of the carriage and felt Ethan's hand on her shoulder, steadying her. The connection comforted her, a reminder she wasn't alone. But he released her all too soon, avoiding her gaze, and turned away, his anger not lost on her.

Panting heavily, heart pounding, Jenna backed up against the wall and tried to catch her breath. Her lungs burned and her body throbbed. She was relieved they were alone, surrounded by graffiti-covered walls and the hum of the train.

But her relief was short-lived when she looked up to see Ethan walking toward her like a thundercloud.

****

He stopped in front her, keeping his hands balled into fists, despite the urge to touch her. He ignored the flash of apprehension that crossed her face, adrenaline and anger and fatigue working a shitstorm inside his head.

And his shoulder hurt like hell.

He glowered at her, inhaling a few long, deep breaths. She had wild eyes, flushed cheeks, her shoulders rising and falling with every choppy breath. Her skin shimmered from a thin sheen of sweat, her face coloured in a golden glow from the yellow light behind him.

A warrior woman he'd face a war with on any given day. A woman who'd lied to him. Misled him.

And damn nearly got herself killed.

Her hair was damp and she smelt of dirt and blood. He zoned in on the cut on her throat. Her wounds had been brutal and deep, but she'd still fought alongside him, fled the cats and the vampires, and matched his pace through the city.

Her ripped t-shirt exposed her bra, her abdomen, and neck smeared in blood. A hot wave of alarm washed over him, over-riding everything else – even the rage. He grimaced. "Shit, the vamps must've smelt you from a mile away."

"I'm fine. The wounds have already healed." Her voice was husky, soft, and she cleared her throat.

He thought about her pinned to the wall, at Hazel's mercy as the witch had sliced and diced at parts of her while he'd watched. Hot fury rose up inside him all over again. "You took on Hazel alone," he said quietly, unable to keep the lethal tone from his voice. "*Alone*, Jenna. Are you insane?"

"You're angry with me for what I told you earlier –"

A goddamn understatement. "And that surprises you? But that's not what this is about, dammit."

"I had no choice, Ethan. The opportunity came up and I –"

"Almost got yourself killed! What the hell were you thinking?" He placed a hand on the wall beside her head and leaned in.

"You're a goldmine to someone like Hazel and we both know it's not your magic she'll want."

Her breathing hitched, her mouth opened. But she didn't argue because she knew it was the damn truth. Hazel wouldn't care for Jenna's healing powers – they were useless on anyone evil. No, Hazel would be after the secret Jenna's lineage had guarded for years.

The location of the witch massacre.

"If Hazel figures out what you are –"

"I'm nothing to her."

"That's bullshit. You're a Salubrious! Your ancestors were there the night those witches died. They knew the location and when Hazel figures this shit out, she's going to assume that *you* know too."

"I don't. None of us do. The Circle wiped the location from the memories of everyone involved, Keepers included. It's the truth, Ethan, I swear."

His eyes narrowed and he stared at her in silence for a long moment, trying to decide if he believed her. But something in her eyes, the honesty he saw there, gave him his answer. Well, shit.

She inhaled quietly and placed a hand on his chest. Whether that was to keep him at a distance or calm him, he wasn't sure. "I should've told you about all this before we came to Ameera."

"No, Jenna. You should've told me a long, long time ago. Way back when you befriended my sister and came into our home. At worst, when you took on the role to protect Kate, a woman with the ability to change our war or crush my brother in a heart-beat should our enemies reach her." He snapped his fingers, the sound loud and intrusive in the silence beating around them. He dipped his head closer, their noses almost touching. "And when we decided to take on Ameera, I deserved to know that the only person *watching my back* had her own damn agenda that had nothing to do with mine."

"That's unfair, Ethan!"

He slammed the wall beside her head, cursing loudly. "This whole fucking place is unfair. You should've told me, dammit! And you should never, *ever*, have gone in there alone."

They stared at each other in heated silence, electricity sizzling between them, heightened in a way they'd never felt before. Her gaze held his, her shoulders rising and falling with every shallow breath she took. Her eyes were a storm of emotion that softened when she reached out to cup his cheek with the palm of her hand.

His first instinct was to recoil, but something in her eyes kept him transfixed, unable to look away.

She licked her lips, her thumb stroking his face. "You're right about everything. I should've told you and I'm sorry I didn't. I was afraid and I was wrong."

He didn't trust himself to reply and stood staring at her, trying to ignore the calm she'd suddenly injected into their conversation. Needed, but unwanted. He was still angry, dammit.

"You came for me," she murmured. "Despite everything, you came for me."

"I should've left you to rot," he grumbled, trying to think of all the reasons why he hadn't.

"But you didn't."

"Of course not." His fingers closed around her wrist, stilling her movement. "I'm a Keeper. I would never abandon one of my own. Even you." *Especially you.*

A thought that only irked him more.

"I wouldn't either, Ethan."

Breathing deeply through his nose, he glanced at her lips, torn between the urge to throttle her and . . . hell, he had no fucking idea. He was still a dozen shades of pissed off, but he couldn't ignore the fact that she was here, in front of him, safe.

Everything he'd just risked his life for.

"You have a right to be angry with me," she said, "but I didn't lie to you, Ethan. Be mad, but don't hate me –"

"I don't hate you. I hate that you've brought this between us."

204

"This?"

"Distrust." She flinched, just a fraction, but enough for him to see the hurt in her eyes. "I can't trust you, Jenna."

She didn't reply, but the words stung. He saw it in the way her brows drew together and her jaw tightened. But it was the damn truth and he refused to soften the blow that came with it.

He exhaled noisily, willing himself to calm the hell down. Before he did something he'd regret. Or burst a blood vessel. "I will always watch your back, Jen, but right now, I have serious doubts about you watching mine."

"I told you I'm on your side, Ethan."

His brows shot up. "Are you really, Jenna?"

"I told you –"

"Because the way I see, we're anything *but* on the same side." He moved closer, taking small satisfaction knowing she couldn't back away, trapped between him and the wall. Again. He dipped his head, his breath fanning her face, unable to tear his eyes away from her lips. They stood in silence for a long while, their bodies rocking gently together to the rhythm of the train. When he finally lifted his head to meet her gaze, he was all too aware that she'd stopped breathing.

"I'm not wrong, am I?" he murmured, not surprised when she turned her head, looking away. But she didn't deny it. He tipped her chin upward, bringing her gaze back to his. "My only goal for this stupid trip to Ameera is to close the damn portal, preferably with Hazel inside. And we both know that when I do, you won't *let* me."

CHAPTER THIRTY FIVE

Jenna closed the door of Susan's apartment and slid the locks into place. Without saying anything, Ethan disappeared into the bathroom. A moment later, the rattling of old pipes was followed by the gush of water as he turned on the shower.

They hadn't said much on the walk home, quietly stewing in their own thoughts. Their argument, their differences, and everything that had happened since coming to Ameera, had wedged between them like a lead weight she wasn't sure how to sidestep. The anger had subsided, settling into a silent animosity between them that felt unfamiliar – and stung like hell.

She thought of what he'd said about her stopping him from closing the portal. Even though her Keeper instincts had screamed in objection at the time, she hadn't denied it.

Because she couldn't.

If they found a way to close the portal, would she let him do it?

A shiver ran through her, evoking a layer of goosebumps. She rubbed her arms and walked to the window, gazing out at the city. It looked so quiet, but she knew the turmoil and danger that lurked beneath the surface. She also knew that Hazel would've launched a full-out search for them. With Axel as her ally, they were in more danger than ever.

The shower turned off, accompanied by another quick groan of pipes. When Ethan emerged a moment later, a towel around his waist, and rummaged in their bag for clothing, she couldn't help but stare at him.

He was magnificent.

Tanned skin, every muscle clearly defined. He had sturdy shoulders and a broad chest. Powerful biceps she'd clung to the night before as she'd climaxed in his arms.

The memory sparked a blush and she averted her gaze.

Even though she'd hurt him, misled him, and he'd walked out on her in a fit of rage, he'd come for her.

She swallowed, trying to dislodge the lump in her throat.

He pulled out a fresh t-shirt but cursed beneath his breath and stilled. He had his back to her so she couldn't see his face, but instincts had her scanning the length of him, searching for injuries. His bruises and cuts had already begun to heal, although it would be a while until they were completely gone. But he was hurting. She was sure of it.

Her suspicions were confirmed when he used one arm to tug the t-shirt over his head, favouring the other.

A flash of worry had her in front of him before he'd finished dressing.

****

Ethan blinked, surprised she'd moved so fast. He hadn't even heard her, the damn pain in his shoulder causing havoc with his senses. Frowning, he adjusted the t-shirt and tightened the towel around his waist.

"You're hurting," she said softly, her delicate brows creased.

He almost laughed at the statement when he saw the amount of blood on her. He'd taken the shower first, a feeble attempt to wash away some of the frustration, when, in fact, he should've offered it to her. She looked like crap. A bloody, torn mess.

And yet, here she was, worried about him.

Not trusting himself yet to speak, he turned away, but gritted his teeth when she took his arm and pain tore through his shoulder.

"Your shoulder?" she asked without releasing him.

He sighed, figuring he wouldn't be able to shirk her. "It'll heal soon. It was dislocated in the struggle with the vamp. I popped it back into place, but it still hurts like a bitch. A wicked one. With scary teeth."

A small smile twisted the corner of her mouth but disappeared before it developed into one of the full grins he adored. She held her hand above his injury and he clenched his jaw, anticipating feeling the bitch again.

Instead, he felt warmth.

The pain eased as the warmth intensified, penetrating flesh and bones, healing everything it touched. A swirl of energy, unlike his own, something he'd never felt before. Surprised, he looked at his shoulder and flexed his fingers. No pain.

She pulled away, taking a step back, but not before he caught the flash of fear in her eyes. She suddenly seemed unsure and the vulnerability that crossed her expression tore at him. Not surprising, considering how their last conversation had ended. But despite that, she'd lowered her guard and used her magic to heal him.

"We should get some sleep," he said, forcing himself to release her. He walked to the front door – the only door in the apartment – and checked that it was locked before removing the key. When he turned around, the scowl she shot him was one he'd expected. Ignoring her, he crossed the room, snagging the couch along the way and pushing it up against the only window that could open. When he went to retrieve a blanket from the bed, she cut him off.

She folded her arms and gave a defiant lift of her chin. "Seriously? You're barricading the exits so I can't leave?"

"Are you planning to?"

"No."

"So there's no problem."

She held out her hand. "Give me the key, Ethan."

He almost laughed at her. "*Right*. No." When she tried to take the key from him, he extended his arm, out of her reach. Her strength might almost match his, but she was still smaller.

"Really, Ethan? You're locking me in here with you?"

"You'd rather be out with them?" he challenged, nodding in the direction of the city.

"I told you –"

"Everything you told me is questionable, Jenna. Everything."

Her eyes flared and she grabbed his wrist. Not an ordinary grab one would expect from a woman. No, she was all strength, glaring at him with a challenge he easily recognised. He closed his fist around the key, keeping his arm out of her reach.

He might be bigger, stronger even, but he wasn't a fool. He knew her strength and how lethal she could be when cornered.

She moved in, clutching his fist between her hands. The scuffle was brief and breathless, ending when they tripped over the couch. He went down, taking her with him as he fell, and landed on the cushions.

"Stop that!" She slapped a palm against his chest. "You're being a bastard."

"Maybe, but I'm the only bastard in this city that cares about you."

"I didn't ask you to care."

"Well I do, dammit, so it makes this crap situation you've put us in even harder." He moved so fast that she gasped, twisting around so that she was beneath him. She blinked and tried to wiggle free, but he took her wrists, pinning them to the couch beside her head.

They glared at each other, breathing quietly, as electricity ignited between them.

It was always like that with her. An overwhelming rush of heat that rose up whenever they touched, challenging the foundation of their relationship – their friendship – and the unspoken agreement that kept them apart. And he hated that he had no damn control over it.

Her expression remained unreadable, but her heartbeat gave her away. As always. He could feel the frantic rhythm and knew he was the cause of it.

The thought sent a surge of arousal through him, feeding a possessiveness he'd always felt toward her, one he'd never been able to shed. He wanted her – hell, he'd always wanted her. But he'd always held back, kept his distance. And suddenly, with the breathless, wriggling woman beneath him, he couldn't remember why. Damn her.

She chose that moment to lower her gaze to his lips and he felt his resolve wavering. He frowned at her, trying to ignore the way she felt beneath him. Her breasts pressed against his chest. Her body a combination of soft and firm, athletic but feminine, a strength that turned him on like no other woman ever had.

She shifted to alleviate his full weight on her, and raised her knee. When all it did was nestle him between her legs even more, her eyes rounded.

His cock surged and he felt the last of his damn resolve crash and burn.

She twisted beneath him, pushing at his shoulders with both hands, but her resistance lacked conviction. As though she'd realised it, she stopped fighting and released a frustrated groan. Her eyes had gone a shade darker and her cheeks were flushed, a look he instantly recognised.

Arousal.

He glanced at her lips, trying to remind himself that he was still furious with her. He shouldn't want her. If anything, he wanted to hate her, find a way to close the stupid portal and leave her here in this crappy city. With her secrets and lies and omissions and whatever the hell she had going on. But he couldn't and he had no damn idea why.

Or maybe he did and just refused to admit it yet.

She blew out air and closed her eyes in surrender. "Fine, keep the key."

"Like you had an option."

"Don't underestimate me, Ethan," she warned, lifting her lashes. "If I wanted to leave this apartment, I would. Rapunzel act be damned. I screwed up, I apologised. But we're in danger and need each other and I'm not going anywhere. So can you stop with the big-bad-wolf glares and get the hell off me?"

"I have a right to be angry, Jenna. What you did was an ass manoeuvre."

"And it frustrates the hell out of you that I'm the ass you want." Not giving him a chance to reply, she gave a hard shove, rolled out from beneath him, and stomped to the bathroom.

CHAPTER THIRTY SIX

The shower was hot and blissful and helped to wash away the blood.

But did nothing to erase the wicked thoughts that had plagued her the moment he'd pinned her to the couch and slid between her legs.

She wanted him. So damn bad that her entire body ached. More so now that she'd had a taste of what it felt like to be in his arms. *To be his.* Since she'd seen the desire in his eyes, felt his arousal pressed against her. Knew that he wanted her.

The man blazed heat, pure passion, and had sparked something inside of her she'd thought dormant. Thanks to the adrenaline rushes, fear and worry of the last few days, her body felt wired in a way that made her uneasy. She longed to lose herself in him, a brief respite from the ugliness of their surroundings and everything they faced.

Which was crazy considering he was still furious with her.

Groaning, she cradled the soap but froze when the door opened. Her breath quickened and her heart skipped a beat.

He stood in the doorway, the lights from the city behind him. A silhouette of pure masculine beauty. His still wore the towel and t-shirt, his face hazed in a gentle yellow from the two flickering candles. His eyes burned with something dark and determined. Desire, hunger – both of which she shared.

God.

Their eyes connected across the room, but neither of them moved, stilled by the intensity of the moment. A prickly sensation swept across the back of her neck and she shivered, despite the warm, moist air.

"Ethan, what are we doing?" she murmured in a deep, throaty voice that had him taking a step closer.

In two strides, he crossed the room. And then he was there, in the shower, his hands around her waist, drawing her closer. Water cascaded over them, soaking him.

"You're right," he grunted in a low, gruff voice. "I want you and it frustrates the hell out of me that I do. I should be mad, but all I want is you naked, in my bed, at my mercy."

A thrill of excitement trailed through her and she lifted her head to look at him. "So what's stopping you?"

With a low growl, his mouth came down on hers, hungry and heated, a kiss that sparked the need for more. Wild, hot, a rush of desire that had always been there since the day they'd met. His kisses were firm, demanding, his facial fuzz deliciously rugged against her skin.

His satisfied grunt reverberated against her, through her, along with the steady beat of the water pouring over them. It was surreal, beautiful, an excitement like no other. She snagged his wet t-shirt, tugging it over his head, and tossed it to the floor. Her fingers trailed across the slick wall of muscles.

Solid, hard. Pure power.

The colour of his eyes had darkened, a shade she'd never seen before, and he studied her with a hunger that fired her own.

"You're so damn beautiful," he murmured.

"Ethan."

The whisper of his name gave him all the invitation he needed. With a brief growl that came from the back of his throat, he hoisted her into his arms, nudging her legs so that they came up around him. His arousal pressed into her, extracting a gasp from her. He grinned as he slammed off the water and returned to the living room. They clung to each other while his mouth plundered hers again.

Water dripped everywhere, but the mess went ignored.

He stopped halfway to the bed to shove her up against the wall, kissing her senseless. She caught a glimpse of them in the mirror behind him, bodies entwined, breathless, and trapped against the wall by solid heat and sexiness.

A flicker of common sense tugged at her, wedging itself between them and she broke away, just an inch, trying to let her senses take root. But all she wanted was him. Now. Here. Nothing else.

"Wait. Ethan, stop," she groaned when he tried to kiss her again. Her husky voice sounded foreign. He gave her a slow, heated stare before lowering his gaze to her breasts, devouring her. He'd never looked at her like that before. Pure desire. Possessive. Like she would be his.

Only his.

"This," she murmured. "Are you sure?"

He placed a palm against the wall to steady himself, shoulders rising and falling as he dragged in a few deep breaths. He lacked his usual self-control and composure. Wild eyes, ruffled hair. A side of him she'd never seen.

"Hell, yes," he breathed. "But if you're not, Jen, you need to tell me now, because any more of this and I won't be able to stop."

The coarseness of his voice rumbled through her, so sexy, but that damn flicker of common sense wouldn't relent. "We're friends. We live together. This is wrong. It's a complication we don't need."

"Complicated can feel good. So damn good that nothing else matters. I feel it and I bet you do too."

"It's still wrong."

"It still feels good." He pressed closer, his gaze never unwavering from hers. "Right now, we're in this crazy city and probably the most hunted couple in Ameera. I need you, I need to forget, and I suspect beneath all the protest bullshit, you feel the same way too."

He nibbled the corner of her mouth and she sighed into him, not caring when she felt the last of her resolve slip away. Her shiver brought a smirk to his lips, triggering that dimple she found so irresistible.

"Deny it," he whispered, edging forward until his mouth was an inch from hers. "I dare you. Deny it and I'll back away."

"Ethan . . ."

But she'd didn't push him away. Or deny it.

CHAPTER THIRTY SEVEN

Ethan grinned.

Hot arousal chased the brief moment of victory when her gaze lowered to his lips. He ached to ravish her, to kiss her until she was senseless and breathless and pliable to anything he wanted from her.

He wanted her. Naked. Exposed. Vulnerable. Writhing and groaning as she gave herself to him, took everything he offered.

He clutched her waist with both hands, her body pinned to the wall by his. He looked at her mouth, hungering for her, knowing it would take a lot to back away. Thank God she hadn't asked him to.

So he kissed her.

When she immediately relaxed in his arms and tangled her fingers in his hair, he devoured her. Hard and hot and demanding. There was no gentleness, no holding back, and he kissed her until they were panting and shaking, heat and desire burning between them.

He broke away, just enough to meet her gaze, questioning, but she moved her hand behind his neck, applying soft pressure, all the answer he needed.

Grinning, he seated her on the drawers beside them and settled himself between her legs. His hips ground against hers in delicious torment that extracted a soft moan from her. He left a trail of kisses along her jaw, her neck, her earlobe. Inhaling, he took a deep breath of her incredible, womanly scent.

He leaned back to look at her, feasting on her feminine beauty. Flawless, tanned skin, still damp and warm from the shower. Nipples puckered with arousal. Flat stomach and curvy hips.

When he ran the back of his fingers across her body to cup a full breast, she released a breathy sigh and arched her back. His abdomen tightened in anticipation. He caught her nipple between his fingers, offering leisurely strokes, and then traced the movements with his mouth.

"Oh God," she groaned, dropping her head back against the wall, her eyes closed. Her heartbeat raced and her body trembled. "I'm quivering like an aroused teen."

He lifted his head, grinning. "But with so much more experience and energy."

She visibly gulped, her eyes widening. "Wow, this could be fun."

"Guaranteed."

Smiling, she cupped his head within her palms and brought his mouth back to hers. She ran her fingers across his chest, over his muscles, down to his waist. She unhooked his towel, grinning when it fell to the floor, and then her mouth was on his.

Her hands brushed across his abdomen, triggering a jerk from him. He groaned when her fingers closed around his length.

Everything around him disappeared. All he saw was her. All he wanted was her.

Fierce, avid hunger.

She grabbed his hips with an impatient jerk. He backed away, leaving her panting on the drawers, but couldn't tear his eyes away from her. So beautiful.

He reached for their rucksack on the floor and withdrew a foil packet. When he returned to her, she lowered her gaze, taking her fill, and smiled a heated, sexy smirk that took his breath away.

"I was wrong about your female fans," she said, her voice husky, dreamy. "It's not about the money."

He grinned and nibbled her lip. "Trust me, it's *definitely* not about the money."

She laughed, a beautiful lyrical sound that echoed through the room. "Oh, this is so wrong, but feels so damn good."

"And when it's over, we'll do it again. And again," he whispered between soft kisses. "Especially once you've had the advantage the other women haven't."

"What's that?"

He grinned. "You'll be the only woman to know what it's like, *really like*, to be in my bed."

Her breath caught and she lifted her head, the meaning behind his words surprising her. Just as he'd intended. "You've been holding back with them?"

"Of course." With a mammoth effort that had grown increasingly frustrating over time. But he'd done it. Reigned in his strength and power, despite the overwhelming urge to let go. He'd had no choice. Anything less and he would've hurt them. No woman he'd ever bedded had matched his strength.

But Jenna would and he couldn't wait to have her. Alone, together, they could let go, using their inner strength and speed with a freedom they'd never had before.

His cock pulsed at the thought. *Hell, yeah.*

A small smile lit up her face and she slid her arms around his neck. "So I'm your first?"

He couldn't answer, the thought making him restless. Instead, he kissed her again.

"I've never been with a Keeper either," she whispered between kisses.

Damn, just when he thought he couldn't be more aroused.

He grunted, sounding like an uncaged beast, and caught her hips. "Shall we find out what we've been missing?"

She shivered, her tongue darting out to mingle with his.

Another kiss, another sigh. "Yes," she breathed heavily. "Now."

Heat and desire and a wanting like he'd never experienced before engulfed him. He pressed forward, using his hips to spread her thighs, relishing in the feel of her naked flesh against his.

"Are you sure?" he asked, sliding a hand into her hair. "Last chance to stop this, Jen. Last chance."

Her elbows came up to rest on either side of his shoulders, her fingers toying with his hair. "Do you want to stop?"

"Not on your life."

She smiled. "So don't."

A deep-throated growl emerged from the back of his throat and he clenched his fist, gathering a mound of hair with it, drawing her head back to expose the long line of her throat. He kissed her neck, tasting, nipping, licking, working his way across her jaw until he found her mouth again.

His other hand grazed the skin along her thigh and dipped between her legs and he was all too aware of how close he was to claiming her as his.

She dropped her head back, releasing a soft sigh, and gripped the side of the drawers with both hands. The movement exposed her breasts, exposed her. He untangled his fingers from her hair to cup a breast with one hand whilst stroking her with the other. Slow, leisurely strokes that extracted soft murmurs of pleasure that sent his libido into overdrive.

She was so wet and ready and he had to employ every ounce of willpower he had not to grab her hips and plunge into her. But he held back, torn between the urge to ravish her and savour her.

He upped his strokes and sucked a nipple into his mouth, grinning when she gasped. He felt the shivers increase, the build of tension, that moment before everything exploded into pure pleasure.

He lifted his head, wanting to watch her while it happened.

She released a soft groan as the climax rolled through her, her body shuddering from the ripples of pleasure. Her eyes were closed, her face a mixture of surprise and ecstasy, a vulnerable beauty he'd never seen in her.

Still quivering from the aftermaths of her fierce climax, she lifted her head, all wild eyes and breathless. She reached for him, her expression clouded with longing.

Screw the waiting. He knew what she wanted. Hell, he wanted it more.

With a possessive, caveman-like grunt, he gathered her in his arms. He placed her on the bed and leaned back to revel in the beauty of the woman sprawled out in front of him.

Fuck, yeah.

He tore open the foil packet, quickly sheathing himself, his cock pulsing beneath his fingers. He pressed his hips forward, nestling between her legs, and groaned when her wetness enveloped him. She gave a soft, impatient murmur of encouragement.

So he thrust.

Her head dropped back and she released a long, husky moan. His fingers laced with hers and he drew her arms up above her head, pressing her hands into the sheet. She was trapped beneath him, around him, at his mercy. Writhing and longing and breathless. She'd never looked more exquisite.

He thrust again, the movement extracting a soft gasp from her that he swallowed with another kiss. This time, the kiss was slower, evenly matched with the rhythm of his hips.

She shifted, drawing him in deeper. They moved together, a moment where only they existed. Frozen in time, when nothing else mattered. Only them, here, now. Absolute ecstasy.

Her fingers gripped his, her nails digging into his skin, her heart pounding against his. She tore her mouth away from his, gasping as pleasure rippled through her, the breathy cry of her climax triggering his own. He came with a force so powerful that a burst of energy surged through him. A gush of air rushed through the room, dislodging a lamp that crashed to the floor.

She groaned his name as she gave herself over to the wave of sensations, fuelled by the energy that had unleashed within him. She'd felt it too and she clung to him, her eyes squeezed shut, her fingers curled around his.

Total surrender.

When it was over, they were left exhausted, panting. Overwhelmed by the sheer force of the moment. There'd been pleasure, an avalanche of incredible sensations that had rocked his world. But above that, there'd been something else. He'd felt her. Connected with her. Lowered his guard enough to let go in a way he'd never thought possible.

His magic was sacred, treasured, a part of him he'd never shared with another woman before. But he'd let go. With her.

Releasing her hand, breathing heavily, he touched a finger to her chin, needing to look at her. Her body trembled beneath his and he wanted her all over again.

They should shower, get dressed, and formulate a plan to get them the hell home. Hazel would be fuming. The storm would've relented and by now; she'd have unleashed a full hunt for them.

"Ethan," she whispered, burying her face into his neck. She left soft kisses across his skin, his jaw, until her mouth claimed his. Her lips were soft, her breathing heavy, and when he lifted his head to look at her, all he saw were eyes filled with desire, questioning, searching.

Yes. They should shower, get dressed, and formulate a plan. *Later.*

CHAPTER THIRTY EIGHT

Ethan awoke, instinctively knowing she wasn't beside him.

He sat upright, searching for her, surprised he'd dozed off. He'd relented – to the sex and the sleep. Despite knowing they had time for neither.

But damn, he hadn't been able to resist Jenna. Not anymore. Sex with her had been something else. The freedom of letting go with a woman who matched his strength and speed had been sensational. A level of pleasure he'd never thought possible.

The thought made him instantly hard. Again.

The air felt cold, the room mostly in darkness. Jenna sat on the floor in front of the couch, her features lit by the flickering glow of candlelight. She'd gathered her hair into a messy knot at the nape of her neck. Her brows were furrowed as she paged through a small book. She wore his shirt, the sleeves rolled up, and socks.

The woman who'd crept under his skin.

That thought alone should make him uneasy, but dammit, he liked her and they were in this crappy city with death nipping at their heels and life was too goddamn short for pussyfooting around.

Now that he'd tasted her, he only wanted more. No matter who – or what – she was. When she'd told him, all he'd felt was a blind rage that had threatened to consume him.

But something inside him had altered when he'd found her at Hazel's mercy.

Watching Hazel slice her open, knowing that at any moment, she could plunge the knife into Jenna's heart, killing her, had paled everything else – his anger, Jenna's confession, her motives for coming to Ameera, and their fight.

At that moment, none of it had mattered. Only Jenna. Because despite her secrecy, he believed they were on the same side, fighting for the same thing. Her love for Kate was real, a bond he understood all too well. It wasn't something a Keeper could forge and that bond would prevail over everything else. Even her demons.

He simply had to remind her of that.

The fact that she'd kept it from him still smarted, but he'd mastered the art of keeping his agitation in check. Now wasn't the time to be at loggerheads anyway. And it had nothing to do with the sex. Okay, maybe *a little*. But in truth, the only way they'd get out of Ameera alive was if they relied on each other.

He tugged on jeans and went to her. The floor felt icy beneath his feet and he grabbed a blanket, discarded on the floor. Her eyes lit up when she saw him approaching but did nothing to hide the worry on her features. Covering her shoulders with the blanket, he crouched behind her and pulled her into his arms. He couldn't resist, needing to hold her again before allowing reality to take its roots. The warmth of her eased the chill but did little to ease the angst brewing in his gut.

She breathed in quietly and leaned into him, seemingly needing the feel of him just as much as he needed her.

He kissed her head, allowing the stillness to take its beat. "Did you get some sleep?"

"Yes."

"Any bad dreams again?" He'd known she'd been having them, had often heard her pacing around the house at night back home. She'd always evaded his questions, like she so often did when he nudged too close.

223

"Surprisingly, no. First time in ages I didn't dream at all."

"You were exhausted. It was a rough night."

"No, stud muffin, the dreams are usually worse when I'm tired." She tilted her head toward his, a smile playing on her lips. "I think I have you to thank."

Her admission surprised him, sparking a rush of manly satisfaction. He smiled and kissed her cheek. "If sex keeps the monsters at bay, then I'm all for another round."

She laughed, the sound easy and light. "I bet you are." Sobering, she leaned into him and sighed. "To be honest, I've never slept beside anyone before."

"You've had other lovers." He would've known if she hadn't.

"Yes, but none that made me want to stay."

Another admission that surprised him. But this time, the satisfaction gave way to something else. A protectiveness he'd always felt for her, one that had magnified in the last few hours. His throat tightened. Adjusting his arms around her, he pressed his face into her hair and breathed her in. She was so beautiful, so quiet, unlike the fierce warrior who'd kicked ass a few hours ago. Her walls were down, first time he'd ever seen her without them, and he knew it wouldn't be long before they returned.

"I'm glad you stayed," he whispered, kissing her temple.

"How did you find me last night?" she asked softly.

"I followed Axel, which led me to you."

"You risked your life to help me."

"Because I protect what's mine, Jenna. Always."

She tensed, a reaction he'd expected. "That's a pretty loaded statement."

"Just stating it like it is."

"I'm not a woman who can be owned. You know that, right?

"Of course."

"And the sex doesn't change anything."

"Oh, it changes everything."

"Ethan —"

When she turned her head to look up at him, he flashed her a wild grin and kissed the groove between her brows. "Relax, I'm not about to plant a flagpost and start demanding ownership rights." Sensing he was pressing a panic button, he decided to change the subject. "What are you reading?"

Her expression fell. "My father's journal. He kept it hidden behind a loose brick in the living room. I found it after you left last night. Fortunately, Hazel never saw it in my back pocket."

Her father.

He looked at the book, a reminder that she'd once had family and a life here. A life he knew nothing about. The thought stirred a fresh bout of anger and for a moment, all he could do was stare at it.

She cleared her throat and peered up at him. "Ethan, about all this . . ." Her words were spoken softly, hesitantly, her lower lip caught between her teeth.

"Why didn't you tell me, Jen?"

"I'm a Salubrious. I've been taught not to acknowledge that to anyone. Over the years, my ancestors were hunted and killed because of what they were and the secret they refused to share. Admitting what I am puts me in so much danger, not only from our enemies but from Keepers too."

"You think we're a danger to you?"

"I come from a family banished to a prison world as punishment for killing the very thing you'd die to protect. We stand for everything you and your brothers loathe." Her gaze met his, eyes full of sorrow. "I planned to tell you but kept delaying it. I didn't want you to see me differently."

"You're still a Keeper."

"I saw the way you looked at me last night."

"I needed a beat, time to think." He laced their fingers, glancing down at her graceful hands. "Which, in a place like Ameera, was stupid. When I saw what they were doing to you, none of that mattered anymore."

Dark eyelashes lifted, revealing light blue eyes glistening with emotion. "My family –"

"Doesn't define you. *You* define you, Jen. You." He cupped her cheeks between his hands, not missing the way her breath caught. "Not your family or their crimes. Not the rumours and accusations. You."

Her eyes widened, her lips thinned, and she watched him in silence. When her eyes went glossy, she blinked several times, but didn't look away. "You were so furious with me."

"Yes. Not because you're a Salubrious, or from Ameera, but because you kept it from me. We spend our lives defending ourselves and our witches – and each other. Trust is everything." Especially in a place like Ameera with enemies like Hazel. He took her hand, hesitating with his next words, but needing to voice them anyway. "And, to be honest, Jen, I'm worried that when the time comes to seal that portal, you won't want to."

Her eyes closed and she nodded. She stayed quiet for a long while before her lids fluttered open again. "And I'm worried that when the time comes to seal the portal, I'll be forced to."

"You know we have to. Especially if Hazel's still in Ameera."

"My parents are here, Ethan. Or at least, they were. Not knowing what happened to them is slowly destroying me." She gave a half-shrug. "But I don't even know who to ask or where to look for them without bringing suspicion on myself."

Her voice sounded so small, soft, tugging at the worry he'd felt when he'd discovered her sneaking out the night before. But he felt her pain, even understood it. When Sienna had vanished a few years back, he'd witnessed Archer go half insane with worry for her. The not-knowing had almost killed him. Ethan had shared his brother's anguish, but for Archer, it had been different. "Let's start with Susan. She might have answers for you."

"She's a Sage. That doesn't make her all-knowing."

"I know, but right now she might be your only hope. Besides, we should warn her that Hazel's onto her. I also want to talk to her about the portal spell." He paused, hesitating, a ball of agitation tightening in his chest. "If Hazel's talk of Mason and the Brogan Grimoire hold any truth, we're running out of time and options. We have to get home soon."

"You really think that Mason's free and they have the Brogan Grimoire?" Their gazes met, a heaviness wedging between them. They both knew what that meant, if it was true.

"No. Because that would mean they reached either Sienna or Kate." And *that* would mean they'd gotten through his brothers. A thought he refused to embrace. No freaking way.

"We should get dressed and get to Susan." She shifted, rising, but paused when he tugged her back to him.

He laced their fingers. "Jen . . . we have to leave as soon as possible, preferably with that spell. If by any miracle we find it before you find your parents, you know there'd be no choice, right?" He studied her expression, not missing the slight flinch or her quick attempt to cover it by looking down at the journal. Silent, her lashes lowered, she traced the leather-bound cover of the book with her fingers. "We're Keepers, Jen. Our witches and our duties come first. We don't get to put ourselves before that. Not even for this."

Her eyes glistened and she blinked, averting her gaze to the city outside. But she didn't say anything.

Probably because she knew he was right.

CHAPTER THIRTY NINE

They were marked.

Jenna knew it the moment they boarded the train, but the doors closed and the train began to move before she could issue a warning to Ethan.

But he sensed it too. She could see it in his narrowed eyes and stiff body. He placed a hand on her lower back, staying close to the door, and eyed the two men at the back of the carriage. Both had beards and wore t-shirts, unperturbed by the icy chill in the air. Neither budged from their spot against the wall or bothered toning down their fierce scrutiny.

Jenna glanced outside, trying to judge the distance to their next stop. She heard howling in the distance. Hellhounds or werewolves, she couldn't tell, but hoped they met neither. They passed a crowd of youths outside a store, swinging baseball bats at the windows.

They weren't the only ones. The streets were full of people clutching a variety of weapons. Warehouses, stores, and bars were all victims of their destruction and looting.

"What the hell's going on?" Ethan asked. "Everyone's gone crazy."

"Something's wrong." Unease worked its way through her as the looting and violence sparked memories of the night she'd left

Ameera. *The Annex.* She glanced at the moon. Clouds patched most of it, but she could tell it hadn't peaked yet.

The train began to shake. Brakes screeched, lights flickered. A harsh jerk had Ethan and Jenna grasping the nearest railing.

"*Jenna.*" Ethan's murmured warning had her turning around.

The two men pushed themselves away from the wall, baring their teeth and clenching their fists. She swore she heard them growl. And then they were running. But Ethan and Jenna were ready for them, moving swiftly as they fielded the first round of punches. Ethan bolted forward, targeting the closest man, and delivered several blows in lightning-quick speed.

Jenna ducked as the second man took a swing at her. She pivoted around and gave a powerful kick at his face. He crashed into the railing, bellowing with rage as blood spurted from his nose. Straightening, he leapt forward, landing on all fours, snarling. The colour of his eyes had darkened.

The motion sparked old memories and fears and Jenna gasped. "Ethan, we have to go!"

"You think?"

"Now!"

Turning to the nearest door, they leapt. They were both on their feet and running before the train sped by.

"What the hell are they?" Ethan panted.

She pointed to the sky, coloured with grey clouds that spotted the moon. "It's nearing a full moon."

His brows hitched. "Crap. They're werewolves?"

"They will be when the moon peaks."

"Aren't their bites –?"

"Yes, fatal to Keepers. But my magic will heal it."

"Thank God, 'cause mine won't."

A thought she refused to embrace. "In that case, stay clear of their jaws."

"Noted. I thought they kept to their district?"

"They never come into the city unless it's the Annex." She

229

shrugged, looking at the chaos around them. "But something's changed. I think the boundaries have already lowered, which explains the violence. There are always casualties during an Annex, but an early one is lethal. People are unprepared, more vulnerable and confused. They're panicking. It's simply going to snowball from here and if it's anything like last time, the violence will be unlike anything you've ever seen before."

"This has Hazel's stench all over it. All the more reason we need to get the hell out of Ameera."

The streets were a beehive of activity. Two rival crowds had gathered in the middle of the street further up, their arguments ripe with tension. Several clutched baseball bats and knives. Cats scurried along the sidewalks, shifting in and out of human form at will.

Another earth tremor rumbled through the streets, evoking an outcry. Glass shattered and a loud crack from the roof above sent a nearby crowd dashing for shelter. A cement statue landed in the centre of the street, exploding into dozens of smaller pieces.

Ethan pulled Jenna into a doorway of a nearby store. It was deserted, the windows boarded up with wood. Lights flickered several times before going out.

The darkness added to the chaos and everyone went mad.

****

Reaching Susan's bar was easier than Ethan expected.

The darkness offered a cloak from their predators. They merged into the chaos, dodging flames and irate crowds, and raced through the streets with a speed they usually avoided in public. But everyone was so wrapped up in the fighting that no one noticed.

Susan's grim expression brightened when she opened her kitchen door. Ushering them inside, she hurriedly slammed the locks into place. Her hair was dishevelled, like it had been repeatedly finger-combed. "You shouldn't be here. It's not safe!"

Jenna swivelled around, flushed and breathless. "We had to talk to you, warn you. You're in danger, Susan. Hazel's onto you."

Susan's lips thinned. "You're the one in danger. Hazel's issued a bounty on your head in exchange for a portal trip to the mortal world."

Ethan cursed softly beneath his breath, a new kind of worry flaring in his chest. He turned to Jenna, sharing a long look. "Hazel knows what you are."

Jenna scowled at him, her eyes flashing with panic. He knew why. Her background and connection with Ameera was a fiercely guarded secret. One he'd just blurted out. But he figured Susan knew it anyway.

"It's impossible, Ethan. I've been so careful. You're the only one who knows." Her brows tightened as she glanced at Susan. "And now, thanks to your big mouth, Susan knows too."

Susan's lips curled into a small smile, but there was no surprise, a testament that she had.

"What about Megan?" he asked. "She lived with you."

Jenna shook her head. "She doesn't know. My parents insisted we don't tell her. And even if she did know, ratting me out will rat *her* out. Hazel would see her secrecy as a betrayal. Megan won't risk it."

Ethan ran a hand across his face and took a deep breath, trying to calm the shit in his head. He was wired, on edge, his mind racing with an exit route out of this damn city. "So explain the bounty. Hazel's officially made it public that the portal's open. She's roped in the entire city to search for you – and possibly evoked an early Annex, which puts her in danger too. Why would she risk that? For vengeance?"

Jenna's covered her face with her hands and released a frustrated groan. She shook her head and looked up. "Lord knows I've given her enough reason –" She froze, staring at her arm. And then she gasped, yanking back the sleeve of her jacket. "Unless . . , unless it's this? Her bracelet . . . maybe that's what she's after?"

Ethan leaned in, his stomach dipping. Hazel's silver scorpion bracelet. The sound of her frantic screeches when she'd lost it echoed in his mind. He'd never thought to examine why. "You picked it up?"

"I figured it had to have some value. She was so distracted by losing it that she failed to retaliate. That's not like her at all."

He jerked his thumb toward the kitchen door. "That's what possibly sparked all this chaos? A damn bracelet?"

She looked up, her eyes shining with excitement. "I think it's more than that. Maybe a talisman of sorts? She always wore it, sometimes two. You saw how she reacted when she lost –"

"Wait . . . a bracelet?" Susan cut in, reaching for Jenna's arm. She gasped, pointing at the intricate design. "I saw this in one of my visions. It made no sense at the time."

Ethan squinted at the bracelet, his mind racing. And then it hit him. *A key.*

"We were wrong," he said. "It's not a spell we need to close the portal. It's a key. Hazel's bracelet."

CHAPTER FORTY

Jenna's jaw dropped, but a thud from the roof above had her pivoting toward the window.

Keeping her back to the wall, she peered through the blinds, but the alley was empty. She turned back to Ethan, shaking her head, and glanced up at the roof.

But gasped when the window behind her suddenly exploded. A large creature hurtled through the air, crashing into her.

She twisted around as they fell, crying out when it nipped her. She tried to shove it away. Snarling, it lunged repeatedly, snapping viciously, spittle dripping from its mouth. The stench was unbearable, putrid meat and wild animal.

But it had a human-like resemblance.

Ethan grabbed it from behind and flung it across the room. It crashed into the cupboard, splintering wood.

Gritting her teeth at the pain in her arm, Jenna rushed to Susan. "There'll be more. You need to hide! Now!"

"But –"

"They're not here for you. Go! We'll lead them away." She ushered Susan into the next room and shut the door.

They ran into the bar, but changed direction when another two human-like figures crashed through the windows. The men were still clothed, but moved like wolves, on all fours. They had distorted, fierce expressions. Their dark eyes had a yellow glow to them, their lips upturned to reveal sharp canines. Teeth bared, growling, one of the wolves took a step forward, a movement the pack replicated.

"What the hell's happening?" Ethan grunted, taking Jenna's arm.

"The moon. They're in transition. Werewolves."

****

Ethan glared at them, breathless, his heart racing as he sized up their attackers. They were huge, emanating a strength and viciousness that had him on full alert. It wasn't often he came across enemies that matched his strength.

But the werewolves came close – and in numbers.

Energy flooded his veins, evoking a gust of wind that swept through the broken windows.

Jenna's hand slipped into his, the gentle motion igniting a fierce protective streak. "Ready?"

But he heard her and replied with a single nod.

In unison, they released war-like cries and barrelled forward like tank trucks. The wolves snapped and snarled as they collided. The brawl was brutal and swift. Bones splintered, furniture toppled over and the sound of savage growls filled the air.

The wind increased, rattling the windows, the air charged with a sizzle of electricity.

The wolves kept coming, so damn powerful, and so many. Ethan cursed when claws slashed his back and he spun around to fend off his attacker. But the wolf ducked, bolted forward, and delivered a harsh punch to his jaw. The impact slammed Ethan into the wolf behind him. Teeth bared, the wolf bit him on the shoulder.

Fuck!

It stung like hell, but adrenaline spurred him on, overshadowing the pain. His arm came up in a ruthless punch. He felt the satisfying crunch of bone beneath the blow and backed it up with several more.

"Jenna, we have to go!"

Side by side, they backed toward the door, adrenaline pumping, senses alert. The scent of blood filled his nostrils. He glanced behind them, drawing on his energy. Together, they turned around and sped outside, the wolves hot on their heels.

The air crackled with electricity. The sky brightened as lightning struck, zapping the ground around them. The wolves backed away, but hovered, ready to attack at any moment. Ethan drew on more power and the street became a mirage of white from the continuous flash of lightning bolts that created a protective cage around him and Jenna.

The wolves mock-charged, but kept their distance.

Jenna tilted her head upward, taking in the lightning chaos. "The cocoon of lightning . . . you're doing that?" His lips twitched at the incredulous look on her face. "Now you're just showing off."

"I have a few injuries if you want to show off too." He gave her a quick grin. One that faded the moment he turned around. Hazel stood at the entrance to The Square, her warlocks and witch behind her. He heard Jenna's sharp intake of air, a sign she'd spotted them too.

Diverting the flow of energy, he sent several bolts of lightning their way. But Hazel stood still, unperturbed, feet planted firmly apart, glaring at them.

All at once, the windows in the courtyard exploded, the sound deafening. Ethan grabbed Jenna, tucking her into him, covering her head with his hands. Shards of glass flew through the air in all directions. Howling, the wolves retreated to the roof of a nearby warehouse. People screamed.

"Are you okay?" he shouted, straightening, but didn't hear her reply as more windows exploded.

Simultaneously, they turned around and bolted. Hazel sent her full wrath after them as they ran. Light bulbs imploded, doors flew off their hinges, more windows shattered.

The werewolves chased from above, their vicious growls charged with fury and excitement.

Ethan drew on more lightning, lashing out at everything around them. More power, more fury, and the entire street became a sizzle of electricity. He glanced back at Hazel. She hadn't moved, but a black cloud approached from behind her. Ear-piercing screeches added to the noise as thousands of bats soared above the courtyard and chased down the street.

"We need shelter!" Jenna screamed above the noise as they ran. "Think we can make the portal?"

She scaled a cement slab and glanced up, grimacing at the wolves sprinting across the rooftops. "We'll never make it in time. There's just too many of them."

She squealed as the ground cracked beneath their feet, jerking with a sudden force that sent them both sprawling onto the sidewalk. Another crack and the tar split. The ground rumbled as it tore apart, destroying the road and sidewalks. They hurried to their feet, stumbling from the unsteady ground.

Hazel's high-pitched laughter pierced the din. She closed her fists, jerking her arms toward her chest.

A searing pain tore through Ethan's head. He groaned and collapsed to his knees. Jenna screamed his name and he searched for her, but everything had turned blurry. Gritting his teeth, grunting, he reached out. "Jenna!"

"I'm here. Hold on." Her arms were around him, clinging to him. Her voice trembled, edged with panic. "You have to stand up. Ethan!"

He clenched his fists, his knuckles scraping the tar. Squeezing his eyes closed, he released another groan. He was vaguely aware of her tugging him upward, supporting him. He felt the hitch in his energy supply, overwhelmed by the pain that threatened to explode his brain.

Still crouched beside him, holding him, she moved around him, her desperate cry feeding his fear. "Ethan, you have to get up!"

The ground rumbled, accompanied by a loud crack as the sidewalk split with a force and speed that knocked Jenna off her feet.

Fighting the darkness that threatened, he searched for her. He couldn't see. Couldn't stand. All he felt was pain. "Jenna!"

As the blackness engulfed him, he heard a vicious roar echoing around him.

His roar.

CHAPTER FORTY ONE

He reeked of blood.

And it was so damn cold.

The city was mostly in darkness, a glow of white from the near-full moon. He was high up. Perhaps another warehouse? There were no windows, only wide gaping holes built in preparation for them. Fire blazed in the two drums in the middle of the room, but did nothing to ward off the icy wind. Construction equipment had been abandoned in the corner. A project that would most likely never be completed if the rest of the city was anything to go by.

They'd finally left him alone, tied by thick chains attached to the metal beam in the roof. Pain had become a bitch of a companion, unrelenting and fierce. Hazel had cast a paralysis spell on him. He couldn't move but he felt everything. They'd cut him, several long slashes across his body, and stuck shards of glass into the wounds to prevent them from healing.

Old-school voodoo crap that had worked like a charm.

The blood loss and beatings had left him weak, voiding the permanent flow of energy he thrived on. It was the weakness he loathed more than the pain. Now, all he felt was numbness and silent fury that grew increasingly lethal the more they'd tortured him.

But all he could think about was her. *Jenna.* Where the hell was she?

Hot fury stirred all over again. He tried to move, yank at the chains that held him captive, and cursed when his body refused to cooperate. A movement in the doorway had him lifting his head. He kept his expression blank, refusing to give them anything else.

Hazel approached. The dim light softened the harshness of her tattooed face. Her black coat swayed around her legs as she walked. She stopped in front of him and raked a gaze across his injuries, her lips curling into a small smile. He stifled the urge to lash out and almost laughed at the absurdity of it. Even if he wanted to, the goddamn paralysis spell made it impossible.

She circled him, making a show of ogling him, taking great pleasure in his condition. Raising a hand, she flicked at his torn shirt. "How's that paralysis spelling working for you?"

He bit back a reply.

"You really think you could follow me here, steal my bracelet, and . . ." her jaw line of inked teeth cracked a smile, ". . . leave me here?"

"A city of crazies who thrive on violence and chaos? You'd fit right in."

She poked him in the ribs and he gritted his teeth as the pain flared. "I'm glad you consider Ameera so charming. Perhaps I should keep you alive and leave you here. That seems a more fitting punishment than the slow death I had in mind."

"You'd have to close the portal for that. Hard to do if you don't have the key."

"Oh, but Jenna has it." She twisted around him, watching his expression. "And I have you."

Which gave Hazel all the leverage she needed. "She won't give it up easily."

"Then she'll die. Or you will and somehow I doubt she'd let that happen. Either way, I'll get what I want. We always do."

"Yeah, I'm sure Mason and Warrick would agree with you."

"Antagonising me with memories of my nephews – men you and your brothers destroyed. Not a smart move, Bennett."

"I'm not antagonising. Just reminding."

"I don't need reminding that your family destroyed mine." Another poke. Harder. Another flare of pain. This time, more severe. "Payback's a bitch."

"Yeah, so is karma."

"And you're about to taste both soon. By the time I'm done, you'll be begging for mercy. I'll ruin your family and still get what I want. I'm almost giddy at the thought of watching you squirm."

"Fuck you, Hazel."

"Tempting, but I prefer like-minded men."

"Do they prefer you or do you spell them to?"

Her smile lessened, just a fraction. Her eyes narrowed. "You're hurting, tied up, weak. You're alone, forgotten, and yet you're baiting me. I can't quite figure out if that's desperation or stupidity."

"Either way, it's working, isn't it?" He risked a smile, not sure why he was goading. But it felt damn good.

She ran a finger along the veins that bulged in his neck. He couldn't see them, but he felt them. Throbbing and swollen, like they'd explode at any moment. "I figure it's desperation because you know that you've run out of options and soon your brothers will be less one sibling. Again."

He forced himself not to take her bait. Refused to think about Sarah. Instead, he scowled. "You might get your bracelet back, Hazel, but you still don't know where all that magic is buried. You're the one that's desperate."

Her face twisted. "As soon as Jenna returns my bracelet, I'll have control of the portal again. I'll close it, when it suits me. Until then, that should keep your brothers busy."

"Leaving the portal open will destroy both worlds and you know it."

"Nothing a little magic won't fix. But there'll be nothing *little* about my magic once I access that energy."

"Energy from good witches. You really think they'd relinquish it so easily?"

"They're dead. They have no choice."

"You'd be a fool to underestimate them."

"They'd be fools to underestimate me."

"Exposing our existence is risky. What makes you think the humans can be so easily controlled? They're not stupid or defenceless, Hazel. The witch massacre proves how resourceful they can be when threatened."

"Ah, but they had help that night."

He kept his features unreadable; refusing to react to the reference of the Keepers who'd stood by and watched their witches die. "And since then, the humans have technology and weapons that have made them stronger."

Hazel moved around him, tugging at the chains that bound him. The rattle of metal echoed through the quiet room, accompanied only by the sound of the wind that whined through the building. "You Keepers are always on about nobility and honour. You're always so damned determined to protect your witches and the balance of nature. And yet, all those witches died because of their Keepers."

"They died because they exposed themselves to the humans." Ethan cleared his throat, his body bristling with anger. The lethal kind he'd felt many times before but had forced himself to control. He cocked his head, fixing a narrow gaze on her. "I will do whatever it takes to protect Sienna and defend what's mine," he said softly, his voice clipped with an icy edge. "But you'd be stupid to mistake my nobility and honour as a weakness. 'Cause when it comes to the crunch, Hazel, neither will stop me from ripping your fucking head off."

Hazel blinked. "Such strong words for a man who's paralysed and dying. Besides, you're a Keeper. You're bound to the code that comes with that. Murdering your enemies won't bide well with The Circle or your brothers."

"Like I give a damn."

"Like you'd take them on."

He squinted at her, unable to resist a challenging smirk. "I'm in Ameera. What makes you think I haven't already?"

CHAPTER FORTY TWO

Jenna heard voices. *His* voice.

The sound sparked an overwhelming relief that took every effort to stifle. She quickened her steps through the hallway, Rick and John directly behind her. They hadn't bound or hurt her at first. But their questions and threats had grown more forceful when they couldn't find the bracelet.

A bracelet Megan had veiled with a spell.

Subtly and quickly, the moment they'd captured Jenna in The Square. She'd kept her mouth shut, employing a bulletproof front for their taunts and increasing violence.

So they'd brought her to Ethan. Clever.

Bracing herself for what she'd find, she took a right at the next door. The room was dark, like the rest of the warehouse, lit by the fading blaze of the fire. The air was icy cold and smelt of blood and sweat. Hazel stood in front of Ethan. His arms were stretched above his head, secured by chains.

Jenna froze, staring at him, her breath caught in her chest. His expression remained blank, but she heard the sudden increase in his heartbeat when he saw her. Blood dripped down his body, pooling onto the floor. She could hear it, a slow, repetitive sound that made her want to cringe. His breathing was shallow, but his eyes shimmered with fierce determination and fury.

Which softened the moment he saw her. Their gazes met and held, unspoken words filling the space between them, and all she wanted was to run to him. Free him, hold him. A spurt of fear overruled her relief, a whirlwind of emotions she fought to contain. This is what they'd been counting on. Leverage.

She moved into the room, the two warlocks following behind. "What have you done to him?"

Hazel turned, lifting her brows. She held out a hand. "You have something for me?"

"You have your leverage." Jenna glanced at Ethan. "The bracelet is mine."

"You'd risk his life for a bracelet?"

"You'd risk your bracelet for his life?"

"Ooh, word games." Hazel smiled. She sauntered closer to Ethan, her gaze gliding across his body. She ran a finger across his cheek, his jaw line. Her closeness to him, the way she looked at him, sent a bolt of objection through Jenna.

Her gut clenched in response and she stepped forward, hesitating when John's hand curled around her elbow.

"One thing you're forgetting, Jenna. Your leverage can't be hurt." Hazel drove an elbow into Ethan's ribs, grinning when he flinched. She kicked his legs, smiling when he didn't respond. "But even if I did release him, he couldn't move anyway."

"Ethan?" Jenna said softly, trying to read his expression, but all she saw was a simmering hatred.

"We spelled him with a paralysis spell and used a few old tricks to stop that annoying healing thing. Painful and inconvenient but not fatal." Hazel ripped his shirt, exposing the bleeding gashes, bruises, and scratches. She ran a finger along his arm, stopping at the open wound on his shoulder. She made a *tsk tsk* sound and shook her head. "But considering his werewolf bite, I'd say the magic is the least of your worries."

An icy chill swept through Jenna. *A werewolf bite.* Lethal to

Keepers. An injury his magic couldn't heal. Untreated, it would kill him. Dammit, she hadn't realised he'd been bitten too. Her gaze sought out Ethan's, but he'd bowed his head. Every part of her being ached for him.

Hazel's smile faded as she sauntered toward Jenna. A glance at John had him tightening his grip on Jenna's arms. "Ethan's injuries are deep and he's not healing. It won't be long before he bleeds out."

A soft rumble echoed in the distance and the building quivered as another tremor swept through the city. Steady and persistent. Glass shattered from somewhere below. A murmur of alarm erupted from the streets. They waited it out until the tremor finally lessened, leaving an eerie silence.

"We're running out of time, Hazel." Rick's accented voice boomed through the room. He circled Ethan, withdrawing a hunting knife from his jacket pocket. "Give us the bracelet, Jenna. Either way, he dies. The question is how painful it'll be."

Rick's eyes sparkled with a fierceness that had Jenna on edge. She'd seen what he was capable of. A level of violence and pain he executed flawlessly, without a hint of conscience.

"Jenna, don't," Ethan said, groaning when Rick plunged the knife into his leg. Rick withdrew the weapon, smiling when blood gushed from the wound. Raising his arm, he plunged it into Ethan's shoulder.

"Stop!" Jenna yelled.

Ethan grunted through gritted teeth. His face hardened and even though he refused to relent, Jenna could see that he was weakening at a rate that frightened her. His body sagged, relying on the chains that held him upright. His head rolled to the side, his chin lowered. He murmured something, so quietly that Jenna hardly heard it.

"Have something to say, Keeper?" Rick taunted, twisting the knife again. He tilted his head closer to Ethan's. "Speak up. I can't hear your mumbling."

"Yeah," Ethan muttered, louder this time. "Fuck you." His head bolted up and he lunged forward, biting Rick on the ear. With a gruff grunt, he jerked his head back, tearing flesh. Rick reeled back, bellowing in rage. He clutched his ear and punched Ethan in the ribs.

Ethan sucked in air, the chains rattling around him as his body swayed from the impact. He spat out blood, his lips curling.

"Rick, stop!" Hazel's snapped order reverberated through the room, instantly halting his retaliation.

"He bit my fucking ear!"

"A good thing you have two. Let's get this over with." She slid behind Ethan and held a knife to his throat. Jenna's heart lurched when she saw the blood seeping out from beneath the blade. "I've had enough of your meddling, Jenna. Give me the bracelet before I slit his damn throat."

Jenna stared at her, breathless, her body heaving from the adrenaline and a fear she'd never tasted before. She was revved for another fight, high on anger and vengeance and the desperate fight for survival. But the knife on Ethan's throat curbed her.

"Jenna," Ethan grunted when her gaze shifted to her wrist. "Don't. You give her the bracelet and she wins."

Jenna balled her hands into fists, loathing the slight tremble. Her mind scrambled for an escape. But there was no way out and she knew it. Her cry of frustration broke the silence, sounding nothing like her. More like a trapped animal facing its death.

"You're out of options, Jenna," Hazel called. "But I'll make you one last deal. Give me the bracelet and I'll leave you both alive."

"Your word's as good as your nephews' and we all know their stellar record at promises."

"You'll have to take your chances, then."

Their gazes met, challenge dripping between them. Hazel was lying. Jenna knew it. The only way Hazel would leave them alive was if she intended trapping them in Ameera. The thought of being stuck here for eternity, separated from Kate, sparked another wave of angst.

But the thought of leaving Ameera hurt just as much. If by any chance, they made it to the portal before Hazel closed it, Jenna would never see her parents again and *they* would be trapped in Ameera.

If they're alive.

Overwhelmed with panic, she sought out Ethan, blinking back desperate tears, torn between the family she'd known and the man she'd fallen for. She hadn't known until now, faced with the possibility of losing him – and the choice to save him – how much he meant to her. And of course, there was Kate too. A witch she'd vowed to protect; one who'd become her closest friend.

Her parents. Kate. Ethan.

"Jenna," Ethan whispered, his words a murmur only she could hear. When she met his gaze, all she saw were eyes filled with worry. A quiet strength emanated from him, despite his wounds and weakness. "Don't do it. Get out of here."

"I can't leave you," she murmured and when he closed his eyes, she knew he'd heard her. She'd already let him down once and he'd suffered so much because of it. She had a responsibility to the people, to her witch. She knew what she had to do, how to fix the wrongs she'd made. It was time to let go. But as a decision took hold, she had to bite back the unbearable ache that came with it.

"I'm sorry," she breathed. An apology not meant for Ethan, or her. No, the words were meant for the parents who'd never hear them. The ones she'd be leaving behind. "I'm so, so sorry."

Stifling the agonising scream that bubbled inside her, she raised her arm and pulled back her sleeve. "It's hidden by a veiling spell."

"Remind me to have a word with the witch who's helping you," Hazel said, rolling her eyes. She released Ethan and tossed the knife. After wiping her bloody hands across Ethan's jeans, she went to Jenna. She whispered the unveiling spell, her expression brightening when the bracelet appeared. Like a greedy child reaching for candy, she snatched the bracelet off Jenna's wrist and slid it on her own.

The ground trembled again.

"Hazel," Rick called out. "We have the bracelet. We should leave."

Hazel cast a slow gaze across Jenna's body, lingering on the wound where the werewolf's bite had been – now healed. Her eyes narrowed.

Loathing the scrutiny, Jenna jerked back, but Rick came up behind her and rammed an elbow into her ribs. Air slammed out her lungs, leaving her breathless and gasping. He grasped her arms.

"What have we here?" Hazel plucked at Jenna's shirt. The material tore, exposing more flesh, and she zeroed in on the dried blood. She poked Jenna, searching for the wound, her expression a mixture of puzzlement and pleasure when she found no sign of one.

Dark lashes lifted as Hazel's cold gaze found hers. The whites of her eyes seemed brighter against the circled tattoos. "Outside on the street, you and Ethan were spelled the same way, both bitten by the werewolves," Hazel said slowly, her voice dripping with suspicion. "So how's it possible that he's dying and you're not?"

CHAPTER FORTY THREE

Icy needles crept down Jenna's spine and she fought the urge to cringe. Her mind raced for a response, an excuse, a denial. Anything to preserve her secret.

But Hazel was onto her and wouldn't easily be fooled.

She'd felt the twinges of pain from Hazel's spell – one that created a mini aneurysm, painful and debilitating. Witches loved them. She'd also been bitten but her magic had healed her before either one could set in.

"After you took Kate from us at the cemetery, there was one thing I could never figure out," Hazel said casually. She circled, fiddling with Jenna's braided hair. "Her wrists were slit. She was bleeding out and then suddenly, she wasn't."

"She's half Keeper, we heal quickly."

"Not that fast." Hazel's eyes sparkled when she realigned the rip on Jenna's sleeve to the patch of blood on her arm. She raised her inked brows, a smirk on her lips. "So tell me, Jenna. How the hell did she heal so fast?"

"Next time I see her, I'll ask her." But Jenna already knew. When she'd rescued Kate, she'd given her a potion to drink, one she'd doctored with her own magic. It had rapidly stopped Kate's bleeding and healed her injuries.

"It all makes sense now." Hazel's breath quickened, her body bristling with anticipation. "For so long, we searched for a Salubrious and all this time you've been under my damn nose."

A spurt of fear, cold and paralysing, swept through Jenna. She kept her gaze on Hazel refusing the cringe her body demanded.

The tattooed lines on Hazel's face creased when she cracked a wide grin. "My sister suspected there was a child."

"I have no idea what you're talking about." She was pleased her voice sounded calm, unwavering, even though her insides were a mess.

"We never thought of looking for a child in the mortal world. That explains where your mother disappeared to that night. The portal. And you have no idea what happened afterwards, do you?"

Jenna clamped her jaw so tightly that it hurt. Her racing heart-beat pulsed in her throat, her wrists.

Hazel crossed her arms, her eyes glistening. "She returned, found your father's body, and everything turned so . . . messy." Jenna's body jerked as though the words had struck her. Hazel grinned. "Ah, so you *do* know what I'm talking about."

Jenna fought for composure, even though she wanted to scream. Rip Hazel's fucking throat out. When the anger took a grip on her, she went with that, knowing it would shield the emotions that could cripple her.

"My sister and her husband were smart," Hazel continued. "Without our family Grimoire, we were stumped for the location of the massacre. She had the bright idea of searching for a descendent of one of the Keepers who'd witnessed the witches' slaughter that night. She thought they'd know the location."

"A bummer The Circle took care of them."

"It wasn't hard to figure out they'd been sent to Ameera. The Circle never understood what had transpired that night. They'd never murder their own, which is why they exiled them here." She smiled, waving her hands at the city in the distance. "How

250

fortunate for us that those old bitches are so transparent and that we now hold the only key to Ameera."

A key Jenna had in her possession only moments before. Guilt trickled through her and she glanced at Ethan, her heart tightening. If she'd figured it out sooner, taken the time to process the nagging voice in the back of her mind. . .

Stupid. Stupid. Stupid.

Hazel's forehead crinkled when she frowned. "Unfortunately, Ameera had already taken care of most of the Keepers and the few brats they left behind had no knowledge of the location. The Circle had altered the memories of all the Keepers at the massacre. A little spell-casting confirmed they were telling the truth."

"But you killed them anyway."

"They're Keepers," Hazel said with a careless shrug, as if that justified everything. "We tracked down all the lineages but one. Yours."

It took sheer willpower not to flinch.

"And then one night, my sister and her husband received a tip." Her smile was one of pure pride and awe. "She roped in the locals, triggered an early Annex and all hell broke loose. But she found them."

Horror flared in Jenna's chest. She'd been right. The attack on her neighbourhood that night hadn't been random. They'd been searching for a Salubrious.

"She didn't mean to kill them," Hazel said casually, not taking her eyes off Jenna. "That was rather unfortunate. They wouldn't talk and she couldn't spell them too. A fire broke out and . . ." she snapped her fingers, ". . . *poof.*"

Jenna blinked, the words slicing through her, just as Hazel had intended. Pursing her lips together, she bit back a retort, and tried to keep herself from unravelling. She'd wanted the truth. A truth so crippling that breathing was impossible.

"Did you know my family destroyed yours?" Hazel taunted. "Is that why you pretended to side with us all those years ago? Revenge?"

"If it's revenge I wanted, I would've set you alight in your sleep."

"So why didn't you, Jenna?" They glared at each other in silence. Hazel's eyes widened as understanding dawned. "Ah, *Ameera*. You needed a way in and I was it. Kate was never the priority, Ameera was."

"You really think I'd spend two torturous years biding by your evil if Kate wasn't a priority? I risked my life to save her from you!"

"But the first chance you got, you left her behind to return to Ameera. Oh, honey," Hazel gushed, giving an exaggerated gasp. "Is that why you returned? You think your parents are alive?"

"*Jenna*," Ethan's voice cut through the taunts. "Don't listen to her. She's trying to rattle you."

She knew that and it took a mammoth effort to maintain her equilibrium. Even though it felt like her heart had been ripped into pieces. She clung to the little composure she had left, refusing to allow the guilt to take root.

Kate had always come first, even when her longing to return home had been unbearable. But the truth was, when the opportunity she'd been waiting for finally arose and knowing that her witch was safe with Ethan's brothers, she *had* left for Ameera.

And she couldn't deny that her quest for the portal spell had been outranked by her need to find her parents.

Hazel chuckled, almost as though she'd read Jenna's inner struggle. But then she sobered. "Now that we've established you're a Salubrious love child . . ."

The blow came from behind, vicious and sudden, as something connected with Jenna's head. Pain arrowed through her and she collapsed. On her hands and knees, she tried to rise, hampered when Rick delivered another two punches. Everything went blurry. She turned her head, tasting blood.

"Jenna!" Ethan shouted, rattling his chains.

Hazel knelt in front of her and captured Jenna's head between her bony fingers. Her eyes danced with excitement and a sick smile twisted her tattooed features. She whispered a chant.

Jenna cried out as heat seared through her, powerful and overwhelming. A blinding pain pierced her skull. Her vision clouded and she fought the darkness that threatened.

And then the images struck. Brief, flashing moments of Jenna's life. Her parents, her home, the city. Even grandparents she'd hardly known. Ethan and his brothers, Kate, the night she'd saved her at the cemetery.

The memories rolled through her, snatches of her life, like clips of a movie – but out of order. Moments she'd treasured, memories she'd buried – like the one of her mother when she'd given Jenna the doll. But it disappeared too soon and Jenna cried out, aching to cling to that moment – a time when they'd been happy, before everything had changed. She saw a blurred image of Megan, the night her parents had brought her home. Small and helpless, her head bowed and covered in a hoodie.

Dozens more images followed, brief and murky. But Jenna recognised them all, her body shaking with the familiar ache of despair.

The night of the attack replayed itself in her mind. The fire, the fear, her father's desperate attempt to protect them. Her mother's mad dash for the portal and the moment she'd separated them.

NO!

A scream echoed through the room, long and desperate, and Jenna fought the panic and terror. She vaguely heard Ethan shouting her name, the frantic jerking of chains. But the memories kept coming.

And just like that, they vanished and the pain subsided.

Jenna felt the pressure ease and when Rick released her, stepping back, she couldn't move. She felt broken. All over again. Her self-preservation shattered. Tears welled in her eyes and she lifted her head, hating Hazel's close scrutiny.

The witch had seen everything. Invaded every goddamn memory.

"Anything?" Rick prompted, helping Hazel up. She shook her

head, evoking a curse from him. "We finally find one and she doesn't know?"

"Those crazy bitches wiped their memories. All of them. Even her lineage. She doesn't know where the massacre took place. Just like the others." Hazel said the last words through pinched lips, her inked jaw clasped in fury.

"Your sister –"

"Was wrong." His outraged roar split the silence and he spun around, aiming a furious kick into Jenna's side. The pain exploded through her and she curled into a foetal position, gasping air. "Rick, stop that!"

But he lunged for Jenna, settling on her back like a lead weight. "We have no use for this treacherous bitch anymore."

"STOP!" Megan burst out, appearing in the doorway. "Rick, leave her alone!"

"She deserves to die, Megan."

Megan hurried forward, breathless, clutching the Brogan Grimoire in her arms. "Mason's a genius. It worked."

"What do you mean?" Hazel asked, reaching for the book. Her eyes widened and her face lit up like a kid whose wish had just been granted. She hugged the Grimoire to her chest, threw her head back and released a croaky laugh.

The location?

Before Jenna could process that revelation, the earth rumbled again, rolling in faster and stronger than before. The room shook with a frightening force.

"Hazel, we have what we need. Let's deal with these two," Rick prompted, nodding at Ethan and Jenna, "and get out of here."

"In a minute. I have an idea. One far more satisfying than the quick death you have in mind." Hazel knelt over Jenna. "Have you ever wondered why those Keepers betrayed their witches?"

Dozens of times, but she refused to take the bait and ask.

"I'll give you a hint," Hazel whispered, telling her anyway. "A Behesting spell."

"They were spelled to ignore their witches?"

"Want to see how it works?" Hazel laughed and stood, fading in and out of Jenna's view as she walked to Ethan.

Jenna tried to push herself off the floor, stumbling as dizziness overwhelmed her. But another blow from Rick sent her sprawling to the ground. "NO!" Her cry came out as a gurgle of blood. She spat it out, grimacing at the vile taste, and tried to make sense of the blurry images in the distance. Chains jerked as Hazel removed the glass embedded in Ethan's body. His body swayed with the harsh movement. She murmured something in his ear.

"Ethan!" Jenna cried, her voice croaky. Her cheeks were wet, either from tears or blood, she wasn't sure. She didn't care. "Leave him alone!"

As the darkness overwhelmed her, she saw Hazel step away from Ethan. With a brief nod at Rick, they walked out.

Leaving them alone. Alive.

CHAPTER FORTY FOUR

Jenna awoke to another earth tremor.

They were becoming more powerful, lasting longer. She waited it out, her cheek pressed to the cement floor. Her teeth chattered and her body shivered uncontrollably.

The wind had grown stronger, colder, the room a whirlwind of dust.

She lifted her head, the scent of blood in her nostrils. Her injuries had healed while she'd been out, leaving her bloody and wet. The flames of the fire had died but orange embers floated in the wind, a sign she hadn't been out too long. Without the light from the fire, she had to rely on the glow of the moon, sporadic from the movement of the clouds.

Her heart soared when she saw Ethan. Still chained, quiet, staring at her.

"Ethan!" He didn't respond and she struggled to her feet, crossing the room, holding up her arm in front of her face to shield herself from the wind. It was dark, his features almost unreadable in the dim light. He stood in a puddle of blood.

A hard yank to the chains broke the lock and both clattered to the ground at his feet. He slumped but stayed upright, staring at her. She glanced at the wounds, relieved the bleeding had stopped. Which meant he was healing.

"She left us alive. They're gone, Ethan. We made it!" Breathless, shivering, she threw her arms around him.

But he remained rigid, his arms beside him, feet planted firmly apart. A shiver of trepidation ran through her.

Confused, she drew back, searching his expression. "Ethan?" Her heartbeat sped up when he ignored her. She took his hand, fiddling with the shackles around his wrist. The chains rattled from the jerky movement. "Ethan?"

An icy wind blasted into her.

The force propelled her backward and she crashed into the fire drums. Orange embers exploded, raining down on her. A wheelbarrow swept across the floor toward the gaping window, the metal screeching on the floor. It skidded past her and disappeared over the edge.

She gasped when the temperature suddenly dropped – a cold like she'd never experienced before. Her shivering intensified and her eyes watered.

Ethan still hadn't moved, but his expression had hardened. The way it always did when he connected with his elemental power.

Dread curled her insides when she realised the cause of the wind. *Ethan.*

She crouched against the drums, terrified the wind would push her toward the edge of the room. Her cheeks burned and every breath she took hurt like hell. "Ethan!"

His ferocious glare turned on her. Teeth bared, fists clenched beside his thighs, he stomped forward, dragging the chains behind him. The wind hampered his movements, but he kept coming.

An unstoppable force.

"Stop it! What are you doing?"

And then it struck her.

Want to see how it works?

Hazel's words came to mind, along with a new kind of terror.

A Behesting spell. She'd spelled him. It had to be. He'd never hurt her otherwise. Oh, no.

"Look at me, damn you! It's me. Jenna. It's Jenna!" Her teeth chattered and the wind muffled her cry. "Ethan!"

He spread his hands and a powerful whirlwind gathered force around them.

It twisted through the room, jarring tools and rubble. The chains slid across the floor, anchored by his body weight. The wind wrapped around her, fierce and unrelenting. She clutched onto the drums, leaning into them, crying out when they shifted and skidded toward the ledge. One toppled over, breaking her hold and surrendering her to the mercy of the wind. She screamed as she slid, horrified when the drum rolled ahead and catapulted out the window.

"Ethan!"

She frantically searched for something to grasp onto and cried out in relief when her fingers found one of the chains still attached to his wrist. She clutched on with both hands, rolling onto her stomach.

The sudden, harsh movement unbalanced him. Fuelled by the wind at his back, he tumbled forward. His chest collided with the floor and the momentum slid them along the ground toward the gaping hole of the window. As they reached the edge, she screamed as she went over, her body jerking violently when he grabbed onto a steel rod sticking out from the wall.

She felt the ground vanish beneath her and she swayed mid-air, clinging to the chain, anchored by his body. She looked up, unable to breathe, horror and fear freezing everything inside. He lay on his stomach, one arm outstretched toward her, trapped by the chain that supported her weight. The other arm clutched the steel rod behind him, all that stood between them and the horrific fall.

Her body trembled viciously and it was so damn cold. She glanced over her shoulder. The city loomed below, dark and ominous.

"You're stronger than her spell!" she screamed, looking up at him. "*We're* stronger. Fight it. Please, Ethan, you have to fight it!"

He gritted his teeth and tried to jerk free.

"Don't let me fall," she cried, her words a screech of terror. The chain rattled when she jiggled it, trying to reach him, terrified it was too late. "Please don't do this. You have to fight it. ETHAN!"

She saw the moment it changed for him.

That flash of recognition.

"Come back to me!" she cried, louder this time, hope spreading through her like wildfire when his brows furrowed and his eyes softened. The wind eased.

He blinked rapidly. "Jenna?" With a loud grunt, he hauled her up, dragging them away from the ledge. Scanning the room, he cradled her, breathless and panicked. "You're so cold. What the hell happened?"

Words escaped her, joy joining the ranks of her terror. She clung to him and closed her eyes, trying to catch her breath. Everything felt numb.

"You're frozen —" He stilled and his frown grew more pronounced. "Oh shit, *I* did this to you?"

She tried to answer him, but the words remained trapped between her chattering teeth and shivers.

His low curse rumbled through her as a wave of energy emanated off him, fierce and sudden, followed by a trickle of heat. A warm wind wrapped around them, lessening the chill. She took a few deep breaths as her body temperature rose, easing the shivers.

"You were spelled," she said, her voice croaky. "That's why Hazel left you alive. She spelled you to kill me."

He released her as though her words had scorched him. With a low growl that came from the back of his throat, he stood, clenching his fists.

"Ethan —"

"She almost succeeded! If the temperature drop didn't kill you, the fall would've."

"It didn't. I'm fine. We're fine."

"I used my magic on you!" He jabbed a finger toward the window. "I almost killed you!"

"It wasn't you, Ethan. You were under her spell." She took his hands and drew them up between them. They were so warm, a contrast to when she'd first found him. "But you broke through. You came back. Hazel didn't win. *You* did, Ethan."

His gorgeous blue eyes were glossy with emotion. He captured her face with shaky fingers. "I saw Sarah. But then it was you."

She gasped. "The dreams you've had of Sarah. Maybe this is why. When I fell off the roller coaster, it jarred something inside you and now again, enough to reach you."

He closed his eyes and cradled her head against his chest. "I'm so damn sorry."

"You beat her, Ethan," she said, grinning up at him. "You beat her spell. You're so bad-ass."

His lips twitched, but he didn't reply.

Jenna drew back, lacing their fingers. "Even in her death, Sarah saved us." Her face came to mind, sparking a fresh wave of longing.

He nodded slowly and swallowed. He cleared his throat. "How long since Hazel left?"

"The fire was still smouldering when I woke up."

"Jen." His eyes flashed with newfound worry. "You gave her the bracelet. She has control of the portal again. Your parents –"

"I did what I had to do, Ethan." She lowered her gaze, biting back hot disappointment. "She would've killed you if I hadn't. Your brothers can't lose another sibling. Losing you would destroy them – and me."

It was true. Somehow, despite her walls and precautions, she'd fallen for him. Hard. She'd been numb for so many years, kept her distance from others, but he'd broken through when no one else could.

"Handing over that bracelet was one of the hardest choices I've ever made, but I had to." She drew her lower lip into her teeth.

"What about your parents?"

"Hazel said they're dead."

"Do you believe her?"

"I don't know what to believe anymore." A part of her refused to accept Hazel's version. She couldn't let go of her parents yet.

They stared at each other in silence, words unnecessary, so many emotions between them. He pressed his lips to hers, a slow, gentle kiss that held the promises of everything she'd always lacked. Friendship, passion, safety.

She lifted her head, reaching for the courage required to voice the next sentence. "We should go home, Ethan. Kate and Sienna need us and I think Megan's found a way to break the spell on the Brogan Grimoire."

"How the hell could she do that?"

Jenna shrugged, but couldn't reply, refusing to embrace the realm of possibilities that came with that thought. She reached for his arm and turned to the door.

But he grimaced and covered his shoulder with one hand.

"Oh crap, the werewolf bite!" she gasped, hurriedly shifting the torn material aside to expose the wound. How could she have forgotten? She winced at the ugly stench of rotting flesh. His magic had begun to heal his other wounds, but not this one. Never this one.

"The paralysis spell must've numbed the side effects of the bite," he said through gritted teeth. "But now that it's worn off, it hurts so damn bad."

"Guess it's my turn to show off now."

He grinned and she held out her hand above the wound. An instant energy surged between them. Warm and healing, it worked its way through her, healing everything it touched. The stench lessened and the colour changed as his flesh knitted together.

She stilled, looking up at him, suddenly clear on why Hazel had left them alive. Her heart plummeted at the sick thought and she expelled a shaky breath. "Hazel's spell . . . she was so sure you'd kill me and that the bite would kill you. That's why she left us both alive. She never expected us to make it out of here."

They shared a long, dark look, the magnitude of what they'd overcome weighing between them. But they had. Against the odds. Against Hazel's devious plan and crazy magic.

"Fortunately, Hazel underestimated two things. My bond with my sister and . . . *this*." He jerked her toward him and pressed his lips to hers, smiling when she gasped at the rush of heat ignited by the movement. He withdrew and slung an arm around her shoulder. "Let's get the hell out of here."

CHAPTER FORTY FIVE

Home.

Ethan closed the front door and pocketed his key. The house was mostly in darkness, sparsely lit by a few scattered lamps. He turned around, revelling in the solace of home, and pulled Jenna into his arms. Tucking her head beneath his chin, he kissed her forehead. "It's so damn good to be back."

"It feels like a lifetime ago since we left."

They were both filthy, their clothes torn, their bodies smeared in dry blood. At least their injuries had healed.

The resistance they'd encountered along the way to the portal hadn't stood a chance against their fury and determination to leave Ameera. Finding the portal had been tricky. They'd panicked at first, thinking Hazel had closed it, but thanks to Jenna's wrist tattoo, they'd discovered it had been moved. There'd been no sign of her on either side.

He grinned when footsteps approached at the top of the stairs and pulled away from Jenna.

Declan bolted down the steps, tugging a t-shirt over his head.

He slammed into Ethan, grabbing him into a fierce hug. His heart raced, his relief and emotion evident in his tight grip and silence. A novelty for his brother. But Ethan felt it too and he wrapped his arms around his brother's neck.

Declan withdrew and caught Ethan's head in his hands. "You ass, you had me worried."

"I missed you too, brother. Sienna okay?"

"She's fine. She's sleeping." Declan slung an arm around Jenna's shoulders. "Dammit, Blondie. I never thought I'd be so damn happy to see you."

"Thanks. I think." She smiled and returned the hug. "Where's Kate?"

"She's on her way."

"She's awake? She's okay?"

"We heard the car and yes, she's fine. We're all fine."

Jenna grinned and bolted up the stairs in search of her witch.

"Has anyone checked on Mason recently?" Ethan asked, his stomach twisting at the question.

Declan's brows dipped. "Yes, Archer's checked on him several times. He's still a mummified beauty."

"No signs of anyone trying to free him?"

"Nope."

"Are you sure?"

"Yes. Why?"

Ethan frowned and put an arm around his brother's shoulders. "I need a drink, brother, and then you can help me figure this shit out."

Declan shoved him away, frowning at his appearance. "You need a shower. What the hell happened to you?"

"It's more like what the hell *didn't* happen. Pour me a drink and I'll tell you all about it. The quick version." His brother was right. He did need a shower. And Jenna.

He wanted her alone, in the safety of his home, his room. His bed.

Damn, he could hardly wait.

They walked into the pool room. The lights turned on automatically when they entered. The pool water glistened in the reflection of the dim glow. Wide glass doors overlooked a lush green garden, most of it in darkness. The bar and lounge were on the other side of the room, the wall decorated in natural stone. A favourite gathering spot in the house.

While Declan poured drinks, Ethan took a quick shower in the en-suite bathroom. It was brief and hot and he took satisfaction in watching the water, coloured red, disappear down the drain. Grabbing a white towel, he tucked it around his hips, and joined his brother.

Declan eyed his appearance, holding out a glass in one hand, a clean t-shirt in the other. Ethan pulled on the t-shirt and took the whiskey, downing it in one go. Not his drink of choice, but Declan loved his whiskey and assumed everyone else did too.

He took a beer from the fridge, frowning when he saw Declan glowering at him. "What's with the aneurysm glare?"

"I'm torn between kicking your ass for leaving or shutting the hell up and listening to what you have to say."

Ethan snorted. "Trust me, brother, I've had enough ass-kicking to last me a lifetime."

"That bad?"

"It was crap. All of it. Everything about the city, the people, the way they live."

"Did you find the witch bitch and her minions?"

"Yeah. We kicked their asses." He frowned and took a large sip of beer. "But then they kicked ours and spelled me to kill Jenna after they left."

Declan froze, his glass mid-air to his lips. "Sounds like you had an eventful trip."

"I haven't even started." He explained what had happened, leaving out the details of Jenna's connection with Ameera. That was her story to tell. By the time he was done, he was on his second

265

beer. As for Declan, Ethan never counted his brother's impressive whiskey consumption.

"So Hazel's back in our world?" Declan asked.

"Yes, and she's left the portal open. She –" He paused, turning toward the door at the sound of hurried footsteps approaching. Sienna skidded into the room, wide-eyed and breathless. She sported messy hair and pyjamas. With a whoop of joy, she rushed forward and threw her arms around him. He laughed and kissed her head. He had to swallow a few times to get rid of the damn tightness in his throat. Apparently, he'd been more worried about her than he'd been willing to admit to himself. "I'm fine, Sienna."

She swatted his back. "Don't do that again! You had us worried sick."

He kissed her again, breathing in her scent, one that reminded him of everything he fought for. His entire body was hard-wired to protect this woman, his magic linked to hers. An indescribable bond. And he adored her.

"Archer's going to be so relieved you're back," she said.

Declan grunted. "Yeah, 'cause he's been a dick since you left."

Sienna shot him a frown and took a seat at the bar. "He's been worried, Declan."

"I've been worried too, but I've kept myself in check. Archer, on the hand, brought out the big guns."

Sienna sighed but didn't deny it. She looked up at Ethan. "Did you find the spell?"

"It's a key. A scorpion bracelet that activates the spell, but Hazel got away with it." He left out the details, deciding his brother could do without the elevated blood pressure.

"A key? At least we know what to look for." Sienna stood and walked around the bar, turning on the kettle. "We have to stop her. Since the portal's been opened, so many cities and towns have been harmed by earthquakes and storms."

"It's a result of the open portal. Ameera's the same. The portal makes both worlds unstable."

"There've been animal attacks, insect infestations, Keepers disappearing –"

"It's all part of Hazel's diabolical plan." Ethan explained what they'd discovered, not surprised when Declan poured another drink. This time, with more agitation and haste. "The open portal, her attack on the witches and their Keepers, and her army of beefed-up supernatural freaks . . . she has it all worked out."

"She still doesn't know where the location of the massacre is," Sienna said.

Ah, crap. He shifted, wondering how the hell he should break it to them.

"Oh, no," she gasped, her eyes widening. Apparently, his witch knew him well. "She found it? How –?"

Declan choked on his whiskey and bolted off his chair. "How on earth did you let that happen?"

"That's a dick thing to say and you know it, brother."

"She's found the fucking magic, Ethan!"

"We don't know that for sure. But yelling at me won't help shit. Instead, let's figure out a way to find her."

"Right, like *that* should be easy."

"Stop yelling at me, dammit!"

Kate's appearance in the doorway curbed Declan's reply. She shot Declan a fierce frown before looking at Ethan. Relief crossed her expression and she hurried toward him, hugging him. "I'm so glad you're home. Your brother's been driving me insane."

Curbing his agitation, he smiled and kissed her cheek, glancing over her head at Declan. "I told you before . . . it's his trademark. Like his messy hair and whiskey addiction."

Declan flipped him the middle finger.

Kate grinned. "I had no idea he was capable of such colourful language."

Ethan's lips twitched and he pulled away, ignoring his brother's scowl.

"How did Hazel find the location?" Sienna asked.

"She has her Grimoire. Supposedly."

She gasped. "That's impossible."

"Have you checked on the Grimoires recently?"

"Not since we locked them away a day or two ago. There's no way she could access it."

"Can you check?" Although something told him it would be fruitless. Somehow, Hazel had found a way to summon her Grimoire – and open it. He had no idea how, but he knew that she had. She'd practically drooled when Megan had showed up with the book.

"Even if Hazel has her book, how on earth could she break my mother's spell?" Sienna asked. "And why would she only take her Grimoire and not mine too?"

Ethan shrugged. "I don't know, Sienna, but . . ."

A bristle of awareness crept down his spine and his heart sped up in response. Turning, he looked at the door, not surprised when Jenna appeared a moment later.

He'd felt her presence. One that was as comforting as it was arousing. She'd always done that to him, but now, after everything they'd been through together, those feelings had magnified to a whole new level.

She'd showered, her wet hair tied in a knot at the top of her head. She wore a t-shirt and yoga pants, both items hugging luscious curves he'd spent hours exploring. She looked so beautiful, feminine, and so different to the warrior who'd saved his butt in Ameera.

The thought made him smile and he motioned to her with the wave of a hand. "You want a drink?"

"Or tea," Sienna added, rolling her eyes. "Not everyone wants a drink at this time of the morning."

Jenna smiled, one that didn't reach her eyes, and walked into the room. "I'll have a drink, please. Something strong."

The way she said it, and the way she hovered at a distance, had Ethan's brows knitting together as he poured the whiskey. Holding out the glass, he went to her, deliberately towering over her, using his body to shield her from his family. She lifted her gaze to his, took the glass, and released a shaky breath.

Leaning closer, he put his mouth to her ear. "You took on Ameera. You're bad ass. You can do this." Her lashes fluttered and her lips twitched. "Declan will be a walk in the park compared to what you've faced."

"Easy for you to say. You share the same blood. That automatically gives you a safe pass."

He chuckled, running a hand down her arm. He couldn't help himself, needing to touch her. Hell, he wanted to ignore his family – doing a great job of pretending not to listen – and take her upstairs. Now. But he knew that wouldn't happen. Not with the fire that burned in her eyes.

She was on a mission to tell them the truth, one that was necessary.

"It's okay," he whispered in her ear, drawing back to offer a reassuring smile.

Swallowing the whiskey in one gulp, she stiffened, stepped around him and walked to the counter to pour another drink. They all watched in silence, sensing she wanted to say something.

When she'd swallowed half the liquid in the glass, she placed it on the counter and folded her arms. "I have something to tell you."

CHAPTER FORTY SIX

Ethan didn't say much during the conversation that followed.

But he was there, beside her, ready to reel in Declan on more than one occasion. Archer had joined them at some point but he'd kept his distance and hadn't said much. He'd worn a permanent scowl, apparently still pissed at them. Probably more so when he heard what she had to say.

Their reactions were . . . colourful. But Jenna couldn't blame them.

So she answered all their questions honestly, with as much patience as anyone in the firing line, exhausted from lack of sleep, food and too many adrenaline rushes, could muster. But couldn't bring herself to tell them about the bracelet. The fact that she'd had it and been so close to ending this, only to fail, had burned a hole of shame inside her.

An hour and a gazillion questions later, they were still there. But at least their surprise and agitation had eased. She wished she could say the same for their questions. When her stomach growled and a yawn slipped out before she could stifle it, Ethan quietly stood. He disappeared, returning a few minutes later with a bottle of water and some sandwiches. Her heart leapt at the sight and her stomach growled again. Not surprising considering she hadn't eaten much in the last few days.

"It's late." He reached for her hand, tugging her up. "We'll pick this up in the morning."

"Ethan, we're not done here," Declan grumbled, reaching for a sandwich.

Ethan moved the plate out of his reach and led Jenna to the door. "Damn right we are. For now at least."

Relief rolled through her, easing the knots between her shoulders, a testament to how tense she'd been. She followed him quietly, stifling the urge to grin. Or kiss him. But someone was about to get very, very lucky.

She wasn't much for playing a damsel in distress – and hadn't been *in* distress – but exhaustion and hunger had taken their toll. Right now, he was her knight in gorgeous, shiny, much-needed armour – and she was totally fine with that. Oh yes.

"Where the hell are you going?" Declan asked, raising a brow.

"To bed," Ethan replied without looking back. "It's been a rough couple of days, with little sleep. We'll see you in a few hours."

"Jenna's room is in the other direction," Declan called after them, his voice laced with amusement.

"She won't need it."

****

Ethan revelled in the feel of the naked woman nestled in his arms. They lay in bed, a mixture of tangled limbs and sheets.

She was sleepy, peaceful, a contagious combination that had him relaxing beside her. He pressed a kiss into her hair, trailing his fingers up and down her arm, allowing the stillness to take its beat.

He laced their fingers and drew her hand to his mouth. He kissed her wrist, looking at the tattoo she loathed.

"The tattoo on my side has grown again," she said softly.

He lifted his head to peer down at her. "You never said anything."

271

She smiled, her eyes glistening with that playful gleam he loved. "You had me rather occupied."

"Want to get occupied again?"

"I don't think I can move."

Chuckling, he kissed her head. "We should rest. My brothers will be banging down my door in a few hours."

"Even though they know I'm in here?"

"Afraid so."

"Don't you have a guy code or a signal that lets them know you're . . . busy? You know, like a tie on the door handle or a –"

He laughed. "We hung a red cap outside the door at the academy."

"Time for you to haul it out then."

"I can't. It stayed behind. Got passed down to the new recruits."

"So what do you use here?"

"Nothing. I've never needed one here." Her delicate brows furrowed in confusion. "I don't bring women home."

"Like ever?"

"Never."

"Why not?"

"I live with five other supernatural beings that use their magic freely at home. Explain *that* over morning coffee."

Her expression held a combination of surprise and amusement. "So how come I got to be your first bed buddy?"

The satisfaction in her voice pleased him. He wasn't sure why, but it did. "Because you're different and I'd say you're a little more than a bed buddy, don't you think?"

A lot more. But he left it at that.

Her expression faltered, just a little, but she didn't respond. Instead, she propped herself up on her elbows and peered up at him. "Think your brothers are mad with me?"

"They'll get over it."

"I never lied to them, you know. Every question I ever answered or piece of information I offered was as close to the truth as possible."

It was true. She'd said she'd lost her parents several years ago and taken shelter at the academy. An only child. A Keeper. All the truth – with a whole lot of blank spaces in between. But she'd had her reasons and even though he loathed the secrets, he couldn't hold them against her. Provided there were no more lies or omissions. With him at least.

He said as much to her and she frowned. "Does that mean I have to tell them that I had the bracelet?"

"No," he said, shaking his head, knowing instinctively she wouldn't want that. "*I* know and that's all that matters. Seriously, Jen, no more secrets between us."

She nodded, but was silent for a while before releasing a soft sigh. "We should get out of bed and come up with a way to find Hazel."

"Soon," he said, tugging her back down. For now, all he wanted was her, in his bed, without the memories of Ameera and the threat of Hazel between them. If only for a few hours. He shook his head and touched a finger to her lips. "Later. She doesn't belong here, in bed with us. We'll figure out what to do later, when we're rested and dressed. And not horny."

"Speak for yourself, stud muffin." She laughed, the sound easing her mood. Her fingers trailed across his abdomen, causing his muscles to tighten. She brushed the scar along his side, a small frown tightening her brows. "Will you tell me about your scar?"

He stilled, not particularly in the mood to dredge up old memories, but figured if he insisted on honesty he owed her the same. He rested his head on the pillow, staring up at the ceiling, dread curling up inside him as he remembered the night they'd lost Sarah. "After we bound Mason to the tomb, Warrick attacked Declan. Sarah got in the way. She died in Sienna's arms. In her grief and rage, Sienna tapped into her powers, ours too. She set the tomb alight. Without our magic, we were weak and struggled to get out of the burning tomb. My shirt caught alight, but Declan was quick to smother the flames." He didn't say anything more, didn't have to. Jenna would know the reason his scar had never healed.

Because it was caused by a witch. His witch. And to this day, he carried the permanent reminder of that night. Archer had one too, on his arm, and Ethan had often caught Sienna looking at it.

"I've never shown Sienna," he added, "so please don't tell her. She carries enough guilt over what happened." They all did. In different ways. A tragedy that had changed them forever. They'd lost their parents and Rose, grieved for them all, but somehow losing their sister had cut the deepest.

"You can't blame yourself, Ethan."

"I don't blame myself that it happened," he replied quietly. "I blame myself that it happened to *her*. Mason had spelled three cats, like the ones Hazel had in Ameera. Archer and Sarah were about to leave to check on them, but I stopped her and told her I'd go instead."

"So you blame yourself because you switched places with her?"

"If I hadn't she would've still been alive."

"Not necessarily, Ethan. You must know that."

"I guess the logical side of me does. The side that grieves her . . ." He left it there, already having said too much. Which surprised him as he'd never told anyone before.

Her fingers toyed with the leather necklace around his neck, closing over the pendant. "Is that why you wear her necklace?"

Her perceptiveness surprised him. "How do you know it belonged to her?"

"I gave it to her." She shook her head, looking at the pendant in her hand. "I miss her so much."

"Me too."

"And I wish I could change the last thing I said to her."

"Your argument?"

"We'd hardly spoken before she died as I'd already joined Hazel's people. I couldn't risk blowing my cover. But I wanted her to know. Unfortunately, she saw me with Megan before I could tell her."

"That's why you were fighting?"

She nodded. "She was so furious that she uprooted that tree. I left and she died thinking I betrayed you all."

Her eyes held a storm of emotion. So much sadness, loss, regrets. Guilt.

"Sarah loved you," he said softly, stroking her chin with his thumb. "You and Sienna were her best friends."

"She was my only friend."

"Not anymore."

She tilted her head, considering his words, and then she smiled. With a slight nod, she placed her cheek on his chest.

They fell silent and he held her, stroking her arm. Her breathing deepened, her body warm and heavy against his. He pulled the sheet up to cover her, purposefully brushing his fingers along her skin. So soft and feminine. *His.*

The thought made him smile and he kissed her head, breathing her in. Settling back into the cushions, he debated whether he should attempt sleep or go search for his brothers. The sun would be up soon. Another day. Another fight. The same damn war.

It wasn't long after that sleep won.

CHAPTER FORTY SEVEN

She felt invincible.

A silly notion. Jenna knew that. But from the balcony of Ethan's bedroom, with the stillness of the mountains in front of her and the naked body of the man who'd rocked her world asleep in the bed behind her, it was impossible to feel anything less.

Her skin tingled and she felt lighter than she had in a long time, a few hours in Ethan's bed easing her tension and permanent sense of dread. For now, at least.

She knew reality would come crashing back as sure as the sunrise. It was inevitable, but for now, she simply wanted to revel in that brief moment of peace before memories, responsibilities, and fears crept in.

She tightened the belt of her satin robe, turned her face toward the sky, and breathed in.

Blissful silence.

It was hard to reconcile the peace and beauty with the violence they'd experienced in Ameera.

A movement in the bedroom made her smile. Grateful for the distraction, she looked over her shoulder as Ethan appeared in the doorway.

Ruffled hair, bright blue eyes and early morning stubble. He'd tugged the sheet around his waist. Her gaze lingered on the ripple of rock-hard abs she'd explored many times over.

The man was breathtaking.

And now that he'd made her his, sex with anyone else would pale in comparison. The freedom, the ability to let go, the lack of inhibitions. Total mind-blowing, toe-curling . . . *holy cow*.

He slid his arms around her waist and nuzzled her neck. "Hi."

She leaned into him, her back against his chest, revelling in the masculine strength that enveloped her. Smiling, she turned her face inward, her cheek brushing his stubble.

His caresses, the scent of him, felt familiar – a sensation that warmed her in places deep inside.

"Did you get some sleep?" he murmured against her ear. She nodded. "Any dreams?"

"No."

He caught her earlobe between his teeth, grinning when she breathed in sharply. His hand slid between the folds of her robe to cup a breast. This time it was her turn to smile when he inhaled deeply.

"I can't get enough of you," he murmured, turning her to face him.

A stir of wanting ignited inside her. "So don't."

He grinned and his mouth found hers. Electricity fired and he deepened their kiss. More pressure. More heat. So much hunger.

His breathing grew heavier and he captured her hip with one hand. A rough jerk had her pressed against him, the evidence of his arousal triggering a rush of excitement. With a low growl, he gave her a hard kiss on the mouth before pulling away. She was about to protest, but he took her hand and led her inside.

She followed him toward the bathroom, pausing to gape at the mess. The sheets were tangled to within an inch of their lives, furniture had been rearranged, pillows and clothes littered the floor. An overturned lamp, a skewed headboard. Even the damn bed had shifted!

Hell, she'd known they'd let go, revelled in a sense of freedom and safety that came with being back home, but. . .

"You're blushing," he whispered in her ear, the breathy words sending a fresh shiver through her.

"We did that?"

"Ashamed?"

"No. But . . ." She gawked at the bed, uneven and out of place. "Oh, shit, *we broke the bed*?"

"It was an old bed."

"Old or used?"

"I told you, other than Sienna, you're the only woman who's ever been up here." His words stroked something inside her and she smiled. "Don't worry about the mess. I'll sort it out."

"We destroyed the room!"

A wicked grin broke free. "Want to destroy the bathroom?"

"Ethan!" But she didn't protest when he took her hand and headed for the door across the room. Still grinning, he turned on the shower.

He rummaged through the drawer, extracting a pair of earplugs and a foil packet. She glanced at the earplugs and lifted her eyebrows.

"Do you trust me?" he asked softly, kissing her earlobe.

"Of course."

"Then close your eyes."

"Why?"

He brushed away the hair covering her ears, his touch sending a shiver of wanting through her. "Just close your eyes, Jen."

But she didn't. "We really should get downstairs."

He sighed, his eyes flashing with brief irritation at the reminder. "The moment we do, we'll be swept away with all the hell about to break loose, and before that happens I want you to know something." She opened her mouth to question him, but he kissed her, cutting her off. "Close your eyes. And keep them closed. I dare you."

Curious, overwhelmed by him, she closed her eyes. But when he placed an earplug in her ear, they flew open again.

He pressed his lips against her eyebrows, his kisses light and soothing. "Trust me. Close your eyes," he whispered.

So she did.

He plugged her other ear and a cocoon of darkness and silence enveloped her. In a world where heightened hearing was the norm for her, the absolute silence was disconcerting. Her nerve endings fired, the urge to regain control of her surroundings stronger than her desire for the man in front her.

But his hands captured her face and his lips found hers in a gentle, reassuring kiss that eased the rush of panic. He loosened her robe and the material slithered down her body, the soft material stroking her flesh in a sensual caress. His hands moved to her hips, his body against hers. He'd lost the sheet and was naked and aroused.

He guided her under the water. She gasped and drew back, but he was there, coaxing her forward, his arms around her, his body anchoring hers.

She stilled, the sound of her breathing echoing in her ears. Her heart pounded, her body tingled. Wrapped in darkness and silence, every touch receptor and nerve ending sharpened in a way that had her shivering.

Every touch. Every kiss. The feel of his body against hers. The water raining down on her. She felt it.

Everywhere.

So she gave herself over to him – not something she'd ever thought she'd do, but with him, *this*, it felt right. A moment of pure bliss. Trust. Overwhelming peace.

Her mind shut down, along with her need for control, and she allowed herself to be guided by him, accepting everything he offered.

He took her to heights she'd never experienced before, her body a quivering mess of wild sensations that had her moaning in his arms, begging for release. But he was on his own schedule, one that revolved around her pleasure, and he wasn't ready for it to be over yet.

When he lay her down on the tiles, water cascading over them, and spread her legs, she cried out. Her back arched in anticipation, but she kept her eyes closed, relishing in the intensity of the experience.

She gasped when his mouth closed over the sensitive nub between her legs, the action taking her by surprise. Renewed desire burst through her and she spread her arms, her body, giving him the access he sought.

He nibbled, kissed, touched, and licked until she could barely catch her breath through the shivers that rippled through her. When he finally, finally pushed her over the edge with another stroke of his tongue, she cried out and arched her back again, her fingers spread against the floor.

Her body soared, enveloped in darkness and stillness and pleasure. Receptive to him and only him. Incredible, breathtaking sensations that had her writhing on the floor, trembling beneath him.

And when he covered her body with his, she clung to his shoulders, needing to feel him there.

He claimed her body with a hard thrust, extracting another low moan from her. She widened her legs to accommodate him, the movement drawing him in deeper. His growl vibrated through her, his heart slammed against hers. It excited her, knowing his arousal matched hers.

If that was even possible.

He reached up, untangling her arms from around his neck. Lacing their fingers, he placed their hands above her head, the movement firm and possessive. His mouth crushed hers and he rocked his hips, filling her in a way that transcended more than something physical.

She met him thrust for thrust in a rhythmic dance. When she

positioned her legs around his waist, he released another animal-like growl that vibrated to the very core of her. With a final, deep thrust, they came together in an explosion of sensations that had them rocking, gasping, clinging to each other.

When it was over, she kept her eyes closed, savouring the breathy remains of their climax. The feel of his body against hers, slick and breathless and aroused. The rush of satisfaction. That moment of pure joy.

When she finally opened them, he pressed his lips to hers in a powerful, gentle kiss before lifting his head to look at her. But it wasn't pleasure she saw. He was frowning and his eyes reflected a struggle that surprised her.

She tugged the earplugs out of her ears and lifted a hand to his cheek. "Ethan?"

He blew out air, his expression pensive, worried, and she knew it was reality returning with a bite. "You're right. We should get downstairs." He adjusted his weight onto his elbows and dipped his forehead to hers. "But before we do and get wrapped up in this damn war all over again, I want you to know something."

"No." His words, the intensity in his eyes, suddenly frightened her and she shook her head. "Ethan, don't. Not now."

"There might not be a later, Jen. If Hazel's headed for that magic, things are about to turn a shade of ugly we've never seen before. But we'll stop her. We'll win. We always do."

He said the words with such sincerity and conviction that she ached to believe him. "We have no idea where that magic is, Ethan. How –?"

"We'll find a way to get the bracelet back and when we do, I want you to know something." He swallowed, his heart beating a steady, slow rhythm against hers. "You've become a part of me I wish I didn't need. But I do. So damn fiercely that the thought of losing you scares me. And I know you feel it too."

"Ethan –"

"I will do whatever it takes to protect you, to protect what we have." The raw emotion behind his words stilled her. Inhaling deeply, the movement shaky, he lowered his head, touching his forehead to hers. "You're not alone anymore. Remember that when the time comes to close the portal."

His words resonated through her, so powerful and meaningful. Unable to voice a reply, all she could do was nod. Because he was right. She felt it too. Everything. So much that it terrified her.

And that changed everything.

CHAPTER FORTY EIGHT

The sound of Archer and Sienna's clipped voices in the living room had Ethan slowing his stride on the stairs.

He shifted uncomfortably, never one for eavesdropping, but thanks to his enhanced hearing, it was hard not to. He debated giving them their privacy and returning to his room – sound-proofed – but the tension in Sienna's voice had him rooted to the spot.

Privacy or not, she was still his witch and tuning *her* out, especially when she was upset, was impossible. So he waited, listening. Unashamed.

Archer sounded agitated. Nothing new lately, but the heat of their argument was.

"How could you let this happen?" Sienna snapped in a hushed tone. "You said you'd put the Grimoires away!"

"I did. And that's unfair, don't you think? You were with me. You spelled the damned door shut."

"Then how the hell did Hazel get her hands on the Brogan Grimoire? The house and the books are protected by a spell. There's no way Hazel could crack that without me knowing."

"Perhaps your magic isn't as foolproof as you think."

"I'm a Beckham witch –"

"Stop underestimating Hazel, dammit!"

"Don't yell at me, Archer. Being furious with your brother doesn't give you the right –"

"You have no fucking idea how furious I am, Sienna. No idea."

Something about Archer's tone had Ethan taking the last few steps, but it was the sound of shattering glass and Sienna's soft cry that had him bolting into the living room like a discharged bullet.

Archer had her pressed against the back of the couch. Sienna gaped at him, her hands on his chest, her bare feet surrounded by a broken vase. Her main Grimoire rested in its secret place in the hole in the wall behind her, the door ajar.

Ethan glanced at the mess on the floor and shot his brother an icy stare. "Archer?"

"Go away, Ethan."

Sienna took a step backward, dodging the glass. Ethan was beside her before she took another step, but Archer threw up a hand, stopping him.

Screw that.

Ethan shoved him away, with more force than intended. Archer slid across the floor, slamming into the mantelpiece. The three daggers on the wall rattled from the impact. He lifted Sienna over the glass and tucked her behind him, not sure why he felt the need to. Archer would never hurt her. Duty aside, his brother adored her. But something about their argument had his protective instincts lit up like an airstrip and until he was sure Archer was calm, he wasn't getting anywhere near her.

Ethan met his brother's lethal stare. When Archer took three strides toward him, he didn't budge. Didn't even blink. "Who peed in your coffee this morning?"

"Butting your ass in the middle of our arguments now?"

"A given if Sienna's in danger."

"She's not in danger, dammit! Not from me at least."

"Then stop acting like an overbearing ogre and calm the fuck down."

"Screw you, Ethan."

He was vaguely aware of Jenna entering the room, but his gaze remained locked with his brother's. Archer seldom lost his cool and seeing him like this surprised him. "If you're angry that I went to Ameera —"

"Damn right I am."

"Get over it, brother. I did what I had to do."

Archer released a low growl at the back of his throat and grabbed Ethan's shirt. "What did you accomplish, huh? All you did was aggravate Hazel." As he spoke, he pressed forward, their noses almost touching. "And while you were gone, she somehow found a way to the Brogan Grimoire, which means they were here, in our damn home, with access to Sienna. She's your witch and you weren't here for her!"

"Archer —" Jenna said, placing a hand on Archer's shoulder.

"You!" Archer bellowed. He spun around, shoving her off him with such force that she dropped her book and crashed into the coffee table.

She gaped at him. "What the hell's wrong with you?"

Ethan bolted forward, grabbing his brother by the shirt in his stride, and didn't stop until he had him pinned to the wall. "You need to leave, brother. Now."

Declan skidded into the doorway, Kate behind him. He frowned when he saw them, but seemed unsurprised at the scuffle.

"Get your hands off me," Archer said in a low tone, pushing Ethan away. He straightened his shirt, scowling at them, and jabbed a finger in the direction of the Beckham Grimoire. "The book's gone and it sounds like Megan found a way to open it. It's only a matter of time before they track the location of that magic and all hell breaks loose. Do I need to remind you of your duties, brother?"

"Sienna will always be my first concern."

"Make sure she stays your first concern." He sent Jenna a final glare and walked out, slamming the door behind him.

Ethan blew out air. He glanced over his shoulder at Jenna, already knowing she hadn't been hurt – and that Archer hadn't meant to harm her.

But . . . *shit*.

Declan raised his brows and spread his hands in question, but Ethan shook his head, not up for another rehash. Jenna retrieved her book off the floor, placed it on the table, and picked up the glass.

Sienna sighed. "I'm sorry. Archer's so angry lately."

"That we left?" Ethan asked.

"It's more than that. He's mad at everyone. Me included."

"He's worried."

"We're all worried, but . . ." She paused, her shoulder lifting in a half-shrug.

"There's a lot at stake." Ethan went to her, pulling her into his arms, and kissed her forehead. "He'll be okay, Sienna. Give him a chance to cool off. He'll come around."

"How did Hazel get the book, Ethan?" When he shrugged and didn't reply, she sighed and walked to the wall that housed her Grimoire. Closing the door, she whispered a chant that would seal it. "We were browsing my Grimoire recently, but we put it back beside the Brogan book. I spelled the door. What if Archer's right and my magic isn't foolproof?"

"I think he's right in that you shouldn't underestimate Hazel."

She nodded and he loathed the angst he saw in her eyes. "I should go talk to him." She paused as her gaze found Jenna's book. Reaching for it, she ran her fingers across the leather cover.

Jenna dumped the glass into the bin and came up behind her. "I brought that to show you. It was my father's journal. I found it in Ameera. It's mostly his notes about healing potions, but I found this . . ." She flipped through the pages and slid a finger to a roughly drawn sketch. Three small interlinked circles.

Judging by Sienna's gasp, she recognised it instantly. Her head bolted up, her eyes brightening with excitement. "It's the same symbol as the one on Kate's scroll."

Ethan's brows rose. "*The* scroll?"

The impossible one they'd all but given up trying to decode. The one that hinted at a legend they'd heard countless times growing up. Kate had found it in her late mother's Grimoire. The faded sketch consisted of a smaller triangle with a symbol at each corner – fire, three daggers, and a Keeper. The triangle was embedded within a larger one, a protection symbol at each corner. A black shadow filled the centre and according to the legend it depicted the evil that would one day descend upon them. The symbols were the keys to defeating it.

Which would help tremendously if they were able to decipher the damn thing.

Until now, every time they tried, they came to the same conclusion. It appeared that a Keeper, with the element of fire, and three daggers would be their hero. But they had no idea who that was or when it would happen.

Sienna hurried to the coffee table. It was covered in old books, dusty and worn. Grimoires. She pulled one out of the pile and showed them the cover. "While you were away, we discovered this old Grimoire in my grandmother's attic. It has the same interlinked circles on the front."

Jenna pointed to her father's scribbled notes. "He labelled it *The Pure –*"

"Oh my God," Sienna breathed, cutting her off. "Before my grandmother died, she told me I was a chosen one. *The Pure.* I thought she was just rambling at the time."

"Rose never rambled," Declan cut in, crossing his arms. "And what's with the number three cropping up all over the place?"

"Because it's significant." Ethan's heart upped its rhythm, his gaze flickering between the women. "Three circles that appear on three family heirlooms. Belonging to three women."

"That's crazy." Jenna gaped at him, her brows creased. "You think we're all linked?"

"It's the same symbol. And you're all here. Together."

"That's a coincidence, Ethan."

"Whoa, Jenna's right, let's not get ahead of ourselves," Declan grumbled, holding out a hand. "Sienna, don't you think if you were part of some big-assed legend, we'd know about it?"

She stared at him and Ethan could tell her mind raced to connect the dots. And they weren't far off. He could feel it. Hot damn.

"Maybe that's why my grandmother gave me her powers," she murmured. "She said I wouldn't understand at first, but it was a journey I had to discover. Maybe that journey has something to do with everything that's happening now."

Ethan caught the way her voice had lowered at the mention of her grandmother. A potent witch with the ability to control all four elements of nature at once. Sienna had once been a simple elemental witch, a fire witch, until Rose had passed her magic on to her. Sienna had fiercely rejected it at first, terrified at the strength of her magic.

"Rose sacrificed herself for me," Sienna said softly. "I never understood why."

Ethan frowned at the memory. "Before she died, she kept saying you're meant for greater things. Maybe she —" Levi's loud growl cut him off. The hairs on the back of her neck stood on end, her attention on something outside. Another growl, followed by the faint sound of squawking in the distance.

Ethan moved to the window, vaguely aware of his brother coming up behind him, and traced Levi's gaze. The noise grew louder as a flock of birds flew past the window, trailed by dozens more. Four deers bolted out of the forest and raced across the lawn in the same direction.

The ground began to tremble and Levi barked. A deep, agitated bark that always hinted at trouble.

"We need to close that damn portal," Declan grumbled, staring outside.

"I think we have a bigger problem," Sienna said softly, coming up behind them, her expression twisted with worry. She pointed to the sky, the ominous clouds marred with dozens of birds flying in the same direction. "It's a full moon tonight. The tremors, storms, and now the birds . . . it's starting. Hazel's begun to harvest the magic."

CHAPTER FORTY NINE

If that damn scroll meant anything, the darkness had started.

Hot fury, mixed with fear, burned through Jenna as she moved through the water. She'd hoped a swim would uncoil the tension, but other than aching muscles and a shortage of breath, she still felt the overwhelming urge to scream. Or punch something.

Hard.

News reports had trickled in all day, the media splashed with repeated warnings of impending storms. Earth tremors and heavy weather had swept through dozens of cities and towns, threatening thousands of homes and people. So far, the damage was mild, but people were in a frenzy as they made the necessary preparations for what the media had dubbed "the worst weather crisis in decades."

The sheer magnitude of so many storms at the same time had Hazel's name all over it. According to Sienna, it would take a mammoth amount of energy to summon such destruction.

The kind of energy that came from dozens of dead witches.

But it was Hazel. They were sure of it. Which meant that Hazel had found the location of the massacre. And they couldn't stop her because they had no idea where that was.

They'd spent the day scouring Grimoires, her father's journal, and making notes. They'd made dozens of phones calls, tossed around multiple theories, watched the news, and paced a hole in the living room floor.

And they were still no damn closer to finding Hazel.

Jenna released a frustrated scream underneath the water. She did several laps, pumping her legs and arms harder and faster. As if she could outswim the grim reality they faced. And the nagging voice that kept bothering her.

The Pure.

Had her parents known this would happen? Had they known she was part of a stupid legend that no one could understand? Is that why her mother had pushed her through the portal?

You're made for greater things, Jen. Things that can't be accomplished here.

Agitation coursed through her, spurring her on. She increased her pace. Hard, fast, furious. Anything to relieve the ache burning in her chest, a permanent companion slowly driving her crazy.

A dozen laps later, breathless and exhausted, she reached the edge of the pool, her face emerging from the water with a powerful gasp of air. Before she could catch her breath, a force came out of nowhere, grabbed her shoulders, and shoved her back down.

The water engulfed her cry as she went under. She fought the grip, thrashing her arms, stunned by the sudden attack. Adrenaline took flight, accompanied by a spurt of horror when she couldn't break free.

She surged upward, sucking air. "ETHAN!"

But her words were muffled as she disappeared beneath the water again. *No!*

Her chest burned, her muscles were on fire, and just as the panic set in, strong hands grabbed her by the shoulders and hauled her out of the water. Coughing, spluttering, she lashed out.

"Jenna, stop it! It's me, dammit!" Archer said quickly, kneeling in front of her.

The air slammed out of her in relief when she recognised the voice. "Archer?" she breathed, trying to catch her breath. She grabbed his shirt between her fists and looked around for her attacker. "Where did he go?"

"Where did who go?" He swiped the hair away from her face, glancing over his shoulder.

She shoved his chest, tried to stand, but her legs wouldn't cooperate. "Where's Kate?"

"She's with Declan." He looked at her as though she'd gone mad. "I thought you could swim. What the hell happened?"

"There was someone here, holding me under the water. I couldn't see anyone but –"

"There's no one here, Jen."

A bolt of anger landed in her chest. Her gaze flew to his. "I felt it, Archer! I'm not imagining things. There was someone here."

"Jenna . . . the alarm is still activated, the patio doors are locked, and the remaining exit to this room is the one I just came through. There's no one here."

****

Ethan tore into the room, almost dislodging the hinges from the door, and skidded to a halt when he saw his brother kneeling in front of Jenna. Her scream had evoked a level of terror inside him he never knew was there.

"What happened?" he burst out, dropping to his knees beside them. "What's wrong?"

She was shaking, breathless, her eyes wide as she gaped at Archer.

Ethan took her arm. "Hey, are you okay?"

"She said someone tried to drown her."

His head snapped up, his gaze finding his brothers. "How –? The alarm –"

"There was no one here and still armed," Archer grunted,

292

standing up. "I saw her fighting beneath the water but . . . she was alone."

They shared a long, quiet stare as an icy chill crept down Ethan's spine. He scanned the patio outside. "Did you check the doors?"

"There's no one here, Ethan. I saw the whole damn thing."

Jenna muttered something and stood. Her panic had subsided, replaced by irritation. She shot them both a glare. "Then explain what just happened. I'm an excellent swimmer. Someone was here."

Archer didn't comment, but looked at her quietly, his narrowed eyes clouded with worry.

Ethan took her arm, not missing the way she tried to suppress a shiver. Her wet hair clung to her skin and goosebumps had erupted across her flesh. He tucked her against him. "Check all the windows and doors," he said over his shoulder, leading her to the bathroom. "And the alarm too."

"Ethan —"

"Just do it, Archer!" Ethan shut the door behind them, exhaling loudly as he pulled Jenna into his arms. She stiffened and tried to pull away, but he tightened his grip.

"Stop it," she breathed, trying to wiggle loose. "I'm not a damn kid who lost her arm bands."

"I know. But you scared the crap out of me." That seemed to appease her and she relaxed against him, placing her cheek against his chest. He grabbed a nearby towel and covered her, a new kind of worry taking a beat inside his chest.

She'd just been attacked. In their home, without a physical presence. *Shit.*

"I felt it, Ethan," she murmured into his shirt. Her head lifted, her brows furrowed. "There was someone holding me under."

But Archer swore there hadn't been.

"Could this be magical? Hazel?"

Her eyes widened. "But . . . how? Sienna's spelled the house with a new protection spell. No one can get in or out without an invitation. That would extend to any unwanted magic too."

"Hazel's obviously found a way around it." Which left them exposed and in a shitload of danger. Clenching his jaw, he turned on the shower behind him. "Get showered and dressed and we'll check with Sienna."

Her bikini came loose with a small tug, revealing perky breasts and smooth skin.

God.

Without taking his eyes off her, he tossed the skimpy material into the bath. She was naked, not counting the scrap of floss that covered her hips, on display for his eyes only.

That thought tugged at a manly possessiveness he'd only experienced with her. It also wreaked havoc with his libido. His body surged with renewed wanting and he dipped his head to capture her mouth with his. Her breath caught and she opened up to him, tangling her fingers into his hair.

He ravished her, feasting on her as though he'd been starved. And maybe he had been. For so long, his sexual encounters had been so . . . meaningless. Quick, fun, mindless.

But this was different. *She* was different.

He palmed a breast, rolling a nipple between his fingers, grinning at the soft sound she made at the back of her throat. She was so damn beautiful and he couldn't get enough of her. Not when she'd moulded into him like she was meant to be there. A perfect, tight, incredible fit.

But dammit, his timing sucked.

Reluctantly, he pulled away, breathless and wanting and irritated with himself for his dog-assed lack of restraint. She'd just been attacked by some voodoo crap and he couldn't keep his hands off her.

Go figure.

Frowning, he stepped around her, testing the water and reached for her hand. He caught a glimpse of her in the mirror. Feminine and beautiful and so damn sexy. All slender curves and tanned

294

skin, marked with the dark brown tattoo that stretched from her hip upward.

He zoned in on the mark, tilting his head as the steam blurred the image in the mirror. It was longer, more detailed.

He stilled as something blasted through him. Recognition. For a moment, he simply stared, speechless, wondering if he could be wrong.

But he wasn't. Even as the image disappeared completely, he knew what he'd seen. Sure, the mark was prettied up with some fancy patterns and intricate designs but. . .

"Ethan?" His gaze snapped to hers. "Are you okay?"

"Your tattoo," he murmured, moving around her to wipe the mirror. "Look."

She glanced over her shoulder at her reflection. Her eyes narrowed, her brows creasing as she studied the mark. Then she gasped and jerked her gaze back to his.

"That's why we couldn't figure it out," he said, excitement coursing through him. "It's mirror-imaged. It's not just a tattoo. It's a map."

CHAPTER FIFTY

They were trapped.

All dressed and armoured and standing on the porch raring to go and they couldn't get out of the damn house.

"What the hell?" Ethan grumbled, slamming a fist on the invisible wall at the bottom of the steps. He searched the ground and cursed when he spotted the thin white line that trailed along the ground. Frustration and fury boiled inside him. He glanced at his brothers charging down the stairs toward him. "We can't get out. They've used a salt spell."

A spell designed to trap a Keeper. Around their goddamn house.

Declan spread his palms against the barrier. "You gotta be shitting me."

He wished he was. And the timing couldn't have been worse. "This means Sienna's right. Hazel's already here, in Rapid Falls." No doubt, on the estate.

Jenna adjusted her bow and arrow around her shoulders, glancing at the sky. "Ciphering that magic on tonight's full moon."

Declan snorted. "Not if we can stop her."

"How the hell are we going to stop her if we can't leave the house, Declan?"

"You can't," Sienna said from the top step, "but I can."

They all stared at her, the magnitude of her words striking them all. The spell would trap them all inside the house, Kate included, because of her hybrid blood, but Sienna would be free.

"Over my dead body, Sienna," Declan snapped, waving a finger at her, his eyes flashing with irritation. "Uh, uh, witchy. Don't even think about it."

"Declan —"

"You're not going anywhere," Ethan cut in, his tone clipped with anger. "It's too dangerous, Sienna. We're stronger if we're together. All of us."

"She doesn't know that we know where the location is," Kate said. "Or that Ethan and Jenna are home. So why the salt spell?"

"They're watching us," Sienna replied. "Hazel's waited so long for this. There's no way she's taking any chances."

Declan sent Sienna a raised brow. "So what's the witchy worka-round for the spell?"

Sienna lowered her gaze and shook her head. "Only Hazel can —" She gasped as Kate brushed past her and hurried down the stairs, holding up her hands. "Kate, no!"

The moment Kate touched the barrier, her body jerked backward as though she'd been shocked. Jenna was behind her in a heartbeat, gritting her teeth at the charge of electricity.

Cursing, Declan reached for Kate, but she elbowed him away and tried again, feeding her magic into the spell in an attempt to break it. When her body trembled vigorously, Jenna and Declan tugged her away.

"Dammit, Kate," he grumbled, "you're going to hurt yourself!"

"I can do it, Declan!" she snapped, pushing him off her. "I broke the salt spell before, I can do it again!"

"Kate," Sienna said, stepping forward. "This is different. It's Hazel. Last time, it was Megan who cast the spell. She's nowhere near as powerful as Hazel and she's most likely already tapping into some of that magic. If that's the case, breaking her spell won't be easy. Even for you."

The air sizzled with frustration as they stared at each other helplessly. And helpless was a stupid emotion Ethan loathed.

"Wait, what about the tunnel?" Jenna asked, her face brightening. "No one knows about it."

Ethan spun around to stare at her, cracking a wild grin. *Oh, yeah.*

****

Leaving the stuffy tunnel was a relief felt by all.

But it came with a lot of angst too. They were away from the safety of their home, surrounded by dark forests and a ton of danger. The weather was crap, thick clouds covered the sky, patching the near-full moon. It had turned cold and windy, causing the trees to sway in a gentle rhythm.

Ethan was grateful for the darkness. It cloaked their emotions as they walked through the woods in silence, the mood sombre. Tension ruled, knowing what they faced.

Hazel had found the location of the massacre. On the Bennett Estate. *Their home.*

Shit, how could they not have known?

His parents, once Keepers to Sienna's mother and grandmother, had built them each a house on their estate as a way of striking a balance between privacy and protection. Two families, bound by a destiny, love and loyalty. Sienna's home – hell, the entire estate – had become a platform for hundreds of childhood encounters together.

On the site of the damn witch massacre.

But what better way to hide something so valuable and dangerous than in clear sight? Genius.

It didn't take long to find the path that led to her old house. Heaviness enveloped them as they walked. Returning to Sienna's old home, once ravished by the fire that had claimed both their parents, was a weight they all shared.

The path was overgrown, abandoned. They'd all avoided

returning since that night and now, years later, the once well-worn path had almost vanished. The charred remains of the house, the memories of that night, and the heartache that came with it were painful reminders of everything they'd lost.

All at the hands of the Brogan family.

And tonight, several years and dozens of battles later, was a culmination of the war they'd fought for so long. Hazel had found the magic her family had been searching for. The very magic Ethan and his family would do anything to protect.

Thunder rumbled in the distance, the sky marred with frequent flashes of lightning. The closer they got to Sienna's house, the more the air sizzled with energy.

"I can feel her," Sienna muttered, shuddering. She swiped a lock of red hair away from her face. "I've always felt an energy buzz in Rapid Falls, especially here."

Not surprising, their town – her home – was fuelled by the energy of many dead witches. Right under their damn noses. Imagine that.

"At least now we know why," he said.

"But tonight it's different."

Ethan put an arm around her shoulders and gave her a quick squeeze. Although tall, she was small beside him. "Those witches were killed on the land beneath your home, Sienna. Good witches. That counts for something. We simply have to figure out how to use that."

"If Hazel ciphers that magic, Ethan, she'll be evil on steroids. That terrifies me."

"She's still mortal." He gave her an encouraging smile. "And you're a Beckham witch. You can handle her."

He released her and glanced at Jenna. She walked closely beside Kate, a bow and arrow strapped to her back, eyeing her surroundings. Her expression remained unreadable, her hair braided into a single concoction that hung down her back. She'd been quiet since they'd decoded her tattoo earlier. Probably trying to figure out how the hell the map of the massacre location had ended up on her back.

The magic. The map. The damn *Pure* symbols – whatever the hell that meant. They were all connected. Somehow. A thought that had plagued them all since the discovery.

A witch, a hybrid warrior, and a Keeper. Three women that meant far more than loyalty or duty to him and his brothers.

Ethan's gut tightened at the thought, and for a moment, he wished it had stayed just that. *A duty.* But the emotions that rang between them had screwed up everything. Raised the stakes to more than simply preserving the balance of nature and fulfilling a destiny they were born for.

He heard the faint rustling of bushes and the snap of a twig a moment before he heard the soft growl.

Hellhounds. Six of them.

Creatures he'd never seen before, large and vicious. Their eyes were a glow of orange. Their lips upturned, showing sharp teeth and drool. They were all growling softly, bodies poised in stalk mode.

And they stank like hell.

Declan and Archer moved silently beside him, a barrier of brotherhood and duty between the beasts and the women. Ethan heard the quickening of heartbeats around him, the rush of adrenaline and fierceness that came with the overwhelming need to protect. Defend. To get their witch – and women – home safely.

Ethan released a heavy sigh, all too aware of the hostility that emanated from his brothers. "Ready?"

"Hell yes," Declan grunted.

Ethan frowned when Archer grabbed his arm. "Now's not the time for a nobility speech, Archer."

"I wasn't planning on one."

"Good, 'cause tonight . . ." Ethan turned toward the hellhounds, a glowing ember of evil in the darkness, "all gloves are off."

CHAPTER FIFTY ONE

Jenna's stomach clenched as three of the hellhounds sauntered closer, bodies crouched, eyes on their prey. The other three hung back, but kept to the sides, circling them.

They were all growling, a chorus of warning that sent a chill down her spine. They were huge, their viciousness and strength more scary in reality than the ones she'd imagined as a child.

And there were so many of them.

She heard a rush of air as a flame sparked on the ground in front of the three women. It trailed off into a thin line, a barrier between them and the hounds, and formed a protective circle around them. Jenna stepped out before it closed.

"Jenna!" Kate gasped, reaching for her, but reared back when the flames flared.

Without looking back, Jenna shook her head. "If they're anything like the ones we saw the other day, it's not the witches they're after, Kate."

"All the more reason you should've stayed in the circle!"

"Declan, they're –" Jenna's words were trapped in her throat as the hellhounds charged. Jenna dove for the nearest one, kicking and punching in synchronised movements, effortlessly slipping into the training that had saved her so many times.

"Jenna, behind you!" Ethan yelled. He held out his arms and she jumped forward, grabbing his hands. He dug in his heels, using his body as an anchor, the movement giving her the momentum she needed to swing her body around him. As she came full circle, she delivered a powerful kick, slamming her boot into the hellhound's face.

Bone crunched, a satisfying sound, but it lunged for her, snapping its jaws. Archer came up behind it, grabbed the hound around the neck and snapped. Its eyes bulged and it went limp instantly, sagging in Archer's grip.

"Declan," Jenna shouted. "They're afraid of fire!"

"Why the hell didn't you say so?" Declan grunted. Two fireballs sprang to life in his hands. The remaining hellhounds hesitated, the wariness in their eyes fuelling Declan into action. He tossed both fireballs at once, following it up with several more in quick succession, striking them all. Still flaming, they continued to approach, snarling furiously, but their movements were unsteady and slower and it wasn't long before they collapsed. The stench was unbearable.

Panting, the brothers circled, back to back, searching for more threats. The bodies of the smouldering beasts lay scattered around them.

But there was one unaccounted for.

Jenna counted again, whirling around when Sienna's protection circle faded. A hound had crept out from behind a tree and stood in the shadows behind Kate, body poised in attack mode. "NO!" Jenna screamed and started running.

Declan had seen it too and they simultaneously lunged for it. But instead of taking down the hellhound, they crashed into each other. Pain seared through Jenna as her shoulder took the impact of the fall. The hound charged for the witches, spittle flying from its mouth, but veered off track when Ethan slammed into it from the side. He twisted around as they fell and snapped its neck.

The silence was instant, marred only by the sound of the crackling of flames as the fire receded.

Breathless, heart pounding, torn between gratitude and fury, Jenna shoved Declan off her. They rose quickly, glaring at each other. "Dammit, Declan, why'd you do that? You almost got us both killed!"

"Stupid question, Blondie. It was about to attack Kate." He swiped a hand across the shimmer of moisture that covered his forehead.

"I know, I was there, but you got in my way, dammit!"

"More like you got in *my* way."

"And while we were fumbling over each other, the hound had a red carpet directly to Kate! She –" The rest of her sentence vanished as something in the distance behind Declan caught her attention. Her heart leapt as she traced the shadow emerging from the bushes. It was one of Hazel's warlocks and she caught a glimpse of a shiny machete in his hand.

Without missing a beat, she withdrew an arrow from her shoulder pouch, readied her weapon and aimed.

"Jenna, what the hell?" Declan shouted, his jaw dropping as the arrow flew toward him. But it missed his shoulder by inches and slammed into the warlock behind him.

She had the next arrow ready to go as two more warlocks stepped out of the bushes and quickly released another two lethal rounds. The speed at which she moved was exhilarating, a skill that had taken years to master. The men collapsed to the ground with soft groans, their weapons clattering to the ground.

Declan swivelled around to face her, his mouth parted in surprise.

"Next time," she said, slinging her weapon across her shoulders, "let me do my job and protect my witch."

****

They reached the edge of the forest without any more resistance.

Although that would be short-lived, Ethan knew that. The moment Hazel saw them, she'd be onto them like vultures at a kill.

The old Beckham house stood in a clearing in the distance, the backdrop of tall trees behind it. A double-storey house with a pointed roof and a wrap-around porch. Both had been devoured by the flames, leaving behind blackened walls. The garden was messy and overgrown, the grass at knee height. Old, dilapidated, charred ruins – a shadow of what it had once been.

They should've cleared it years ago, but no one had the heart or courage for it. So the house had gone ignored, a permanent reminder of the catastrophe that had claimed their parents. Four people with a vision of living in harmony amongst the ordinary folk.

A dream Ethan, his brothers and Sienna still fought for. A never-ending war.

They moved in silence along the edge of the forest, until the back of the house came into view. A ring of fire surrounded the house, illuminating the walls in a yellow haze. No doubt a protection circle.

"Hazel's smart," Declan muttered beside him, although his tone lacked surprise. They'd expected one.

"So are we," Ethan replied. "Difference is we have the element of surprise on our side. She doesn't know we're here."

Declan snorted. "That witch bitch seems to know all our movements lately, brother. We shouldn't underestimate her."

It wasn't hard to spot Hazel amongst the crowd. She stood in the centre of the circle, Megan, Rick, and John hovering beside her. They were surrounded by a crowd of followers – loyal warlocks and witches with the same vision. Destruction, power, control. A vision that had destroyed Hazel's entire family and so many others.

They were mostly men of different races and ages, but they all wore menacing expressions and clutched a variety of weapons.

They were chanting quietly, a repetitive sound that echoed in the darkness.

Ethan stole a glance at Jenna. She stood beside Kate, watching Hazel and Megan. Her expression remained blank, but her eyes gave her away. Fear. An emotion he hadn't often seen in her. But tonight was different. She'd spent two years with these people, pretending to be like them. Her betrayal had marked her in the eyes of every single enemy that stood before them.

His gut twisted at the thought of anything happening to her and he had to take a few deep breaths to expel the rising panic inside him.

Thunder rumbled above them, followed by flashes of lightning that danced across the sky. Clouds hovered above, a dark grey of gloom that warned of a massive storm.

"The full moon hasn't peaked yet," Sienna said softly, breaking the silence. "Hazel's already harvesting the energy, but she'll only be at her strongest when it does."

"She's in a protection circle," Kate said. "I'm a Null. I should be able to break it, Sienna."

"It's risky. That circle was created by Hazel's magic, fuelled by the power of the dead witches. Absorbing that much energy could kill you."

"Then how will we reach her?"

"Let's start with the warlocks outside the protection circle first and work our way in," Ethan said. "It's a process of elimination."

But Sienna hesitated, her eyes flashing with worry. "She's protected. Reaching her won't be easy."

"We'll figure something out. We have to." He shared a long, quiet look with her, packed with an urgency and emotion that needed no words.

Because they all knew that anything else wasn't an option.

CHAPTER FIFTY TWO

An ear-piercing screech tore through the darkness.

Jenna slapped her hands over her ears and swung around to see her friends replicating the motion. They groaned, gritting their teeth at the overwhelming noise.

And then suddenly, the sound grew muffled as a familiar energy washed over them. Kate. Her brows were furrowed and she wore an agonised expression that matched the others. But there was more. Her eyes blazed with fierce objection.

She'd tapped into her powers, using her magic to create an invisible dome of protection around them. It was shaky, a new skill she'd recently mastered, but enough to lessen the noise and pain, leaving them breathless and fighting the disorientation.

When Hazel realised her banshee screeching had been nullified, she stopped, leaving a stunned silence.

A cold wind blew through the forest, an eerie murmur that sent a shiver down Jenna's spine. The wind gathered force, spreading along the edge of the forest, rustling trees along the way. Ethan and Sienna's magic at work. An elemental connection to air only they shared.

Jenna watched in fascination as the whirlwind gathered momentum around the house. A wailing of earth and air that

306

caused a stir amongst Hazel's people. The circle of fire flared brighter, the flames fighting the harsh wind.

But the chanting continued.

Without missing a beat, Hazel scanned the forest. There was a rumble as the ground began to tremble. It parted with a loud crack, creating a ripple effect of exploding earth that sped toward the trees.

Dust clouded their vision and they backed away, scurrying for cover. When the ground parted, Jenna lunged for Kate and leapt for solid ground.

"Are you okay?" Jenna panted, glancing at her.

She nodded, but pointed at the sand. "Look!"

Dozens of snakes and scorpions surrounded them, their bodies almost invisible in the dark grit. But they were lifeless.

"What the hell?" Jenna gasped, tugging Kate behind her. "Watch your footing! They're everywhere!"

Ethan nudged a snake with his boot, easily turning it over. "It's dead." He tested another, glancing around them. "They're all dead."

"This creepy bitch is really pissing me off," Declan grumbled, stepping forward, dodging the creatures.

Hazel's chanting grew louder and faster. Rick barked out orders. Fierce war cries broke out as the men readied their weapons and started running.

Jenna hauled out an arrow from the pouch on her back. She took aim and released it, swiftly reaching for another. Within moments, she'd injured several men. Their screams of rage and pain went ignored as others pressed forward, keeping their heads low, fighting the wind beating down on them.

But they were fast and determined and so damn fierce. They kept coming.

Ethan and Sienna increased the torment, adding more power. Declan joined in. Lashes of fire whipped across the sky, striking warlocks along the way. The whirlwind turned faster, harder, the motion scooping up two men along the way. The others kept running, shouting and waving their weapons. They plundered forward, dodging the unsteady ground and fire. Lightning flashed, a buzz of electricity that sparked around them.

And then they were upon them, roaring as they lashed out with their weapons. They broke out in a vicious battle, a brutal hand-to-hand combat charged with hatred and desperation.

Jenna heard a whoosh of air and jerked around, staring in horror as an axe hurtled past her, missing her by inches.

And slammed into Ethan's shoulder.

"ETHAN!" she screamed, horror clutching her insides, but ducked as another axe soared through the air.

A warlock charged her and she aimed a low, lethal kick that connected with his knees. He dropped instantly and she backed it up with a punch. Another warlock came from behind and she ducked his swing but took a blow to the jaw when she whirled around.

Pain exploded through her and she staggered backward. Archer leapt above them, colliding with the warlock and took him down with a single strike. Jenna hurried toward Ethan, her movements shaky from the trembling ground. She reached him as he tugged out the axe, cursing loudly. Blood spurted from the wound. She glanced around them, relieved to see they'd taken down several of Hazel's warlocks. The others had retreated to the safety of her circle.

"I'm fine," Ethan grunted, but when she reached for him, he didn't pull away. This was a fight they couldn't win if injured or weak and he knew that. She placed her hand on his shoulder, grimacing at the gushing blood. Forcing herself to breathe, she exuded energy as her heart pounded with a fear she'd never known before. The wound was deep, making her more grateful than ever for her ability to heal instantly.

He exhaled loudly and took her hand, giving her a brief nod.

Her throat thick with emotion, she stood and offered a hand, pulling him up.

308

The crack of thunder startled her. It was followed by a loud hissing sound as the snakes and scorpions reared to life. They shifted into attack mode instantly, slithering and scurrying along the ground, striking at everything in sight.

"Sienna!" Archer yelled, scooping Sienna out of the way as a snake went for her.

"They were dead!" Kate gasped, edging backward.

"They must've been dormant," Sienna called out. "Most likely a nifty black magic trick. Probably used for guarding perimeters. Get back!" She held out her hands. Flames flared and swept across the ground, scorching everything it touched.

When it grew quiet, Sienna withdrew the fire and scanned the carnage. The bodies of dead warlocks and creatures surrounded them, a smoking, mangled mess. She frowned at her Keepers' bloody appearance. Her attention turned to Hazel, still chanting in the distance, her warlocks around her. "She's untouchable. There's no point to all this. All this fighting will only weaken us."

"We have no other choice, Sienna," Ethan said. His shirt was blood-soaked. He pointed toward the injured warlocks that had retreated to the circle. "They won't let us near Hazel and we have no idea when her army of supernatural beefcakes from Ameera will arrive. The more we eliminate now, the less we have to deal with later."

"Which helps shit if we can't get to Hazel, brother," Declan grumbled. "We can pick off her minions of evil all we like, but if we can't stop her channelling that magic, we're screwed."

"So we'll improvise," Sienna said quietly, something in her tone sparking Jenna's interest.

"Sienna?" Jenna prompted, her heart picking up speed.

"When the moon peaks, she'll be channelling more energy than ever. Until then, she's vulnerable," Sienna said, her voice packed with a sudden urgency and excitement. Her gaze flickered between Kate and Jenna. "There's a reason Rose chose to sacrifice herself for me. And there's a reason you're both here, with me. A hybrid

Null and a Salubrious. I have no idea what *The Pure* means, but somehow that symbol links us. Maybe . . ." she turned her attention back to Hazel, her expression thoughtful. "Maybe this is why."

"Sienna?" Ethan asked, moving around her, his brows narrowed as he studied his witch. "You have a plan."

There was no question, because Sienna radiated one. Her eyes gleamed and her body bristled with restless energy.

"Between us, we have so much magic," she continued. "Combined, we're a lethal force."

"Cut the witch-speak and get to the point, Sienna," Declan interrupted, never one for beating around the bush. "If you have an idea, spit it out."

"I'm thinking, Declan!"

"Well, think a little faster, witchy. Before we're all toast."

She rolled her eyes at him and faced the house. "There's only so much magic one witch can manage until she overloads."

They all waited for her to elaborate.

Jenna gasped as the meaning of her words fell into place. And then she grinned. "Even Hazel?"

She nodded again, a small smile breaking free. "Even Hazel."

CHAPTER FIFTY THREE

They withdrew into the forest, using the darkness as a shield, and thrashed out a plan.

They all paced restlessly, itching to move in, but knew that without one they stood no chance.

Ethan glanced at his brothers, sharing a long, quiet look with them that needed no words. So much fear and emotion. But they had no choice.

Jenna took Sienna and Kate's hands. "We can do this. I'll be here for you both when you weaken."

"We won't have long to pull this off," Sienna said. "The moment she realises what we're trying to do, she'll go crazy."

"She'll still be vulnerable. Let's go." Jenna moved forward, but paused when Ethan touched her wrist.

"Jen." Dammit, he hated the gritty, desperate sound to his voice. But didn't bother covering it up. Now wasn't the time for some macho crap anyway. He pulled her to him, his body beating with tension. Her eyes were a mixture of worry and determination and she had a smear of dirt on her cheek. But she was so damn beautiful.

His woman.

He glanced at Sienna, the witch he'd devoted his life to. For a moment, all he could do was stare at them, caught between the urge to hold them and let them go.

Jenna leaned in and pressed her lips to his in a soft, sweet kiss that tugged at something inside him. He closed his eyes and inhaled her. "We can do this," she whispered against his lips.

He nodded before withdrawing, despite the caveman instincts demanding he take her home. Both women were powerful in different ways. They could take care of themselves.

But dammit, it still stung like a bitch to watch them walk away. Without looking back, they headed into the clearing around the house. Ethan and his brothers spread out, even though every instinct he possessed told him not to.

But Sienna had a plan. One that might just work. So he forced the nagging voice of caution to the back of his mind and walked away.

He took shelter against a tree and waited for his brothers to move around the house. They stayed in the shadows at the edge of the forest, keeping hidden. When they were all in place, the women upped their pace.

It was then that Ethan lost the ability to breathe.

It was so quiet, the edge of the forest a yellow haze from the flaming protection circle that safeguarded Hazel.

Their plan had to work or Declan was right – they were toast.

Jenna had her bow and arrow ready, the warrior in her on full alert as she walked beside the two witches. Hell, they were all warriors. All three women. Despite the dangers and their fears and knowing they might not survive tonight, they were here, willing to fight to protect everything they were born to defend.

It was admirable. And no one but them knew it. In a world where they lived in secrecy, their friends had no idea what they faced in their quest to maintain the balance of nature.

The rumble of thunder echoed across the sky. He felt the vibrations beneath his feet, a steady drum of warning that the energy field around him was intensifying. An eerie whisper broke out, an agitated murmur of voices, and Ethan wondered if they belonged to the slaughtered witches buried here.

Sienna began chanting.

When Rick spotted the women, his snapped orders triggered the stampede of three warlocks. But between Declan's fireball and Jenna's arrow, they stood no chance.

The wind increased its pace, creating whirlwinds of sand. Lightning struck, a sizzle of flashes around the house. The clouds grew darker, rain inevitable.

Hazel's chanting grew louder. Her gaze fell on the three approaching women, surprise crossing her expression when she found them alone. Still chanting, she scanned the forest in search of the Keepers.

Of course she'd expect an ambush, a plan. The witch wasn't stupid and knew the resistance she faced. She stopped chanting, but the others continued. A repetitive drone of voices that filled the air.

She held out her hands, the light of the fire catching both bracelets on her arms, and whispered a spell. Within moments, a swirl of lights signalled the opening of a portal. She pointed at Megan. "Go," she ordered. "Find Axel."

"I thought you weren't going to –"

"We may have no choice. Tell him it's time. And hurry!"

A portal to Ameera.

The dark caster was worried. Damn right. But she'd roped in reinforcements. Big, scary-assed, feeding, scavenging reinforcements.

Ethan shifted, growing edgier. He searched for his brothers, each backed up against a tree on opposite sides of the clearing. They were well hidden in the darkness and he could barely make out their shapes. But he knew they were there.

The thought comforted him, as their presence always did, but it brought a lot of angst too. He'd already lost a sibling. Losing another. . .

An energy rush like he'd never experienced before blasted

313

through him. One that had nothing to do with the thought of losing a brother. He inhaled deeply, suddenly uncomfortable with the sheer magnitude of power rolling through him. He glanced at the women, sensing they'd felt it too. They were moving faster, with more urgency, and Sienna's chanting had upped a pace in speed and volume.

Jenna moved between Sienna and Kate, taking their hands, and together they faced the fray.

Thunder cracked above. Everyone jumped, even Hazel. But she remained unperturbed at the sight of the women and continued to channel the magic that was almost hers.

Sienna glared at her, clutching Jenna's hand, her voice mingling with the eerie whispers around them – now a loud murmur of angry voices.

No doubt the dead witches objecting to the ritual.

The women reached the edge of the protection circle and Sienna released Jenna's hand. While the mayhem continued, Kate towered over the invisible barrier.

And drew on her magic.

Within moments, she began to tremble as her body fought the dark magic. She fell to her knees, crying out. Jenna wrapped her arms around her, fuelling Kate's strength with her own.

"NOW!" Sienna screamed, throwing up her arms.

Ethan grunted as the magic stormed through him, that connection of energy he shared with her. And only her. His brothers would feel it too as she drew on them all, that magical bond that bound them to her.

And together, the power of their combined energy was a force like no other.

It swirled through him, an energy blast he'd only ever felt once before. The night his sister had died and Sienna had tapped into their powers after weakening hers. But this time, instead of fighting it, he let go. He gave in to her, feeding her magic with his.

It began to rain. Flames flared. The ground quivered. The house rattled furiously. Windows shattered. Lightning flashed, striking everything it touched. The angry whispers continued, faster and noisier. The clash of energy, along with the storm, culminated in a terrifying force that threatened to explode around them.

Sienna in all her magical glory. Hazel in all of hers.

"The protection spell's weakening!" Kate cried out as Ethan and his brothers walked closer. They were bristling with a fierce protectiveness that matched his. "I can feel her! I can feel Hazel!"

Kate sagged to the ground, leaning into her Keeper. Jenna tightened her arms around her, shouting her name. They were both pale and breathless, a sign they were weakening at a rapid rate.

Trembling violently, Sienna held up her hands in the direction of Hazel. An explosion ripped through the house behind the witch, splintering doors and shattering glass. So much power, anger, and a fierce fortitude to win the struggle between right and wrong. A combination of magic – *their magic* – that was lethal when channelled all at once.

And Sienna channelled it all toward Hazel.

There's only so much magic one witch can manage until she overloads.

Sienna's words ringing in his mind, Ethan saw the moment it reached Hazel. Her body jerked, her head hung back, arms outstretched. She looked like someone about to be sacrificed. She screamed and fell to her knees as the energy engulfed her.

Sienna, Kate, and Jenna joined hands, gritting their teeth, and continued their torment. They staggered, their bodies straining from the force of magic.

Sensing their distress, Ethan and his brothers closed in around them, ready to protect the three women and annihilate anyone who harmed them. They had no control over their magic. Sienna owned them all, but they gave to her freely, feeding her, strengthening her.

They shared the same goal. To weaken Hazel. And they were.

The witch released a long, furious wail, overwhelmed by the

315

flood of magic belonging to the dozens of dead witches – and the six people who fought to stop her.

A witch and a hybrid warrior – both on the brink of collapse from the exertion of energy – fuelled and strengthened by a Keeper's healing magic. Surrounded, *protected*, by him and his brothers.

Fighting the darkness that threatened them all.

Ethan jerked as recognition landed in his gut with a punch like no other. A *fire* witch, a warrior, and a Keeper.

The Scroll.

****

Rick and John rallied around Hazel, shouting orders at the men.

Jenna screamed a warning as they charged. A fresh spurt of adrenaline overrode the weakness she'd felt after helping Sienna and Kate. She staggered to her feet, stepping in front of them.

The four Keepers sprang into action, side by side, a barricade of anger and unyielding determination as they fought to protect their witches.

But even though they were stronger, they were heavily outnumbered.

Black smoke rose up around them, clouding the fight as the warlocks surrounded them. Rick and John joined the brawl, their strength and speed a challenge the others lacked. They were scavengers and had spent years feeding off the magic of others. A vicious desperation fuelled the battle.

Shouts rang out, mingling with the creepy voices of the dead witches. The air had turned icy, the wind and rain relentless.

Hazel was on her hands and knees, glaring at them, her tattooed teeth bared in a terrifying snarl. She was drenched. Her hair and clothes clung to her. Her expression had twisted in agony from the overwhelming energy flushing through her.

But she refused to surrender.

When John leapt through the air toward Kate, Jenna was there in lightning speed. They erupted into a rapid fight, martial arts in all its glory. But her vision spotted when he elbowed her in the face. Fighting the disorientation, she staggered, grunting. John spat out blood, grinning, but reeled around as Kate pounced. She dropped low, delivering a hard kick to his knee.

"You bitch!" he yelled as he collapsed, clutching his leg – the same one Ethan had speared back in Ameera.

Declan's roar of rage had Jenna pivoting around. He staggered and fell to his knees. Rick stood behind him, a spear clutched in his hand, the blade embedded deep in Declan's back. The warlock swung around as Ethan charged him.

"Declan!" Kate screamed, struggling to her feet. But she was weak and stumbled into Jenna.

Jenna grasped her witch with both hands and together they hurried toward Declan. "Twice in one night I've had to save your ass, Declan," she grumbled, tugging out the spear and healing him. "It's about time you pulled your weight!"

"Shut up, Blondie."

She helped him up, searching for Ethan and Archer. Her eyes burned from the black smoke, her vision foggy, but she was able to track them. They fought with such strength and speed, but were exhausted and outnumbered.

Breathless, she forced down the rising panic as their enemies closed in. NO! Her gaze found Hazel, the woman behind the torture.

It all ended with her.

"Stay with Sienna and Declan!" she told Kate as an idea came to mind. "Ethan! Archer!" Without looking back, she raced through the carnage, dodging their enemies. As the two brothers fought their way toward her, Jenna hurtled over Rick and crashed into Hazel.

"Get the hell off me!" Hazel screamed, pounding Jenna with her fists.

317

"The witches who died were good witches!" Jenna shouted. She twisted around, using her body weight to pin Hazel, and grabbed her wrists. "I will die before I let you steal their legacy."

"And I will die before I let you stop me!"

An invisible force slammed into Jenna's chest, launching her backward. Hazel stood, arms beside her thighs, her hands curled. She released an eerie laugh, one that held more crazy than humour, but it was cut short when Jenna unclenched her fingers.

Hazel's jaw unhinged when she saw the bracelet in Jenna's hand and she quickly searched her wrist, crying out when she couldn't find it.

"Sienna!" Jenna shouted, tossing her the bracelet. "The portal!"

Hazel went mad.

"No!" she screeched, picking up a discarded knife beside her. Straightening, she threw it at Sienna.

"SIENNA!" Jenna screamed as Archer dove in front of her, fielding the attack.

Hazel clapped her hands together and the ground exploded. Sand erupted; the house tore apart, a frightening rumble of absolute destruction.

Ethan came up behind Jenna, Archer staggering after him. Panting, their gazes met briefly before they glanced at the portal.

As a new plan unfolded, they turned toward Hazel. Together, they charged, crashing into her in one synchronised movement.

And catapulted through the portal.

CHAPTER FIFTY FOUR

Ethan grunted as they burst through the portal and skidded across the sand.

They were in the overgrown amusement park, the roller coaster looming behind them. Thank God Hazel had moved the opening to ground level.

Hazel scrambled away and he lunged for her, grabbing her ankle. The witch's frantic kick was accompanied by a mind blast like no other. Groaning, Ethan released her and clutched his head, vaguely aware of Archer mimicking his movements behind him.

Fighting the pain, he staggered after her, but the snap of his name stopped him.

"Ethan, your brother!" Jenna yelled.

The mind blast eased and Ethan glanced over his shoulder, his vision blurry from the pain. But he saw the horror splashed across her face and knew that something was wrong. And then he saw Archer's face. Twisted in pain, gasping air.

Ethan searched his brother for injuries and scanned for Hazel, not surprised to see her hurrying away. His instinct was to chase after her, stop her. *End this.* Everything they'd fought so hard and long for. It would all be over. Absorbing the energy of all the dead witches, along with theirs, had exhausted her and she'd been separated from her people. Now might be his only chance.

He was about to follow, charged with an adrenaline rush and rage that urged him forward, but he hesitated and glanced back at Archer, divided in a way he loathed. *One chance.*

Archer collapsed, clutching his chest.

Jenna was beside him in an instant. "You're hurt! There's so much blood! Ethan!"

Dammit. He gave a growl of frustration and raced back to his brother.

He slung an arm around Archer and hoisted him upward, leading him behind an old shed. It was dark, the only light from the full moon, and so damn cold. He placed Archer on the ground, panic sweeping through him when he heard his brother's wheezing. Blood soaked his shirt, the smell filling Ethan's nostrils in a way that made him cringe.

"Oh no," Jenna gasped, gaping at the knife lodged in Archer's chest.

Ethan's entire universe shifted at the sight of the blade embedded in his brother's flesh. Way too fucking close to his heart – lethal to a Keeper. Ethan's ability to breathe had disappeared as he pulled out the knife. It released with a sickly, sucking sound. He tossed the weapon aside and grabbed his brother's head between his hands. "Don't you dare do this, Archer. Don't you dare!"

"Dammit, that bitch stabbed me . . ." Archer muttered, but the words came out as a grunt. He spat out blood and took Ethan's arm.

"Stay still," Jenna said, kneeling beside them. She spread her hands over the wound, blood pooling around her fingers. Archer coughed, gasping air, spitting out blood. She lifted her head to meet Ethan's gaze and he hated the panic he saw in her eyes. "It's not working!"

"What the hell? Heal him, dammit!"

"I'm trying!"

Her movements grew more frantic and she jerked Archer's shoulders, crying out when her second attempt to heal him made no difference.

"*Jen*," Ethan choked, that single word a pathetic plea of desperation. He leaned over his brother, dipping his head so they were on eye-level. "Archer, don't you leave us, brother. Sienna's waiting for you –"

Archer caught his wrist with one hand. "Tell her . . ." he wheezed. "Tell her I love her."

"You tell her yourself, damn you."

"Why can't I heal him?" Jenna cried, her voice tinged with panic. "We're losing him, Ethan. Oh, my God."

Archer stilled. His eyes widened, his expression twisted in agony. But it was the fear in his eyes that struck Ethan. Raw terror. The kind that came when faced with death.

"NO!" Ethan shouted, a bolt of hot denial landing in his gut. "Why can't I heal him? Oh, my God. Archer!"

Ethan felt for a pulse, a roar of rage erupting from him when he found none. *No, no, no.* He grabbed his brother's shoulders, shaking him. He pressed his fists onto Archer's chest, locked his fingers together, and pumped.

"ARCHER!" Jenna cried when he simply stared at them. She scrambled around him, cradling his head, and released a soft wail that sounded nothing like her.

Ethan kept pumping, muttering to his brother, willing life back into him. And then he froze, his heart pounding, devastation and denial competing inside him. Because somewhere between that he knew it was over. Too late. Too goddamn late.

He could see it in his brother's vacant eyes and blank expression. Archer lay slumped against Jenna, his head limp. No! NO!

He gasped air and buckled over, as though he'd taken a punch to the gut. He grunted, unable to breath. His vision blurred and he grabbed his brother's hand, but it was ice-cold and slippery from the blood.

He released Archer's hand as though it had scalded him and looked at his own, his fingers dripping with blood. His brother's blood.

It took every ounce of strength he had to stifle the loud roar of fury that bubbled inside him; one so powerful and brutal that it felt like it would rip him apart, tearing everything on the way out.

"I'm so sorry, brother," he whispered. "I'm so goddamn sorry."

He ran his trembling fingers over his brother's face, closing his eyes, and turned away. Cursing softly, he paced, gasping air, anything to calm the rage and pain. He wiped his bloody hands on his jeans and squeezed his eyes shut to block out the image of his brother's lifeless body sprawled against the side of an abandoned shed.

Archer. *Oh shit. Oh shit. Oh shit.*

Ethan lifted his head when he heard movement nearby, his senses snapping forward. It was easier to deal with a physical threat than the shitstorm of emotions about to erupt inside him. So he went with that and stood, keeping to the shadows of the shed, and peered around it.

A crowd of people had gathered around Hazel, men and women he recognised from the warehouse a few days ago. The night they'd slain two Keepers and scavenged their powers. And now, another Keeper had been slain at the hands of their enemies.

His brother.

He clenched his fists, biting back the wave of rage, vaguely aware of Jenna peering over his shoulder.

Axel shoved Megan to her knees in front of them and glared at Hazel. "We had a fucking deal, Hazel."

Hazel's tattooed features twisted in anger. She waved a fist at him. "The Bennetts and their stupid witch just attacked. Where the hell were you?"

"Waiting for your word, which never came. What game are you playing, witch?"

She pinned Megan with a lethal stare. "Megan was sent to summon you through the portal."

"Pity she was so damn tight-lipped with the location."

Hazel stomped forward, crouching in front of Megan. The younger witch kept her head high, despite her trembling. Hazel stared at her for a long moment before slapping her. Hard. "You betrayed me. Like that damn Keeper bitch? How could you?"

Megan swiped a hand across her face, smearing the blood. "I'm all for your cause, Hazel, but you've gone too far."

"So you left us there to die? Are you insane?"

"You've made it clear that nothing matters besides getting your magical fix. Nothing. Screw the rest of the world. You're a danger to everyone around you, us included."

"You're right," Hazel hissed, rising. "Nothing else . . . *matters*." A quick nod to Axel had him sliding an arm around Megan's shoulders. With a loud grunt, he snapped her neck.

"NO!" Jenna cried, her words muffled when Ethan shoved a hand over her mouth.

"Where's the portal, Hazel?" Axel shouted.

"It's still open, but Jenna and her Bennett friends are here," Hazel called out. "Sienna won't close it until they're safe. Find them! They're our leverage for getting my bracelet back and regaining control of the portal. Find them and bring them to me! Let's end this!"

Her words triggered an eruption of cheers, along with a shuffle of movement as they all spread out.

Fresh fear gripped Ethan as he searched for the portal, their way home. He ducked as something flew past his head on a whoosh of air. An arrow slammed into the wall of the shed. A moment later, dozens more followed, striking at their enemies.

Shouts rang out as the men and women scattered for cover. Another batch of arrows took flight, raining down on them.

"Jen, we have to go," Ethan said, a fresh spurt of adrenaline flushing his veins. He looked over his shoulder, trying to track the archers, but they were concealed within the shadows of the trees. "Jenna!"

She shook her head, looking at Archer. "We can't leave him. Sienna –"

"We gotta go!" He took Jenna's hand, glancing at the portal, a swirl of lights in the distance. It wouldn't take long to reach it, but even at a full run they'd be exposed to Hazel, her people and the arrows. He turned back to his brother. Everything inside him clenched at the idea of leaving him here, but they had no choice. They were outnumbered and in danger. And Sienna needed to close the damn portal.

More arrows. More shouts.

Not stopping to consider how much he'd regret this later, he tugged off his jacket and covered his brother's head and shoulders. "I'm so sorry, brother. I'm so damn sorry." His voice cracked and he hurriedly turned away. Biting back the stab of pain, he took Jenna's hand. "We have to run for the portal."

"We can't leave Archer –"

"He's gone, Jen. We can't help him. He died protecting his witch. We owe it to him to do the same and if we don't leave now –" He froze as a cloaked figure stepped behind Jenna. The face was hidden, but the person's presence jarred the protective surge inside him.

"I mean you no harm," the figure said quickly. The voice belonged to a woman.

"Ethan!" Jenna gasped and went slack against him.

His arms came up around her and he turned, taking her with him, shielding her body with his own. He glanced over his shoulder at the stranger. "Who the hell are you?"

"*Catherine*," Jenna croaked. "Her name's Catherine. She's my mother."

CHAPTER FIFTY FIVE

A whirlwind of emotions flooded Jenna, shock being the front-runner.

"Mom?" she muttered, her voice sounding childlike. Her breath felt trapped in her lungs and her body shivered as though she'd been doused in icy water. When Ethan held her against him, she let him, needing him to ground her because . . . *shit*. She felt the slight tremble in his hold, even though his tight expression masked the grief and anger she saw in his eyes.

"Get to the portal!" Hazel screamed. Her people began running, a stampede of aggression that scattered when another round of arrows soared toward them.

"You have to get to the portal before she does," Catherine said breathlessly, shoving back the hoodie. She wore her blond hair braided, like she always had, but the years in Ameera had aged her. Her eyes gleamed with a combination of joy and worry. She adjusted the bow and arrow on her back and glanced over her shoulder before taking Jenna's hand and pulling her into the shadows beside the shed. "We'll hold them off as long as we can."

"Is it really you?" Jenna asked, her voice cracking.

Catherine hesitated, her gaze flickering between their enemies and her daughter. With a soft sigh, she tugged Jenna into her arms. But she pulled away quickly, her fleeting smile triggering so many memories Jenna had clung to. "My dear child . . ." she said in a shaky voice, stroking Jenna's hair. "You're so beautiful, so strong, everything I imagined all these years. How I've longed to see you again."

Jenna swallowed repeatedly, unable to dislodge the lump in her throat. Her vision blurred and she blinked. "I didn't think we ever would. Where's Dad?" Catherine's smile faded, her mouth tightened, and she shook her head. Jenna swallowed the sob, biting back the tears. "You've been alone all this time?"

Catherine nodded toward the trees behind her. "I have them."

"I'm assuming they mean us no harm?" Ethan asked, glancing at the trees.

Catherine's gaze shifted to Ethan. "No. They're with me. All of them." She glanced at Archer. "I'm so sorry for your loss."

Ethan didn't comment, but Jenna heard his soft intake of air, the rapid increase of his heartbeat. And knew he was employing every ounce of strength he had to keep it together. He gave a brief nod before turning away. "Our witches are weak. We have to get back so they can close the portal."

"My people will ensure your safe passage." As if they'd heard her, they released another round of arrows, fending off Hazel and her people. "You should go. We can't hold them back for much longer."

Jenna's heart skipped a beat. "You're coming with me?" But she already knew. She could see it on her mother's face.

"This is my home, Jenna."

"You will die here!"

"My purpose here is incomplete." She glanced at her people, emerging from the trees behind them. Dozens of cloaked figures, shadows in the moonlight, clutching bows and arrows, their focus on Hazel and her army. "We fight for the good of Ameera, for the people like Megan caught up in the evil. I can't leave now. They need me."

326

"Then I'll stay!" Jenna loathed the childlike cry to her voice, but her heart felt as though it would shatter all over again. And this time, she wasn't sure if she'd ever recover. But even as she said the words, she knew they held no weight.

Because *her* purpose in the mortal world was incomplete.

And she had Kate . . . and Ethan.

"You have to go home, Jen." Catherine glanced at Ethan and the lifeless body of Archer behind them. "They'll need you now more than ever."

"Mom —" she cried, but her words were lost as the discarded arrows rattled on the ground. They softened, altering their shape, taking on a new life form. A product of Hazel's magic Jenna instantly recognised. She'd seen it the night she'd saved Kate in the cemetery.

The arrows shifted into large black birds, screeching furiously as they transformed.

"GO!" Catherine shouted. She handed Jenna a few arrows and readied her weapon with a fresh one. "We'll hold them back. Get to the portal!"

Dodging the screeching birds that took flight around them, they kept to the outskirts of the clearing, out of the aim of the arrows, and raced for the portal. It was a shimmer of blue in the darkness, a hint of home and safety. A reprieve from the madness of Hazel, Ameera, and so much violence.

When they skidded to a stop nearby, Jenna's arrows were depleted. She ducked as a bird dove for her, squawking loudly, and swung around, hitting it with her bow.

Catherine took her arm, her face a mixture of love and worry. "Listen to me," she panted. "We all have a purpose. I've found mine. You're finding yours. It's our duty, our destiny."

"I can't leave you here, Mom."

"You have to close that portal."

"If we do, I might never see you again!"

"I'll find a way back to you, Jen. I promise." Catherine tightened her grip, ducking them both to dodge another bird. "If not in this lifetime then the next, but I'll find you." She cupped Jenna's face in her hands. "I love you more than anything else in this world. I fight for you and others like you. Pure and precious and meant for so much more than this. Your duty is in the mortal world. Not here."

"No –"

"If Hazel's trapped here, my people will need me more than ever. I built this army, I have to protect them."

Jenna glanced over her shoulder at the faceless men and women delivering one arrow after the next in the distance. Her mother's friends, strangers who'd rallied together to protect them – and the balance of nature.

A purpose. *Their* purpose.

Even here in Ameera.

And Catherine was their leader, a warrior woman in her own right. A Keeper, a Salubrious. Her mother.

Jenna's sob rang out as she realised the depth of the woman in front of her. Her eyes held so much sorrow and pain, like they had all those years ago, and beneath it all was a strength that Jenna recognised.

Because she'd seen it in herself all too often.

"Jenna, we have to go!" Ethan said, backing up against her as Hazel's army raced toward them, dodging arrows and birds. But sensing the battle shifting against them had made them fearless and they fought their way forward.

Catherine turned to Ethan. "I'll make sure your brother gets the burial he deserves."

"And I'll take care of your daughter."

"That's all I ask."

"There's a woman who helped us. Her name is Susan –"

"We'll protect her." They shared a brief look, an ocean of understanding between them. She gave Jenna a final hug and pulled away. "I love you. Be safe."

Jenna swallowed another cry as Ethan took her hand. "My mother, Archer . . ." she choked as he pulled her into the protective curve of his arm. "We can't leave them here."

"I know." His voice was gruff with a sorrow that matched hers. "I know we can't leave them, Jen."

But they both knew they would. Anything else meant they'd never see home again and Hazel and her people would be unleashed on the mortal world. They were destined to protect two powerful witches. Together, they protected the innocent people in the mortal world. And of course, the balance between good and evil.

They were warriors. Broken, bruised.

But not defeated.

Jenna watched her mother hurry away without looking back, her bow and arrow raised as she joined her people. Drawing on every ounce of strength she possessed, Jenna laced her fingers with Ethan's and turned toward the portal.

As they stepped into the blue light, the tears came.

And this time, she let them.

CHAPTER FIFTY SIX

THREE DAYS LATER
BENNETT ESTATE

Jenna needed air.

A respite from the sadness that had crept into every corner of the house. The kind that hurt and crippled beyond repair.

They'd closed the portal, trapping Hazel and her people. But the victory had come with a mammoth loss. A brother, a lover, a friend.

Archer.

She'd lost her parents. And Megan, a woman caught up in Hazel's madness. But in the end, the goodness Jenna's parents had seen in her had prevailed and she'd risked her life to make things right.

So much grief and loss and Jenna wondered if they'd ever be whole again. The tears had ceased, leaving behind bewildered shells of the people she'd grown to love, lost in a sea of emotion and grief. She shared their pain and loathed the constant ache in her heart that had become a permanent companion.

But at least Jenna knew her mother was alive and where she wanted to be. It gave her hope. Closure. But the reality of Archer's death had plunged them into the deepest, darkest hole of despair. Absolute destruction.

An agony no one should ever have to endure.

Would time really mend this? They'd recovered – and only just – from Sarah's death. Could they survive another?

Sienna placed the mug onto the kitchen counter with a sigh and ran her hands through her hair. Her eyes were swollen, her face pale. She stood, her movements unsteady, and waved Ethan away.

"You haven't slept for days, Sienna," Ethan said. "You should rest."

"That's the last thing I need." Her words were lined with a venom they seldom heard from her.

"Sienna –"

Several lights bulbs suddenly exploded.

"I don't need rest!" she cried, clenching her fists against her chest. Pain and rage twisted her features. Gone was the tearful, grieving woman who had said so little in the wake of Archer's death. She swiped her arm across the counter, smashing the mugs onto the floor. "I don't want tea or any damn thing I've been offered since Archer died! I want him. Not rest. ARCHER!"

And then she screamed. A long, distraught wail that echoed through the house, sending chills down Jenna's spine. Tears poured down her face and she crouched, clutching her stomach, crying Archer's name over and over.

A single name that resembled her entire existence. Gone in a blink of an eye, ripping her apart in ways that could never be healed.

The walls rattled, a soft, insistent sound that hinted of trouble.

"Sienna," Ethan warned, coming closer. His anguished expression tore at Jenna. "Stop. Ssh, it'll be okay."

"It won't be *okay*, Ethan. He's gone and I'll never get to tell him how sorry I am for the way things ended between us."

"Sienna –"

"He was consumed by so much rage that it frightened me. *He* frightened *me*." The words came out in choked horror, sparking a fresh flood of tears. "And I loathe myself for admitting it because he'd be devastated to know!"

"Because he loved you, Sienna. So much that he died to protect you. We were all under tremendous stress, maybe more so for him because he's the oldest and took it upon himself decades ago to be the damn patriarch of this family." His voice cracked and he paused, clearing his throat. "But he loved you to the end."

Shaking violently, she buried her face in her hands and sobbed.

Ethan put his arms around her. "No one will ever replace him, but I'm here, Sienna. Declan's here. We'll get through this. I promise."

She sank against him and they went to their knees, clinging to each other, tears flowing without shame. Ethan held onto her as she cried, a fierce frown creasing his brows, his eyes closed. Declan knelt beside them, wrapping his arms around them both, and buried his face in Sienna's hair.

And whilst Jenna watched their sorrow, there was only one thought that kept playing in her mind.

She hadn't saved Archer.

****

Jenna closed the door to the attic and leaned against it, forcing a few deep, calming breaths into her lungs.

"You okay?" Kate asked from the desk at the far end of the room. She swiped away a curl that had escaped from the messy knot on top of her head.

"Watching them grieve for Archer is gonna kill me."

Kate grimaced. "I know. That's why I've spent the day up here."

Jenna raised her arms, holding up a bottle of wine and two glasses. "Is it too early for this?"

"Never."

The reply sparked a smile. Jenna pushed herself forward and

went to her, glancing at the desk. Notebooks, colourful pens, an iPad, and a Grimoire covered the table. Pouring the wine, Jenna took a seat opposite her. "Did you get a chance to read my notes?"

"Where's Declan?"

"With Sienna, why?"

"He sees us with this and he'll pop a vein." Kate nodded at the notebooks before sipping her wine.

"So don't tell him."

"You're questioning his brother, Jenna –"

"He doesn't have to know." Jenna held up the book, scribbled with dozens of notes she'd made in the wake of Archer's death.

Because something didn't add up.

Jenna raised a brow at Kate. "So you gonna help me figure this out?"

"Yes. Maybe." But Kate still looked doubtful.

"Come on, Kate, something's wrong. Look at my notes, dammit." She jabbed a finger at the book. "How the hell did Hazel know all our movements? How did they gain access to our house? How did they steal the Grimoire? The guys think she somehow broke through Sienna's spell, but that's bullshit. She's a damn Beckham witch."

"And Hazel's a dark caster, Jen. She –"

"Couldn't break the veiling spell on the Brogan Grimoire in Ameera!" Jenna cried. "And why? Because it's spelled by a Beckham witch. I saw her, Kate. She couldn't do it."

"But she *did*."

"And who was the last person with the Grimoire before it went missing?"

They stared at each other in silence, Archer's name ringing between them, along with an intense denial neither of them could shake.

Because Archer would never betray them, right?

Jenna stood so abruptly that her chair toppled over. She gulped her wine, waving the glass at the table. "Will you stop crashing my detective work and help me, dammit? Please."

Kate squinted at her. "You're not going to let this go, are you?"

"Hell, no."

Kate sighed and leaned back in her chair, folding her arms. "If Ethan and Declan find out that we doubt Archer's loyalties, they'll be livid."

"We're not questioning his loyalties, Kate. We're questioning his actions. He was off the last few days. We all sensed something was up, but put it down to the stress of everything happening."

"They'll still be livid."

"Maybe I'm wrong. Maybe Hazel spelled him. That's the point, Kate. We don't know. But something's way off and you know it."

"I'm not denying that or saying I won't help you. All I'm saying is what we're doing, *this* . . ." she waved at hand at the desk, ". . . is delicate. We have to be careful they don't know what we're up to until *we* know."

Jenna inhaled deeply and blew out air slowly, puffing her cheeks. "Fair enough."

Kate pointed a finger at Jenna's hair and clothes. Rumpled and mismatched. "You need to sort that out, Jen. You look like crap." Jenna opened her mouth to protest, but Kate shook her head. "And when last did you get some sleep?"

She hadn't.

Instead, she'd spent hours holed up in the attic, trying to makes sense of everything. Kate had bust her last night when she'd found her rambling quietly to herself in the darkened room.

But Kate was right. She did look like crap and she was beyond the point of exhaustion because sleep had evaded her for days, worse than ever. Since returning from Ameera, nightmares tainted the little bit of sleep she'd attempted. Dreams that had nothing to do with burning witches or her family. Not even Hazel. No, they were wrought with images of Archer and his death.

Not surprising, considering he'd died in her arms. And she'd failed to save him.

What the hell was with that? She was a Salubrious. She healed. She saved people, dammit. She was a goddamn supernatural *doctor*.

Which had meant nothing for her friend.

"Jenna, you're doing that thing again," Kate blurted, rising. When Jenna raised a brow, Kate walked around the desk and took her arm. "Silently stewing in that way that makes you look like you're suffering a migraine or something."

"Nothing makes sense, Kate, and it kills me that I can't figure it out."

"I said I'll help you. I'll have another look. Go take a shower, grab another bottle of wine, and we'll go over the notes together."

Jenna hesitated and then smiled when Kate gave an exaggerated grimace at her clothing. "Fine, I'll go. Fifteen minutes and I'll be back."

"Fine. But don't forget the wine when you're done. Red – and steal a bottle of the good stuff."

Jenna's brows hitched. They both knew how the brothers treasured their prized bottles.

"If I'm going to help you plot your crazy theory about Archer and risk the wrath of his brothers, it's the least you can do."

"Will you have another look at my notes while I'm gone?"

"Yes, now go."

Sighing, Jenna went to the door, but turned, a small smile breaking free. "You're my girl, Kate."

"Yeah, yeah, I know." She waved her away, but her eyes flashed with amusement. "Go. You're a mess and I need a refill."

CHAPTER FIFTY SEVEN

Her hair damp from her shower, Jenna headed for the attic via the pool room.

Because she'd promised Kate a bottle of wine. And she swore she'd seen a box of the Bennett reserve wine on the bottom shelf at the bar. She hoped so, otherwise she'd have to risk the cellar beside the kitchen – and face Ethan and his family.

She'd rather drink coffee.

She circled the pool slowly, recalling what had happened the last time she'd used it.

Frustration burned a hole in her stomach.

Something was off, way off, and it frustrated the hell out of her that she couldn't figure out what. But there was something more. A trickle of suspicion she'd been unable to shed.

And it had to do with Archer.

She'd searched the locks on all the windows and doors in the pool room, but nothing had been tampered with.

But someone had attacked her. Here, in the pool, and the only person in the room at the time was Archer.

The Brogan Grimoire, the broken spell. None of it made any damn sense.

He frightened me.

Sienna's words kept replaying in her mind – words that would have Archer turning in his grave if he'd heard them. Sienna had been his entire existence. He'd never betray her or his brothers.

God, why the hell was she questioning him?

Groaning, she walked to the bar, but paused when Archer's jacket on the couch caught her eye.

Unable to stop herself, her heart torn between doubts and longing, she went to it. Her fingers stroked the leather, her mind flashing with memories of the last time she'd seen him wearing it. The night the hellhounds and shifters had attacked Rapid Falls.

She picked it up, biting back tears, and drew the jacket to her nose. She sniffed, allowing the scent of her friend to wash over her.

Despite her worries and doubts, he was a good man and she missed him.

"Jenna?"

She gasped and pivoted around, horrified to see Ethan standing in the doorway. He had ruffled hair and thick stubble across his jaw. She lowered the jacket, her cheeks reddening.

He glanced at the jacket and edged forward. "What are you doing?"

"Just thinking of your brother." She turned away, terrified he'd read more into that statement. Because there was so much more and he couldn't know that yet.

He took the jacket from her and tossed it over the couch. It slid to the floor. His arms curled around her and he buried his face into her neck, breathing her in.

"Are you okay?" she whispered.

"Ssh, I just want to hold you for a minute."

She remained quiet, revelling in the feel of him. Turning, she kissed his mouth. The longer fuzz on his cheeks felt softer. The scent of him filled her nostrils, familiar and beautiful and everything hers. "I'm so sorry, Ethan."

His head lifted and he raised a brow, stroking her hair.

"I'm sorry I couldn't save him."

337

He shook his head and pulled her into his arms, kissing her head. "You did everything you could." He gave her another kiss before breaking away. "I have to call Pam. She's left a dozen messages on my phone and it sounds urgent."

Jenna nodded and watched him walk away to call the sheriff, wishing she had the power to heal emotional pain too. She loathed seeing them all so devastated and lost.

Turning, she picked up the jacket and stilled when she saw the rolled-up ball of material on the floor beneath it. It must've fallen out of the pocket. She reached for it, unravelling it.

Her heart sped up as she recognised the ripped t-shirt, recoiling at the telltale signs of dried blood. It belonged to Kate and she'd worn it the night they were attacked by hellhounds. She was sure of it.

Why on earth would Archer have it?

Cursing softly, she bolted for the door, forgetting all about the wine.

****

Jenna found Kate pacing the attic floor, clutching an iPad in her hands. But it was her worried expression that caught Jenna.

"What's wrong?" Jenna asked, glancing at the iPad.

"Has Ethan or Declan spoken to Pam yet?"

"He's calling her now, why?"

"I saw something on the news." She lowered her gaze and looked at the iPad. "We won the battle, Jen. Hazel's in Ameera, the portal's closed . . ." She activated the screen and held it out. "But we've been exposed."

Jenna frowned and leaned in for a closer look. The screen contained a news report, along with a video, images that she instantly recognised from the battle at Sienna's house. "How did they get this?"

"Someone filmed us fighting. It's a quick clip, but enough to have made the news and cause a lot of panic and confusion."

338

That explained Pam's frantic messages left on Ethan's phone. *Shit.*

"One of Hazel's people?" Kate shrugged and Jenna exhaled loudly. "This could ruin us."

"We'll find a way around it, but it won't be easy. At least they can't make out our faces."

It was true. The video was blurry, shaky, and filmed from a distance. It captured the three women from behind, moving toward the house, wielding a shitload of magic that smacked of supernatural. It also showed the shadows of Ethan and his brothers waiting in the forest.

"For so long, we've fought to protect our existence and in the blink of a damn phone recording, we're so screwed," Jenna breathed. "The last time our kind was exposed . . ." Her voice trailed off as she caught a glimpse of a shadow on the screen. Holding her breath, she swiped a finger across the glass, replaying the video, and almost dropped the iPad when she saw it again.

"Jenna?"

She jabbed the pause button, freezing the image, bringing it closer for a better look. She tugged on the neckline of her t-shirt, suddenly breathless, and studied the image she'd originally thought was Archer.

Only, it wasn't.

The image was blurry, captured in the shadows of the tree. But it was a man. A man with a black and white tattooed face.

Mason gave it to me himself. An icy hand raked down Jenna's spine as she recalled Megan's words in Ameera about the Brogan Grimoire.

"Jen, what's wrong?"

Archer's unaccustomed rage. His mood swings. The fights with Sienna. The missing Grimoire. The drowning.

"Did anyone other than Archer check on Mason recently?" Jenna asked breathlessly.

"No, Archer took care of it."

"That's how Hazel knew all our movements." Jenna swivelled around, her heart pounding so loud that she could hear it in her ears. Her breathing had turned choppy. She went to the window, peering out at the peaceful vineyards, mentally trying to shift the puzzle into place.

"You're making no sense, Jenna," Kate grumbled, her eyes narrowing as she looked at the stained material in Jenna's hand. "And where on earth did you find my t-shirt?"

Jenna tossed it to her. "I found it in Archer's jacket."

"He said he'd burn it. Where's the rest of it?" Frowning, she dangled the torn material on one finger. "Why would Archer have kept –?" She gasped, her eyes rounded and she gaped at the t-shirt. "Oh, no."

Their gazes met and held, the truth nudging between them in a way they both loathed. But they couldn't pretend none of this mattered.

Jenna pointed to the t-shirt. "That's how they broke the spell on the Brogan Grimoire. They used your blood."

"Archer wouldn't give them my blood, Jenna. He knows what that means."

"Kate . . . they had *your blood*."

Which meant any spell ever cast was at risk. Even a spell cast by a Beckham witch.

Kate paled. "If that's true, then they could . . ."

"Yes," she finished as adrenaline flooded her veins. "They could free Mason."

CHAPTER FIFTY EIGHT

Ethan sipped his beer from his spot on the porch.

The air was cooler, the sky painted pink from the sunset. A beauty that meant so little in the wake of their grief.

He lowered the bottle when he saw Jenna and Kate running across the lawn in all their Keeper glory. Where were they off to?

Curiosity spiked, a welcome change to the gloom that seemed to follow him everywhere. A given considering he'd just lost another sibling. Archer's death had created an unbearable ache that seemed determined to claw its way through him in an attempt to get the attention it deserved.

But he couldn't.

His parents, Rose, Sarah. And now Archer.

So much damn heartache and crap he couldn't deal with now. Not when Sienna was struggling to hold it together. She'd been so strong, quiet, moving through the last few days in robotic mode. But this evening, she'd crashed as the pain and grief had overwhelmed her.

An inevitable crash they all faced.

Fuck that.

Needing a distraction, he glanced through the window, loathe to leave Sienna alone. But Declan hovered around her like a damn helicopter.

When Jenna and Kate disappeared into the forest, Ethan discarded his beer and followed.

The sun had begun to set, its rays filtering through the umbrella of trees in the forest. It was so quiet, too quiet, and he paused to listen for signs of the women. He tracked them instantly and took off at a run, following their trace with ease. They were in a hurry and uncaring about leaving one.

He drew to an abrupt stop as he recognised the route the women had taken. The underground storage rooms. The ones that housed Mason Brogan.

What the hell?

Dodging bushes and fallen tree branches, he searched for the small door that led to the underground tunnel. It was overgrown and concealed by greenery. He might have missed it had it not been left ajar.

He hovered, debating whether he should follow them, but the stuffy air was torture and triggered memories he'd rather avoid. So he waited, listening, his senses tuned into every sound.

It wasn't long before voices drifted through the tunnel, hurried and breathless, accompanied by movement. When the heavy door opened, Jenna emerged carrying a flashlight and inhaled deeply. She sensed his presence instantly and swung around, gasping when she saw him. Her eyes sparkled and her cheeks were flushed. She stared at him in silence, her mouth parted.

"What are you doing here?" he asked.

A smile broke free, softening her expression. "Ethan . . ."

And then everything changed. Just like that. In a blink of an eye as Kate stepped out of the tunnel and all Ethan could do was stare, feasting on the vision that made no sense.

A man stood between them, leaning heavily on Kate.

Archer.

The air slammed out of Ethan's lungs and he gaped in stunned silence.

Archer shifted his weight, his movements slow and weak. He wore torn jeans, his chest covered in dried blood. His wrists were bruised and red. He lifted his head, surprise brightening his features when he saw Ethan. "What took you so damn long, brother?"

"Archer?" Ethan croaked.

Not understanding what was happening, or bothering to question it, Ethan bolted forward. He engulfed his brother into his arms, shouting his name, ignoring the stupid-assed tears that blurred his vision.

"Ouch, Ethan, that hurts," Archer groaned, drawing back. But he grinned – the best damn sight Ethan had ever seen.

Ethan glanced at Kate and Jenna. They were both crying. He caught his brother's head between his hands and leaned in, their foreheads touching.

"We saw you die," he said in a choked voice that sounded nothing like his. He swallowed at the memory, willing away the goddamn lump in his throat. "Hazel stabbed you. How are you here? How's this –"

"That wasn't me. It was Mason."

"Mason?"

Jenna slid Archer's arm around her shoulders. "Archer checked on Mason the night we left for Ameera. A desiccating, mummified body was *not* what he found."

"Hazel broke Sienna's spell on Mason? How?"

"I destroyed the blood they'd harvested from Kate in the cemetery that night in New Orleans. But Hazel must've salvaged enough to break the spell that's kept Mason in a desiccating state." She adjusted Archer's arm, taking his weight. "Sienna sealed the tunnels with a separate spell so they were unable to access him."

"Why not use Kate's blood to break it?"

"They only had enough blood for one ritual," Archer replied.

343

"Although free, Mason was trapped underground," Kate added, motioning to the door with a nod. "So when Archer came to check on him . . . *surprise*."

Ethan rubbed his face and shook his head, trying to make sense of it all. "But you died. I was there."

"No, Mason died," Archer muttered, his brows narrowing. "After he attacked, he knocked me out cold and shackled me to the goddamn wall. Then he mimicked me and returned to the house, pretending to *be* me. Asshole."

Holy shit, a damn Mimic. It was a favourite trick of Mason's. He'd fooled Sienna once before, pretending to be Sarah. The night they'd lost her. And now again. But this time, his trickery had killed him. Ironic considering that after everything Hazel had done to free her nephew, she'd ended up killing him. *Sweet justice.*

"That's how the Grimoire went missing?" Ethan asked.

Jenna nodded. "Without Sienna knowing, Mason took the book and gave it to Megan, along with a piece of Kate's bloody t-shirt. That's how they opened the book and found the location."

"That bastard's been living in our house! He had access to everything."

Archer grunted. "If he touched Sienna in any way –"

"I wouldn't worry about that, Archer," Kate said. "Things were pretty tense between them the last few days. Sienna spent most of the time furious with . . . you."

"Did he hurt her?"

"No," Ethan replied. "In fact, Mason saved her."

Surprise crossed Archer's expression. "She's the one who bound him to the tomb."

"But when Hazel threw a knife at Sienna, he didn't hesitate to protect her. He always had a weird obsession with her. Fortunately, it worked in our favour this time."

"He's still an asshole."

Ethan put his arms around his brother and hugged him tightly,

344

a big ball of emotion wedged in his throat as he recalled the moment they'd lost him in Ameera. Unbelievable.

"I'm okay, brother," Archer grunted, returning the hug. "I've been stuck in this hellhole for days. It's about time you guys figured it out. I've been worried sick and I'm starving."

"At least it was a safe hellhole. And it explains why you've been such a dick lately." God, was Declan in for a surprise.

Ethan grinned.

"I felt Sienna connect to my magic. What happened? Where's Hazel?"

Ethan adjusted his brother's weight, all too aware of how weak he was. "We'll fill you in on the walk home."

Holy crap, Sienna was about to receive the surprise of her life too. His smile faded and his throat tightened as relief rolled through him.

"How is she?" Archer asked, as though he'd read Ethan's mind.

He didn't reply and lowered his gaze. But it was all the answer Archer needed. Cursing softly beneath his breath, he limped forward.

****

The first thing Jenna saw as they came out of the forest was Declan nursing a glass of whiskey on the patio. He sported dishevelled hair and an old t-shirt of Archer's.

"Where the hell have you all been?" Declan called out, sipping his drink. "I've been looking everywhere for you."

She saw the moment it all fell into place for him. That beautiful moment when his entire world shifted so that everything was finally, finally right again.

His glass shattered and then he was running, shouting Archer's name, calling for Sienna. He reached them on a rush of air and power and engulfed Archer into a hug.

"What the hell is this?" Declan choked, his expression a mixture of relief and joy. He leaned back to study his brother, holding his head between both hands. "How's this possible? How are you here?"

Ethan stepped up, slinging his arms around both brothers. "It's a long story."

"You said Archer died!"

"We were fooled. It wasn't Archer who died. It was Mason mimicking him."

"*Mason?*" Declan's brows shot up and his jaw went slack. Then he frowned and slapped Archer's head with the back of his hand. "Dying was a dick move, brother. Don't you dare do that again."

Archer grinned and Declan threw his head back and released a long, joyful roar before pulling his brother in for another hug. Archer groaned at the force of his brother's embrace, but didn't pull away.

And then they were laughing, hugging, all talking at once, and crying, the moment as touching as it was joyous. Archer took a deep breath and pulled away, suddenly searching.

Sienna.

His expression changed the moment he saw her. She'd reached the bottom of the stairs, but her legs buckled and she sank to her knees on the grass. Her hands covered her mouth, almost as though she dared not breathe. Or hope.

She made no sound, but tears streaked her cheeks. She looked so small against the massive house looming behind her, the empty expanses of grass on either side of her.

Archer's strangled grunt broke the silence and he pulled away from his brothers, his movements unsteady.

"Whoa. Easy, brother," Declan said, sliding his arm around Archer's shoulders.

"Sienna," Archer murmured in a gutted tone. "She thought . . ." His words trailed off on a groan and he limped forward.

Declan and Kate went with him, supporting his brother's weight as they walked.

Jenna's eyes swelled with fresh tears. She felt Ethan's presence behind her moments before he touched her. Strong arms slid around her waist, enveloping her in a tight hug. Her back pressed against his chest and he rested his chin on her shoulder, his cheek beside hers.

A small sob escaped her before she could reel it in and he kissed her cheek, inhaling deeply against her. "How did you know?"

A hunch that wouldn't let go. And from now on, she'd never disregard another one. "I knew something was off when I couldn't heal him, but Kate helped me piece it all together." Her stomach rolled at the thought of what might have happened if she'd ignored the hunch. If their fight hadn't been filmed or Kate hadn't seen it on the news, they might not have found Archer in time.

"You didn't say anything."

"I couldn't until I was sure."

"My brother's home, Jen. Because of you, he's home." He pushed his face into her hair, breathing her in, and whispered, "Thank you."

She felt the emotion behind that single word and nodded through her tears.

Archer stopped in front of Sienna, still crouched on the ground, staring up at him, her entire body a quiver of hope.

"Really?" Sienna asked, her voice barely audible. A sob escaped her when he nodded and knelt.

They stared at each other in silence, a poignant moment Jenna would never forget.

"How's this possible?" Sienna whispered.

"I would've come sooner, but I couldn't get out of the damn storage room." He cupped her cheeks within his palms. "I'll explain everything later. For now, I just need to hold you."

Her hands covered his as she searched his gaze. "Is this really happening? Is this really you?"

He smiled and nodded. Her sob tore at them all, muffled against his shirt when he pulled her into his arms.

347

Jenna heard Ethan's sharp intake of breath. She tilted her head to look up at him. Ruffled hair, bloodshot eyes, and a clenched jaw. A mess. But he was beautiful.

Her beautiful.

"We're going to be okay," she whispered, stroking the leather bracelet on his wrist. "It's over."

Mason was dead. They'd beaten Hazel, trapped her in Ameera, and had power of the portal. Hazel had achieved her goal of exposure.

But *they'd* won the war.

Their secret was out, which likely meant that a new battle was on the horizon. But they'd deal with it like they always did. Together.

All six of them.

Grinning, Jenna averted her gaze to Kate. The incredible witch she'd defend with everything in her. When she'd accepted the duty of being Kate's Keeper, she'd never expected to find new friends too. Ethan.

A family.

"Jenna!" Kate called, beckoning them closer.

Ethan adjusted his arm around Jenna, tugging her into the curve of his shoulder. She leaned her head against him and smiled when he pressed a kiss into her hair.

As they walked to the two couples, Jenna thought of her mother. She'd left her in Ameera and the pain that came with that would never leave entirely. She'd always long for Catherine, but she was comforted by the fact that her mother had been right.

Jenna had a purpose here. She was walking toward it and they needed her.

As much as she needed them.

CHAPTER FIFTY NINE

BENNETT ESTATE
THREE MONTHS LATER

Jenna stood beside the photographer, a young woman laden with two cameras and an assortment of lenses.

She had striking black hair and a friendly smile that remained in place despite the challenges of trying to organise a group of people for a photograph.

A group of people more concerned with champagne and laughter than having their photograph taken – both of which were needed after all the time they'd spent putting out the fires that followed the release of the video.

Thankfully, without any more public displays of magic, things had started quieting down.

Sienna looked gorgeous in her wedding gown, a vision of white beauty amongst the backdrop of greenery and aqua-blue sky. It was warm and sunny; the air permeated with the smell of freshly cut grass and the sound of music and chatter from the guests in the marquee.

Archer slid his arm around his bride, drawing her closer. Declan and Ethan gathered beside the couple, arms around each other.

Dark hair, tanned skin, and black tuxedos. The sunlight caught their Keeper rings. They were smiling, relaxed, holding on to everything they treasured. Family. Love. Laughter.

Moments of pure joy amongst the darkness of their world.

And Jenna knew in that moment that the image of Sienna with her Keepers would be forever captured in her mind, just as the photographer captured the moment with several clicks of her camera.

Three warrior men and the witch they were duty-bound to defend. So fiercely protective of life and each other. So powerful. They emanated pure joy. Courage. Honour. Loyalty. Love. A perfect image of everything that mattered.

Sienna's laughter broke the brief silence as everyone posed for a photograph. She hung her head back, giggling at something Archer had whispered in her ear, her veil hanging freely down her back.

"They're breathtaking," Kate said, coming up behind Jenna. She hooked her arm through Jenna's, giving it a gentle squeeze. Their gazes met and Jenna smiled.

The witch *she* was duty-bound to defend. Her entire being was connected to her, to them all.

And because of them, since returning to Rapid Falls a few months ago, Jenna had realised there was more to life – the balance – than simply fighting for it.

They carried the responsibilities and burden of their birthrights without question or resentment. A duty they'd embraced. But there was more. They had each other.

Jenna's throat tightened as she looked at Kate and Sienna. Her gaze drifted to Declan and Archer, settling on Ethan.

Her love for him had surprised her. She knew they faced more battles and challenges that came with protecting two powerful witches. But she loved him. More than she ever thought she could love someone.

He was her friend, her lover. *Her partner.*

As if he sensed her watching him, he looked up, his gaze finding hers. A boyish grin curled his lips into one of those beautiful smiles she adored. He looked relaxed, happy, his eyes filled with quiet satisfaction.

The photographer lowered her camera and waved at Kate and Jenna. "Now for a photo of the whole family."

****

Ethan slid his arms around Jenna and kissed her cheek, savouring the feel of her. She settled against him, owning the space that belonged to her.

He grinned at the thought, knowing he'd never hold another woman the way he held her. *Loved her.*

She tilted her head, laughing as he delivered a soft kiss to her lips. He became vaguely aware of the photographer clicking away.

She eventually lowered the camera, checked the images on the screen, her lips twitching into a grin. "I think I'm done here."

"Thank God," Declan drawled in exaggerated relief. "Time for a whiskey."

"Make that two," Archer said.

"And champagne for us," Sienna added as Jenna and Kate adjusted her veil.

They looked so delicate and feminine. It was hard to reconcile the image of Sienna in her wedding gown and her two beautiful bridesmaids to the warrior women who had fought so hard beside them.

He and his brothers were warriors at heart, determined and powerful, but he'd be the first to admit that the three women strengthened them in more ways than one.

And not only physically.

He watched them walk ahead, their arms linked, laughing. Sienna's veil trailed behind them, the white of the gown a contrast to her bright red hair. A fire witch, a hybrid warrior, and a Keeper.

The Pure.

351

Incredible to think they were all part of an ancient legend.

He grinned at the thought and turned back to his brothers, but paused when a movement in the vineyards caught his attention.

The glare of sunlight behind the figure made it impossible to see much, but judging by the petite frame it appeared to be a woman.

She stood unmoving, watching them, a silhouette in the sunlight.

Something niggled inside and for an insane moment, the image of his sister's smiling face came to mind. Beautiful, sweet, kind Sarah.

He felt the familiar tug of sadness always triggered by thoughts of her. She would've loved this. Weddings had always been a firm favourite for her and Archer and Sienna's wedding would've been a highlight.

"Ready for a fun night?" Archer asked, coming up behind him, his jacket slung over one arm. He'd loosened his tie, officially ending the formalities of the wedding ceremony.

"Absolutely." Ethan glanced back at the woman in the vineyards, surprised to find no one there. She'd disappeared. Like a mirage in the distance that had vanished in the blink of an eye.

Maybe he'd imagined her? She'd seemed so real.

Declan joined them, a perfect distraction from thoughts of their sister. His jacket and tie hung over one arm. "Tonight's all about whiskey, women, and the biggest celebration of the year."

Ethan raised a brow. "In that order?"

"No. Definitely not." He grinned at the three women waiting for them and slapped a hand on Ethan's back. "As for you, brother, this party will be a first for you. No scouring the room for female company tonight."

Ethan smiled and sought out Jenna. The sunlight highlighted her hair and skin in a golden glow. The olive-green gown she wore clung to her hips like a second skin, accentuating curves and shapely legs he'd explored many times over.

God, she was beautiful.

Mine.

Not taking his eyes off her, Ethan shook his head. "I have everything I want."

"Excellent choice, brother."

"Can I tell her you said that?"

"Hell, no."

Ethan laughed and slid an arm around his brother's shoulder. "How about those drinks?"

As they reached the women, Ethan glanced back at the vineyards, the silhouetted image etched in his mind.

Frowning, he slipped his hand into Jenna's, lacing their fingers, bringing them to a stop. Her bright smile tugged at parts of him he'd always kept hidden from women.

But not her.

She'd penetrated every wall, every barricade, and he loved her more for it.

He leaned forward and kissed her, his lips lingering longer than usual. His body tightened in response, auto-tuned to everything *her*. Desire sparked and he had the insane urge to toss her over his shoulder and haul her back to bed. Wedding or no wedding.

"Hm," she murmured against his lips, her hips brushing against his, the movement as arousing as it was subtle. "Any more of that and you're going to have a problem, stud muffin."

He chuckled and captured her mouth with his, their kiss a promise of everything to come.

A shiver ran through her and with a dreamy sigh, she tipped her head back, just an inch, and peered up at him. "Will you dance with me tonight?"

He caught her chin between his thumb and finger, his lips close to hers, and smiled. "Always, my love."

Her mouth curled into a beautiful smile that took his breath away. He kissed her, slow, lingering, absorbing everything about her. Breathing her in, he pressed his lips to her forehead.

Always.

ACKNOWLEDGEMENTS

A few years ago, I was driving home from an inspirational lunch with my best friend when the idea of Sienna and her Keepers came to mind. By the time I got home, my mind was racing and I was buzzing with excitement. I went straight to my desk and started making notes that eventually developed into a tale of three brothers, four books, and an epic adventure.

And wow, what an epic adventure writing this series has been! It's one I could never have completed alone. I am so incredibly grateful to so many people for cheering me on and supporting me:

My precious husband, children, Mom, family and friends. Thank you for your support and love and for being patient with me when I'm distracted, unavailable and lost in a world of my own creation. And as always, thanks to Lisa for always knowing what to say or offering a plot twist when I need one! I love you all.

My editor, Charlotte Ledger (and her team). Your enthusiasm for my Keepers and your guidance, kindness and patience is so appreciated. Thank you!

My incredible author friends. Thank you for your support, love and friendship. You make this journey so fun – and you always understand and believe me when I explain that my Google searches for hot men is for *research*!

And of course, a massive thank you to all the wonderful book bloggers, as well as my incredible readers across the world. Thank you for reading my books and sharing them with your followers, friends and families. Your messages of enthusiasm and support continue to amaze me and I love that you love my stories as much as I do. YOU are my inspiration. I write for you.

I have so many more stories planned for you so if you'd like to keep updated with my book news, please sign up for my newsletter. I can also be found on Facebook, Twitter or my Blog. Your feedback is always appreciated so please leave a review on Amazon or the site where you bought this book.

Thank you for reading!

With love,
Rae Rivers